AMY SACKVILLE was born in 1981. She studied English and Theatre Studies at Leeds, and went on to do an MPhil in English at Exeter College, Oxford, and an MA in Creative and Life Writing at Goldsmiths. Her first novel was *The Still Point*, which was longlisted for the Orange Prize and won the 2010 John Llewellyn Rhys Prize, and her second was *Orkney*, wh̶ ̶ ̶ ̶ ̶ ̶ ̶ ̶ ̶ ̶ ̶ ̶ ̶ ̶ ̶ ̶ ̶ ̶ ̶ ̶n Award. www.amysackville.co.

'Working in luminous and me̶ ̶ ̶ ̶ ̶ ̶ ̶ ̶ ̶ ̶ ̶ ̶ ̶ ̶ ̶ ̶ ̶ achieves an almost miraculous intimacy with her subject. *Painter to the King* is the most engrossing fictional study of visual art I have ever encountered, giving us not only a persuasive account of Velázquez's formation and milieu but a ravishing survey of the very substances and textures of his sensory world. It is, in its own right, an astonishing work of art'
Paraic O'Donnell

'Darkly lyrical ... Stately, lush prose is interspersed with descriptions [and] Sackville uses language that is at once meticulous and rhapsodic ... well worth reading' *Irish Times*

'A transcendent piece of writing that somehow manages to capture Velázquez's art while exploring humans' enduring desire for power, for position and to outlive death itself ... a book that will continue to resonate as more readers discover its wonders'
Emerald Street

'An authentic glimpse into the painter's methods ... superb'
The Times

'For some years now, Amy Sackville has been known for the exquisite quality of her prose. With her third novel, she has tried something different, something more audacious, perhaps, and proves more than equal to the challenge. A work of great subtlety and sophistication, *Painter to the King* is a surprisingly tender portrait of a genius'
Rupert Thomson

Painter
to the King

Amy Sackville

GRANTA

Granta Publications, 12 Addison Avenue, London W11 4QR

First published by Granta Books 2018
This paperback edition published by Granta Books 2019

A CIP catalogue record is available from the British Library

9 8 7 6 5 4 3 2

ISBN 978 1 78378 392 2
eISBN 978 1 78378 391 5

www.granta.com

Typeset in Caslon by M Rules

Printed and bound by CPI Group (UK) Ltd, Croydon, CR0 4YY

to Lucy, my sister

Las palabras son sombra de los hechos: son aquellas las hembras, estos los varones.

Words are the shadows of deeds: the former female, the latter male.

—Baltasar Gracián

. . . que, cierto algunas veces tomo el papel como una cosa boba, que ni s'e qu'e decir ni c'omo comenzar.

. . . for really I sometimes take up my paper, like a perfect fool, with no idea of what to say or of how to begin.

—St Teresa of Ávila

Contents

THREE

        and give nothing   251
XVIII: *Querer por solo querer/Love for love's sake*   263
XIX: *La familia/The family*   274
XX: *Principe vero ea quae digna sunt cogitavit/*
        But he who is noble plans noble things   288
XXI: *Isla de los Faisanes/Île des Faisans/*
        Isle of Pheasants   298

        Expinxit   311

        Image credits   317
        Acknowledgements   321

Frame:

It opens out from this dark corner: halfway along this corridor and— there's the door. Distracted by something perhaps, looking at something on the opposite wall or at someone else or the floor plan or my own tired feet, I pass or almost pass it but—— then the eye just catches and I double-take and stop. Step forward to the archway and aside to just off-centre, letting people pass, buffeted by bodies; I don't see them. I see: opposite, a man is also pausing in a doorway. And everything's stopped. Between us: on my side of the frame, the buzz and brightness of the gallery; and on his a cool grey room, lofty, quiet, dim in its high and far corners. Both of us at a threshold, and the threshold of the frame between. And they are all there— all long familiar, I've been half-seeking them even and yet—— this shock. There they all are! Just as if they always have been, or have just this moment stopped. Looking back. And, just off-centre, just looking, he has just stepped back, he's also just stopped— the painter; there he is, with his long brush. And I——

— I want to pass through this archway I'm stopped in and cross the gallery and step through the frame and into the whole room beyond it, find my way through and between them, their heads all turning to watch me pass or else still staring out as I move invisible among them; pause and stand at the painter's shoulder and find out at last what he's painting, what's on the surface of the canvas, the reverse of that vast framed blank

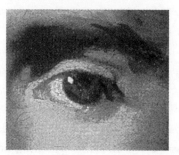

back, what he and only he can see— pause to look and then leave him to it and find my way all the way back to that door at the back, squeeze past the silhouette-man on the stair and see what's beyond in the yellow light, which might be sunshine or lamplight. So I step towards him across the gallery until the gallery vanishes and all the people in it and the frame closes round my peripheral vision and I stand on the brink of the light and regard them——

— the sinuous line of them and how they might easily at any moment join hands and dance a jig: from the girl on the left, offering a red beaker to the girl about to take it, through gesture and curtsey and bow to the poised balancing hands of the delicate dwarf on the right, who is distracted by the dog and seems already to be dancing; and motionless, held here, I dance back across the restless, unresolved cadence of it. From hand to hand, from corner to corner; pointed toe to poised brush; elbow-crook to elbow-crook. It is a strange, cut-off light that lights them— bright lines in the depths— frame to frame to frame. The mirror just off-centre on the back wall is full of that borrowed light. He is interested in mirrors, this painter. I live in a world of them—I want to tell him—cameras, phones, chrome, shop windows, plate glass, screens of all sizes:

reflections everywhere. I can't get away from myself. What would you make of that?

But look how real, in contrast: this illusion he has made. How true to a life that is, itself, illusion; nothing more— but not less, either. Shadows and shams. A life lived as a dream that repeats and retreats and refracts through successions of sometimes impossible frames; I was—— but also at the same time you— I was there and also watching and you— and then—— But— then again—— Step closer, and it's all just a surface of smears; rough daubs, features half-formed, hands that only gesture at the shape of hands. The painter's brush has a long handle— made only of a swipe of that same brush; and so, stepping back, stopped, he sees clearly the illusion of coherence he is bringing into being——

— it is also the whole life of the painter; your whole life, Diego— or some semblance of it— a version— a way to say, to frame it. And at the centre back there in the dimness of a vanishing point, it is an open door; and I pause on the threshold unseen, about to leave or to enter, longing across this distance, dying to go towards it, to move towards you and I can't yet— can't move, can't quite. This wasn't going to be about you, but now— this, it turns out—— this is, you are, what I was looking for, in this hot foreign city. And I've stopped here and everything's stopped. It feels like hours, and every minute passing increases that impossible distance, of centuries, of years, of yards. And from now on, from this moment on, I am always following, always trying to follow; I go out, back into the city and it's been hours and already it's evening and still light, and still hot; I order fino and sit and I'm still there, just— stopped—— just— to find a way to say it; to say——

ONE

I

Bodegón/
Still life

— Say he arrived at night, the painter. In summer the dark comes late, the sky only just deepening blue as he reaches the gates of Madrid. He had a stipend for the journey and some pride, he arrives in style: he has paid for a horse. Just one attendant on a mule with the baggage, who has no features in the dark beyond the torchlight. The gatekeeper is waiting to take their entry tax, greets them with bluff caution, wonders who approaches the city so late? The roads aren't safe after dark——

— True—— he must have been anxious to reach the city, but there's no sense in his arriving in the middle of the night; why risk himself, his goods his horse his faceless servant? He has ridden a long road from Seville——

— Say he stopped for a rest as the sun sank— they are travelling north— so, as the sun sank to his left. The capital already half-shadowed in the distance on the tawny plain. The air full of kicked-up soil and straw-dust from the fields already yellowing and drying into a meagre baked crop. He stops and stays at an inn a few miles away, breaks his journey so that when he arrives he will be rested, fresh, as free of dust as anyone can be from the road coming into the city in summer.

Spends a restless night, worrying, scratching. Glad to rise in the morning; he paid extra to avoid sleeping on straw but the beds are no less infested. Brown piss frothing in a piss-stained pot, a chip dark brown in the rim of it. The smell strong and stinging. He should drink. This dry air. He drinks and then washes quickly with cool water: an earthen ewer and a basin, liquid limpid with dawn light; he sees all of this, the droplet that hangs on the lip— there— the early high dawn caught in it and making the stoneware gleam. He thinks briefly of home and perhaps of the water-seller. Sweet trace of a ripe fig, the fluid clarity, the goblet's shine.

He sighs, gulps the last of the water from the clay mug, sets it down and devotes some time to scratching each bite in turn, noting the night's fresh welts, working around the older scabs—he's been travelling a few days now, and the journey has marked him. Almost there now, almost. Intense, localised pleasure where his nails scrape, knowing when he leaves off it will only make it worse and he should stop, scratching, it feels so good to scratch, he should (scratch) he should stop. Stop. He washes again to soothe the bites, scratches scratches, inhales, holds his breath, holds his hands out steady, exhales and smoothes his hair, runs a finger and thumb across his moustache, his dark eyebrows. Curls with a finger the modest ringlet at his temple. If there's a mirror, he searches his face as if to paint it, his tranquil eyes, which belie his agitation. A last scratch.

He descends the stair and finds his way to the kitchen. He hands his provisions to the old woman, asks her to cook him breakfast, he has eggs, which he has somehow transported from the last hencoop he passed; he watches them in the pan just setting, a semi-opaque gloop, a series of rounds within rounds. The circle of the old iron pan is not quite perfect; so if his brush-line were to follow its form he would include in the foreshortened oval that bentness, that dent.

The boy serves him the eggs— the serious boy with the straight-cut hair sleek like a mole's fur close on the scalp, the planes of the bone beneath——— the boy serves him eggs, and water from a carafe, half-glazed white and painted with a simple leaf design.

The painter has faith in solid objects, arresting their motion through the world and preserving forever their thisness, the quiddity of matter and moisture and shine; transparency, opacity; the exterior that things present to the world, and how much of the world can be seen through them, distorted, distilled. The cool curve in the hand, the rough striation of the clay and the smooth glaze, the fine cracks snagging lightly each ridge of the fingertip; he attends to all of this, plasticity, rigidity, fragility, damage and flaw, detail, surface and shape. Copper, gleaming; a dark knife resting on a bowl, its bent black shadow; the hairy tangle topping a glossy red onion; a melon tied with cord, the pale orange sheen and the dull brown patch like— a map of a new continent——— or like nothing except a blemish on fruit-skin, exactly as it is———

— or a glass, a sherry glass, say, short-stemmed, tulip tapering to a narrow rim with a pink lip-smear where three sips have been taken; the chill condensing on the outside, just higher than the line of the pale fino reduced by three sips. Damp paper napkin, dirty plastic ashtray. A thin black pen, matte to the touch, nib nervously rotated in and out by the bent clip, grasped and ungrasped, loosely tapping at the page. I'm restless since I left you, since I moved off from where I'd stopped, left you stopped. Things look strange to me; the light, it might be. I'm looking. I'd like to borrow your eyes. None of these things, these solid objects on an outdoor table at the centre of this plaza in Madrid this evening, now seem as solid as that glossy red onion that rotted almost four hundred years ago. I've half made them up.

Piss-pot, ewer, bowl; eggs, onion, melon; carafe, woman, boy.

These are the elements of this composition. The sinews of her wrists— his strong large hands— thumbnail shining and long enough to cast a slivered shadow on the skin beneath. Solid objects, solid flesh. Just like any one of us.

So sated, stomach scrambling, the painter is on his way. It is still early and he hopes to avoid the worst of the sun, but the roads into the city are crammed with beasts, a smelly fraught jostle backed up for leagues. He joins the queue of animals, bearing wheat and fruit, wine and fish, silver and gold, goods from all over the country making their way to its heart, here, to keep the court running; the sluggish veins that return the empire's bounty in trickles and clots. He waits, patiently, he picks his way through, his attendant following keeps his baggage close. His gut rebelling as the eggs digest, and as he draws nearer to the inevitable, whatever it may be—whatever's meant for him in this city— but the noise of the road is enormous and no one else can hear it, the eggs, revueltos. At last at the gate he pays his entry tax from the stipend he has been provided, thus returning the coins to the coffers they came from. At last, he enters the city, which is already sleeping in the sun. It is long after noon and the day's meal is eaten; he enters the capital dirty and hungry, gurgling, with the Canon's letter tucked into his shirt: you have been sent for. Come, stay at my house. We Sevillians should stick together. He is still a young man; the King is younger. Not yet twenty, just a man of solid flesh, and the greatest monarch in the world.

Just about the time the painter sets out from the inn, say, the Prime Minister, the King's valido, visits the King in his private chamber. In he strides, or lurches and stumps, too big for most rooms, covered in papers—stuffed into his hat, his belt, between buttons—so that he makes an important rustling sound as he walks, as he swaggers and rolls. He has weight to carry, the Count, the valido, his own considerable bulk and the government of the country on his high humped shoulders—— But he won't be called valido, he won't have it; he is not the favourite, he is only a servant; he has flushed out the corruption of the last king's court and will not have it said that there is favouritism here. He is Prime Minister because someone must be; it is his honour, to bear this duty. He has worked hard to be permitted to the King's chamber, first thing in the morning. He has always worked hard. He must be tired. Yet here he is, already up for hours, fresh from confession, clean of countenance and conscience; so perhaps he doesn't get tired—or doesn't show it.

A new artist has been sent for, Señor, says the Count, and is on his way now from the south. The King looks up, with something akin to interest. The Count passes the King the King's shirt and the King sits on the side of his bed and puts it on. There are portraits to be made of Your Majesty, and this man has, already, a reputation. They say he sees the dignity, the grace of the Lord's creation, just as it is: the truth, the life of it. A young man, a quiet man who will not bore Your Majesty with prattle. A cultured man. Like me, a Sevillian.

The King yawns, quite prettily, covering the stretch of his closed mouth with the back of his hand. Blood comes easily to the surface of his skin. When he opens his eyes again they are pink-rimmed and wet, like a waking child's, fair lashes dew-sprung; or like a night rodent's. He rubs his palms against his bare thin fair-furred thighs, receives his stockings one by one, his breeches. Yes, he's sure the Count is right, he is always right. The Count nods his acknowledgement, and shuffles a paper from his hat, which he is permitted to wear before the King. He gives it a straightening flick, reviews it at length at arm's length—does it merit His Majesty's attention? he hmms. Flick— Hmmmm … But he is performing to an empty hall— His Majesty's attention is currently elsewhere, he is tucking his shirt in ponderously—so his Prime Minister, standing before him like a fat fairground reflection, tucks the petition into his own belt. Coughs. And there is this other matter, which must be attended to. The King groans, throws himself into a chair, throws his head back, lets his mouth hang, lolls (he is just nineteen). Who will marry my sister, is it? That's what you were going to ask? Who, who indeed? You know I've no mind for this. Haven't we some cousin that'll have her? There's surely no shortage of them. (And indeed the King calls everyone of rank cousin, out of respect, and because it's easier, and distantly at least a safe assumption.)

And then Felipe thinks of María, his youngest sister, his playmate, so bright and lively and unlike the rest of them, this sad family, and foresees a time when the court is even duller and darker for her absence, and letting his head hang right off the back of the chair to look upside down at the Count behind him, asks in a throttled whisper, Must we have her married at all?

Obviously a foolish question, which the Count ignores. For now at least, he says, we must deal with her suitor. The English Prince arrived incognito, at some personal risk, and awaits his answer. (This peculiar and unprecedented arrival of a royal guest—in disguise, unannounced, unknown to the English ambassador even—has caused no end of trouble for the Count, ever overburdened as he is.) For years we've talked about it, and now he's here. Will this Prince Charles do for her?

The King snorts. What, this northerner who shows up as T-T-Tom Smith and expects our sister to marry a Protestant, one who goes in the guise of a commoner, no less? This tongue-swallowing incomprehensible P-Prince Ch-Ch-*Charlatan*, whose English is no better than my own?— Your Majesty's English is excellent, of course, improving daily, the Count interjects smoothly— Well what does María think? Can she be persuaded? No, I can imagine; she is ignoring him. She is at all times in his presence very interested in her fan or her dwarves or her little dog. The Count laughs. He will not concede their terms? He will not convert? No, he will not. Then no. She will not marry him; she need not.

Quite right, Señor, nods the Count. He knew the answer already, he had already decided it. But still, Prince Ch-Ch-Charles must be ... attended to ... along with his boyfriend Buckingham (the erstwhile John Smith, to whom the Prime Minister has taken particular exception, his pompoms and his white stockings and his shapely solid calves, his garter, his bad reputation and his tassels); they must be detained ... eh ... that is *enter*tained ... a little; it is embarrassing ... It is delicate. How to get rid of them, and keep the peace? How to play this?

How, indeed, says the King, sounding bored. His valido can work out the details. Appease him. Festivities. Feasts. Conferences in the afternoon. And yet more festivities. A parade, every day, for the English Prince! The King throws himself back in his chair again, so low that the royal backside is in danger of slipping from the edge of it and his chin rests on his chest, and he digs it into his sternum and then lifts it, jutting, a proud and famous chin indeed it is. He puts a hand to it. A little fuzzy. He will need to be shaved. This painter of yours . . . he covers a brisk yawn, pulls himself upright, pats his newly trousered knees decisively— what is he?

This is more in Felipe's line. He has a collection to build on. It will be magnificent—it is already—the King's chamber is hung with works acquired by his forefathers. The flesh of these nymphs and goddesses, these flanks and flushes and arrested flights—his great-grandfather and grandfather and father have enjoyed them all before him. His forefathers who are, of course, all dead, or he would not sit in these chambers, or yet be king. Here, on this morning, almost all of his reign is yet to come, and the two years of it passed have been much taken up with grieving. (There is another servant of the family, always on hand, a hooded old woman who's been here longer than any of them, and will outlast us all—keeping quiet in the shadows, inhabiting the draughts. And there are so many draughts in this old fortress; though she, patient, fleshless, doesn't feel them.) The outward show of masses and candles and black, a semblance to mask the unshown grief that the Count has seen in the King, in these private rooms, sometimes, and which hasn't entirely to do with his father's or any other individual passing. It was there already, he was already grieving for something greater, or less particular, than one man; which is to say, mourning suits him.

Anyway the King's spirits are high, today, as a reed instrument can be thin and high and carry a brittle melody over low-strung notes. Thinly. He does not gambol or jape. But he is at least lively in his distraction; it's restlessness rather than lethargy. He is enthused, as far as he can be, as far as he's willing to show it. The Count, twice his age and bumptious, rustles about him, regards his features—the chin (which wants shaving), the nose, the golden hair, the pout which manhood will not retract. The Count has known these features all his life, he has worked hard and served and now he is needed, when once he was an irritant to the weary little Prince— This man wearies me, he'd said. Remember this, Your Majesty? How your servant lifted the Prince's pot to his lips and kissed it, kissed the receptacle of the pettish Prince's stool; how he had then quietly, with only the faintest yellow slosh, withdrawn from the chamber, taking the pot with him; remember how he suffered all those years under the Prince's disdain, how he acquiesced, how he humbled himself, how he devised days of entertainment to be yawned and stropped through, how he schooled his pupil not to show it, the impatience, the fatigue, the strop; how he brought tutors of language, of drawing, of history and law; how he oversaw the slaughter of the Prince's first boar, and the spilling of his seed into his first whore (actress, whore, let's not split hairs), until at last this most devoted servant was tolerated, then trusted, and then slowly by degrees at last indispensable ... and remember above all how, as the last King was dying, this faithful servant said: Everything is mine now; everything.

And yes, this young King will do better; his father was weak, too easily swayed, but with the Count beside him (his servant and the servant of the court), this fourth Felipe will do better. They will revive the country's fortunes before they are even seen to be failing. There are many facets to being a king;

and yet all edges must appear burnished to a perfect smooth orb, shining at the centre of his empire. A Planet King, a golden king to warm and shine upon this golden age, which can't be allowed to end, or be seen to be ending.

And so, Señor, there must be portraits painted. There are treaties and matches and strategies to be made, but images also. Of course, the King assures the Count; when the time comes he will sit patiently for this painter. He gathers himself, a straight back, a jut and a pout. He tosses his chin and puts out a hand in regal pose, in readiness. Not a smile, which would be unseemly, but the possibility of one. Yes, this morning, he is at least lively——

— Later they'll say he laughed only three times in his life, but this is a rumour that spores in the dank silence of his ageing; now he is young and golden, and his people love him, and although he is melancholy by temperament he hasn't yet known many of the many sadnesses that will later come to weigh him down and pull at the corners of his eyes and cast the court into muttering silence, chafing in the draughts; all this is to come and if anyone can see it they won't speak, won't say it, or won't be listened to; only a fool would tell a truth like that one, that it's all already ending——

Yes, he is laughing today, in this private chamber where a laugh is admissible, his laugh that comes out as a sigh.

The painter waits what seems a long time for the call. It seems there's an English Prince at court, come for the hand of the King's sister, and the streets are filled every day with festivity— processions and puppets and plays. No doubt the painter sees the King at a distance, sometimes, a dark-clothed white figure at his balcony of marble, unmoved and marmoreal as below him the people of the city lick the syrup from paper-wrapped fruits and crack nuts and strew the broken dry shells on the paving and watch as bulls stamp and scrape and vomit blood in the Plaza Mayor. And he walks through the husk-strewn sometimes-bloody streets waiting. He is well looked after in his friend, the Canon's, home. He sketches and paints when he has a mind to; he eats and sleeps well; he doesn't want for company. He sees old friends. His master's house in Seville must be empty, since all the former guests are here—the wits, the poets, the men of letters, have all followed the shining stream of the quinto, the tithe that the court takes from every cargo; the Sevillians have followed the flow of silver and gold to seek their fortune, hoping for favour from the valido Count who claims to be one of them. Likewise, of course, the painter.

He walks, and paints, and waits; he misses Seville's wide river, misses the silt-salt airs off the Guadalquivir. This is a strange high inland city, without the currents of trade, without the tides that bring it. He has moved, they say, to the capital of his country from the capital of the world. He misses Juana, and their little daughter; and is anxious, and impatient, and full of hope; all of this. Hopeful and telling himself to hope for nothing, to expect nothing, although the Count has asked for him, and he is living here on the Count's stipend—and the Count is the most powerful man in the country— so they say, and for the time being at least.

He paints his host, the Canon, to please him and to keep his hand in, and as a calling card, and to acquaint his eye with the dry blue light here. As he pricks the last catchlight in the Canon's pupil, he turns to find he has an audience—his host's guests have gathered in the shade in the courtyard behind him to watch as features form upon planes of light and shadow, as the semblance of life comes into the eyes. Among them is a chamberlain to the Infante Don Carlos. This man comes forward and says to the finished portrait: Father, I would make confession. And the Canon maintains his wise silence— the painter has made the eyes wise. The chamberlain says, Are you listening, Father? What, have you no interest in my sins? Am I to have no penance? The animate mortal Canon and his guests are amused; the chamberlain, gratified, spins the joke out a while longer; the painter smiles, modestly. Doesn't push his advantage. Lets the work, which remains silent, speak for itself. The chamberlain announces that he will take the canvas with him to court that evening. The painter sends a boy with him. So again, he's waiting, and this small specific wait seems longer than the weeks that have gone before; he shifts about the Canon's house, can't settle to supper, then feels hungry, takes up and abandons snacks, cleans brushes, straightens things, cleans his fingernails of the paint that's always under them. And it's growing dark before the boy comes racing back. This boy is attached to the painter; he has come up from Seville, he's the attendant at the gate, who's been here in the background the whole time; the painter has owned him since he was no more than an infant. The painter sometimes sketches him, and the boy now fancies himself an actor, so successful are his masks of weeping, laughter, fury. With the charcoal face held up beside his own dark one he'll make the same face back at himself in the master's mirror, so that there are four of him: the sad boy in the drawing, the sad boy in the mirror, the sad boy in the drawing in the mirror, and the boy himself, and this last is the only one he cannot see, his true self, not really sad at all, and when he explained all this to the painter, the painter smiled and nodded and offered him chalk, paper, and mirror, and let him sketch— so he loves the painter, this boy, he's excited and races back from the palace to tell them: The Prince, Don Carlos, approves. His younger brother, the

Cardinal Fernando, approves. And their older brother approves too; and their older brother is King.

The festivities continue. The nights are full of fireworks. The painter waits.

At last, word comes. The Canon brings the note to him in the evening, pleased for his young friend, full of reflected glory. It is the Canon's task to raise and lower the King's canopy at mass, so he is accustomed to these spells of basking in the King's dazzle, is responsible, indeed, for its public exposure, and metes and measures it scrupulously, according to ceremony. He has the King's ear, he explains, and a splendid shell-pink ear it is, he says, which the painter will see for himself, because— Yes because? says the painter, unusually unable to restrain his impatience, Am I to paint the King's brother? So Don Carlos' chamberlain had hinted. But no! says the Canon, all the more delighted to exceed his expectations— *Because*, the King and the Count have decided that so fine a painter, it would be only proper— he pauses to pour out water and drinks and swallows and the painter with dry throat also swallows deliberately— in short, you are to go to court and paint the King. In short, the Count has sent the Canon home with a note for the painter, to come in the morning, first thing.

But before that there's the night, and the night is terrible; hot and droning with flies and the buzz of his own thoughts, all the distance he's come and the weeks he's waited, the damp tangle of blanket pushed to his feet, and he must be up early and on form in the morning and he must sleep so he looks presentable so he can think and see and paint straight with clean and steady hands, and he goes over what he must take with him tomorrow which he has already set out but might have forgotten something and maybe needs more white and he's actually forgotten all his brushes or can't think where to find them and no, he's awake—— but everything is fine; he'll go to sleep; why are these flies so loud, tonight of all nights?— but, sleep; he thinks about the Canon and the image he made of him and tries to recall it and the Canon's face, remembering the eyes and— it was good, wasn't it? The King and his whole family liked it— and then the King's face: what he knows of it already and how he imagines it and how he might paint it. He envisions the canvas the first marks he'll make on it his hands moving across twitching at the sheet he walks through a palace and it has rooms and rooms and they are all full of paintings they are full of windows the palace is yellow and glass and things start to blur the borders of sense seem to thicken and the edges of these things he sees begin to shift and every time the world slides and softens and begins to become senseless, every time he thinks ah, now I'm sleeping! that treacherous thought wakes him and he's back to the hot room in the Canon's house and the drone of his own thoughts and the flies. Oh, poor painter— I am with him, I have been here, this hot room; I can't bear nights like this, I know too well, I have not-slept through too many of them. And oh, he needs to sleep.

Morning comes and he splashes his face and rubs it and shaves carefully with nervy steadied hands. Smoothes eyebrows, moustache, ringlet. Drinks a thick chocolate. Washes his hands and cleans his nails, and sets out into the city. Everything's edges are brightly unreal with tiredness. He would like to keep more to the shade, of which there is little, even in the narrower alleyways, under the already high sun. It is decreed that the King has a right to all second storeys, so they just don't build that high; no one wants a lodger from the court taking rooms. He finds his way through the close, low streets. La Corte they call it, this synonymous city, clustering up to the hulk of the palace, the city an excrescence of the thing that gives it meaning, spreading out from it like a stain. Everything here exists to serve the court, to bake its bread and cure its meat and weave and starch its linens and sew its sleeves and tunics and undergarments; an ersatz city at the axis of a cross drawn through the country, and built upon a high dry plain across which hot winds in summer and ice winds in winter wander and gallop like madness.

The painter would like to keep more to the shade— but the shade is mostly occupied. He squints. The sluggish river that chugs past the palace is as clogged with dust as the streets are. The dust is mostly dry shit. The high sharp air dries out everything and, he has heard, will shrivel any foul thing before it can begin to putrefy; if that is the case then he is glad of it, because as it is there are some streets he struggles to pass without gagging——

— But then again, he is himself from a city that stinks, and where the stink hangs heavy in the thicker air, a city famed for soap and so the stink of tallow, a port and so the stink of fish, of sailors; and the lame, the unwashed beggars, the war-torn, the thieves throng the shit-clogged shade just as they do here; he will have seen them all his life, although here perhaps they are dustier. So he is accustomed to all this— or something different but no better. But still, he sees them, the unfortunate and criminal and crippled and poor, in the shadows of the city that they call la Corte. Their frayed hems and fingernails, their chipped begging bowls. Other shadows passing veiled, intent upon their own assignations, faceless blur against the walls. Papered windows and women unseen within and he doesn't even try to look in to see them, since the noblemen who linger at the windows carry swords with them. And who knows what knives the beggars might be hiding, if they can afford to keep them—who knows what price you could get on a knife? Who knows what you'd choose between bread, wine and protection. So he keeps his eyes down and his purse with its few coins close, ignores the comments that his canvas roll draws, clasps the long wrap of brushes to his body; a gift from his mentor who is also his wife's father, the brushes with which he has already outstripped him. But he's not thinking of Juana's father; he has added his own brushes to the set and discarded others and is used to them, they are used to him, so he rarely thinks about them at all, and anyway he has other things on his mind, now.

At last he enters the palace gate; it has not been a long walk but heat, nerves and threat have made it seem so. He is within the walls——

— What was it like then, this palace? The Alcázar he enters, which was not a fairy-tale thing but a fortress, is gone—and four hundred years after, I can't follow. A visitor to this city, come looking for him, will find that the towers, the ramparts, the halls and passageways and corridors are gone, the draughts and dark corners swept out by fire a hundred years after him, the hulking façade blackened and crumbled and cleared away. In its place, an unlovely grey square-cornered horseshoe enclosing an open forecourt that is tiring and boring to walk across in the sun, and empty and nothing like it was then. So that I stand lost at the centre of this hot grey open space, a northern foreigner, and feel sick and woozy with the heat—it is July and although I love the sunlight, it's cruel to me in return; standing in this vast and lifeless courtyard feeling sick and tired and dusty, feeling dizzy also with the thought of the old palace that once stood here, with the thought of its absolute absence. Of the lives obliterated along with its hidden courtyards, corridors; the heavy hangings and carved gilded ceilings, and the dank poky discomfort of it. Whether it would be as hot as this in there, in the narrow shadows, or cool, or hotter. These shoes are stupid or the feet are, swollen, too soft, pink and weepy where the strap's rubbed, pale on the instep and bright red toes. Feeling sick and stupid and foreign and hot as a dog and dizzy. Listening for any aural trace, footsteps, voices. Thinking maybe something like a version of the place could be managed— like something from an old play. Asking the audience to imagine that the actors on a lit stage are whispering in a corner in the dark, and the characters they are playing don't know they're being played, and think themselves unseen. So——

—— What is it like then—— this fortress where the painter finds himself, at last? It is … incoherent. Kind of a mess. Disjointed, repurposed to look like a palace, with towers re-roofed and a new façade that fails to unite its disparate elements … Bulky, blocky, busy. At its centre, within, in its central squares and rooms of state, there is grandeur; it is spacious and broad; high sculpted ceilings in the old Moorish style; windows open to the blue cloudless cloche of sky, a vast glass arc full of the heat of the sun, which never quite reaches within—although it pounds at the walls all through the day; it scorches the air that carries the arid dust, scouring at the stones in hot gusts. So the stones of the castle as it faces out might be too hot to touch, but deep within it is— yes, it is chilly, gloomy, the light pale and strained as it passes through the casements.

Already the forecourt is filled with people: litigants and their bored lawyers waiting for days; pretenders petitioning, striking poses, clutching their cuffs of grubby linen; imperious officials and attentive pages and magistrates and ministers and soldiers and statues, busts lining the porticos, looking on, impassive. The walls are thick and high and their shadow when he reaches it at last is deep and cool, and the painter's sun-blind eyes can't make out the colour or the texture of the earth, closing up dark beneath him; only the reiterated brilliance of the sun on the opposite stone wall, its bright white balconies— These walls will close him in for the rest of his life now. Not these particular walls, not always; but the court is not bound by a single building. Even when we travel, into the country, into woods and mountains, even when we pour in a great procession from this high plain down to convents and churches and country palaces, when we go to hunt or pray or to war, as we follow the King wherever he would go, we are not out of it.

The painter hitches the brushes under his arm, his hand sticky on the dusty cloth. No one sees him. He feels awkward, hot, an interloper. Far from the south, far from the sea. But, also, thinks yes— I have arrived at last— yes. He looks up and sees many windows, a succession of grilles, of frames paned and glassed or open and only black within.

On the first floor, the King awaits. His Prime Minister, the Count, at his side with papers to sign and a reminder of the painter's visit. The Count tuts. Who attended your dress this morning? If Your Majesty would permit me . . . even the King's private chamberlains are not to be trusted above the Count. He straightens the wide stiff collar, and Felipe presses his lips together so that they blossom out into a reddened pout; he is virtuous but not without vanity.

The English Prince paces, though his weak ankles ache. He dreads the afternoon's processions, the Count's impatience, the

Infanta's contempt. He tries to rehearse a pleasantry and can't get the f . . . first word out. He puts on Tom Smith's hat in the mirror and wishes, for a moment, he could wear it always.

The King's brother Carlos: reclining, happily idle.

María's head is surrounded by hands, brushing and plaiting and knotting in bows. She's bored. In the mirror she is haughty, big eyes, pearls, blurred.

From a high window the sun is ripe behind the golden tower and the swifts are wheeling, thin and high their crying, an augury; they fall past the window, sweep up and wheel and fall. It is a long drop, over the sill, rolling and turning and falling wings outstretched to the courtyard below. A fool at the window, maybe, to see what there is to foresee. An arrival.

The painter stands in the forecourt, just within the gate, with his roll under his arm and looks up, and looking up into the brightness can't see anyone within looking down from the windows. He finds someone who finds someone who finds a steward who comes to find him at the gate and greets him and leads him through endless darkened antechambers and stairways and doorways, which the steward unlocks and locks behind them. The locks run smooth in the palace, because they are in constant use (and it is someone's duty to ensure they do so). Not everyone has every key but every lock has its keepers. The painter makes no attempt at small talk—and the steward doesn't either—he is silent and deferential and wears sober clothing that is nonetheless, the painter sees, expensive. Fine black silk embroidery tracing its way through black satin, sliding noiseless through each door. The painter

feels a stir of envy and regrets again the dust that clings to
him, to his dark green worsted suit, the dust that he thinks
he can feel stuck in the sweat that clags his thin moustache.
Then they climb a flight of stairs much balustraded and
the ceilings soar suddenly above them as they reach what must
be the King's public rooms. Why they have come what must be
the long way round, the painter cannot fathom. They pass at
a tortuous pace through one grand chamber after another,
each grander than the last, each unpeopled and chairless,
without apparent purpose; tapestries of hunting scenes and
battles, the shine of armour, the vibrant red of insignia and
blood and dogs' gums; inlaid tables whose only function is to
hold things made of silver and gold, which things in turn hold
nothing but their own surprising gold and silver light; solid
objects but barely so; and paintings, everywhere, glimpses
of saints and gods which the painter would long to stop and
study if he were not so anxious to progress, to move from this
chamber to the next and to the next until at last— the King.
The steward announces the painter to a chamberlain who
announces the painter to the room beyond and turning, with
an odd salute by way of leave-taking—tapping two fingers to
his forehead, staring, a moue, a shrug—withdraws, closing
the door behind him. A key turns.

The painter bows, and wants to cough; his throat feels
sticky and coated, he would like to lick his dry lips but resists
putting his tongue out, even for a moment, before— the King.
At last.

The King stands at a console table and looks as if he has
stood for centuries since he was sculpted there, unblinking,
a basilisk. He raises one hand, slowly, slowly, to his brow in
greeting; the painter hurriedly pulls his hat from his head (that
salute!) and bows again. The Count has an easel ready for him

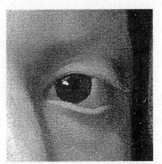

and a canvas primed; the painter unrolls his wrap and lays out his brushes, prepares his palette under the Count's attention and the King's sublime indifference, and when all is ready and still the King is at his console he suggests to the Count that His Majesty might sit, wondering if it is in his power to make such a suggestion. But the King somehow achieves his throne without seeming to move any muscle or limb and sits, graciously, and the Count takes his gloves from him. His movements, his gestures, are seamless, smooth, and he does not breathe discernibly, or blink. He is thin, but not feeble; young—five, six years younger than the painter, and looks younger still; wet eyes, wet coralline lips just bitten, just licked, and yet seeming now without utterance and unlikely ever to part. Fairer than any one of his subjects, thinks the painter, feeling sunburnt and southern and itchy and coarse. Moving forward a pace, his hands go out to turn the shoulders, and stop and gesture in the air instead, and he hopes that the air in which he gestures is not too close to the King's body; the King, mildly, does as he is bid. Over the last nineteen years he's had many portraits painted. By now he knows the process.

The painter's nerves are fizzing—he almost left his hat on!—now he has to, now, get this right; he must make the

right impression; he knows he's capable he is sure he can except
what if he can't; he is so tired—but his hand is sure. He works
quickly, so quickly it's amazing, straight onto the canvas: the
length of the head the width of the head the shoulders and how
they are set. The fleshy chin which he sees the King hold forth;
the jut but not the excess of pride in it; the faintest boyish fold
of skin below; the pale skin that he makes paler— glowing;
the fair lights in the hair, glossing them, the red full lips reddened. The pink flush of the cheek, the tip of the ear. But also,
the faintest traces of tiredness and care already, which he sees
and knows and doesn't paint over, which make a divot in the
forehead and hang about the eye sockets— the skull under the
skin— the veins below the thin temple skin; the same carmine
from the lips at the lids, almost lashless; dark pupils glinting,
but glinting in the distance. It is a portrait of a man, just a man,
a very radiant regal man in simple black and plain collar and no
crown— they do not wear crowns, these kings. All the weight
of the reign is worn invisibly; perhaps it is this invisible crown
that dents his brow. The painter works at it all day, unstinting; sometimes there are other people there; sometimes he is
brought refreshment; sometimes he glances out of the window
and sees that the sun has moved and hours have passed and
that's why the light has shifted, and he compensates. The work
is finished by the time evening comes.

The King doesn't smile exactly but makes a sound through
his nose like a sigh, which might be a laugh. He is appar-
ently pleased. His family are pleased. His brothers Carlos
and Fernando are pleased. The Queen? Well. The Queen's
view is undisclosed; she is perhaps indisposed; perhaps the
Count doesn't think to ask her in. But otherwise, they are
all astounded— he did this in a day? And they all agree, the
painter has painted a true portrait—— or, even better, has

found a way to flatter without seeming to resort to falsehood. See, the sincere care that haunts the eyes, the pallor of the fair skin, the perfect proportion of the regal chin. The Count tells him: no other has caught the King as you have. No other has truly painted the King before now. And the painter, as he exhales for what seems the first time that day, spreads out his stiff oily painty fingers and feels them tremble, and bows.

And word like this gets around; in every studio can be heard the hiss, who is this Sevillian?

The Count says— The King has instructed that you will come to the court and live in the city and when His Majesty asks, you will paint whatever he pleases. You will paint his family, his heirs, his— children, when they come, God willing ... his ... well. Well, perhaps you will paint his wife. That is up to Her Majesty. Perhaps, if you find time and it pleases the King, you will paint me. But not only this. Listen: You alone will paint the King from hereon, my lad. Of all the King's painters, *only you* may paint the King himself. So, you belong here, now. Send for your people. You will be a part of this household until you die, now, if you're lucky, if you play it right, if you stay in favour; you may find advancement. You are, already, an important man, having access to the King's person, having sole right to convey His Majesty's image, the majesty of his person, to his people.

Or words to this effect. The Count likes to talk. The painter listens. You are the King's painter, the only painter of the King. Stay here in Madrid and send for your people. Not a request but an instruction—but after all, why else did he come?

Charles paces in the fine rooms they gave him when he revealed the royal face he wore below Tom's cap. This face is

now furious. Ten years of promises and all of them hollow.
Ffireworks and f-. And ff ... (Buckingham raises a finely
formed eyebrow) and ffffucking *fiestas*. He came here for a
princess and has been sent a p ... a ... p*painter*. Although, in
truth, he likes painting better than politics ... *p*erhaps yes, a
little ... *portrait*.

Which is painted, at least partially, and lost, somewhere
along the way. The English Prince may or may not take it with
him; in his haste he leaves behind several gifts that he's been
given. Rude, after such a show of hospitality. Enraged, embarrassed, and bellicose, he leaves also without his princess. Before
he goes, he bestows 100 ducats on the painter.

II

¿Retratas, o animas?/
Do you portray, or give life?

The painter begins to settle; the days shorten and cool; he takes a residence near the palace, a few steps from the Plaza Mayor. His wife comes, bringing their daughter Francisca. His wife with the face of the Virgin, humble and mild: an attitude perhaps adopted for the role, or indeed superimposed by the painter. Juana's father was the painter's master, at the centre of a circle of clever, cultured Sevillians; and she has spent her life in her father's salon; so Juana, actually, is not so humble. Juana sets about putting their new apartments in order; no knowing how long they might stay, here in Madrid, in this house——

—— A hundred tourists an hour might now walk unknowing down Calle Concepcion Jerónima, but a traveller who's gone to look for it can stand back, being careful of the cars that pass between the narrow pavements and the parking bays across the street, and see a yellow plaque that bears the painter's name and attests to this fact, that he lived here once; the plaque is fixed to a storey that wouldn't have existed then, and the plaque and the street are a little grubby, nondescript, it's an unloved little thoroughfare close to the throng of tourist tat and tapas, and there is nothing more there to be found of him. There are these traces of remembrance scattered through the city, a statue on a plinth, a figure on a rooftop if you look up, a plaque— he lived here, once, in a house that was here. While the city passes on below this plaque, I stand all gauche and hot and gawkish and take a photo of it— Are you at home? I came calling for you . . .

He works, rests, visits friends, thinks he might become accustomed to the dry air, to the winter cold coming, the wind— or perhaps he never will. Sometimes in the evening the sky is low and purple and hunkers down close upon the city, and the air feels sweaty, and he feels at home then and walks in the liquid dusk until he's soaked; but the rain that comes is cold and torrential and he must choose to either keep to the walls for shelter, where the beggars wallow in the night's slops still running fresh, or get wet. He is given a studio in the east wing, and every morning makes his way there, very early, while the shadows still sleep. The room is not large but it is light, light enough to work in, and high, and he is brought water in little red clay jugs—how sweet the water is, here! Beneath the filthy city it runs pure and clear from the rock—and fresh oranges when he asks for fruit, which make him think of home, the orange trees in the ochre-walled courtyards of Seville, maybe they are brought all the way from there. A porcelain bowl of them, tart and dimpled and sweet.

His neighbours, other, older painters of the court, nod to him as he passes but do not speak, and he feels their suspicion, muttering, sneers. This Sevillian . . . If he even is that. Half Portuguese, isn't he? His father's people are merchants, aren't they? Probably conversos . . . Half a Portuguese Jew, then, and what's the other half? Some spurious noble ancestry, reckons his mother's lot are hidalgo . . . So that's why he uses her name, then . . . but he's a southerner after all, that's how they do things down there. Well, he certainly knows how to paint heads, doesn't he, and pots and pans too, these ah— these bodegones of his . . . An old woman cooking eggs, very *original*; such deep shadows in the hollows of her cheeks, there, such a shock to see such *contrast*, so ill-fed she is—the common touch, very fashionable, no doubt. An old man drinking with two boys, as they do in the south no doubt. A miserable maid— ha! a Sevillian *maid*? *most* likely— with a bucket of fish. It's all so exceedingly *real*, isn't it, they say, surveying. Reality *can* be so rough around the edges . . . The painter says politely, he would rather be first in coarseness than second in delicacy. He means second to Raphael, whose work they love and he doesn't, although he doesn't say so. If he thinks himself second to any other, in any other aspect, he doesn't say so. But he is so polite that they don't at first register the jibe, and can't work out if it is one. First in *coarseness* . . . And this, according to the Count, the King's valido (as they persist in calling him), is the only man who now can paint the King?

Their work can be glimpsed through open doors and in the rooms where they hang: martyrs, miracles and histories; formal, traditional, stiff stuff, he finds it, but doesn't say so. (Some of these works hang still, formulaic, unremarked, in shadowy chapels, lost among the profusion of so many others like them.) He has no interest in doing things their way. He does things his own way and always has and even his father-in-law trying to school him had to admit that it works. Straight to canvas and straight from life. It's not about beauty, if by beauty what's meant is proportion; is grace; is easeful transition, from dark to lightness, from youth to ageing, from stillness to life; and no roughness, no rough edges, no deep hollows. It's not about appraisal. It's about opening the eye onto the world and looking; the world as he sees it, as anyone can see it if they choose to look; isn't this what the world looks like? Pull away the veil of custom to show the world just so, and don't they see what he sees, the way he sees it? Don't they? He'll show them how to see it that way, then. He'll show them. He's here now by royal appointment. He has the Prime Minister's favour. He belongs here. He will come to belong here.

The Prime Minister, the painter's patron and the King's favour-ite—— the King's servant— has been awarded a dukedom and so acquired the title he will be known for, unwilling to forsake the first for the other. The painter paints the new-made Count-Duke huge and broad and powerful, with key and spurs at his waist, meaning Groom of the Stole *and* Master of the Horse; he is at the King's side when he dresses and at any time he leaves the palace walls, at the ready any hour of day or night. He is the only member of the court to hold such a double office, just as he is the only one to hold two titles. He fills the frame with massive black bulk just as he fills any space that he enters, forcing the edges of it. His huge head; the painter shows the weight of it, all the cunning and the power of the brow, but does not make it monstrous.

Above the entrance to the Alcázar a new room has lately come into being. The King's father imposed upon the palace a façade, thinking to unite all its incongruous parts, hoping to make the place less hideous; and within this screen, slung between two towers, there is a new gallery to be filled. And so the royal collection has been reshuffled and a king, it seems, is missing from the pack. The Count-Duke says: You are to paint a grand portrait, for the New Room.

So sittings are arranged and the King is brought to the painter's studio with the usual retinue of key-turners and attendants, who variously, discreetly, attend or disperse, and the King takes his seat. He looks well, hair and armour shining, golden indoors on this dull day. If he is hot in his armour, bored, he doesn't show it, or show anything; he is pouting but he can't help that, it's the way his mouth is, and the general's sash gives peachy sensuous life to his lips. He is young, and in command of armies, although he has not yet been in the field. He is almost, almost smiling.

They might speak, a little; the King is well-schooled in politesse and might ask after the painter's family and so the painter tells him about Juana, how they are finding their way around the city, smaller than Seville, yes, cold, now, it's refreshing, the—— breeze ... they are settling in and like it very much, thank you, Your Majesty; and tells him about Francisca his daughter; but not about her sister little Ignacia who's dead, some years since, died in Seville, because the Queen is heavily pregnant and he doesn't want to trouble the King, or make him frown while he works on the eyes; instead he tells him how he has enjoyed the oranges, and thanks him: His Majesty is most generous; thank you, Your Majesty, for Your Majesty's hospitality. The King says, I am glad you enjoyed the oranges.

I think perhaps, like you, they have come from Seville? And please, Diego, call me Señor. It makes things easier.

Behind him there is a bristling rustle as the valido's paper hackles briefly rise and settle. The painter turns; the Count-Duke appears occupied with his stack of statutes, but his attention is palpable, just as surely as if he had taken a note and tucked it into his doublet, secreted away close to his heart; yes, he has noted the King's favour of the painter. Which was the point in the first place—the painter will be loyal to his first patron—but still, the corner of that note sticks, just a little, into the Count-Duke's ribs, and he feels it as he moves and works. And that little paper-prick is useful; he must be vigilant, even among friends, especially then. The Count-Duke is covered in paper-pricks. They are his hair shirt. He says, I shall send for more oranges, Señor.

The painter's colleagues come to assess the work in progress, to offer their professional opinion, which he graciously accepts as if he's asked for it. There are, they suggest, many *fine* examples, here in the palace, of the equestrian mode; the King's new pet might profit from a little study of them. Many of the court's most distinguished painters—some of us ourselves, indeed—have assayed this noble subject, and although of course we would not think to rival you for *coarseness*, perhaps a little refinement might be called for now, Sevillian? And as they walk away, they snigger: The King after all is not a southern peasant; he doesn't ride a mule. Have you seen that horse?

By royal appointment. He'll show them, what that means—they'll see— see as he sees—— In the royal stables, the painter watches, sketches, sketches, observing, sketches the hind-leg the foreleg the rump, the mane the tail tensing;

sheen on the sleek sides, deep chestnut flank, the foreleg rearing; the groomsmen are patient or some are not, but he is the King's painter and they do as they're bid, they skim a crop at the sleek sides and the horse rears and foams and flicks the tail and the painter at a distance watches and sketches——— foreleg tail flick, front to back, nose ears bridle between. Soft whinny breathing and the black chalk soft scrape——— rough paper under fingertips—— hours pass. Warm spice of horse-smell and low horsey noises; the King's horses stand with quiet dignity and only the occasional nicker or ear-flick or nostril-flare, and when one of them must relieve herself she does so with the same decorum, barely a shuffle and clop of the feet and a quiet, dignified succession of thuds. He breathes it in and the chalk soft-scrapes over the page—he will not be mocked.

He works and reworks over it, turning and pressing the brush upon the palette, swiping the excess off on the corner of the canvas, his habit—— dip, swipe, dip, swipe: The leg of the horse curves up and into the belly here, like—— Here, the top of the leg rounding into the socket like—— The curve of the belly barrel-like—

—— No

The curve of the belly and the legs little like—— The legs longer—— The legs rearing and the hooves curled under and the barrel of the belly like

No

The swish and the thickness the ropes of horse-hair thick at the root of it muscle thick at the root lifting the swish of it into a plume like——

Like—— Like it's about to shit in the street. No.

———————

— The hind legs leaning into the charge— Leaning
— Like it will topple
— Poking from the bottom of the belly-barrel the legs of some other animal like they're sewn on horribly—grotesque—not attached at all———

Again— the forelegs again rearing again foreshortened no too short— Like stumps— Like they wouldn't meet the ground when it topples like they couldn't take the weight of the massive barrel-belly———

Like———
No
—— No ——

_____

Unpaint it again
Again

———

—

Unpaint it

He starts over.

There's a passage below the Alcázar that acts as a sort of store-room, for the discarded, the unwanted, the rejected; a corner where the palace's shameful things, impossible to entirely extirpate, can be kept from sight. There are several such corners. Canvases are stacked and hung, painted nobles alongside kitchen maids, tavern boys on top of saints, all awaiting their turn on a gallery or chamber wall or to be repurposed, covered over with another work. There is a half-formed king riding a ghosted horse, half-erased by a pale clay wash, the contours of its bulbous belly, its crooked legs, just showing through. And here's a signature—he doesn't sign his finished works, but here it is, his name, and— Pictor Regis, expinxit— 'the Painter to the King unpainted this'——

— Vanished now. Time has entirely unpainted it. No trace left of that obscure horse or of the painter's pique, his shame.

The second attempt is finished. The family comes to appraise it.

The King's brothers approve. His valido approves. The Queen ... Queen Isabel's fool takes up reins and mounts an imaginary horse, his bandy legs in a wobbly squat under him, arms akimbo, back pulled straight; his horse turns wild, his arms strain with the effort, it whinnies and bucks and canters around the chamber mad-eyed and snorting until the fool is thrown high and tumbled and rolls forward over his shoulder and up into a deep bow grinning at Her Majesty's feet. Isabel says it is well done. Her ladies applaud. The painter is not fool-ish enough to presume she means his painting.

(Isabel gives birth to a girl around now. One night not a month after, an old woman hooded and passing unseen lays a cold hard hand upon a hot brow; the infant gurgles once and hiccups, a little laughing rattle and sigh, and she's gone before the painter can even paint her—— He is just nineteen, the King, but they've been trying for an heir five years now and this is the third child miscarried or lost. The Queen, who keeps her own counsel, mourns for Catharina and rests, makes her womb ready, awaits her husband's visit to her chamber.)

In the city's grand square, the poets exalt the new equestrian portrait: A royal copy exceeding all likeness! So gallant! So gracious! So fierce! Painter, do you portray, or do you give life? He is rewarded with ducats, with a pension from the Pope, he is made Painter to the Bedchamber. Brought one doorway closer. The mournful King is pleased with his Sevillian.

✝

Juana's father is in town. Filled with pride, he is the first to
acclaim his former pupil; and when the old guard sneer at his
son-in-law's still lives and bodegones, he says, you do it then.
Go on. Have a go at it. And then, looking at the painter's
world of solid objects, looking at the jugs and jars and eggs,
he thinks he might have a go himself. Alberti, in his treatise,
advises: to describe a thing, you describe the space around it;
the first part of painting is circumscription. He looks at the
things and the space around them. And it's so refreshing, this
carafe of Madrid water before him and a handful of fruit; no
careful geometries or schemes or drawings, just himself in the
world with the things in it, within hand's reach. And when he's
finished he thinks; that might just be the best I've done— and,
well. It comes nowhere close. This boy— but look at him now
with his moustache, with his new hat— this courtier, my pupil,
my daughter's husband; that's the best thing I've done.

Juana says— You have what you wanted, then? You're a painter
of the court. You are painter to the King. And the painter
says— Yes, I have what I wanted. She sets down a dish at his
elbow; makes no move to touch him; she waits. There's probably more; but only if she waits for it, doesn't press. He pares his
fingernails. He says— There are no poets' laurels for painters
to rest on. I take nothing for granted ... He spreads his fingers
upon the table. She waits. He says— There are so many rooms
in that palace, and so many doors, and they all have a key, and
all the keys have someone to hold them. Usher, Chamberlain,
Major-domo. And there are so many doors still closed to me;
there are chambers still closer, still further within. And ...
there are so many walls in that palace, Juana, and half of them

are covered in rubbish. And I know I could do better. And then there are things in there . . . things the King owns . . . the Venetians, Juana, the colours, you should see them . . . works I've waited so long to see, to stop and sketch and study and learn from if I can. And now I can. Do better. So . . . I don't stop wanting.

Throughout this unemphatic speech he pares his fingernails and worries at the cuticles. Do you like it here, Juana? Do you think you will like it? She smiles, comes to lean against the table at his side, takes his hand and holds it up; They're clean, she says. Look at mine. What a ruffian I am beside you. She kisses each scoured nail in turn and says, I'm proud of you. He says— Just wait, Juana. You haven't seen anything yet.

III

La Corte/
Court

The King: official and in sombre mood, black cloak and pale skin; standing back, held in reserve; a princely ankle points the toe outwards, a hand bent around the corner of a standing-desk; a document folded with a finger in the crease— this too is command, in paper there is power—— A thought across the brow there— Mutual scrutiny: they are both immobile a long moment, the King and his personal painter—until the pout pouts and the King has had enough and the painter goes back to his palace duties and his other projects.

There is no shortage of them. He is in the King's favour, and so, in demand. In attending to these duties, these commissions, the painter comes to know the Alcázar, the old fortress—the parts he is permitted access to—and those who occupy them. He sees who moves between places, and how freely; who is constrained; the nature of their restraints. This most restrained of courts. He acquaints himself, always observing as he walks: he reads the angle of the light from the open windows, the angle of the shadow of the frame across the sill, he reads the shadows to know which way he's walking, but the sun is high and hard to steer by and the light is diffuse and he quickly becomes lost on these walks, at first. So he recruits an attendant to take him through grand chambers and galleries and narrow passages to small stores and they wind their way through and between, down, back, up, around (walls of stone to brick to mud). He trusts the attendant to know the way back, to know the keys as they're needed (not everyone has every key but every lock has its keepers). They venture into council rooms and peek into empty chambers of state; pause to listen in the mentideros, the salons of the liars/literary wits that lead off the forecourts; on into kitchens and stables and backyards of brick, up into the stifling rooms in the roof where the servants and fools stay. Closed doors to guessed-at small chambers. A shriek like a wild bird or someone doing an impression of one. It repeats, once, twice, and turns into laughter that is also shrieking. Drunks, laughing or crying. From the windows, this high, the swallows can be seen rising, diving. The sound of rattles and inflated bladders and wooden sticks, of routines practised behind doors, of dropped clubs falling, a yell, an under-breath oath. A guitar. A man ascends the stairs ahead of them in military costume, fine scarlet and gold, and stops when he sees them and bows grandly; but the hat he sweeps off his head, when returned to it, half-slips over an eye; the hose are dusty and rumpled; the uniform is fifty years or so out of date, to the painter's uncertain eye.

Good day, Don John, says his guide, and the man returns the greeting, with a salute which is almost exaggerated, somehow awry, and hesitates there shyly, shuffling back to allow them to pass, and they pass him and walk on. The painter looks back up the stairwell to see him still standing, framed in the gloom and the filtered light of the dusty sloping corridor, looking down at his own pointed toe as if waiting to see if it will make a new step. Who was that, asks the painter.

That was Don John of Austria, says the attendant,

straight-faced, didn't you know him? Don John, that's what we call him. He doesn't seem to mind it.

A boy without a family is taken in from— where? He doesn't toddle in off the street unchallenged; the Queen does not walk the city in a rough shawl disguise and gather foundlings; but this man is here now in the court nonetheless. A kitchen boy maybe, who turned out too funny or useless for the task and had the good fortune to amuse someone important. Or else someone important's unacknowledged bastard, kept close for sentimental reasons. No shortage of bastards in la Corte. So they say. Named as a joke or to honour a bastard before him.

The attendant is laughing— That great admiral, the Emperor Charles' bastard—don't you see the resemblance? Can't you just see him, leading our armada? The painter doesn't react but the man laughs anyway, claps him on the arm. Don John of Austria! The man's hands are as clean as his own are. They are on equal terms, then. Servant, artisan.

So the painter can be anywhere; he is known but unobtrusive, and he spends quiet intent hours in the varied company of the court and among the things of it. The scholars and accountants and chamberlains, the grandees, the dandies in crimson-trimmed silk; groomsmen and smiths and stable boys and girls in the kitchen cracking eggs, scaling fish, cooks turning and basting and shaping pastries and he sees the different shine of glaze, of fat, of dog-gnawed bone. There are dogs all around, little lapdogs and big mastiffs, pets and gundogs for the hunt, and he is fond of dogs— and whenever I see a dog in Madrid I think of him, and how he might paint it. He sees, knows, spends time with physicians, astrologers, advisers, architects, key-holders, keepers of every obscure office; the men of pleasure, the drinkers and topers, the bastards and priests and canons; poets, playwrights, even other painters.

And others, lost, silent and nameless, loafing and clutching to the periphery of the court. Scholars clerks and clerics. All of them, all these men—yes, all men—white-collared, all in black, carrying their hats in their hands and putting them on when it is proper to. This court is a pious court, or dresses like one. The King has worked carefully on new sumptuary laws, with a junta selected by the King's own hand. With, of course, the Count-Duke on hand to guide it. These are the clothes we are to wear, and these are the ranks we are to acknowledge and the ways we will acknowledge them, these are the words we are to speak and when and this is what may be written. A court of Stoics: temperate, constant, disciplined. That's the idea anyway.

There will be no silliness in the Count-Duke's court—— in, that is, the King's court, which the Count-Duke serves most humbly. We are to move through this world unmoved by it. We are to be prudent and patient as we see out these last days. No silliness, no silver embroidery, no silk. The exuberance of huge frilled ruffs and bows has given way to sobriety and the golilla, the simple square white collar—the King designed it himself and overnight, of course, the court followed in the King's adoption of it. The fantastic plumage of former years has been plucked; officials stalk the halls with scissors, on the watch for illicit finery. A young gallant flashes a bright silken flourish at knee and neck; a clatter of heeled slippers, a giggle and shriek, neatly silenced by a long silver snip; he clutches his neck as if it's been slit; crimson spills to the stone floor in ribbons. We will not give way to fashions, distractions, passions and opinions. Or desire or fear, or sorrow, or joy.

The court wears black, black heavy capes over thick black garments, and the plain white golilla close to the throat, and they move, in emulation of the King, without exterior show of discomfort or excessive sorrow or joy through the dark and treacherous halls of the fortress. They move through the shadows with their dark beards and dark eyes, with their soft tread in soft black leather slippers, and they sweat, their bodies inside their black clothes in the dark, they sweat like animals.

The painter is, at once, embedded and removed, in his new black suit, paid for on credit; standing apart at the distance of a long-handled brush. The Sevillian, they call him, and he makes no effort to drop his accent; the son of a merchant with the name of an aristocrat; a palace official, discreet, obedient, with access to any secret that can be observed by a keen observer of fingers and faces, of mouths and their corners, of eyes and where and how and on what they focus, of solid objects and the hands that hold them. He paints for private rooms, for private posterity, small commissions, without statecraft or symbols. His colleagues in their dark garb, sneering— Another portrait! The man can only paint faces. That's all there is to him—likenesses—portraits and peasants. How little this artist's intellect comes between the canvas and the world. He does not invent, he transcribes. He *observes*.

⚔

So, observe: the court as he observes it: before a ready canvas, attending to the forms— lay in a dark ground— behind everything, beneath everything brilliant and particular, there is this: a foundation of Seville clay, dug from the ground we'll be buried in; the dark earth to which we all return. Begin here, and then find the contour, the shadows, and the lights. Let it show through rough, or deepen it, add oil, give it lustre, add calcite to degloss it; there are the different thicknesses of a folded shadow, of a velvet robe. The painter attends to the gradations, where a pupil meets the inkwell of a man's eye, where a beard fades out in filaments against the plain dark ground; a smokiness to the edge of things, and under the surface, always, the earth, the dark. Without it only colour, without depth. This is the palette: ochres red and yellow; lead white; charcoal, bone and vegetable blacks. Why pay for fugitive imported pigments? Paint the world as it is, in the colours it is made from.

Observe: the Infante Don Carlos, long nose and full pout, at leisure to do as he will; the same pose as his sombre brother but without papers of state to concern him, a version less troubled, less burdened, perhaps a little more handsome, and carefully glossed. Hard to read if the purse of the mouth is sweetness or sneer; but no threat, surely no threat. All in black but for the gold chain, the crafted links blurred by their own dull sparkle— one brown-gloved hand bending down the brim of a soft wide hat— the other glove in the other hand in place of a folded paper, dangling from this nonchalant Prince's clasp like a rabbit glove puppet. How many others are permitted, to observe this nonchalance so closely, to come so close?

Observe this young man: a hand about there on the hip— more or less; there's the space for it— the other here resting, fingers curled with four, five, six or so bony strokes. The face: the planes of it, the hint of hair at the surface of the skin, bone under the flesh, the dark of the eyes watching quietly, thoughtfully, sunk in their own depths. No props. There is no worldly thing to distract from this gaze and what can be read in its shadows; no book or quill to say this man is learned, no skull to say that he is mortal— but for his own, under the skin. He is young; his beard— lighter than that—— the beard is fine, his skin is clear, quite fair, perhaps he wears no blush or perhaps the painter unpaints him, preferring the pallor below.

Soft hair furring with a soft brush. Soft sable brush, pulled to
a point with spit between the lips. His shoulders not so wide,
no, nor so set—— bring the ground back in around him. The
body a dark mass of garments. Blocked and sketched. He
paints him for his own, or the young man's pleasure, or both.
This is his friend, surely, who looks so sincerely, who doesn't
mind his hands unfinished.

Observe Pablillos, the jester-philosopher, the man of pleasure,
posing as a jolly Democritus; once a man of the world, now
retired to his gardens, and coming out sometimes to walk
to the harbour and watch life's ridiculous intrigues unfold.
Ridiculous because there's nothing real but atoms, and the
void, and everything else is convention. Smooth white atoms
cast no shadow; and shadows are cast by jagged black atoms—
so this court must be stuffed with black atoms, as well as
conventions. Colour—the umbers and earths and whites that
make this surface— and the solid clay ground that we build
palaces as well as paintings on— colour is consensus, convention. As are bitter, sour, sweet; heat and cold. And all the
atoms you're made of will never perish, although they will one
day fly apart or dissipate— and we call this dissipation death,
by convention. Pablillos-Democritus, slight and sun-worn and
grinning with his globe, its surface meticulously rendered,
coastline and greenish sea and umber underside shadow, this
world which is one of an infinite number stilled in its rotation
to observe it, and Pablillos passing through; the fool Pablillos
passing through the arrangement of atoms that we call the
world and pausing to point and laugh at it.

Observe the old poet: his tall forehead, rising into darkness,
crowned with bay leaves then on second thought— this court

does not do crowns for kings and not for poets either——
unpaint it. But observe how the forehead goes up and up
from the cross brow to the bald crown, a crucible for the cul-
tivation of verbal curlicues; still distilling acid drops, which
might be what is in his mouth to make him look so sourly.
Observe the deep-graved lines; the whole right side enshad-
owed, ageing acetic face corroded with years of vinegar wit;
mouth close-clamped, creasy chin. To finish— bruisey contused shine on nose's bridge— in the eyes no light, no, but
darkly fulgent— a mole upon the temple, distinct and dark,
the last mark—

He is falling out of fashion. The poets that nest in the
mentideros are a mean and vicious bunch, and the arrogant
and insecure will always fall in unison upon a common
enemy, pecking away until all the sinews are shown exposed,
and then plucking at them to see how they sound: without
these hundred words for nothing, what is left of you, old
man? They are talon-deep in a cruel fad for parody: who can
stretch an absurd verb the wordiest. See him in all his glory,
they say: stuck-on superlative nose; gambler; flatterer; sodo-
mite. His foremost rival buys his house from under him and
kicks him out of it and writes cruel verses about his forehead
and the purpleness of his prose and his nose. His rival is
a favourite of the Count-Duke's (for the moment). So this
old poet's works are suppressed, and everyone loses interest
and as he is forgotten he begins to forget; he retreats, to the
town he came from and into his own dementia, with no final
rile and caustic flourish; in a pall of bitterness, sickness, and
finally no more to be said. The traces of the laurel crown
will come to the surface in time. Who heard, who heard,
who saw what I saw?

And so observe: the new favourite poet. There's a red cross on this poet's breast—poets can be knights, because they don't get their hands dirty; poetry is the exercise of mental invention, not the work of an artisan—and the painter, observing this, paints the cross on very precisely. Two heavy black circles round his eyes, as if drawn on by a schoolboy in marker pen. The dandies, noting this favour the poet is enjoying, have taken to wearing the same large dark-rimmed glasses, which they do not need to see by; even the ladies are at it. It's as old as frames and lenses, this association: myopia is a symptom of intellect, and just now it's hip to be a wit, or at least to look like one. But if the poet is actually as well as fashionably short-sighted, he sees clearly enough to see all the tireless work of the Prime Minister—clinging tenuously to his newfound favour, he is full of praises for the Count-Duke, despite the chattering and whispers of the palace's shadowy periphery. This is the life the Count-Duke leads, he writes. Look at him in his prison of paper. Look at him bound to his oar. What thanks he gets. If you envy him, much good may it do you. You gossips, and your lies.

Observe the Stoical Count-Duke, as exemplar: where once he faced head-on as if to withstand a charge, now he is oblique, and the badges of office are worn less boldly, the key just seen (or perhaps jealously guarded). Pride without earthly vanity, which the court as it lives under this man condemns; it is austere, this image, without any trappings or frippery. The privacy of a public man. This left hand carefully moulded, resting casually on a cloaked sword. (And what is that in his other hand? A whip? That sounds about right . . .) Having secured this power, he will bear it as his burden, modestly.

✝

The chattering figures on the periphery change shape, change
title, as the Count-Duke riffles his notes. Ushers crumpled in
his big fist and discarded, left to roll themselves into disregarded corners and unfurl with crackle and whisper, to smooth
out the creases which will make whatever's written there all
the harder to decipher; the dangerous rustle of disgrace running all around the Alcázar. One must take care with these
tossed-out fragments; take note of where they land. But the
Count-Duke has an eye for it, has his eye on it at all times,
the text and texture of the times. So if it is written that the
valido is a hunchback as they say and mad or that the King is
fucking this actress or that it is just as soon censored and thus
unwritten. The Count-Duke is in control. He is the scourge of
all corruption, lawlessness, heresy and discord. Heresy whispering, treachery, treason, the Count-Duke everywhere hears
it; heretics everywhere conspiring against us, ranked against us,
from all sides and within, hidden in plain black among us—he
will show no mercy. He will cast it all out.

He is a model of temperate authority. He can tear up those
pamphlets and tear down those pasquinades as fast as his
whispering critics can post them. Can't he? Can't he rely on
the opacity of his best Indian ink? Can't he keep track of every
slip and scrap, every scrap that might be slipped into the King's
hand or under his napkin even? (Your Majesty, do your limbs
not ache from the jerking of the Count-Duke's strings?)

Here he is in his office: the door is always open, or may as
well be, to permit the numbers that pass through it hourly.
Here are today's agendas for the juntas: he will sit on every
council. Here are forty supplicants, each with their petition.
Here is an arbitrista with an idea to save the country that's so

secret, and so good, that he can share it only with the Prime
Minister directly; and this particular petitioner, because of
who he is and the people he knows, must be indulged by the
Count-Duke, directly; and it might just after all be the idea
they are looking for, the key to restoring Spain's glories, or then
again it might be another fabulous grand strategy to unite with
Scotland or Malta or some other place, or a marriage proposal
for the King's sister María, or a brand-new infallible formula
for gold! And in any of these cases the Count-Duke must hear
the man out. Here is his new Chief Secretary, Don Jerónimo
(that shadowy man, of whom it is said that he built a nunnery
next to his house that serves as a brothel), with sixty sheaves of
letters. Here is the Count-Duke surrounded by his creatures:
they set out in his carriage so he can take his work with him
and they all squash in together and clutch papers and each
other as they all get thrown about on the pot-holed road—he
makes a note: fill the pot-holes. Here he is bellowing, bullying,
berating, sticking his cane under his hairpiece to scratch. In
spare snatched moments he prays and takes small frugal meals
and grinds herbs and mixes his tinctures, ever wary of sickness,
ever on the edge of fever, so busy, so sweaty, so big. (Crazy. Just
look at him twitch and scratch.)

The Count-Duke has nothing left, nothing but the King he
serves and the country and the family of the King—including,
now, an heir of sorts—another Princess has been born, and
survived birth, and lived more than a day, a week, and still
lives. Whereas the Count-Duke has lately lost his only daughter, dying as she gave birth to a dead granddaughter—there
she goes, that bony busy midwife—and he has also lately lost
his nephew, who was his own heir. He is nothing but a man
of paper, now. He is willingly folded into it, this paper prison.
Sheaf upon sheaf torn and tucked and torched, folded and

fanned, issued and received, assessed and censored and signed and when absolutely necessary, placed before the King.

The Count-Duke comes into the King's chamber, as he does every morning—he has been up for hours— Good morning, Your Majesty, Señor ... here is your shirt ... The barber is on his way already, yes ... now, if I may—to business! If you are dressed now, Señor ... These writs, these laws ... if you are ready for your desk, now ... We must look to our borders. We must look to our tithes, we must look to our coffers. We must look to our insides. To whom we allow inside. There is coffee here, Señor. The world is a series of guarded walls and we must be vigilant, we must keep our keys close. Traitors at the gates, and in our midst, even. Heretics. These new laws, then, it's vital that ... I'm sorry, Señor, I know it's tedious, but it's important, it's important that we do this. That *you* do this, that you are seen to do this. That you are seen to be involved, that you ... that you take an interest.

He is treading a line, here. He doesn't say, So that everyone can see that you are not your father. Forgive me for saying it, he doesn't say. But I knew him, I saw what they did to him, how swaddled he was, how he allowed them to enfeeble him, and you are not him, I know you are not feeble; and I am not a schemer, I am in your service, I will not be a valido. You are the head of this state, of this Empire. You. You are not the puppet of your favourites, whatever you've heard muttered. I am trying, Señor, to purge that corruption, to rid us of this poison, this knot of snakes we must cut down the middle and cast the pieces, wriggling, out. And the King must be seen to wield both the sword, and the pen, to do so. The King's grand-father, that most prudent monarch, was said to rule the world with two inches of paper. So, says the Count-Duke, there are just a few more documents, there is just a little more that we must do this morning, and then to your studies.

Among his many other attributes, the Count-Duke is a pedagogue, and has devised a thorough and broad curriculum for the sons of courtiers and for princes and kings. And so every day, when their business is done, he puts the papers away and brings out the King's books; tests him on his French; leaves him learning of the history of Castile, which is his own history, which has shaped him, which his own family has shaped, which is the history of the future he——they— will shape.

As he moves to the door behind him, he offers assurance: Two hours more, Señor, and then perhaps we can seek some other diversion (for the King, there is a programme of extra-curricular activity also).

Felipe at his books, alone; thinking he is unobserved he heaves a huge sigh, slumps on one hand. The Count-Duke ordinarily leaves the King to his reading, but today thinks better of it; waits, watches from the doorway to see how his pupil is faring. The King is to show himself to be a model: sovereign, sports-man, scholar—and now doting father to the Infanta, María Eugenia. A better man than any in the court.

The King smoothes and strokes the fine hair at his temple where the bone is, taps the skull under the skin. Then stops himself and straightens his back and sits completely still for long minutes, before stiffly turning a page and reading without even bowing his head. He is trying hard.

I wonder, the Count-Duke says from the doorway. The King doesn't even jump. Turns slowly, impassive, enquiring. Oh, he is good, he can be good, when he wants to be. There is another thing, I'm sorry, Señor. While I'm here. (When isn't he?) I have been thinking. I have been thinking of your father, Señor. The last king—for all his faults, his ... tenderness, forgive me— (he doesn't say, for all his foolishness and feebleness and lack of independence—for all his cosseting and all his validos ...)— the last king was your father still, and while we look to *his* father, your grandfather, as a more ... fitting model, and you so diligently make study of your illustrious forebears ... still, we can't pretend he didn't happen. It's been some years now. Perhaps it would be prudent to acknowledge him.

The point being that with all those old favourites out, those families gone (and carefully replaced), things need to be consolidated; things need to seem seamless. A new PR campaign is needed, to glorify the reign of the King's father, and by extension his own succession—and that of his children, now that this claim to Spain's future is so tenuously established. A subject is needed. The material is scant. The King his father was ... well. He was good at delegating? No, best avoid that. He was of a quiet sort of nature, peaceful ... yet this never-ending complicated war he got us into has been going on for years now ... He was ... well, he was really pious. Yes! This can be said for him, this can be emphasised, reiterated; kingship and its continuance, let's not forget, are in turn ordained by God. And Spain, to be restored, must look to her glorious uncontaminated past and her God-given right to govern in all her territories. Good. This is useful, on-message.

The King announces a competition to glorify the reign of his father. In recognition of this pious king's holy achievements, the court's painters are invited to glorify the expulsion of the heretic and traitor Moriscos from his kingdom.

And what will the Sevillian do now? the old guard snigger. He will have to exercise his *intellect*—oh dear!—his *imagination*—ha! He'll have to show a bit of draughtsmanship now, won't he. They look forward to the result.

And perhaps the King extends this opportunity quite purposely (or perhaps his valido has suggested it); perhaps the King requires his favourite painter now to prove his worth, to paint something other than portraits—which, after all, have been his only commission.

So how is he to construct this scene? His father-in-law spent long hours teaching him the rules of composition and there must be some use he can make of the lessons he's spent the last few years largely disregarding ... And he knows how to paint people, real people, better than any of his rivals: that's his thing. The world as it is. When were any of that lot last in the streets, in a tavern, at the market, at a dock? (When was he, for that matter?) No, he can hardly work from life; there are hardly any Moriscos left to sit for him; that being precisely the point of the brief. But as a boy in Seville, he saw it (he must have seen it)— and works back to it, as he remembers it— as he tries to remember the world as it was, as he saw it, as a boy— how the city had been, then——

— How that city is now: the streets he must have known, and the church they wet his head in—where now a child is baptised under the same dark carved ceiling. I step out from the gloom of San Pedro and into the bright heat to find the street he owned a house on—maybe he was raised round here—there are dogs everywhere, but they are scrappy and uncombed and he might find this neighbourhood beneath him, how it is these days. All the scrawled walls, all the women in the street in the early afternoon, smoking, bored, waiting for the hours of their business. Not the sort of place a purported nobleman would want to come from. Everyone seems to keep birds; the air above street level full of the squawk of budgerigars out of open apartment windows; browned curtains and plants on the sills and dark within, looking up from the street and not knowing which window—

—— there was sickness in the city in those years, he remembers; and there were Moors. The long train of them leaving; the colours of their clothing; their goods in packs and hands, carrying all that they could, because as they went they weren't allowed to use a cart or mule, even. The fabric of shawls and bedding bunched in fists and pulling taut over the shoulder, full of stuff. Weeping, were they? Some must have been weeping; the children, the elderly, waiting on the wide banks of the Guadalquivir, he must have, he saw them, sees them, the colours and the weeping and all their goods (and the pleasure of painting coloured patterned cloth!)— arms full of all their possessions; all the solid objects they can carry. Clay and woven strands and sacking bound with string. He sets his studio to grinding quantities of bright pigment, and they go to work merrily, reds and yellows and greens and blues as well as the endless brown, brown, brown! And then, at the centre, he'll place the armoured King imperious, expelling them with a gesture; and Spain at his side majestic, her proud and pious countenance. There is to be no mercy.

The broad river glittering as they line up for the ships, waiting to pay for their own enforced passage, leaving the only home they've known and some of them shedding, perhaps, since they may as well, the obligation of their new faith—they have practised the rituals required of them, and yet no one believes them, and they still have no right to remain. They are still, after all these years, after generations some of them, taken for heathens and heretics. The boy he was watches: they weep, some of them weep, children his own age and younger. Ordinary faces inscribed with dark lines. He sees them. No histrionics. They wait for transit and quietly weep or reach out or hold each other hold back anger or try to make an adventure of it for their children or stop their babies crying, and he studies in turn each hand and where it's resting, the hollow of each cheek; he pictures Francisca as a small child, reaching out her little hand, distraught, and uses that (because a child's grief is equal to any occasion, the loss of a home or a sibling or a doll); a mother holding her infant close and swaddled in a red cloth threaded yellow, head bent over him, tears wetting his face as he sleeps; an old man resigned and crooked under his years and his pack, the set of his mouth and the deep lines around it suggesting missing teeth; a woman walking rigid straight, as the women of Seville walk on their high chopines, defiant. And the King with his gesture, casting them out, and he needs to make it glorious and grand, this gesture, because this is the point of the painting after all, the piety of it, the glory of the King's act; not the Moriscos' exiled grief. Not the unhousing of these men and women and children who have lived in this country all their lives and are now sent to a continent some of them have never known; leaving their masters with no one to work for them, leaving their emptied homes and the goods they couldn't carry, the glassware and blue ceramic and beaten copper pans abandoned. With Spain at the King's side, holy and triumphant——

— it is lost, this work, no trace remains but hearsay and I am trying to see how he might have seen it—

He asks his assistant to sit for him. The boy with the charcoal face in the mirror, grown now and a grinder of pigments and still a slave among the students of his master. He sits still and he cries a little as he used to on command. He asks if he may use his master's brush, if he may make some mark of his own on this scene. Remembering a friend or uncle or mother perhaps. The painter says no— I don't know why. I don't want to think this of him. But he did and I can't paint it out——

His colleagues present their own variations on the theme. But look, they gasp theatrically: the Sevillian has excelled himself! It is as if the heretics are once again among us! Truly, where did you find such filthy, dusky peasants to pose for you, Diego? Surely you can't have simply *imagined* them? And to themselves, not letting the others hear, they each mutter: It's good, though—it is good.

And the painter remains silent, thinking I *saw* them, I *remember*, as you must too; and when the works are hung together for the court's inspection, it is obvious who has won. The judges advise His Majesty that this, the Sevillian's piece, is modern, is novel, is most interesting; and the King agrees. A useful ally for the painter, this Italian judge, who is the King's taste-maker; an artist but also an aristocrat, and a knight of Santiago—since he doesn't need to paint to make his living, he can join the Order. Only a hobbyist could receive this honour. The painter observes this.

The King declares himself moved—without which declaration we would not know it; he views each work in turn without a tear or smile. He announces: the King's private painter is hereby appointed an Usher to our Chamber. His work shall hang in the New Room, where all shall see the triumph of my father's piety.

The painter is also given a new per diem, equal to that of the royal barbers. Also an annual allowance for clothing, which he spends before he has even received it; the law-abiding portion of his wardrobe is sparse and growing worn, he needs more cloaks and doublets in black, and he really does like a nice hat; he picks out the fabrics for their lustre and sheen. He's dressed as a noble, now, and no one can call him otherwise, can they? He indulges his assistant with a new suit, or one of his old ones— and I'd also have him give a scrap of board to draw on, the loan of a brush, a palette, an hour. Buys Juana a new veil, Francisca a ribbon. Juana says, You won, then? I knew you'd win.

Juana, what is Juana doing with her days? Not cleaning, not shopping for groceries, because they have people to do that for them, they are not poor and never have been. So she sends someone out to run their errands, every morning: meat and fish if it's come in fresh, bread and eggs and fruit and sweets. The people of this city live day to day, each night the cupboard lies all but bare and every provision is measured carefully; they are not permitted to stockpile. She receives her guests and they drink chocolate, and sometimes she puts on cloak and veil and high Sevillian shoes and visits her friends and drinks their chocolate instead. Who are her friends? She sits on cushions and drinks chocolate and chews chunks of the clay jugs it's served in and feels wired from the cocoa and the clay that's supposed to make the skin white, and maybe she is bored, bored, bored. Or maybe she isn't and has other things to do.

She reads and sews and bickers with her daughter's duenna or ignores her or conspires or cohabits peacefully, plays with Francisca, oversees her schooling, such as it is; and watches as Francisca grows older, as she sets her veil more carefully; listens as she asks for a new pair of shoes, as she turns her tongue easily to the slang of the city, expresses opinions all her own, her shy sophistication as she asks after one of her father's protégés, turning her ribbon around her finger, I wonder, do you think Juan Bautista would like this in my hair? Because he says that blue is his favourite colour and my father needs too little of it grinding. Juana encourages this, tells stories of when she was once a painter's daughter and of his house in Seville—does Francisca remember much? It's five years since we left, now; you remember Grandpa, she says, well he had a big house full of artists and clever men, and your father was one of them; and she tells her daughter how she met her husband there, the best of Grandpa's studio, and how she fell in love with him, if she did fall in love. Grandpa thought he'd make a good match for me because he's so well-mannered, your father, and he was so chaste, that's what Grandpa said and I suppose he saw what was what with his boys and what they got up to, I suppose he'd know, and I certainly never had reason to think otherwise, neither before or after we married. Ah little chick don't blush, okay, you don't want to hear this; but mostly, mostly Grandpa thought he'd found me a good match because he was so talented, your father, and Grandpa could see even then he'd go far. And that's why we're here in Madrid, Francisca, my little Madrileña, that's how we ended up here, to see how far he can go. And your boy, your beau, your Juan Bautista—oh it's a very pretty blush!—he'll go far too, I think (she's far-sighted, Juana, and has a keen eye), especially if all the ladies start wearing blue for their portraits. She ties the ribbon neatly into Francisca's new hairstyle. So we'll see what your father has to say about it, shall we. If you'll just hang on a few years; you're young yet.

She awaits her husband's return from the palace and when he gets home, drawn and tired and filled with his observations and frustrations and saying nothing about them, Juana is aglow with the restored youth of nostalgia and is bright and girlish even and soothes him and waits out his silence patiently and asks about his work and about the King and the court, his latest commissions. Maybe she isn't really interested but she'll always encourage his advancement, seeing that it matters to him, and it can't do her any harm either. Juana who was once the Virgin with a coronet of stars. I've been thinking of home, today, she says.

He asks, Has Francisca changed her hair? Quite the lady. Quite the little Madrileña … Always observing. Always an eye for a ribbon.

IV

La dama duende/
Phantom lady

This is a fortress of closely ordered shadows, but also, within its courtyards and out, up the Calle Mayor, into the Plaza Mayor, and out from it in every direction, out into the streets, out into the barrios, and on into the parks, seeping out across the permeable borders where the court in the fortress becomes the city la Corte: brightness, frivolity, unstoppably rules broken. The Count-Duke's reach is not as long and strong and octopoid as he'd have us all believe; even he cannot circumscribe this riot. And why would he? He can have it both ways ... This is a Golden Age, and it is a sober, pious, proud— and *fabulous* court that his most cultured monarch presides over; a glittering galaxy revolves about the Planet King.

The streets of the city as it stirs from its siesta: capes and cloaks and habits and veils emerge from doorways; drifting, spendthrift young nobles, frittering their funds and their affections; shopkeepers, disdaining their own wares, stalls barely attended while they preen and strut, flashing their knives; the streetwalkers setting their scarlet capes; the hawkers, scriveners, hookers and hired killers of all orders, available for business; priests and clerics, brothers and sisters of unclosed orders; the equerries, the errand boys, the blind chanting orisons. A lady in a veil, on the arm of her escort on the brink of the street; suitors lingering at windows. Everywhere, the carriages, illegally splendid and gaudy, the women within curtained from the gallants' attentions and the smell of their own horses' dung.

In the afternoons there are plays to be seen; the ladies safe in their hen-basket up at the back, the nobles in boxes and balconies; sometimes even the King or the rumour of him; and below in the pit the daily hustle and punch-up for benches, that leaves men sometimes bleeding; the spacer with his paddle stuck between bums to wiggle another seat in; the cloaks and daggers of the connoisseur caballeros, so they call themselves, crowding the front and sat up on the stage, dressed to the nines and witty with wine and spoiling for a fight; rattles, bells and whistles, the volleys of catcalls and nutshells . . .

There is a brand new bill at the Corral de la Cruz. A new actress, too: a redhead; she is already much discussed. They say she's a beauty. They say she's just sixteen and looks fresh as a daisy but you can tell she knows what she's about. They say she's been seeing this duke or that. They say that as a child she was left on the doorstep of the playwright Don Pedro, who is in favour with the King, by the way, these days, you couldn't get a seat at his Corpus shows last summer for love nor blood nor money; and now he's written this play for her; and a quiet word has murmured that it's quite a performance, worth a visit, just for this girl alone. So on this afternoon in May all the seats are filled and two men among many take their place in the gallery. A large one and a lithe one, a bull all in black, and a youth with a wide hat to shade his fairness from the sun's glare. They are respectfully acknowledged and allowed just a little more room than they need, than there is, on the cushioned benches, so that the pressed-up nobles on either side are feeling quite cosy. They jostle and murmur and laugh at the dandies and preen discreetly, brushing dust off black knees and shoulders, a sleeking and furling of moustaches, an ostentatious lifting and straightening of specs, and when not occupied with this fidgeting they half-watch the stage, and half-watch their incognito neighbours, from out of the sides of their spectacles. The large one largely looks at his folded hands, as if praying, but no doubt has an eye on what's happening. The lithe one watches the stage intently from under his hat; he sits very straight, not leaning back or letting his shoulders fall, and will sit that way for the whole afternoon.

There is the usual preamble. Skits and speeches, a little music, words and phrases snatched out of the din. And so it goes on, the usual thing: Something about love and pining, about anger, longing. Someone mistaken for another. Somewhere secret they'll meet, late at night, seeking each other out blindly in the afternoon daylight. Something about honour, and the meaning of it; everything, really, is about that.

And here she comes, red hair firing in the sun at midnight when she tosses her veil: she dissembles, she stamps; she is aflame with ire, with desire; she is novelty and passion and dis-traction and all the things they've come for. And in the gallery no one looks directly at the slim young man in their midst but everyone wonders if he's watching, everyone knows who he's watching, no one says anything yet but there are nudges and smirks that promise gossip.

A new scene begins; the women are scheming (as women do). Stay hidden, they say; stay veiled; sneak in the back way; keep behind this door and I shall use the other, cover it with a curtain and they'll never know it's there. The valido, ever attuned, feels the charge of his companion's attention. She's

new, this Calderona ... the valido has his eye out for a new
distraction. The King has grown impatient, and difficult to
manage, and nearing despondent, of late. It's difficult, sometimes, to keep him occupied and to swerve despair. But it seems
this is holding his attention; it seems she is.

They say, Come in, leave that way, in here, quick, keep
quiet. He will never know where he is or whose house he's
in. He'll never know you're here. They leave through hidden
exits and hide in secret spaces. The Count-Duke sits through
it all; lately plays bore him. But he does what he must, in the
service of ...

In the final scene of course they're all unveiled and disabused
of their confusion. And after the music, the applause, word
comes down to the company: there is a gallant in the gallery
who'd like to meet La Calderona.

⚜

There are kings and princes, the whole known world over,
who may do as they please and hide in plain sight. Put off
their crowns and unpin their cloaks and lift the heavy chains
of all their offices from their necks, take off their crimson
silks and golden trimmings and bright sash and put on simple
clothes of brown or black, and go out with an ordinary hat
on. Go out as plain Tom Smith, or Felipe, into an ordinary
night, into the semblance of an ordinary life (and what more
can any of us hope for? At least the semblance of it?). Out
into the city to promenade the parks and take their place upon
the balcony to see a show of an afternoon, or pass unwatched
through doorways that open for a fee as they would to any
man. But if there were a king who had no crown to put off ...
if this king wore that same black as everyone else already ...

if this king, say, were more radiant by far than his country-
men, if he stood out a mile even in his cap, with his blond
hair poking out from it ... that king were to be pitied, for he
would surely keep indoors. And yet, on the other hand, in
the dark a fair face is shaded, and rouge makes a nice mask
for the night time, and one black looks much like another,
whether it's of finest cloth or coarse; and if it's fine to a finger's
touch then the lady who touches will put that finger to her
own lips if she's wise.

Pablillos touches his finger to his own lips. Then he presses
his four fingers over his mouth as if— oops— silencing
himself, eyebrows raised; then he lets his hand fold out from
his mouth, palm upward. A pause to look around and an
appeal— a nod that is little more than a slow blink from the
valido: go on. He holds the floor. His stance wide; his neat
sharp eyes.

And this is not to say that *Your Majesty* would wish to sit
among the noble rabble on the balconies, or pass through these
ordinary unseen doorways, would wish to enter such a place
or meet such a discreet lady and her wise fingers. This is not
something Pablillos would say, Your Majesty. (A small bow.)
And yet (finger upheld— he is not quite done), but, there *are*
those who say that a golden-haired youth has been seen abroad
of late, and there are few of those in this city, and they say that
his chin ... his nose ... his forehead (with gestures— long,
regal chin nose and forehead); they say he gazes upwards
always and won't look down at the street; and they say that at
his side there is a sort of bull (with hunchbacked lollop)— Your
Excellency, this is simply a strange fable I have heard about the
place, there is no need to snort so— Not, of course, as a bull
might snort, no ... It's said that these two men, this youth and
his bull, have been seen about. And that this youth, so golden,

seems to have stepped down from on high to test out a mortal frame, to learn the ways of the common man.

And it's said that His Majesty is a dedicated scholar, an apt and willing pupil, and on any afternoon can be found at his books; but all I am saying is I've *also* heard it said that there are some women of the city who'll say likewise. Apt, willing.

Who says? And where?

Oh—phooph!— in those chambers where the poets rumour and chatter, in the mentideros, Your Excellency, which are named thus after all for the lies told within them. I am only reporting to Your Majesty, Your Excellency, their lies, only telling *of* them. A riddle: if a liar confesses to being such, what trust can we put in his confession? Is a man who tells lies always a liar? I wonder. But anyway, in any case, as I say: all this is second hand. Well, you know how these wits like to witter. And I do not think we can trust their eyewitness, since their vision is so sadly afflicted (peering through spectacle-frame fingers). So the man of pleasure peers through his finger-glasses and at the last moment the dandies become the butt of the joke. Laughter. Pablillos lets his circled fingers pop apart and fly from his face in wide arcs—pooph!— and resettle at his sides; he bows again when his arms come to rest; Pablillos again gets away with it.

The summer draws on and the days stretch on into long golden afternoons of entertainment and blue into warm nights full of serenades and danger; and then autumn and the afternoons still long and the shows still going on in the lengthening shadows but La Calderona's flame no longer there to light them, already snuffed after burning briefly so bright. Where's she gone? Retired, they say; something about her profession seeming unseemly, to someone or other ...

In the afternoons the carriages are out, and the gallants are abroad and still she sits in her own private palace by a disregarded window, the wax paper blocking the last of the light. Seated on cushions of the best silk. Chewing on clay, all day and all the long afternoons, pulling at her needle as the punters queue for benches and the nobles take their seats and the new girls take the stage and here she sits, retired before she's twenty; words that were written for her in the mouths of other women. So this is what it is to be the other woman. My only one, he tells her, but she's not a fool and even here she hears; gossip is a long silkworm insinuating and can thread through any crevice. One of the other women. She hates sewing.

Worth it, though, it must be worth it, to have a palace of her own. Where she sits on her little dais, her little stage, her little throne at the window, queen of half-lit shadows, her red hair shining dimly in the shaded yellow daylight, unattended; chewing on clay jittery and waiting. She sits. Watches for someone coming and most days no one comes, and when he does he's often hangdog and penitent and she has to coax it up, coax it out of him. Putting on a performance for him: I've been here at home, entertaining myself by crying, she tells him; this was once her line, when she played the Phantom Lady; she says it as if she's joking, or sometimes, sometimes she storms at him: Here I

am, dying inside these walls, where even the sun can't find me—
might as well be a prisoner—for love of you, I play the phantom
in my house— she quotes her own lines, she mutters them, when
once her voice banged up against the walls of the theatre in the
street, thrown out to the stones and over the catcalls and up to
the open sky; and now this needling little ironic performance
under a low anonymous ceiling with only him or no one or her
horrible manservant to hear her, and she knows it belittles her,
and can't help it. She lives invisibly as he has asked her, forsakes
the stage as he has asked her, keeps quiet, as he has asked her,
keeps occasional acquaintance with only the most discreet and
tedious of ladies, sewing and chewing all day long in this paper-
dark hole. Outside the carriages, the gallants; the world passes
her window, and she watches the shapes of it.

But still, this palace is not a prison. Too easy to give in to
this, to succumb to nothing but waiting indoors patiently, and
he can't expressly ask that of her and she's not patient, really,
that's not in her nature. If he comes and she's out, well, he'll
have to come back later. If she veils herself to venture out, can
he condemn her? They might miss each other, might pass in
the busy street without seeing, all manner of confusions might
arise ... a little like a play, isn't it, the life he's given her. She
laughs and it sounds forced even to herself, and there's no
one else to hear. An echo of laughter out in the street, and a
mandolin. She listens and stabs the linen mindlessly making
no stitch; she's no good at needlework, having little patience;
unable to bear the dull slow pull of the thread and the tight-
ening, stitching herself tighter into this dull obvious irony, a
little like a play, ha ha ... This palace is not a prison. He has
left her with a manservant, an escort, after all. She need only
summon him. Where is he— that odour, is that ... ? — yes,
here he is. Right on cue.

Oh he's made for the role. They'd save a small fortune on stage make-up. His raw eyelids, hairless with mange. Watery-eyed creep. Like a dog in the street, begging for scraps. He'd take a kick as gladly as a pat. Always at her heels, always trailing after her like a bad smell—exactly that! No 'like' about it! Stinking creeping pup.

He brings her cloak. She can tell him he stinks all she likes. He would like to vanish into vapour, fly up her nostril as a tiny particulate and lodge there; he would be happy to spend the rest of his sorry life stuck to the wall of that damp red quivering cavern. How it quivers now! She is all trembling. Come then; so here is her cloak, her veil, her shoes; oh, her perfect feet!

She submits, as she must. But ugh, this man, this terrible man, his terrible yellowy-rinded eyes, his terrible skin, his skin! What isn't a pustule is a scab; the rasp of his fingers scratching at his red-raw wrists, rubbing them together like a cricket with a disease, shkrf shkrf shkrff-ff-ff; in the night sometimes she hears it, feeling those hands on her, waking wet and burning cold, dreading the first itch of his contagion. Skin flying off him as he moves, enough to fill a snow pit with the stuff; putting her tongue to an ice and finding her mouth full of him, full of skin— Ugh. Stop thinking about it.

So here he is with his smell and his scratching and his dandruff covering her cloak, and so she must go out on the street with this wretch; and thank God for the veil to hide the shame of it along with her red hair. Her lover has said, if she *must* go out, then she must have a man to escort her— and she agrees, If she *must* go by foot she must have a man beside her as she makes her way between the carriages that other ladies have, which by the way are pulled by horses, has he noticed the manure in the streets? If he were ever to look down he'd see what she must walk through— And if you *must* have your *own* man beside you, he goes on, over her, then I will gladly employ a man in full-time service on your behalf, and he must be a man that I can trust. If! Would he have her hire an escort from a broker like a common whore every time she wants to step outdoors? No; he'd keep her indoors, of course; of course; he wouldn't have her go out at all.

Well no one will come near her while she's on the arm of this living stinking boil.

They reach the Calle Mayor; it is crowded, as it always is; she stops at its edge and he stops beside her and they teeter as if at the brink of a cliff. She has never seen the sea. He has. There are places he's been, things he's seen, things she doesn't know, fighting battles in the service of her lover; and he keeps them close, these things he knows, and turns them over and thinks one day he'll tell her and he'll watch how she flinches at every livid detail and he'll own her horror. He has lived through worse than her revulsion. He knows why she's stopped. It's not the crowd. He knows the pause a person makes at the brink of disgust; the way you send the mind away, make of yourself a puppet and send the mind out of the flesh that must touch what it despises. For example, a hand without an arm but with rings worth stealing all slippery from a field of faecal gore and bleeding body bits and moaning; or, in her case, his own, living hand.

She inhales, too deeply, regrets it—swallows the *gk* her throat makes and inhales again through her teeth this time. She sets her veil to cover the right eye, an invitation that of course she wouldn't honour, but she's bored and there's no law against flirtation, is there? (She smiles to herself because there is, obviously; there's a law against what she's just done. The left eye of a coquette will bewitch helpless men. Both eyes, or no eyes. Those are the rules that the pious King decrees.) She

glances at her mangy cur and assures herself of his devotion.
He won't tell. She lifts her hand. It is gloved and it is beneath
her cloak, too, a platform raised out of the long black veil, but
when he takes it she can feel him through the layers, still; eager,
flaking, weepy.

He is careful to barely meet her touch, and no more,
although his skin burns at it. He is at her side. They step into
the crowd. Noise, bodies, sour-sickly sweat and bruised fallen
fruit and horseshit and all the other kinds of shit. A carriage
passes and the crowd must adjust and she is jostled, misses her
footing, and he feels her fingers grip his, feels them constrict
under the cloth, ohh such a tight firm grip she has! A living
glove contracting around him; he grips back—he sees her
unveiled eye widen—fury, fear, but her dark pupil is huge,
he is pulled into it, into the grip of it, their faces are close she
is under him, he has his other hand below her shoulder to
steady and right her, and for a second they are dancing and
she has yielded and for only a second longer he won't release
her fingers; and she straightens, too proud to thank him or to
remonstrate or even pull away, she straightens and turns to
the gentleman that knocked her and her hand which is still
gripping contracts for a moment still tighter and then loosens
and he holds on for a second more—and lets her go. Tonight,
alone, that hand, that grip, that huge frightened eye, he can
make use of. The yielding. And then he sees the man that
knocked her— damn—

— And she sees the man that knocked her— Hat in hand
and a coin in the other and tall and trim and his moustache
very long and fine and spread by nostrils flaring. Go buy your
lady a candy. I will stand by her and wait. Holding the coin
out in a pinch with fingers fastidiously spread, to drop it in his
hand. Are you stupid, man? Go!

She doesn't care for sweets. And candied fruits are worst of all. He buys her an apricot drenched in glaze, the stickiest he sees at the stall; two flies must be flicked from it and he takes a surreptitious lick, to clean the shit off from their feet, and oh, it is sweet, it is honey-sweet, he could swoon, to tongue where her mouth will touch even though this honey will disgust her, because he knows already that she will taste it and feign ... The gallant takes the paper from him and bows low and offers it up like Paris with his apple. And she takes it. And she says—ha!— she says, Oh for an apricot I would forgive all manner of sins.

And she lifts her veil away and when the paper comes back he sees she's taken a tiny bite from the fullest reddest part, just where his tongue has been and the flies ...

Lo escatología, my lords. The English you know, and the French, they make a nice distinction: *eschatologie*— (a Frenchman, gasping in terror as death approaches; expiring with much simpering and fainting), *eschatology*— (a harsh and barking accent; an Englishman grossly belching his way to an ending); *scatology* (Englishman squatting, elbows on wide knees, drunk, grunting, shitting, groaning), *scatologie* (he gives this one a while, the Frenchman straining and gurning with mouth drawn down long and nose in the air; every comic knows the value of making them wait ... for it ... fingers fluttering, *phooph!*). But we know, we wise Spaniards know, there's just one word for it; my wise neo-Stoical lords, you know and accept that everything passes, everything runs its inevitable, hidden course, everything gets churned up in time and turns to the same dark matter, and it all comes out the same way in the end.

From an obscure corner, a bony clatter of applause for Pablillos.

At night a nobleman out with his minstrel pageboy in the dark, strolling and strumming through the midnight city; from a lamp-lit window a soft voice calls and the nobleman stops below. Is that a nightingale calling above me? Ah, a lady who would have a song; and the nobleman bows and instructs his boy. She sits at her window all shadowy and smiles, and just for fun she leans out just a little with her lamp, the curve of her cheek shows like the crescent moon, a sliver of her fair skin, a strand of extraordinary red hair falling as if quite by accident it has come loose . . . and the nobleman just like that falls in love, or professes to, puts his hand out and cups the air as if it were her face and then to his own cheek as if his hand were hers, or as if he had her own hand pressed beneath it; she mirrors, soft skin under her palm and bristles under his, and each heart held in the other's hand, and so forth, as his mulatto sings and strums his guitar. And below in a darkened doorway, a grin like the shine on the dagger just drawn, sharp and glinty and over in a flash; shkrf skrf here he comes.

She pulls her head and lamp back quickly and hears the mulatto pageboy shout through a tangle of smashing strings and wood, and peeps out to see him fleeing, his guitar about his neck like an outlawed ruff; and she would laugh but then she sees a brief flash like her man's horrid grin; and it is midnight and so dark and her lamp withdrawn and hidden, so she can't perhaps see her suitor's black blood bubbling over the bone of the flapping right cheek lately touched so tenderly, a frightened eye; and the cur hisses Go and don't come back, my lady isn't into scars. And she puts the lamp out and lies awake in the dark listening to other serenades in other streets. Her eyes closed and streaming and her lips drawn back, teeth dry with the effort of silence sucked through them. Spit thickens and her gullet has a lark's heart stuck in it, her jaw strains and there is a sour thin ache at the join of it, and instead of screaming she is sick into her chamber pot, something else she can do silently. Lies back in the bed she's made for herself. In the morning she'll rise early to tip out her vomit with the slops. Below, the door to the street opens, closes.

☦

In Holy Week the bells are silent and the streets are hushed; the gentry must go on foot, unescorted, and the streets are empty of the usual rattle and tilt. In Holy Week the figure of Christ is borne through the streets, each Station of His suffering intricately carved and coloured, the texture and jaundiced sheen of torn, cut, contused flesh, His Passion mourned with black crepe and crosses and candles carried through the city and the churches open day and night. Those who walk abroad, alone, are on their way to worship, or on their way home from it, souls purged. When the spring rain falls they let it fall upon them, let themselves be cleansed in it and the splashing filth of the streets. There are many places to pray in this city, many small chapels and churches, on street corners, behind small doors in high walls where the orders are sequestered; and if, in the dim and quiet pews, one bent knee happens to encounter and press against another, then who is to see it, this encounter?

In Holy Week a woman walks alone without her cur beside her, through the silent streets, head veiled and bowed, hands clasped and hidden; she plays her part. She walks with cloaked devotional purpose, the glimpse of face kept straight. She keeps her features in order and measures her pilgrim steps. When she hears someone behind her she keeps to this measure. When she hears one before her, coming towards her, the same measure still. And her whole hidden body is thrumming, wound tight as catgut waiting to be plucked. She is an upside down waterspout spinning out in a spiral of sickness or laughter, rushing up from her hips, her womb, whirling through her stomach and into her gullet and about to gush from her mouth. She would like to run or spin or leap and laugh, and laugh; she would like to paint her face with ochre and run laughing like a lunatic, she would love to uncover the red of her hair and the whole of her body and run mad, now. She would like to be sick and would like to laugh spew shriek bellow belch she keeps her face under the veil and the measure of her steps straight. She turns the corner, she does not raise her lowered head and the steps come close and closer through the silent city and the chapel is in sight; moans and murmured chanting, a thud thud thud; below the dark frame of her veil she sees the pointed hoods of penitents approaching, noblemen, disrobed, an extravagance of passion, of suffering, covered in blood, shoulders rubbed raw with the weight of the cross. How they suffer; my lady, see how I suffer for love—he strikes his bare back and the flail flicks his blood upon her robe, and she gasps and glances up and meets his mournful eye but he moves on before she can thank him for the honour of his blood and she looks down again quickly. He will stand below his lady's window and flog himself until he falls and his page comes forward to carry him home. And his lady's husband in his turn more than likely shuffles on a few rows back, also moaning and bloody for another woman, for his sin, and so it goes on, this show of bleeding and bearing of crosses, such a performance, she could never inflict such a performance on her own flesh, and why should she ... The lengths that they will go to, these penitents, for the sake of flirting—and the ladies feign indifference as their suitors' shining eyes blink sweat and blood and roll up to heaven, to their windows. And she makes her way through the bloody muddy silent solemn streets, strung out, alone; but almost there, now, making her way to her silent assignation.

She walks alone, breathing the cleansed bloody air; enters a humble chapel. She prays with red hair veiled. There are so many places to pray in this city that no one else need see when an hour or so later a hat is pulled from a blond head and a supplicant slides alongside her at her pew, and kneels close by so thighs can press together and ungloved backs of hands can find fine fair skin against skin, bones rub bones, knuckling over up and under so two palms meet akin to a prayer; and she drags the hand towards her body and it follows with hopeless reluctance, with a half-hearted feigned reluctance, he knows himself better than that; she pulls it within her cloak; she feels the long fingers pressing and she whispers to him and he smiles despite himself and then he prays, for weeks he prays, and wishes he could whip himself through the streets in penitence. But there is a time for public piety, and places for private penance.

V

Pentimenti/ Repentances

The Chief Secretary sits in his rooms and receives his guests, wreathed in the pale smoke of his personality and what is known or not known about it. (There are rumours about Don Jerónimo. He is a go-between for the King and his valido, discreet and all-pervasive as the Alcázar's shadows. He smoothes and slides his way relaying their most private messages unnoticed unseen unless he needs to be, trusted implicitly. But they say he's ambitious, maybe too ambitious. They say he's a Jew. They say he's a magician. They say he's a fornicator and the Devil's pimp.)

The Secretary's home in the city is admirably, enviably bachelor. No floor-cushions or frivolities or discarded cups of chocolate. A brazier is burning, glinting off the globes of an orrery, all the planets in their golden circuits shining; Don Jerónimo stands surveying them, as if he might pluck one from its orbit or send a satellite shooting with a flick of his finely tapered fingernail. Glossy, rich and dark, Don Jerónimo, and his home is too: leather, brass, well-worn lacquered wood; shelves of intrigue which his visitor, feeling at ease here, pale skin pinking, peruses— And what is this one, and this? That is a traveller's tale, Señor; and— and this little volume explains an ancient system of divination, for that you will need also, I have somewhere, a copy of the Hebrews' holy book . . . Oh yes? says his visitor. How did you come by this Hebrew book? Señor, you know I am a scholar, or pretend to be. The body is willing, the mind is weak . . . Ah. I think you have heard rumours of my heritage. Your M . . . *Señor*, I assure you, I am a thoroughbred enough grandee, I am not Jew enough to owe you taxes! My soul is pledged to Christ, however dark my blood may run.

Ah, now that—his guest is fondling a slender spine of very soft leather, soft as the skin under an ear lobe, he cannot help but stroke it, the Secretary can see— Ah, that is a collection of Eastern prints I had bound, I would be honoured if you would care to borrow it, it is perhaps best enjoyed *alone*, at your leisure, Señor.

Felipe sees a secret smile pass between his host and the Count-Duke (the valido is on hand as ever). His stroking finger lifts and pauses. The Secretary turns smoothly from his guest's silence, a silence changing hue as his flush rises and fades.

Cousin, says the King, tapping the spine firmly back into its space on the shelf. You suggested, I think, that we might visit— that we might make an offering to the convent of San Placido—I had thought we were to visit— I believe you are their patron? Shall we go next door, then?

Señor, the Count-Duke intercedes. As I mentioned, Don Jerónimo has a surprise for you. And here in the wall, where there was a wall, is now a void; and the Secretary lights a torch from the brazier and stands at the brink of it, and the light of his torch shows stairs that lead into darkness, falling from an opening in the dark panelling. But by all means, says the Secretary— Let us go then, Señor.

Go? Go where? Where does this go? The Secretary smiles.

Why, of course, to the chapel of San Placido, Señor. And if ever you should wish to make a prayer or an offering, in private, alone, you are most welcome to come this way. The Count-Duke comes here to pray, often. (The Count-Duke prays for the King, and his country, and also for his own family, what little is left of it; he prays for heirs, an heir to the throne, an heir of his own, daily.)

I am sure you will enjoy their welcome, Señor. They bake biscuits. Let us visit with the sisters.

Through the dark stairs to the convent next door; it is a simple unobtrusive building among the many convents and chapels of the city, and people passing outside in the street below, audible through the vents and small windows, pass all unknowing ... This is one of many hidden passages that the King makes use of. There are others; otherwise he'd have nothing to repent of daily.

(There's a story going round about the King's Chief Secretary, about the lady that left him for God and the convent he built for her, beside his house, attached to his house, accessible from his house maybe so that he can still ... *pray* with her. About the kind of convent this lady, the Prioress, presides over. They say all kinds of things, to pass the time in the mentideros. These days they say there is a young novice in the convent of San Placido who is visited daily by a fair-haired penitent; they say he won't let her alone, they say he goes to pray with her at all hours and begs for forgiveness (but for what?) and she can't refuse him (but what can't she refuse him?) They say one night he came in to find her laid out dead and the abbess holding vigil, the girl's virgin (is she?) skin blooming still so fresh and daisy-like (her name is Margarita, like the flower) that in a daze he reached out for her and had to be restrained

from grasping at her and finding her of course still warm, the
old woman silent in her black cowl scowling. God will forgive
them this deceit; they had no other recourse, the nuns, no other
way to rebuff him.)

✠

The Count-Duke comes to the King's chamber and finds him
still in bed—the Count-Duke has been up for hours— Señor—
your shirt; your coffee; your desk ... here is a pen— pushing
it into a listless pale hand which flops to the side and taps a
heedless splot of ink out. The King, he sees, is going to be hard
work today. I'm sorry, Señor, I know it's tedious ...

The King snatches the paper from him and splashily dips
his pen with a horrid nib-scraping sound and only at the last
moment stops himself scrawling; hand arrested an inch from
the page he signs neatly and blots, and shoves the thing back
at his minister bitterly. Just a few more, he mimics. And then,
cousin? And then, and then? Will it ever be over? These writs
and decrees? When can I rest? When can I spend just an hour
of my own time, in my own chambers, looking at the paintings
that hang in my many dark rooms unseen? Do we still pay that
drawing master? When did I last see him? When can I hunt?
When can I run the course? When can I go out to ...

Señor, please.

The Count-Duke glances at the closed door, briskly switches
the signed paper for an unsigned and holds it out to him. The
King is staring out of the window, a narrow casement from
which, from here, chained as he is by devils to this desk at
the centre of this dreary room, only the pale green sky can be
seen, speaking of a clearing mist, of coolness in the trees. A
good morning for hunting. Cooler, out in the country. None of

this fuss. The little lodge, perhaps, out in the Pardo, out in the woods with just his brothers, the dogs, and in the evening perhaps ... The Count-Duke snaps the paper and the King regards it. It is shaking in the Count-Duke's hands; it is shaking in the King's face. Señor. PLEASE! The King regards his minister in blank-faced surprise. Has he raised his voice?

I am sorry, Señor. It's impossible. This is impossible. This job, I devote my life to, I am glad to, but Your Majesty you make it impossible (his hands are shaking, his shoulders ache), you are a splendid huntsman, the perfect courtier, the model gentleman, I am pleased to attend both your pleasure and your prayers, but while your court may do as it pleases and stuff themselves silly and go to plays and hunt and screw, eat ices in August and put on perfumes and daub their faces with paint and fancy themselves up when they've been TOLD not to and we've— you've— made laws against it and their endless pamphlets and protests and poems and while they can loaf and mince and dance their allemandes while I am working till long past midnight EVERY NIGHT Señor and then up again in the dark I have barely time to pray and I do all this gladly in the service of my country but we need you now to be KING. Señor.

He doesn't say this. He bows and sets down the paper and turns and leaves. But it does have to be said, somehow, and he writes something like it in a letter: This situation is impossible, becoming impossible.

✝

As usual, Felipe dines alone: attended only by his steward, his prelate, his major-domo at his side, and a carver, a butler, a cellarman, and the royal physician, on hand to approve all that is served to him; some mace-bearers, footmen; only the most necessary staff attend the King's lonely, largely silent repast. He would like a sip of cinnamon water, holds out a long hand for it. It is fetched from the dresser. It is uncovered. The physician approves. It is covered and presented; the cellarman kneels, flanked by footmen; the King drinks. The process reverses itself, the cup received re-covered restored to the dresser. And if, a moment later, the King thinks he might like to take another sip—— the glass is fetched again and uncovered and approved and covered and presented and so on and on. Or sometimes perhaps he thinks better of it, prefers to go thirsty for a few minutes more.

Elsewhere, at Queen Isabel's table, things are more relaxed; just one lady to hold and taste her drink, to one side; and on her left a lady who holds her napkin. And across from her a lady who presents dish after dish and the Queen eats a little of everything with a little grimace, it's said—appetite being perhaps unfashionable. And there's the Count-Duke's wife, who resembles her husband (who is also her cousin), in her blobby features, her piety, her cleverness—the Queen feels the weight of this childless woman's sadness, pressing on her own once-more full womb. This Countess has just lately been appointed; she attends on little María Eugenia, the Princess. An infiltrator in the Queen's most private spaces; but the King and his valido insist that it is for the poor lady's benefit, for her distraction. Her daughter died with their granddaughter. They have no heirs. They have only the court and the King and his family, and they serve faithfully. Also like her husband, she is watchful; and the Queen must know full well that's why she's really here. And who else? A man in the corner who has been given this honour, of watching the Queen eat from the corner, although no one speaks with him and he's not sure they know who he is, some diplomat, who cares; and Isabel's jester jumping and japing and burping and gaping, the silence filled with his patter, which the Queen seems to enjoy as far as she appears to enjoy anything, despite the Countess's austere, unspoken disapproval, which really is depressing.

And down in the kitchens, people simply pick up a flask and drink from it; simply tear the bread and pass it to the next hand and set dishes down on unpolished wood, the close walls and ceilings of brick, the blue-glazed tile; and further in, further back, the lesser attendants, the stable boys, the walls of mud closer still, small windows, but it is cool, even though the blazing summer has dragged long into this tail-end of autumn and the dimming evenings are dense with heat.

And somewhere the painter, still, observing.

Sated, or simply exhausted, the King rises. The usual discreet hurry. As if one entered a darkened room bearing a light, and the creatures there have already started, fled, and found corners to hide in before the light has even fully crossed the threshold; the impression of an emptiness recently vacated and of many eyes watching (including those of a hooded old woman unnoticed); so it is, when the King rises from his seat, enters a room, lifts a long hand. This quiet efficiency has surrounded him his whole life. No, he is never without an audience, not even when he rises and retires, not quite even when he's excreting or sleeping or begetting heirs, never, always there is a witness, always someone attending at the doorway, listening out for uncommon noises. Poor King, he has never been alone— or known hunger or squalor or pain, true— but he knows discomfort, has known it so long that it is now a comfort to him. You try standing rigid for hours in the heat; try to know every muscle in order not to move it; try to remain radiant, perfect, luminous, always; try to be always inhabiting the outside of yourself, to meet the perceptions of others; try to rise above the rawness of fear and of grief before you have a chance to feel them. Nothing can touch you and everything is fine. You will have an heir (a legitimate one). Your pregnant Queen will give you a healthy boy. You will win your wars. You will tolerate no traitors. Your people will work, and eat, and be true to God, and heretics will be chased out with their tails burning. Your world will remain stable and your lands will provide, your lands across the whole of the globe will bring forth bounty and will not quake or tremble and neither will your hand. Things are slipping under him and yet he remains, in public, always poised.

So the King rises and the creatures rearrange and are already at their stations, ready to proffer, to close or to open, to fetch or carry, to meet any need before it is even expressed.

But of a sudden, the King sits again. He sits quite heavily. He is pale, paler than usual, one might say pasty when he is usually a little pink, radiant, et cetera ... the King is sweating and he raises one of those regal white hands to his brow, now, and this is not an expected gesture at this juncture and it is not clear, the significance, who should respond to it, or how ... The King grips the table and lifts a finger, two, weakly, and through an exchange of tiny glances and urgent eyelid twitches among the servers and footmen it is interpreted that the King would like some water; and it is brought and uncovered and inspected and covered and presented and the King seems now too weak to raise his hand and take it, and then the physician, who has long been in this family's service, remembering the story about the King's father—that he died of a chill, because his Groom of the Stole was not on hand with a cloak and no one else would step in to supplant the man and supply one— the brave physician steps forward with the goblet and holds it himself to the King's lips. And the King drinks. His eyes are closed and there is an unwholesome blue shine on the eyelids. He puts a hand to his wet mouth. He swivels upon his chair with his shoulders drawn in and his fine head bowed and his hands to his mouth. And the physician suddenly snatches up a silver bowl and throws fruit all over the table and as plums and oranges roll and the footmen watch in alarm as they fall, the King's own vomit splashes into the bowl that the physician has so presciently commandeered for the purpose. It is pink with wine and smells like any man's vomit; the King grips the physician's arm and looks up at him through shining and blurred eyes. Is he poisoned? Is he dying? Should he thank the physician or scold him or have him dealt with more severely? What is he doing, half doubled-over, holding himself up by this man's straining arm?

The physician, an old man now, struggles to bear the King's weight and to keep the dish of vomit steady; cannot think what to do or say to correct the situation; he must not, *must not* drop the King or tip vomit on him, but the King is sinking, sinking, his shining eyes all glassy like a saint in ecstasy, sliding from his chair, the physician bowing to support him, his whole weight, without letting the dish tip and just as he thinks he can hold the King no longer, arm and thighs shaking with the effort, here is the King's valido, rustling and barking at a pageboy who takes the dish from the physician's hands while the valido himself takes the King's weight, kneels beside him with an arm beneath him, and the King is senseless now and limp and they make a sort of strange pieta, the physician thinks, and wants to laugh, he feels senseless and hysterical himself, he needs some tincture, he needs a drink, but he is the King's physician and the King, the King has had some seizure, and if he cannot help then there will be no help for him.

While his brother lies sick, the Infante Don Carlos notices an increased fuss about his own periphery; he resists conversation, resists making eye contact with the meaningful dark looks cast upon him. Knows what they're getting at. The King has no son. And what if, what then? How will he serve and who is to serve him? They are jostling already to get into position. He visits the sickroom and is seen to do so, holds the damp pale hand and perhaps he whispers. No ambitious death wish; no politicking poison to trickle in the ear. Just, It's you who were born to this. Please, leave me out of it.

The King is ill for days. They think near death. Beyond his bedchamber, in the empty place where he usually dines or at his unmanned desk, she waits, the old peasant, his faithful attendant. Something seen only by dogs, or sidelong. Sitting stiffly on a stiff sofa, bony hands on bony knees. She is patient, she has worked this harvest hard and long, she is worn to it, she can wait in these dingy rooms all day. She feels at home here. In her black robes she fits right in. The King's mastiff lies cowed at the foot of the bed, watching through the open door; he whines, from time to time, and death sighs her lungless sigh; you are my servant too, Álvaro, you have run many creatures down for me, so don't you whine at me now. He comes to her, on guard, and she rubs his head with knuckly bone-brown fingers. I'm just keeping the poor lad company; just like you, just keeping an eye on him, old boy. Álvaro snuffles and gnaws on his bone pointedly, and settles; and snores; and then starts and lifts his hunter's head with ears pricked forward, something has passed, he barks, and his master groans but does not stir, so he turns to his new companion— did you hear it did you hear a NOISE! But death has left the room already, and the hurry towards the Queen's quarters flows unknowing around her; there are ladies and major-domos and maids and physicians all rushing to the bedside, the Queen is in trouble, has been heard to cry out; death lets them all fly past; she sees the King's brother, looking drawn, she brushes some fleck or feather from him and he shivers and blurs; but she is in no rush.

And the King recovers; he wakes to the wet tickle of Álvaro's snout. He calls for the Count-Duke, who finds him sitting up, weak but pink again, asking for water, for almond soup and for news. The Count-Duke hesitates. Señor ...

The King's daughter the Infanta, María Eugenia, has died. His little daughter, not yet two, has died.

And also ...

Also, the valido must report, also, Isabel our Queen was brought to bed and another little girl ... I am sorry, Señor. She lived just a night. (The Count-Duke feels this loss almost as he felt his own. Almost.) And the Queen? The Queen is well, Señor. So the King, recovered, must go to his wife again, and try to make another, or better yet a son; and she will be stoical or tearful. Which is worse?

And also ...

No, he doesn't tell him that. Doesn't tell him that when prayers were called for the King's health, the churches were almost empty. Doesn't tell him that his people are tired of fancy processions and squalor and new-minted useless copper coins. Doesn't tell him that they whisper of his mistresses and bastards and his weakness and 'just like his father' and of his valido and all their bad choices and what's to be done about the borders the colonies the costs the foreigners the wars. Doesn't tell him how he, the King's servant, is hated, how he knows it and still goes on.

But still, something must be done, and when the King returns to his desk the Count-Duke explains this. He comes in the morning—up for hours—papers ready—and the King is contrite. He is at his desk with pen in hand already. He will try harder. He is trying. He wishes he could take it all in, understand everything, and fix it. Yes, yes, I know what you will say. Wisdom is not obtained by wishing, but by working. You see? I have at least taken in my Lipsius. But it's just I'm ... still learning ... there's so much ... I need guidance. I don't know what we'd do without you. What I'd do. Cousin. My best counsel.

The Count-Duke bows, and holds the papers out, and explains why they matter and where he should sign, and the King listens and signs, listens and signs, for a whole patient morning. And the King *can* see, he can see for himself: something must be done about the prices, ever inflating, and the vicious frivolity he sees in the streets; war is everywhere or everywhere approaching, all precarious; he has felt the presence of death, at his table, at his door; and so at the moment it is probably not much fun, being King, if it ever was.

He dwells upon his sins; he dwells upon his illness, his near miss, the death of all his children, all his wife's children, all his daughters; of all our children; and everyone and everything he knows and how it passes, and what he will leave behind him, and if he will have sons, if his wife will have sons. Upon all the little blond boys called Felipe living in the city, allowed by God to live, and for them perhaps He has visited punishment on those his wife has borne him; on what he has done, what he persists in doing, on the trifling comforts he so easily derives and then cannot cleanse himself. He must leave something legitimate and strongly built, even though everything passes, as ordure washed out to the river at last by the rain, as fragments of straw. He wears no crown, of gold or straw either, and since it's invisible he can't take it off and leave it lying around for those who covet it to grasp at, hands closing on air; but if any one of the King's subjects knew the troubles that turn and moil within its perimeter then even if they could see it they wouldn't stoop to pick it up. He knows his Lipsius: you don't envy a beggar dressed as a king; you know that under his robes which look so golden from a distance, he is scabbed, filthy, unclean, and if you come close you'll smell him; but the King, too, under his gorgeous black attire, the King is a mortal soul and a body that sweats and shivers and makes waste. And yes, Lipsius, he thinks: that's right, these are gripping griefs indeed, always to be vexed, sorrowful, terrified. And he must bear them and learn to suffer, pay for his sins and offer up his penitence and look to virtue. The sun is on Spain, for now, says Lipsius; and he is the Planet King.

In short, the King has grown serious. He wishes to take his work seriously; the work of rule and the work of prayer. He attends to his education. The Count-Duke is delighted. He leaves off, for the time being, and with some relief, the more clandestine aspects of the curriculum, and together they commit to making a true monarch of him. The King goes to his books with a new dedication, assiduous, every afternoon, the sun sinking unheeded behind him over the city beyond his window; goes out to the country and works as the sun sinks over the mountains around the Escorial, as he sits in the rooms his grandfather furnished, and learns to govern as he did. And the afternoons are short now and he has lamps lit and doesn't languish, and they grow shorter and colder as winter draws on, and tapestries are hung around him to keep the warmth in and among the frozen figures knit forever into their world woven of the same cloth he pulls a rug about him like a poor scholar and by the light of lamps he learns languages, histories, laws. He rarely goes out into the city, now. He is rarely seen. And when he comes back his efforts in work and at prayer are redoubled. He has hidden chambers built and secret windows, so that he can sit still there and listen—and he can sit still for hours—unseen in the walls of his council chambers. Learning how the councils of his kingdoms are run. The Junta for Reform. The Junta for Works and Woods. Juntas for censoring pamphlets, for watering wine, for ribbons and bows.

In Holy Week the King walks among his people. He goes into the crowd as an ordinary man (a clean, luminous, upright, but ordinary man); ordinary but undisguised, bareheaded, and they know him. Today he means to be known. He walks with his chin turned upwards; he was born on another Good Friday, and he has a second sight, they say; he sees the bodies of the murdered in the places where they fell and these streets are littered with the ghosts of corpses; and some of the people know this and it makes them revere him all the more if they do revere him, born on the day the Lord died and gifted with this terrible burden of a gift; and others who don't know or believe it still admire his splendid chin.

The King passes the penitents and they pause for a moment in their flogging, resume with renewed vigour. In Holy Week he walks through the mud humbly to a humble parish church, and there, in the eyes of his God, he kneels before a beggar. He slides his rings from his long fingers and the Count-Duke takes them from him; and the King's own bare hands hold the man's rough heel and he lifts the coarse clay ewer and the sweet pure water of the city pours over the man's brown feet. The feet have already been washed, as far as possible; the state of them an hour ago! They are brown and calloused and common, nonetheless, and the King kneels before them, devout, and the people see this, and they love him, he is assured of this: they love him. But out in the rain, in Holy Week, in the ordinary streets among ordinary people, not actresses or courtiers or courtesans or nuns, and despite the ever-present retinue who surround him and hustle him discreetly from place to place, glancing down it can't be disguised or denied: the populace cannot afford to pay for what it needs; cannot buy an egg for what would last year have bought a week's living; and the King, bare-headed, muddied and humble and soaked to the skin, cannot fail to see it. And he considers that God is angry, despite all of their prayers; He is angry with him— and with his kingdoms and their sins— and in particular with him.

And at his private prayers, every day, the King repents and asks forgiveness for his sins, and prays that his wife should have a son, and promises that he will do better if he is spared this punishment. He will not give way to passions, to sorrow or melancholy or ardour. He prays and chastises his own weakness, his own repeated weakness, the weakness of his ardent flesh; he repents, he repents, on his knees he repents. He can't help himself, he's insatiable. He remembers her red hair and— her hands— her hands in his in prayer he can't help it— alone with no one to see he almost smiles, and then thinks of how God is all-seeing and what else He has seen and renews his prayers alone and in torment. The King seeks absolution for all his sins of thought and deed and he repents, every time, and does it again and repents, and he promises, he prays for a son, he promises to make recompense.

✟

As dusk darkens, the painter's door opens and closes, admitting a brief gape of corridor light along with a footman. He turns his head and registers small surprise, acknowledges his visitor—the footman is the Chief Secretary, bearing a plate—and turns back to the canvas he's still regarding, some feet away from it. I stopped your man on his way in, Diego, the Secretary explains. I hope you don't mind my serving you. I'm afraid I'm not trained. He takes a grape from the plate and slices it neatly in half between his white incisors. See? Now I'm eating your dinner. Is this little plateful dinner? Did you forget to eat again? Munching, he sets the plate down among pots and palette on the painter's table, where he is tidying and cleaning, wiping a thin brush. The Secretary circles, finds the only armchair, lowers himself into it; the painter turns, and the form of Don Jerónimo emerges from the dark, lit red from the brazier; although the eyes remain shaded and illegible, and the smile likewise. Same dark hair, same pointed beard, as all the nobles of the court; the dark robes too, of course; cut from particularly fine cloth, illegally fine cloth in fact, but he is too close to the King and his valido to worry about that. He seems to have made himself comfortable, as he always seems to, wherever he is, though the hand that rests and gestures on the arm of the chair could just as soon grip and he'll be up before you know it. Somehow both languid and taut. The painter waits for him to speak, which eventually, smiling, adjusting his cloak on his knee, he does.

Diego, I come with a commission for you. With the blessing of the King, and of the Count-Duke, of course; in fact, the Count-Duke suggested it. He thought you might have an opening, a gap in your schedule, when you're done with— an elegant unfurling of fingers to the King on the easel— His Majesty. It is to be a gift. It is to be of some scale. For the convent I am neighbour and patron to. It's not, perhaps, in your usual line. But perhaps you'd enjoy the challenge? I mean, the change?

The painter knows when he's being played; but still, his pride is pricked. He nods. They watch each other, or each imagine that this is the case, each unable to see the other's eyes. The Secretary rises and smiles. Your discretion would be appreciated. I know how you tend to let your mouth run away with you.

The painter cracks, breaks his silence, laughs. The Secretary slides off again into the dark corridors he came from. The painter looks again at the dark shape of the King . . . no sense going on with it now . . . and he's already cleaned his brush, in fact; what was he—— endless distractions. What time is it? His stomach growls; he should eat. Ah, supper; that was it.

The painter finds a model willing to stand with arms raised and spread for a few hours. Christ in the dark night of his death, his long lean torso heaven-lit. He observes the body, finds its lines. Thinking, is this what women like, is this what they come to worship, thinking of his daughter and what she'd make of this body so beautiful in its last moments, if she were to encounter it, the body of this young man before him. But he needn't worry about that; the canvas will be carried straight to the convent and the model will put his clothes on before he goes. He needn't worry about her and her presumed urges. Francisca, it seems, is growing up. She has grown out her hair, she is growing breasts, she has grown the faintest trace of facial hair and no doubt hair elsewhere. She wears careful curls that she weaves ribbons through, carefully; and she wears a veil over them so that she can go out and walk with the other ladies. She wears high shoes. She'd like a carriage sometimes, maybe.

His only child, since Ignacia, little Ignacia ... And now she wants to marry his assistant, Juan Bautista. So grandchildren, maybe, if. Perhaps he needn't worry about her at all, sensible, sturdy girl, like her mother, and after all he set the precedent himself: Juana was his master's daughter. More worrying this, maybe, the comparison, since he so far outstripped his master; the thought of being surpassed in turn; no, not likely, though he's not bad, Juan Bautista. Prolific. Works quickly. A boy with hands in hair, bunching up skirts, whispering *your father will crucify me*——

——

————The painter has a deadline. Bleeding wound—— bleeding feet.

The King comes to watch him paint, as he does, sometimes; sits quiet, penitent; he watches as the painter works the nails into the flesh. The model was starting to moan about the ache of holding his arms up, but has shut up since the King came in. The painter doesn't make conversation, is not required to; he works the nails in. His own patience is thin. This is not the first time he has worked to commute the King's guilty conscience, however circumspectly he's been prevailed upon to do so. And he hasn't been paid yet.

Still, he's pleased with it, the geometry of it, the modelling, the blood-run death of the flesh tones. The inscription given three times over, Hebrew, Greek and Latin, because the Secretary is a learned man and will appreciate this detail, or because he's showing off. The painter owns a number of dictionaries and grammars. He is proud of his library, he was brought up to read languages, to be learned also. He owns many books on many subjects. Euclid, Vitruvius, Battista; Vasari, Alberti; Seneca, Lipsius, Democritus; Ovid, Aesop; mythology, history, anatomy, arithmetic, architecture, geometry, archery, armoury;

the tools of his trade, precepts upon painting, perspective, ico-
nographies, yes, all of this. Almost no theology. It holds little
interest for him, the subject itself or the composition of it, all
the rules, maybe because of all the rules, although he's followed
them, he thinks, the feet as his father-in-law stipulates with a
nail each instead of crossed and nailed together, which appar-
ently is important. Will this, master, persuade men to piety?
Will this bring the King closer to God, if there are two separate nails for the feet? He is indifferent to the subject, but not
indifferent to the suffering; his Christ is just a man, meeting his
end. The wounds, though, are invented and painted on, and the
model is young and not really suffering and despite that little
unvoiced whimper can surely manage to hold his arms up a
little longer—— for God's sake—— for the King's sake really,
for the sake of his salvation——— The painter works in silence
until the King departs, taking his sheepish leave as ever discreetly. He rakes the model's lank hair over half his handsome
face. A good effect and far less effort——— Swiped down in
just a few strokes, like it's blood-soaked. An end to suffering.
Maybe dead already. Done.

The sisters of San Placido hang him in the sacristy, a bare and
wretched cell, ill lit by a tiny grated window; and in this obscu-
rity for years he'll suffer for our sins, or someone's.

In a small private palace somewhere in the city behind several
closed doors a woman waits, waits in her own private palace
with its private chambers, its veiled windows; waits for a knock
upon a hidden entrance; knows it will come.

Back in the Alcázar, the King goes to his wife and does his
duty; and every day he goes to pray; he thinks of the nuns of

San Placido offering their prayers for him, and repents again—
and again— and prays daily for a son.

The King in sombre mood, standing back from the canvas all
black cloak and pale skin, all modesty; a slender ankle pointing
the toe outwards, princely—— slender ankles drawn together
one heel an inch off the ground as the foot draws back—the
trace of its retreat shows through the painted layer, the narrow
stance more modest still, and flattering years of maturity shade
the face, hollow the eyes, gravitas; the hint of pain, of loss, of
decisions not taken lightly; cool, impassive; a thought across
the brow there; there; the painter pauses, scrutinises in silence
the King upon the canvas and looks beyond it into the space
where the King stood—five years ago, was it? How they are
passing . . . and calls him into it, seeing him, as he was and as
he is now, the regrets and the care and the prayers he's observed
daily and where they sit, there, upon the brow— *there*——

VI

Los borrachos/ Topers

The famous Fleming has been sent for—the famous artist-ambassador is coming, to meet with the King! His patron the Archduchess, the King's aunt, has released him for this important mission—— this important commission, rather. He's a famous diplomat, but he's only here to paint; he is famous for that, too. He makes haste from Flanders down through France in a southwest sweep, arrives with entourage; the famous Fleming! He is made welcome, he must have space, and so space is to be made for him in the studio the painter uses, here at the King's country place, just a short ride from the city; a monastery-palace, built by the King's grandfather on the refuse of old iron mines, that the court calls the slagheap——

— That is, the Escorial, which despite this inauspicious foundation is still standing, and still known by this igno-minious nickname. A short train ride from the city, into the scrubby mountains, it still lours there, grey and weighty, so that drawing near I feel almost menaced by it; the vertigo of the high blank wall made black against the bright sky as I look up. It is dedicated to San Lorenzo, and is built in the shape of a gridiron, square, rigid and forbidding, a motif which now

recurs on the cast-iron stairheads and movable barriers and the
logo on leaflets and information sheets and the laminated café
menu where I sit and gulp water, exhausted and exhilarated,
for a moment—the gridiron that poor, hilarious Lorenzo was
martyred on. They had him sizzling on the fire, those awful
Romans, and they said well, have you had enough, and he
said— he said!— yes, turn me over, I'm done on this side! Who
says saints have no sense of humour? Medium-rare, please! No,
perhaps even a saint's patience wouldn't stretch this far— the
scale of the place makes me hysterical, facetious—so much
heavy stone and holiness—

The King greets the Fleming in person, and leads a personal tour through his grandfather's house, in all its granite
severity; all its staircases and cells and oratories; they walk
miles of its passageways; they see the tiny cell his grandfather
slept and stank and, gangrenous, died in, and the vast staterooms he ruled from. The Count-Duke accompanies them, of
course. Their guest is to paint a new equestrian portrait of the
King—the painter betrays no reaction—if, in this moment, the
Count-Duke recalls his promise of exclusive access, he is too
much immersed in conversation with the Fleming to acknowledge it. They pause and survey the walls. The new portrait
will hang here, just here where we've got this one that Diego
painted. Oh ... The King hopes his personal painter will not
mind the transposition. Of course he won't, the Count-Duke
assures everyone, the painter assenting with a small bow. It
is a necessary statement, and more to the point an honour, to
have this great man's work at the centre of the scheme for this
grand stateroom; and there is no shortage of other walls in the
palace, Diego's horse will happily trot off and find a new place
to stable, and other witticisms of this sort, and the painter
smiles graciously ...

It is an honour bestowed upon the painter, to host their famous guest and keep him company. To walk with him through the palace, to show him the King's collection, of which he will make study. The Fleming arrives in the afternoon and by the next morning he's in the studio with lackeys in tow, keen to get started, commanding, jocular, this easel here and that trestle there, a folding stool, a sheet pinned to the ceiling, letting light reach places that have never seen it, dispelling gloom; and the boys run around him laying out pigments and oils and grinding stones; all the while he is talking, urbane, expansive: that deposited there, this to be established here, if you don't mind, Don Diego (he says with his drummed northern Ds), if this won't be an encumbrance, no not there *idioot* not you Don Diego . . . Me, I think with God's will, we both may be most comfortably accommodated; with God's will and your forbearance, monsieur . . . so he sets himself up, and a canvas as big as a sail is hoisted, and quickly, he sets to work among them all, and the painter watches as swathes and swatches of fabric, colour, light, come into being upon it.

A fair man with thinning hair, a northern man in this heat—twenty years the painter's senior, his natural quickness is swollen with gout; he sweats as he works and sometimes winces. The painter hears him breathing, hears his exertions, filling up all the space he's been granted and yet somehow, never exceeding it or imposing himself upon his host. The painter finds that it's congenial to match his guest's good manners; he is surprised to enjoy the company.

A week later, he comes into the studio to find the Fleming already at a new canvas, laying down the first forms of the flushed and rubicund-blond flesh. Goedemorgen, Buenos días, Don Diego, he says, nodding briefly but politely before digging back into his palette, all cochineal and coral and ochres and white. It is still quite early. The Fleming will have been at it for hours, after his very early prayers (as observant and impeccably Catholic as the Count-Duke, even); the painter has been Ushering. He watches for a while, and listens to the Fleming's boy reading aloud—the Fleming learns as he works. Seneca is it? A bid to understand where this Stoical court is coming from. The painter has already said he doesn't mind it; he hasn't been in much anyway, hasn't much to be distracted from. He tools with a couple of copies of portraits, directs his apprentices; turns his attention, with a heavy half-heart, to another iteration of the King. He does seem to find it hard these days to get started. And so perhaps it's a relief when the Fleming—completing a flourish of the brush, a line of a leg from hip to heel—standing back to see that the sweep of it is in keeping with the whole, the movement from corner to corner that the whole thing's caught up in (a dynamic balance that the painter admires, but doesn't seek to emulate)— and seeming satisfied— perhaps it's a relief to the painter when he turns, beaming, bids his host good morning again (though it's now past noon), and asks if he might revisit the King's collection. The Venetians, especially. Still splendid, those colours, a hundred years on! So rich, so delicate. He admires the Venetians very much. The painter does too, and this is a welcome and justifiable diversion; he needn't go back to the unfinished canvas just yet. That faceless hole awaiting him.

He takes the Fleming to the King's private chambers, where this most retiring of kings comes to retire—he is no French monarch, to go to bed in public; only the Count-Duke is at his side when night falls, to light his way and see him safe under the sheets and lock the door of the innermost chamber with

the key he keeps close and a man stationed outside. The rooms
are empty now, and the painter, yes, the painter has a key— to
most of them. He observes the way the Fleming moves through
these rooms, the way his attention is given wholly to the works
that hang there, as if he has no interest in the King's other
accoutrements, in his private arrangements. He comes to each
canvas less with surprise than anticipation. Ah, he says before
each (with a little guttural catch to his gasp, quick swollen
fingers tugging his beard). Ach. And the painter, who has
studied these works at length— can he have become used to
them? They are part of the palace's familiar furniture— beside
his guest, he sees them again, diffuse, limpid colour, stillness,
immortal alien faces, full of dreams, intensity, desire—and
enjoys them again, and enjoys that they belong to his King,
that they are his, in a way, by extension, to show off to this
perfect courtier, this artist who's so much in demand in every
court in Europe.

Quickly, effortlessly, the Fleming makes copies. And
freely. The old Adam is stern, cautious and stolid, eyes warily
on the Devil, with staying hand outstretched: Um, Eve, be
careful, I'm not sure that ... But his Flemish double grasps
blindly at her breast, leaning forward with his belly paunch-
ing in his lap, which has lost its fig leaf—life is good in the
garden of Eden, their flesh is dimpled and rippling—he is
aghast: Eve, what are you *doing*? And above them the Devil
with a little cherub's face snaking around one side of the
tree trunk while his forked tail curls out insouciant from the
other—and he has lost all interest in Adam, he is looking las-
civiously at Eve and she reaches up with lips parting to receive
the proffered apple, and on the whole everything is just a
little naughtier, less an inevitable tragedy than a moment's
weakness, which will put paid to the blissful ignorance of

Eden forever; and where there was a space behind old Adam, a red parrot has flown into the frame to fill this obvious hole in the composition.

He paints and paints, banishing darkness. Annunciation! Adoration! Ecstasy and expulsion! And ravishment and revelry and light-struck revelation ... the old gods and the new and all the court too. The painter sends for materials to replenish his guest's stock. Tints and pigments he has never used in quantities he'd take a year or more to work through. And he watches as one by one the canvases fill with colour—portraits and myths, copies and new compositions—he watches as the ground is laid in big grand sweeps, the curve and verve and energy that will show through to the surface there in the first marks. Europa borne into the water by her bull, giving in to her fate, all abandon and inner thigh; such a quantity of ruby-red and peach and golden skin, flushed, ravished, so much flesh, folds of fabric tumbling, the eye unresting unsure where to look but pulled from one corner to another, the flexed toe of a rounded foot, a flung-out hand, the glinting of teeth, the red of ruby-rose lip and nipple and ear lobe; quiet, astonished, the painter watches as his new companion wipes brow and brush and catches his breath and sets to again— tireless.

The King, too, looks on; he visits almost daily. He seems almost relaxed, in their company, as far as he ever does. He stands hatless by the window for an hour or so and watches and they don't appear to mind him, and he's thankful for it. He is like a child in the presence of his heroes, enthralled. Thinking how these worlds they make will outlast them; all of them. How some of these works might still be hanging here, in his grandfather's palace, in hundreds of years' time—— if it would comfort him or not, to know that they will, I don't know; but

they will and I've seen them. Or some of them will; some of
them will burn in the fire at the Alcázar but he'll be dead by
then and so will his sons and his direct line will be smudged
out long since and that, I suppose, would certainly not comfort
him, or in some way, would it? To know they'll be freed from
this earthbound rotary, freed from time into eternity— such a
thought might comfort him, sometimes.

The new portrait is done quickly—the painter looks on as it is
whipped into being, and it is hung in the appointed place, and
in a quiet moment he comes to study it. The King is protected
by pugnacious angels, throwing lightning bolts from a turbu-
lent putti-tumbled sky which exhausts his eye; but below all
this bluster, he sees, how effortless, all the bound-up energy in
the horse's shining, muscled haunch and the Spanish landscape
in the distance rinsed with northern light ...

The Fleming reworks an Adoration already in the King's
collection; the King has suggested he might like to include
himself in the crowd (a thronging writhing crowd lit by stars
and fizzing torchlight). He slips in at the edge, subtle and
stately, a gentleman in royal favour, with chain and sword. He
is a diplomat, an ambassador, although he is on this occasion,
of course, just here to paint. The King tosses a knighthood to
him. The painter thinks, Well that was easy.

Is he jealous? Envious, perhaps, but not jealous; he envies the
accolades but he is proud and sure of his own gift and standing.
But then, he has never seen anything like it, the pace and the
proliferation; and he's not the type to be star-struck but the
Fleming has been a star for a while, now, he's been a name for
as long as the painter's been painting; and so he sees it for what
it is, to share his studio with this man: a privilege. When the
Fleming isn't working and listening to his boys read, he spends

long hours in the company of the Count-Duke; he is close with the painter's first patron, it seems—he is not here to paint at all, they say, the gossiping poets in the mentideros; he's a spy, it's a front, he's here on some mission. But if so it's quite a front—thirty paintings in under a year; it is quite a front.

And while he is here, he would like to see the country, to make some sketches—when he isn't painting, he is drawing, incessantly—will the painter take him? He asks, shall we, you and I, set out upon an expedition in the morning, une petite balade, Don Diego, the weather and God willing?

So they set out early from the Escorial. They carry packs, with bread, cheese, perhaps fruit. Wearing country clothes of simple green cloth. As they reach the sparse woods beyond the palace, the painter passes a tasselled stick to his companion, wordlessly, and they set out on the rough earth path, and provided that they keep up a constant, whisking motion before their faces, the flies are kept at bay. The day is pleasant, temperate, smudged with clouds for depth and texture. They begin to ascend. The painter is little more than half his companion's age, but he finds he is not so robust; the great man climbs, and climbs, sweating, indefatigable. The painter should get out more. Always the walls around him. They reach the seat of the King's grandfather, a niche in the rock where they can rest in shade and look out at the plain, the mountains, the bulking monastery in the distance.

Nothing much else for miles around. The silvery green of oak leaves and pines, growing low and twisting; the dry earth; the mountains purpling around them, the clouds. They take out paper and coloured chalks. They look out and glance down sometimes and let their hands find the forms, find the varied pressures of light and shade, of shadow and leaf, of cloud and

mountain, what impression these things make upon the page
of the world. They work in silence, concentrated, relaxed,
untroubled by flies up here; just the soft shift and susurrus of
chalk and skin on the paper's surface; the wordless passing of
a flask; it is as close as he has come to bliss. How small, next
to the mountains, the palace is. How long he's been inside it.
How many times he's painted this same landscape, a copy from
a copy, without even looking out at it; without being within it.

When they leave the light is softening, blurring violet and
brown. The Fleming claps him on the back gently as a brother
might, and they walk in the quiet dusk sometimes talking of
small things, me and my knees don't much like this downhill,
thank the Lord those flies have retired, and it is almost dark
when they get back. With a relish for their simple, well-earned
thirst, they call for beer to be brought. If the request is unusual
it doesn't show; the painter has his own attendants, who are
paid (or in theory they are paid) to meet the demands of an
Usher of the Chamber, so whatever consternation and flurry
this may cause is kept hidden from them, the diplomat and
the Sevillian. They sit and beer is found in some kitchen or
cellar and brought; they sit and drink beer and the Fleming
tells stories as tirelessly as he paints them: of his travels—of
his work as an artist and of his other work (what he can say
of it—diplomat, spy?)—of his wife who died, who was much
more beautiful than he deserved. He painted her beautiful
even when she'd already died all plague-boiled, as God
willed it—but he couldn't bear to show her pain, he is not a
painter of pain, and that, perhaps, the painter thinks, is why
he's so beloved of monarchs— of everyone, it's impossible
not to like him— they talk long into the night. He speaks of
Italy, of this draughtsman and that, of a splendid ceiling, a
magnificent fountain, naked marble men and goddesses and

gods, and of course it is the home of our mother the Church and our Papa; and I must tell you, the women walk without veils in the streets, laughing; and of course the Basilica, one must visit, you must. The painter is stirred, perhaps; it is not in his nature to feel restless but listening, he feels it; his soul fidgets. He cannot place it, quite, or not at first, what it is that's stirring behind the breastbone; a quivering, an impulse just quelled, although he cannot name this impulse and could not act upon it; something nervy and sanguine, too, as if his blood is tingling close to the surface, as if he cannot keep his fingers still although he does and can. He wants— what? To make something, to go somewhere, to walk, to move, to live, to paint ... He wants to paint— to paint with his fingers, to work at the surface of life and let it get under his fingernails and—— yes— go, Diego, live a little ... So perhaps it is tonight that he thinks he will ask the King for leave to go to Rome. What kind of artist can he hope to be without it? Yes! his new friend claps decisively, pours beer, yes, you *must* see it. Me, I will write for you, I will make introductions, you will meet so many people, you will see so many things, let me tell you ...

When at last the painter is alone his mind is clear and high, and he removes his clothes and smells his own good outdoor sweat and falls into his chair in his shirt and takes up something to read by the last glow of the brazier, not ready quite yet to sleep, not yet, takes up a book, something light, some picaresque, and begins to read and the road is barely embarked upon and here he is, walking it again, the mountains, the earth, the flies, and fountains and frescos in another city and mountains, the distance, the flask, the warm stone, how quiet it is, the crickets even are silent, how deeply he sleeps, how rarely this deeply I sometimes sleep.

While the Fleming is churning out works as fast as his boys can stretch the canvas for them, the painter— because he cannot hope to match his guest? Because he is busy? Because he is lazy? Because he is slow?—— I don't know what his excuse is but maybe he hasn't time, he tells himself, to even be making excuses— oh, I know that one—— the painter produces but a single painting. The King, their regular visitor, has asked for something jolly, enlivened perhaps by their guest's ebullience— How productive our guest is, he notes . . . It has been said, says the King— I have heard it said, that the King's own painter can only paint heads. I am flattered, says the painter, smiling because the King is making a sort of joke, although he also sort of means it. It's not easy, a head. To convey for example your majesty, Your Majesty, but also show the man. How to show the life, in paint, of any man. I don't know anyone that can. And, out of modesty, and because they both know it, doesn't say: anyone else, that is; but I reckon *I* can.

The King lightly sighs, raises a hand to cover his mouth as he smiles in return, the smile creeping to his eyes—how at ease he is here! Nonetheless, he'd like something new, he says; something to further prove the painter's worth, he doesn't say, not in so many words. Something lively and rustic for his private chambers; because, he says, in these days he feels a darkness on him, a grey darkness that he can't shake, and he is tired, tired of mourning, and tired of the views from his windows, even though there are so many windows, so many views, of the busy city and the mountains both, wherever he is, whichever of his several houses and palaces, the sunshine doesn't lift him. And he's sick of the frivolous city and longs for a simple country life and would like to be reminded that such a thing exists somewhere, or could, or at least used to. And the painter plans to leave him soon, and yes—he may go—only the King will miss him, and the King would like to travel too, as if he were a private person, and since he can't do that or ever be that he wants at least some other rude southerner for company here in the palace in the Sevillian's stead, which the painter of course is not, he is a courtier and the son of an arguably noble line, but the King, raising hand to mouth, will have his little joke, and the painter nods, and smiles back at the smile the King is masking.

So: a composition— Bacchus at the feast. Countryside. Out of the same old shadows, into sunshine. A vineyard. The dirt of the real earth. The painter finds a boy with pale skin and paints him paler. He has the mouth for it, the full red mouth always a little wet, ready to drink or kiss, and he is smooth and plumpish and his body hairless, not quite free of his awkward adolescence; he seems, at all times, a little embarrassed, sitting in the painter's studio without his shirt on. And the painter leaves all of this in—the smooth deep-navelled belly, already beginning to pot; the pale hairless white arm like a strong woman's, the lips, the jaw shadowed by the first fluff of a day or two's debauch; and also the awkwardness, the embarrassment. The young god looks askance as he crowns a man with ivy. He is playing his part, but not well.

More vessels needed:

A glass dish propped against— something.

Before them, an earthen jug. It is half-glazed; the spout pinched so that you could fit your fingers just in the place of those that made it; you could heft it by its pointed handle and pour wine; you could lift it right out of the painting and leave just a dark jug-shaped ground where he has superimposed it so it— floats— against Bacchus' pink robe; he—

—— can't quite make it sit.

Each separate thing. Each vessel. Each gesture. Each leaf.

Opposite, the muscular boy holds out a fine-stemmed flute— of yellow glass or else brim-full of yellow wine—— but this boy is in the painter's studio days after Bacchus has departed, so— he's lost the reference— would the stem of the glass be in front of the wreath on his head or— or behind? Where are they in the depth that he's created? He has to rework, rework it—— Maybe his colleagues are right about him; how is it done, this business of composition?

Here— more vessels, a dish, a cup——

Every separate part observed, exact, every solid object. And then what goes here? Then another boy, more muscular, brown, leaning in at the god's shoulder; and following a line through elbows, knees and knives (so maybe he's learned something from the Fleming after all—it all flows), the boy's opposite, a supplicant, grey and dignified; and then at their centre at the side of the god, the southerner, tanned from the fields, his honest grin, each crinkle about his eyes, the sweat in the crease of his chin, every separate tooth; and his buddy at his shoulder with a nose aglow from wine and sunshine, an eyebrow cocked;

they are all perhaps a little tipsy but not dissolute. And at the back of this group, a caped shadow, come to beg for booze or alms, a hand outstretched, a hat, a square of shadow for a face.

To describe a thing, you describe the space around it; until you encounter the brim, the fringe, the outline, where the thing's edges meet the world you find it in.

This world he's making is the same world he lives in, the vineyards, the hills, the earth under the surface and he is out there with them, out of himself, out of time in this afternoon stretching out in the company of this awkward young god and his little gang out in the fields with the farmers, the topers; he is out of himself, only eyes and hands, not here and at the same time only himself, entirely. There is nothing like time only light darkening to mark its passing the shadow shifting as he watches and works reworks it; no ceremonies no anxieties no ambition beyond the immediate object, the next object, the lip the leaf the skin; no longing, no future, no home, no hunger—

————

or—

no—

————

there ... when he stops he finds he *is* hungry, very hungry after all, and thirsty. He drinks from the jug, lifts it right out from the composition, and his hands are clayed with paint and it is dark, beyond the thick-walled windows, all this while the sun has been travelling over the mountains without him, in another world from the one he's made which is, nonetheless, the same one, the same world he lives in, made from its stuff. How long has it been since he felt this, how long has passed? Years are passing in these shadows. In these reiterations. He needs this—this inspiration—this— breathing in. Fresh air. He looks from his studio window at the paths just showing in the gardens and the land rising dim beyond them. His cuticles stained, paint on the ball of the thumb that he catches himself rubbing at, rolling into tiny threads and scurfing off his skin; the lines of his knuckles darkened, as if drawn on. The pale and dark and insect-red sediment marking his hands, the dirt under the nails, hours have passed and the light is gone.

And the clay jug of water on the sill in the light of a candle.

This is what he believes in. The things of the world that he's touched—— And still they remain, these solid objects— I could still almost touch them; things that existed in the world once, in his world, almost in my hands. They have lasted. That seems worth believing in. A toast to the topers: I raise my yellow glass—

He pours out water still seeing how to shape things the fall of water and the clay spout darkens as it wets; he washes his hands carefully, washing off the day's work, revealing the dull shine of the short nails, paring the paint from under them, cuticles ragging, umber like dirt from working the land. His capable hands, his maker's hands, his workman's hands. Art is made with the hands and worked upon with them. And even when they are clean and still as he sits down in the candle-dark his mind is still daubing and drawing, oil-grimed fingers feeling for the forms, still working over surfaces to find the feel of them. Still seeing in the dark how this curve comes out of shadow; how this man's hand, how his own hand, holds the cup, how, like his own, the hand is work-stained, how the man's knee grinds at the grit of the ground, how the flesh is imprinted with it; how the world is worked into the skin. If this sits there then here is its shadow and how it is cast upon what's below it; and that gives shape to the next shape and the next, this basin this leaf and the vine it grows from and the head it sits on and the hair it tangles in; this and this and this hair growing flowing from the bristle of the brush to the temple, the shadow of the slight indent of bone beneath the skin, the shade made of clay and burnt bone. He works with powders ground from earth and stone and things that grow and creep upon them, everything remade from the world, impermanent and everlasting: this glass and this coarse fabric and this gauze, the folds of it, and underneath the flesh and underneath the bone of which he has made study with his mind his eye his hands.

Perhaps it hasn't come out quite as he hoped. But one cannot go on forever reworking. Anyway the King is pleased. He almost smiles, he sighs through his nose, he hangs it in the New Room, to show it off; he says, very well, go then. Go to Rome, Diego. Buy some nice things for me. For yourself, also. Have you been paid lately? Ah . . . then we'll see to that. Come back soon.

VII

Bosquejo/
Sketch

The painter sits in the gardens of the Medici villa. Poplars and stone arches and sky. He has sat all afternoon untroubled, observing, and as evening falls he finds new colours, and sees the light and how to use it—evening greens on a grey ground. Hermes stands watch on his plinth, his shadow behind him, dark and soft in the evening's yellow light, and a woman hangs out a sheet and two men pause— long enough to barely stain the surface, leaving only this brief trace of their anonymous passing, as the earth and stone go on solidly beneath them; the painter sits with his small canvas and his palette quietly as evening comes. And his mind and his eye are entirely at leisure to stretch into grey, into green. He needn't look down at his palette and knows even as the light dims where to dip for each green, each white, each blue, there is no separation now of hand, mind, eye, no body or time; stone, sky, tree, distance, ground, layering opacities in chalk and oil. He has his private rooms and these gardens, this forgotten corner of these gardens, the arches, the ramshackle boards. And there is no one at all to press their impressions upon him or of whom he must sketch his impressions or upon whom he must make an

impression, just people passing and arches and trees, and the
quiet evening——

— There's a swing in a garden in the way-to-the-west of
England, almost Wales, a very green county I have rarely visited; and the sun is out and the day will be hot but in this early
morning, early-ish, it isn't yet. The swing hangs from a big old
tree, the variety obscure to my memory, deciduous, certainly,
apple or linden or beech in full summer leaf and the light
through it deep sap-green; the swing has a cushioned seat to
sink into; things are in bloom and the garden smells of summer
flowers and the green of the pasture fields nearby and the last
moisture of the summer night's dew; and I swing gently with
my eyes closed and am nowhere but here and keep trying to
get back here, will keep trying, for years to come, to come back
here. I have the kind of mild hangover that makes everything
more imminent, that brings the world closer in contact with
the skin. I am waiting to be collected, to go elsewhere, but this
knowledge, for once, only concentrates the instant so I live it
more richly, all senses, all embedded in the present. I try to
get back here sometimes. That's what I see in your Medici
gardens, Diego. I want to somehow simply set down what it
looked like to you, the world, what it felt and smelled like; as
I pass through the same and different world now and it passes
and I try to grasp what's solid and not solid; as if in attending
to it and setting it down I can testify to my passing presence
in it; preserving in the observation not the thing observed but
the fact that I was here to make it. The arrogance of that. The
presumption. The anxiety. The vertigo and yawn of terror,
pre-dawn: What if everything I've ever seen is always gone
already? It is, it is; there's no what if about it. Today, for example, it's April; the fact of a lilac on a cloudy spring evening,
of a greenish dampish evening in London, the scent and the

purple flowers and the different pinks of the paving slabs of an ordinary real world that you don't know, that you're gone from, in a city that you never visited. I have no idea really what your world smelled like. I want to know if—— you know, for example, when you split an almond lengthways in the teeth, and find the perfect smoothness of the nut's inside surface on the tongue— I want to ask—— I want to ask you, do you love that, as I do? The smoothness of it and the sweetly bitter oily tang? No one will remember this about me when I die.

There's a dog, in the garden with the swing, a rust-red dog, maybe a setter. He's gentle, friendly, enquiring, very clean and silky. The kind of dog I think you'd like, Diego.

Boards, scaffold, a sheet hanging. A square arch, then a round, then a square one—

TWO

VIII

Historial
Composition

— Let's say mid-afternoon— bright January cold— the low
sun hazed in the high flat cloud; the pale grey of the plain
continuous with the sky. The fields dry, crisp and barren and
quiet but for the *craak* of hungry crows, and the summer rust
of the earth faded to pewter— to a mute mole-fur softness in
the distance out towards the hills, which haze into the mist
becoming cloud becoming mountains. Everything gone to
ground. Low-lying. Pallid shadows. Villages empty, fallow
farms, no herd or flock of anything, everything faded already
and left to frost. It's been hard to find a bed in places, further
out from the city; on his way here the roads out in the country
have been all but unpeopled and the inns shut up; drawing
closer to the centre, the way to the gate as ever is busy, but
where this influx of jobseekers and aspiring hidalgos have
sprung from is hard to say; come out of the air, out of the
unfarmed earth they've abandoned in favour of flagstones
and la Corte.

The painter pays his tax at the gate, takes a carriage while
his retinue follows by mule. He wraps himself in his dark
warm cloak in the corner of the carriage and breathes the

different air of the city. Over a year since he last breathed it. How many since he first made this journey? Seven ... or eight even ... Since he came from Seville with nothing but a letter and a little stipend and a little hope and his brushes. Tired now. With a carriage to carry him and his palace privileges and his good thick cloak. Half-looking out of the window at the isosceles forms of the veiled ladies, the gallants in their sober dress drunk with pride or wine. Sad to have left Rome; but he's coming to the end of long weeks of travel, of the dragging impatience of a return journey, so the sadness is tempered with leaden relief, in sight of an end to it. Feeling the walls of the old fortress closing on him; thinking of the court encroaching, the backs that may have been stabbed in his absence, the privation, the gossip, the hush; and on the other hand a homecoming— the nearest he has to a home, now. There will have been plays, in his absence, and celebrations for the new Prince—at last, the Queen has borne a son; and mourning for the King's brother Carlos— handsome Carlos with his rabbit-puppet glove— is gone. And new appointments—Juan Bautista, the painter's protégé, doing well he hears, making an impression at court, so Juana in her letters has implied—in his home, also, she has hinted— Francisca, of course, has grown a year older in his absence, just about a woman now— and Juana, what of Juana in his absence? Wrapped in his warm cloak and thinking of his home, Juana bringing in a jug, pouring chocolate for him, a little fatter or a little thinner, laughing at how his beard's grown, taking his cloak. Awaiting him, the re-acquaintance with familiar things, made strange in his absence but soon reabsorbed and the gardens a memory, a separate self; reabsorbed into la Corte, half-seen out of the window ...

A new Prince to be painted. In the painter's absence a boy has been born. That's something. The King called him back for that— to paint his son; won't have anyone else for the job, he wrote, summoning. A new privilege. So, glad to be back, or resigned to it, or both. Sun setting fast now and the streets of grey stone and shadows. The golden tower of the Alcázar's southwest corner gleams dimly in the last of the winter sun, in the long silver winter light, and the swifts are reeling out meanings. Pale grey thoughts; just travel-weary and thinking of not much.

Juana hasn't changed much. He paints her in profile, on a pale grey ground, richly folded in a dark gold robe, her hair wound up and tied in a fashionable wrap he's brought back for her; tight curls falling at the temple, a string of pearls against her pale skin (how much clay have you been chewing, Juana?); he paints her as a sibyl, has her grasp a tablet that she doesn't look down at and her face, too, is a tabula rasa; who knows what she's thinking. The painter, distracted perhaps and much occupied in the first weeks of his return, doesn't quite finish it; leaves her cheek unblushed. She is pleased enough. You have other things to do, she says, Diego. But still, thank you; you've made me look pretty, and not too old—— But after all, she's no older than I am. For now. Like me, a bit unfinished—I'd rather stay that way, not quite seen clearly— and clasping her blank tablet. Pleased to have him back, perhaps.

So, we're back, Diego. And you have other things to do.

The rumour of his return takes little time to percolate. And just look what he's brought back with him! His colleagues arrive one by one, calling in just casually at his studio—a *new* studio, they notice—to say— Welcome back, Sevillian! Peering over his shoulder at the new works he's finishing and framing in there. All lined up, craning necks, old chins pushed forward pulling old necks taut, arms crossed in show of indifference, hanging back, hands to cheeks and mouths to play contemplation, critiquing, assessing, considering; a hand on the shoulder of the Sevillian, brought back to the fold. Well, this is the trouble with these ancient scenes, isn't it—all those unshod appendages. Such a chore. Just chuck a rug over those feet, very wise, Diego, they chuckle—

But. It appears to be true, they admit to each other, once out of earshot and grudgingly. He has made study in Italy, of so much marble, so much musculature, so much modelled flesh and skin. He has learned to invent and people a setting, a scene, a story. As our master Alberti says (so they mutter, his rivals, these Italians and would-be Italians, who wouldn't mind taking a trip to Rome, at the King's expense)—he has learned to make a proper *historia*—these various persons with their varied gestures and attitudes and each with their particular movements; their various states of dress. As it should be. He has it, now: the composition of it:

Jacob's house full of morning light; beyond, a pale blue landscape fading into the hills. Joseph is dead and his brothers have brought his bloody coat to prove it. Two of the brothers are excellent performers, and they've been tasked with the presentation of this humble bloodied garment; they hold the cloth between them, shocked, saddened, downcast. Two others flattened in the shadows are hopeless, smirking, stifling a snigger even? Maybe their brothers told them to hang back, if they can't keep a straight face, because they're not going to convince anyone. Barely formed, these two. Don't even have feet. The little dog on the other hand looks ready to leap right out into your lap, each of his little clawed paws set to scrabble, the shine of tiny canine tooth. He's at bay; he's ready; he's not to be conned. He's on to them.

And then here's Jacob appalled, half sliding off his chair. It's hard to tell the difference between these two griefs: the felt, the feigned. (Maybe there's always this element of performance, maybe the two always coexist—the painter observes this— the one pulled over the other part, which the showing can't reconcile or expel; this other unspeakable grief kept close and hidden in our heavy dark cloaks.)

And then there's more—craning, jostling into the new studio—this new studio he's been given— which is high-ceilinged, north-facing, enviably bright. There's more: drama, action, gesture, horror, bared flesh: who'd have thought it of the stolid Sevillian? *Two* new compositions in a year, and on a large scale, who'd have thought? Biblical and mythical, mastered both? In Vulcan's forge: bright orange hot metal and cloth, and the brilliant blue day outside, beyond. Vulcan's limbs, his stomach, his muscles taut from sweat and labour, powerful, goggle-eyed, his crooked stance, and behind him another workman with the other shoulder dropped in counterpoint, a face, features, barely, only and no more than what's needed. You can feel the heat of the place on their skin, the sheen on it, the sweat deep to the roots of the thick Andalusian heads of hair he's given them (the usual old models), all open-mouthed in disbelief: that Mars, what a git. And his armour still hot on the anvil, too. Glowing orange, and the orange firelight; Vulcan aghast at Apollo's message. But also maybe a little disgusted by the messenger. We're in there with them, one of Vulcan's lads, seeing Apollo as they see him: cool against the blue sky, his radiant laurel halo casting a thin white light that's swallowed up in the orange heat of the forge; raising a pedant's finger, bringing his bad news, golden bright and beaming, his little pointy nose, the little prick.

And they also notice: the painter has abandoned his Seville clay ground forever. Something else he's brought back from Rome: a different kind of shadow, a different way of bringing things out of it, a different way to cast it. How clean your fingernails are, they notice, peering. There is no longer earth under them, just as it has fallen away from under the figures he's learned to arrange; from now on he will always begin with a base of lead white just barely shaded; he has learned the blue of azurite, of smalt, and how to soften and grey them, to lend opacity or gloss; he is learning the art of dilution. This here in the light is solid and bright: the shine of beaten metal, the glaze of a pot, the tension of a forearm flexed; but in the gloom things are no longer so separate, so solid, this face, this hint of form.

The world and its objects, lit by the immanence of God's light; and then, also, the shadows, which will shift as the hour shifts; where light is not absent, just obscured; and the shadows in turn will wait, when the light falls on them, keep hidden until it moves off again.

The new studio in the Gallery of the North Wind is a long narrowish space, with windows running along one side of it. Facing out of them, the Count-Duke's apartments can be seen jutting out to the right; the King's rooms are through the wall at your back.

Looked upon from above, the fortress is a torso, cross-sectioned and imperfectly symmetrical, aired by the two stifled lungs of west and east courtyards; the King's apartments in the west, the Queen's in the east (enclosing the larger of the courtyards, the Alcázar's empty heart); between them and to the back, a central stairwell entered from either side; and that awkward bulk protruding from the spine out to the back where the Count-Duke has his rooms. As the King's buyer it seems the painter has acquitted himself well—he has brought back a choice few purchases, and more are shipping—to be so rewarded, to be brought in so near to the centre. Or else the King has simply missed him, and wants to make sure he's kept close and can't run off again. The King has been waiting for his favourite painter to return. The little Prince has been waiting for his portrait, he says—is that a pout of reproach?— we've been waiting these two years for you to come back. Sixteen months, if that, the painter doesn't say; and besides, you *gave* me two years. I'm early. (The Count-Duke has already commended the prudence of this precipitate return.) The painter says, I am grateful that you honour me thus, Señor. Well, anyway, you're back at last,

Diego, he says; we've waited, my son and I; settle in, be quick about it, there's work to be done.

So the painter makes his way each day, through the southern gate and skirting the inside of the west courtyard and up the spine of the stairs to the main floor, with his deliberate unassuming tread. And the King perhaps begins to listen out for it; he begins to drop in for visits more frequently. At first with the usual ceremony, key-turnings, shuffling, parade of chamberlains; but then one morning not long after his return, the retinue is dismissed. The King makes a small gracious gesture, and they shuffle and scrape away, hats off and bowed bare heads and black cloth, and the King is left alone with the painter. And the next day, and the next. He has a key of his own and lets himself in, although he is always careful to discreetly announce his presence. So this is the pay-off; if he is the King's only and personal painter, then the King can at any time have access to him, painting. Felipe is not bad company; attentive, quiet, at ease almost, alone with the painter. Together they review the painter's purchases as they arrive; he has a good eye and is delighted when it's called upon, and is in good spirits, some days; animated even, his humour restored by his new heir's promise; the painter is glad. There's something very pervasive about the King's sadness, when it comes. Sometimes he'll walk with the painter, show him some item from his collection; he'll say— I'd like to move this, what do you think? This one, this Europa, when I was a boy it was my favourite, you can see why, I used to sneak in to see it; my father didn't much approve but I'm told my grandfather loved it. This collection of his that I've inherited, that I am so grateful to you for enriching . . . how I'd like him to see what you've done; what you'll make of my son. I hope I'll live to meet my son's sons . . . I'd like to have known him, my grandfather. I model my rule upon his but I'd like to have known the *man*. We're only men, after all, Diego. Did you know your father's people? What were they like? That is an ancient name, your father's, isn't it? I'm sorry, I distract you, you must get to your work. I'll just watch.

And certainly there is work to be done. Things are shifting. Lines are unwinding and re-twining. New various positions taken. New arrangements. In the painter's absence—

— The King's youngest brother Fernando, the Cardinal Infante, sent to the war in Flanders to lead their troops—

— The King's brother Carlos— faded into a typhoid haze; mumbling and aching and sweating, knowing death when she comes; she leads him out through the mist of his illness and he goes with her quietly and at court another faction is left with a hole at the centre of their plot. (How convenient; the Count-Duke couldn't have arranged it better himself, could he. Could he?)—

— María, the King's younger sister, married at last, and her new husband's King of Hungary-Bohemia, and heir to the Holy Roman Empire, no less— so things are looking up for the future of the line, if she can manage a daughter; even though this marriage has left her brother abandoned, bereft (this most bereft of kings). The painter crossed her path in Naples—on her way to her waiting husband Ferdinand in Imperial Vienna; on her way to another gloomy court, another melancholy monarch, through all the warring countries in between, a long, dangerous journey of over a year. A beauty, and even more so in maturity, which is a mercy, since they took so long to find her a match. Fair skin and red-blonde curls and green eyes the painter calls the light to, pompoms, feathers in her hair. This image of her the painter brings back for her brother to remember her by; as vibrant and stylish as she is in life. The King will long for her to break out of the moment of arrest that the painter has caught her in, on the point of smiling, and will stand before her willing her to smile and thinking then he'd smile back at her, he'd allow himself a smile for her—— But he won't see her again— never again lively, not in this court. Her daughter will not turn out quite so pretty, which is a pity for the King, as it turns out.

— And so the King's brother is dead and his other brother has left for the north and his sister is gone, too; but on the other hand—— And most of all, above all:

— In the painter's absence, a boy has been born. Blond and seeming strong and still living. The King at last has an heir, thank God, and will not pass out of the world a spectre, without legitimate issue. The little Infante Baltasar's chambers are lit up with an optimism that leaves few shadows for death to hang back to (having all the time in the world, she can be discreet). The painter, still animated by the patterns and tints of Italy, permits these warm and well-kept colours to permeate: red lakes, vermilion, gold. Here is a crimson curtain draped loose to frame the work. Here is a tapestried carpet imported from the East, burnt orange, yellow from Naples. Here is every pink fold and wrinkle and shine upon the little general's sash. Every leaf and curlicue of gold as it's worked into the costume, even and detailed, every stitch; with his fine brush he finds and follows each thread, where it is darkened in a fold, where it creases in an elbow-crook, where it shines. Each strand and loop of lace, one two three four five six points on the cuff the seventh just showing one visible fringe. And within all of this attire: the Prince himself. The princely little chunk of his hand poking out of the lace, curled upon the hilt. He poses uncomplaining in the heavy battle dress, in the close and heavy metal collar and the tickle of lace fronds that line it. Soft and blond, his baby's hair, a duck-tuft at its back like his father's, his luminous flesh like his father's. Such good health he's in. His father is pleased with the boy's patience; his mother too, who stands watching with her husband, at this juncture of their two households, united in their pride and their relief. And the Prince has his own household, his own handmaids to tend him and suckle him and meet his every whim (the Queen's milk, unused, dried up long since and her still heavy puckering breasts tight-hemmed under many layers). Look, how still he can stand! So entirely well cast in this role, from the same plaster as his father. He doesn't even need to be told. Does he? Does he? No he doesn't! What a good little Prince he is. Yes he is. The Count-Duke, too, doting on the Prince— Quite the little general, isn't he, aren't you, my boy; the Prince disregarding him, ah, so like his father when he was a little princeling . . . If at times he does blubber and grizzle and bawl like any baby then the painter shows no trace of it.

Whereas his playmate Francisco Lezcano is restless— Lezcano drafted in for humanity, and balance, and simply a witticism: a visual echo, a dwarf playing at dominion. Because he is not a prince and won't ever be a king, despite his rattle-sceptre, despite his apple-orb, which he has already been prevented from biting into. Glancing back to check that his Prince is still behind him, looking down upon him—so still, so quiet, on his little step! Lezcano is little but won't grow up to be a king, won't grow much at all. He is only here to amuse the Prince, to keep him company, but the painter, set up at his easel and with the Prince in his place, told him wait— stay; stay with the Prince now. He was told, hold this, hold that, and he holds this and that and doesn't bite his apple.

The painter finds relief in the Prince's playmate, in his normal shifts and distractions, because he isn't here to be commemorated, Lezcano, and it doesn't matter if the edges of him aren't so fine-cut. He squirms, blurs. His restless eyes don't settle. He sees something— he is seeing something, looking back over his shoulder and beyond the Prince he sees something of which the Prince, so radiant and sharp-defined, is oblivious. Any curses coming this way will skirt the Prince and fall on his dwarf, so they say, and that's also what Lezcano's here for, and maybe that's what he's seeing when he looks back at his playmate: something inevitable, and indiscriminate, that won't settle for a scapegoat after all.

Ah, sighs the King. Excellent. I see what you have done, here, with the composition ... the dwarf ... The apple and rattle, the orb and sceptre, I see, yes. It is very witty. It is most original. I wonder, if it ... The Lords of Castile, they are to swear allegiance to my heir, you know. It will be quite a ceremony. Naturally. Yes, my boy, a splendid party, just for you! The Prince smiles because his father is smiling at him (before he checks himself); reaches for the rattle and Lezcano willingly gives it, shaking it for him, because Baltasar is only a baby. The Prince doesn't shake it; he wields it, his sceptre, expectantly.

... And the Lords of Castile, they need things to be kept simple. I want no grounds for confusion. The oath is to be sworn to my son, not his playmate; whoever heard of a Spanish King Francis! —Lezcano laughs at the joke, bites his apple, offers it to the Prince and it is smoothly intercepted by the hand of an attendant— So perhaps, in time for the ceremony, it will be early next year, perhaps you might find time for another . . .

By the time the Prince sits again for the painter, his baby blond hair has thickened and reddened and grown into a widow's peak so that, from the front, he has the hair of a middle-aged grandee; but it winds about his ears and sticks out at the side, curled out at the temple, still like his father's. Gleaming at the temple, the thin childish skin, the skull under the skin. The red curtain and cushion . . . this time the carpet rolled back, too much fuss. The same hat with its powder-puff of plumes on the cushion. Same pose. More hair. No dwarf. Threading rich and metallic, less of the labour in it, not so punctilious, points of white there white where the light lights upon it; don't over-worry it; rich red sash, frondy lace; the Prince's pudgy hand now pale and slender, like his father's, rather than fatly baby-pink; and the painter throws all his light upon it, bright in the centre, to show: here is the heir's hand already on his sword. The heir is ready to defend you, Lords of Castile.

The Count-Duke has a suggestion: This auspicious occasion might afford an opportunity for a new official portrait of the King. It has been some years, and the King feels it is needed. Since of course, in your absence, there was no one he might entrust the task to; since he promised you this sole right.

They doubtfully observe the King for signs of enthusiasm. He has taken up his default position—console, window—and his attention is directed beyond it; deferring, for the time being, this conversation. But there's no avoiding it—the King has, indeed, outgrown his portrait. The painter observes. He looks well. In the fullness of his manhood, and a father. Face a little thinner, frame a little bigger. His moustache has filled out. He has grown a small beard (so has everyone else, inevitably; so has the painter). His head drops briefly in resignation; a passing grimace on that impassive face. It's been a while, hasn't it. I've had a suit made for the ceremony. Perhaps I could wear that. Perhaps ... we could get it over with.

Thank you, Señor, says the painter, for keeping your promise to me.

In the royal church of San Jerónimo, just beyond the city's walls, the grandees pledge allegiance to the Prince; his father in his new suit, purple and silver at his son's side; the Queen, his mother, to whom the King is devoted, entirely. At last, an heir. They make a blond, radiant and haughty tableau, at the end of the nave draped in velvet for the occasion; the grandees make their bent-kneed procession, and the air is felty and dense with incense and the little Prince receives their velvet reverence unsneezing. The floor in recent years has been repaired, after the magnificence of the last King's bier broke it—so heavily death has weighed upon this family— but now the King has an heir and she can keep her bony hands off him, back there in the last pew. No one pays her a bit of notice.

(There's a little boy with black hair, who has lately been sent to live in the country up north near León. A few months older than the celebrated Prince. Not unlike him; darker, perhaps a little more robust. He is at liberty, but well looked after, just in case. A safeguard. Juan José doesn't know who he is yet, how can he, he is just a little boy. Or maybe, being just a little boy and only himself, he knows exactly who he is, having never considered the question; has never had to wonder where he ends and his clothes begin. On his back on a blanket he watches the birds wheel over the rough and empty fields, sharp-eyed, dark, frowning.)

(And in a small private palace somewhere in the city behind several closed doors, La Calderona's left alone without career or custody or even her lover, and without that dark changeling child so strong and loud and so soon taken from her; a milk-sour heavy ghost haunting her own private palace with its private chambers, its veiled windows, and its hidden entrances that no one makes use of.)

Richness of red drapes dusking now as light leaves the studio, already the afternoon ending. The painter's door opens and closes, admitting a fragment of corridor shadow, in the shape of the Chief Secretary. The painter is alone with his long fine brush, scrutinising by candlelight; the studio is too dark now

for working, although perhaps he hasn't been anyway. Don
Jerónimo arrives at the painter's side, joins him in his contemplation, candlelit.

Oh, yes. Father— husband— king, complete. A little tension about the mouth, as if he is holding his face that way,
holding something in reserve, his lower lip stiff. Perfectly
turned out. In fact exemplary. A little more at ease, the King
or the depiction, both; the fluid glazes of healthy flesh, thick
crinkle of lace standing proud. Embroidered with the imported
wealth of Spain, intricate silver. And that slip of paper in his
hand there, quite solid: vivid white, coming out of the frame.

Very good, says the Chief Secretary. He steps back a pace or
two into the dark behind the painter. You have been busy, these
last months, haven't you. How *was* Italy? You saw Rome? I
hear you turned down apartments in the Vatican, is that right?
I hear the Medici put you up in your own place ... is that so?
The painter smiles, shrugs ambiguously, palms up; suggesting
humility, or something like it.

And you dined with the Cardinal Sachetti, I hear ... in
Ferrara. I know the Cardinal, says the Secretary. He was in
Madrid a while. He no doubt mentioned it. He likes Spain.
He is, one might say—*he* would, certainly—an Hispanophile.
But I'm sure he told you all about it.

The painter hmms. In fact the Cardinal did mention it, for
some hours, over the many courses of a long lunch just as the
painter was extricating himself from the city of Ferrara, or
attempting to, leaving at last when the sun was already setting; in fact the King's favourite painter, subject to so much
hospitality from everyone he encountered, had to skip through
Bologna with barely a stop and didn't pause to present himself to the further cardinals he had letters for; in fact by the
time he reached the Vatican he wanted only to spend time in

the galleries, alone, at any hour of his choosing, although, he insisted, he couldn't claim to be worthy of accommodation within the city walls, he need not be anyone's guest . . . all these requests graciously granted to the King's painter. His own little villa out on the hill. Stone arches, statues, grey-green evenings. How does the Secretary know all this, anyway? He doesn't ask.

He says, I regret I could spend only an afternoon in the Cardinal's company, on my way out of Ferrara.

Quite, says the Secretary. That is regrettable. He takes the painter's candle and steps closer, to take a better look. Some of the silver threads come loose. Break apart into suggestion. A flicker of light upon the eye turns out to be nothing more than a white paint daub. He stares into it with his own unlit eyes and then steps back so the King's eye is an eye again. Very good, Diego, he says. Haven't you done well.

Alone again (the Secretary dissipated back into shadow), not quite done with this act of commemoration, the painter considers— A white slip in the King's hand— to mean, he commands his councils, he holds the papers of the realm close. In paper too there's power—— It seems a pity to leave that white slip blank. The painter inches his fingers down the brush towards the bristles, making a pen of it, and comes in close. And neatly, there: his name. Pictor Regis. It could be a petition for advancement. It could be a bill (when was he last paid, exactly?). Or just a signature. He'll allow himself that. Why shouldn't he, from time to time? He stands away and the thing swings together. Yes. The King complete. The painter takes up the candle by the canvas and as he turns away the King becomes no more than the silver on his doublet and the paper in his hand——

— In London I come to see him sometimes—he's ended up here— Felipe as grand as he'll ever be, new father to a son in his brand new suit. But it's more brown than purple now and it seems a shame, that he underwent the portrait, that he wanted that opulence recorded and it faded anyway. But the paper in his hand is bright and it's still sharp, the signature on it, your name, you, painter to the King, Diego.

The painter's older colleague in his slightly smaller studio on his slightly lesser salary continues to observe the proprieties of the Florentines, and bemoans what modern painting's coming to. Slapdash brushwork and painting from life. He publishes a thesis upon it; just a general observation. Naming no names. The King listens politely to its presentation. When the painter's daughter marries his apprentice Juan Bautista, the King and the Queen are their patrons.

IX

Buen Retiro/
A retreat

I think, cousin, says the King— he has been pensive all
morning, pausing at his papers, staring at the ceiling even
more than usual, and the Count-Duke has been waiting for
some pronouncement— I think perhaps I might go abroad,
soon. Expand my horizons, as they say. He sets down his pen
and looks back and up over his shoulder to the Count-Duke;
how that bland blond countenance, the blankness of it, can
harden to a challenge, thinks the valido. The King has been
pensive for a while, in fact; he has been difficult to engage,
or to distract—in spite of the daily entertainment of the
Prince, his perfect new teeth, his toddling about, his chatter,
his ever-emerging talents— or, it may be, because of him. It
may be that the King thinks more than ever on death, that
he will die, his son will die, as all things must in God's just
pattern; and time, relentless, passing; it may be that the duties
of fatherhood and the old pleasures he's forgoing leave him
pent-up and ashamed by the strain of self-denial; or it may be
simply the natural cycle of his gloomy temper. But in any case
the Count-Duke has observed that of late the King has lost
interest in everything that can usually be offered to forestall

the fall into full-blown melancholy; listless in the lists and in the field and in the ring, indifferent to any amusement that the Count-Duke and the court and company can provide. However, to leave the country on a whim, a jaunt? Can that be what he means? No; this is not an option. And the King surely knows this.

A tour of Italy, Señor? Hoping to make light of it and move on quickly; another paper slid under the pen, which lifts automatically and the nib comes to rest in the right place but doesn't quite touch, the point of a thought seeking words to express itself and not quite falling. Ah, well— the King nods to indicate he understands the joke— yes, what a pleasure it would be; how I envied Diego; it would be such a pleasure, to see those ancient temples, to visit the collections, the academies, to sit and sketch, I have had so little time for my pencils lately; but—no, of course that's not what I'm suggesting. He looks back at the paper. Something maybe stiffens in the forearms, steeling himself. As you are so keen always to emphasise, cousin, a king must do his duty. So since I can't, in fact, just sit around sketching … since we're hearing, aren't we, that everything's going to pot, up in the north, and in Portugal, and everywhere generally, and they say I don't know what to do about it, say I haven't a clue … since I'm sitting here signing papers that dispense funds and men and resource and whatever this, now—what is this I'm signing? The King breaks off as if he's reading it over; but the Count-Duke knows he's reading something else, something memorised, which the Count-Duke can't confiscate or efface. Without looking up: They say I am not a king, they say I am a person you need to make use of. A puppet that signs papers. Is it not right that I should show myself as leader of my forces? Would that not make an impression? Would that not make me credible? I would like to be believed in. I am not without substance. (A puppet, a phantom, an impotent fool . . .)

This again. So that's it. The valido covers a groan with a cough and then finds he has to cough a bit longer. Needs to mix up more of that electuary, soothe his raw throat a little. That note under the napkin, how did they sneak it by him? (Your Majesty is not a King, you are a Person whom the Count-Duke seeks to conserve . . . a mere Ceremonial Ruler . . .) How perturbed the King was by it, impossible for days. The Count-Duke smiled and tossed it in the brazier, watched it blacken. You are a Person whom th. . . . . .D. . . . . (And in the dark one night a treacherous grandee might easily be taken for an unwise suitor, or be both; who can say how a cheek ends up slit?) The Count-Duke will not have his King bewildered.

Your Majesty. Señor. This is why, this is precisely why, we must work together. So that these accusations cannot stand. So that you understand, so that you know the imperatives of your own government, so that you can sit on any council, any junta, and hold your own there. Must he keep going over this?

Yes, agreed, we agree entirely, says the King. And laughs. Barely a snigger, really, but out loud. Is he growing hysterical?— That's only to be expected, isn't it, that we should be in agreement . . . that's what everyone expects of me . . . So it seems to me that, if we extend this logic, then you in turn agree with *me*. I *should* hold my own. I own a pink sash, cousin, my dutiful painter has made many copies of his good portrait showing me in it, I've been trotted out all across Europe wearing it, I wear my general's guise in many great houses. So since I wear the sash as well as the crown, so to speak, I should perform all of my offices. So I'll go to Flanders. Don't we agree?

It takes days to persuade him out of it. The King capitulates, but still, his agitation is exhausting; enervated mornings and

restless afternoons, pent-up and purposeless, needing occupa-
tion, needing validation, seeking his valido and then dolorous,
impatient, sapped of all vitality then antsy and snappish; he
must have something to do. No, he would not like to hunt. No,
he will not hear music. No, he won't ... well, he might, to get
out of this place for a few hours, some respite, he might pay a
visit ... and then he's back in the evening and lower than ever,
mournful and penitent, miserable. These days, these months,
go on like this. He must have some use, some meaning. Yes,
there is his son. But his brother, the Cardinal, who despite
his mitre was so much at the centre of all revels, is gone to
Brussels—his brother, a soldier before him! And his sister away
to Vienna, matched at last, and taking all her brightness with
her ... And it's so quiet now without them, so close and dark,
this fortress, so damned stuffy, this box of a fortress; and it's
all he can do to get up in the morning and drag himself to his
damned desk. Papers, papers. I am your puppet. I am a paper
cut-out. Yes, yes, I shall play my part. Stand me on the balcony
and hand me my props. Cut me out a paper crown, I may as
well wear a party hat.

The Count-Duke's getting too old for all this. He's gouty, he
couldn't get on his horse today, he is getting fat. In the privacy
of prayer the Count-Duke takes out his greatest treasure and
hugs it to him: the diamond-crusted heart of Saint Teresa. He
must be disciplined. Incision, purgation. The sacred effort of
bleeding. He must bear the burden of his offices and all the
agony that God has sent him; he will not lament or question
when he feels his joints ache and his hardening arteries pinch;
and yet he prays to his saint for a salve for his sicknesses, for
an ebb in the endless headache. He prays for his heart to be
pierced as hers was, prays for a seraphim's lance to relieve him,

for the boiling pressure in his blood to release. He purges.
His head lightens, spirals. It will pass. He scourges and says
to himself all things pass. Teresa looks on glittering. She
whispers: he must find a way to pass through humility and
draw closer to the light within. She says, you dwell among
souls who content themselves with the outer courts of the
soul's castle, who have no thought or knowledge of what is
within, who have no notion of the crystalline, pure place
within; and your soul, which might venture into that interior,
your soul grows accustomed to the vermin and the beasts of
these outer precincts and you are become almost like them . . .
He is everywhere beset by and abetting sin, yes abetting it, a
pimp to a king, never speak of it; but He sees it, and Teresa
sees it; the doors he has opened and those he has closed and
guarded, and so he must be barred from the mansions within,
and lost in this earthly verminous palace where it's cold and
dim; the light of God resides within him, and he can't see it
through the smear of soot and ink and grease. And there is
never an escape from the trials of the world, from its muck,
its councils and commerce and muck; there are shopkeepers
in the patios of the Alcázar, throwing out their slops, the city
comes and goes through the gates, the smell of it, the noise of
it, the poor and their poor stale suppers, the sordid slothful
siesta. And he's brought it on himself perhaps, by making a
seat for himself on every council, by opening the gates and
the windows to the city, by opening the door of his office. But
there is so much talking, so many voices, selling and begging
and petitioning and suggesting, so many suggestions, how we
might restore, redeem, rescue the country from the sin we've
fallen into and the catastrophic bankruptcy of soul and coffers
we can all see coming, so much talk always assailing him and
the scrutiny, the mutter of mutiny, this bloody city that he's

never out of, El cursed Corto. He scourges. He purges. He does what he must in service of his King.

He blasts through the Alcázar, bellowing, a bull with no outlet, limping a little. He barely eats, he barely sleeps. Is he ill? He is getting ill. He eats no fat and barely any meat even lean, he purges, he still feels bilious; his temples are hot and achy and he feels the blood in them, he is cold and sweating; he smells, he thinks, since he can't be having shirts and sheets washed daily, since he can't be known to sweat so, so he has to re-wear the same underclothes he's soaked the day before, and days before that, often still a little damp when he climbs from his damp bed and pulls them back on in the chill of his early rising, and he goes through the day catching whiffs of ill, and knows it's him, it comes from deep within him, this sour yellow stink; he feels the bile rankling through him when he wakes in the morning after so little sleep and gripped under the ribs he retches, spitting at the bowl that he keeps by the bed, analysing the colour and consistency of the content. He mixes tinctures and notes their effects. He prays. He takes his heart out and holds it glittering in his hands. He dissimulates indifference. He is a model of effective statesmanship. He keeps his friends close; close enough to watch them closely.

And on top of all this he must keep the King contented. And there is never quite enough time. Seeking respite, he slips beyond the city's walls and escapes to San Jerónimo, the royal monastery just outside the city, of which he is governor, to pray almost daily; and then he brings his business with him, bustling his protonotaries into a carriage and squashing himself with all his papers in beside them so there's not a moment wasted, because despite himself he's incapable of respite. But the principle of it . . . it gives him an idea; something that might help to assuage these unfortunate royal humours. This is how he puts it in a letter to the Chief Secretary, not how he puts it to the King.

The Chief Secretary has accompanied him to San Jerónimo today and they are inspecting the royal apartment, a modest structure alongside the monastery. And it has occurred to the Count-Duke that it is so convenient, this retreat; peaceful and yet so ... proximate. What does the Secretary make of it, the apartment, these four little rooms?

The Secretary turns full circle, and shrugs elegantly; in this single orbit he has taken in all there is to see. Honestly? Not much. No, the Count-Duke agrees, no, it isn't much. It's no Pardo, no Aranjuez.

Tell me, the Secretary asks, what *should* I make of it?

Aha! The Count-Duke pokes him in the breastbone. Now you're talking! That's just it, the nail on the head, Jerónimo! That's just what I wanted to discuss with you—what *could* you make of it? That is, what could *you* make of it?

He is rustling about now, the small room becoming smaller the longer he's in it, as rooms tend to. The Secretary waits. The Count-Duke raps the window frame with swollen knuckles. It could be something, couldn't it? Think, if these rooms were just enlarged a little; this wall knocked out and another wing added; and the monastery also to have a little enrichment; keep things simple, nothing showy, but a few extra rooms or apartments that we could bring the King to; a few nice things to furnish them ... just last week I was visiting my cousin, who has brought some tapestries back from Genoa, just the sort of thing the King would admire I said to him, just the sort of gift he'd like ... and just this morning a cart arrived, sent by my cousin, and of course you can guess what was on it! You know we've no shortage of generous, loyal ministers ... it needn't cost us anything, you see. There are always resources.

He raps again at the windowsill as if to make a start on the demolition. The Secretary makes no comment. He moves to join the Count-Duke at the window perhaps to look out or perhaps to look into the pages of his own accounts, readily called to the front of his mind, consulting the columns at leisure: income, expenditure, profit, reward. They stand together for some minutes, the silent Secretary listening to the Count-Duke breathe as he raps and clasps his swollen fingers, as he rubs over the stretched dry fluid-filled knuckles to ease them, thinking.

The King ... he is sinking again, the Count-Duke says, splaying his thickened hands out on the sill in the sun, his head bowed—his nails are short and clean but the skin around them is ragged as if bitten or too much scrubbed. The King ... he must always be supported; now more than ever. Now that the line is secured; the Prince is his only joy; we must show him to be solvent, prudent, at peace; unthreatened—and Spain, likewise, all of these things; and we must encourage him to *be* at peace, within himself; and he thinks on sin, and on death. He fears for his son even as he rejoices. He fears for his territories. He is sad, and restless, and at a loss. You may not see it (of course, the Secretary has seen it)—but he is giving way again. He is worried about money, he is worried about tithes and taxes, and he's worried about war ... If there was some place we could spirit him away, for a few days or hours at a stretch, away from the city without having to leave for weeks, without all the trouble of moving the court and all its bits and pieces miles away? Nothing fancy; but isn't it fitting that the King and his new heir should have a private home in which to take their leisure? What king hasn't his own house close to the city to go to? Away from the Alcázar and all its shops and politics clogging up the precincts, all the pamphlets and the peddlers and all the bloody poets. Where is the King to go when he wishes to relax? When *we* wish him to relax? You understand me. Think on it, Don Jerónimo; this is *San* Jerónimo, after all! Don't you like the idea, wouldn't you like to favour your namesake's monastery? We'll work together on this; if you can find the funds, the furnishings, I'll build it— I'd like you to take this on.

They go on looking together out of the window, the Count-Duke knocking with his knuckle. It is a good spot, admittedly, the Secretary says. Peaceful. A little dry, perhaps——

— A traveller might come to this place now and find that it is only parkland, and no trace of the Count-Duke's scheme remaining; and walk in the park as if it were that time again, laying out foundations in the mind as he did; but this park is nothing like the rough land that they built the palace on. This place looks as it does now because the palace was once here, has been and gone already; and now in its place, gravel and planted paths and trees neatly spaced and tended, green grass, and a fountain, even.

All that's left is the name of it. Buen Retiro. The promise of a rest. A public place with litter bins, a baleful mean-eyed cat foraging, as if dipping a paw for fish; and the hot wind blowing up the yellow gravel-dust so that it streaks and cakes the (pale, sweating, pink) skin of my calves. And blisters, too, these stupid shoes, the grit rubbing at the blisters, at the pudge of the round little toe. And here, in the middle of this park, where there was once a palace is another made of steel and glass, a transparent ghost of what stood here, and inside it is even hotter, it is a huge hothouse empty of everything but the sound of birds piped in and the light; the sun slants in and

sweeps the floor the day wheels over and is gone and is gone
and years pass in this way in the sweep of the sun. Light paling
then yellowing, short, then long, the space between shadows
marks the hours, now widening, now narrowing, sleep-stained
yellow light, strained through the dust, long streaks streaming
on the bare floor, which feeling foolish I sat down upon, in the
light, tired, bueno, bueno, rest your blistered gritty feet here,
fool——

Just weeks later all is in motion, and San Jerónimo is no
longer so peaceful. On reflection, looking at the plans, at the
modest planned expansion ... it seems, while they're about it,
that a wing on the other side would be just as well, to balance
it. Towers, at the corners, would look good; and if there are
towers there should be another storey, or else where would the
stairs go to? ... And a hermitage here, in this pleasant quiet
corner, which is surely crying out for one. And an orangery,
we'll have the trees shipped in spring. And a garden here in
the formal style, we'll cut shapes, lions, bulls, all kinds of
fantastical things, gryphons and so forth, yes, for that we'll
need myrtles. And then a courtyard in front so the King can
make sport and there will be fiestas and lances and bullfights.
A walkway between— yes, with more trees. Elms. Planes.
And another hermitage. And another here? So that will need
a garden, too. And actually these rooms are all wrong. If the
King is to receive guests then we'll need a throne room, and
a larger salon; so knock those down, now, the bricks can be
re-used and drawings re-drawn.

Rooms come barely into being, disintegrate, reform. And
here a lake, with a fountain; and then another larger lake with
an island at its centre, what will make these gardens splendid
is water, waterways linking between and nourishing. The soil
is very dry, is almost sand, but there are engineers at work on

that. A green grotto will grow here and those who seek it will find seclusion all year round, depend upon it. And, perhaps, an aviary. In fact the Count-Duke has made a start on that already. He leads the King with him. Come, see the parrots, they are just off the boat. He chucks and coos at the birds in their cages.

The King looks on. On the subject of shipments, in fact, he ventures ... Yes, of course, of course. The need for funding. France is arming herself. There are matters of state to attend to, yes. We will attend to them. But, Señor, just *look* at these parakeets!

And on they walk, among the masons and the scaffold and the earth heaped and dug; the Count-Duke showing off his gift, the new Royal House. A place to retire to, retreat to, withdraw from the world and its noise. Imagine it, in just a few months' time. Buen Retiro. Ahhh. Good. You can imagine it? It's difficult, walking through it now. Buildings at every stage of construction; foundations hastily dug and laid, structures framed and clad and smashed again. Water flooding muddily a pit for a pond. Heaps of brick and sand and lime. Mortar scraped together in a barrel, clunk of brick on brick on brick; chisels chink; timber sawn and plaster dumped out in a whump of powder. The hammer and grind of a thousand labourers. The King picks his way among them and coughs into a dusty square of linen. There is dust under his collar, dust dulling his hair, dust gritting his teeth, in the lining of his gloves when he pulls them onto chalk-dusty fingers; his eyes tear up and itch and the thin skin of his eyelids grows tight and pink and tender; his nostrils are sticky and clogged and his nose is unclearable and obviously he can't be seen to sneeze or blow it. Dust veils everything, these buildings coming out of it like dreams in the desert.

He asks: When shall we be free of all this noise and dust? I would have it finished. I want it done. Do whatever you have to. Order whatever you need. I'll issue a decree—whatever you need, you shall have it.

And the Count-Duke, when the King has departed, renews his hourly urging with fresh intensity— What have you been doing all morning, why is that here and this still there? This: here! move that!

And his architects say: This will hold stronger; this will look better, grander, more Italian; they say integrity, fashion, balance, stability, proportion; endurance; and he says faster. Just do it now. Isn't it done yet? And the architects and master builders, frustrated, perplexed, reply— In these five minutes since you've asked for it, while we've been talking? Well, no, Your Excellency, it's not yet done. But really I'd advise ... if I were you ... that is if I ... And they wilt, they're as much in need of wages as everyone else is. But who am I to advise? No one whose name is even worth remembering. As you command, Your Excellency. You undoubtedly know best. Consider it done. No sooner *said* than done. Who am I to deny our King a miracle?

The Count-Duke is ever more purple of complexion, these days, and for a massive man he is strangely haggard, swollen in places and drawn in others. He's spitting with fury, which comes up as phlegm. He is frugal in his diet, insomniac, and his breath is bad with it, with sleeplessness and hollow guts and long-steeped tinctures. He sweats, hauling his body around with him; it is hot this summer and hot here especially in this part of Madrid; too hot, some might say, for a summer retreat, but not many would say this to his purpling face. And if they did he'd say get out! Did I not give you an instruction? And yet through this window— which by the way wants shifting to the left— I see it's not yet done! Just use brick! Use granite! Use timber! Get it up! This should be square. That, in fact, shall be octagonal, I'll have the new plans brought directly. I'd like my aviary (a snigger from an unseen source)— I'd like the aviary moved. It shall be even more splendid than before. Get it done!

And so it goes on, for months, buildings torn down and flown up at a word, all at the whim of the King, the Count-Duke insists, all of it for the King. It's all done out of donations and gifts (and some cunning secret accounting on the part of the King's Chief Secretary, working his alchemy on invisible hoards of gold). It will cost the people nothing, and the gardens will be open to all—sometimes—gratis. Although, as it happens, it has been necessary to impose new taxes on wine and meat in the city. Which does somewhat sour the grapes. But would you have it said of your monarch that he has nowhere to rest? (Or to roost! The King and his favourites flying to their hutch ... how cosy it must be in their feathery beds there. They call the Count-Duke's new house, with its aviary already famous, the chicken coop. These days a Frenchman can't pass a Spaniard in the city without calling out *cocorico*.)

The famous aviary: in a far corner of the expanded gardens, a series of splendid iron cupolas can be found, filled with squawking. Birds shipped from Africa and the Indies, cooped with the cargo for weeks, confused and moulting and clipped, and some of them have somehow survived and arrived here. The Count-Duke tends to them himself, he visits them and feeds them, he brings his ministers about with him so that they can conduct their business as they walk and then he gathers eggs and offers them as presents; he tuts and chitters in their own language to them, he is often guano-streaked. Bright red parrots such as once observed Adam in the Garden; jays and parakeets; iridescent green-yellow-gold and bronze cockerels proudly plumed; irascible peacocks trailing their trains in the dust resistant to prompting and sometimes, on their own terms, at their own whim, lifting and spreading their tails, shamelessly flouting the sumptuary laws—the Count-Duke carefully gathers their feathers as they fall lest their bright bizarre design should be put to outlawed use, stuck into a hatband or stitched into a fan. And yet all these strutting show-offs are God's creatures, made on the fifth day.

Fair Doña Ana has her quarters here and he comes in quietly and doffs his hat and bows to greet her, my Egyptian princess, he calls her. Perhaps he does this even when alone, a show of affection that is not merely show. He feels below her and she disgruntles a little but lets him rummage, and he lifts the warm eggs still stuck with white feathers from under her. He thanks her for the eggs and she plumply fluffs, resettling, eyeing him with henly familiarity or suspicion, which are not perhaps dissimilar.

⚜

At last it is almost ready. It is all in hand. The courtyard, the salon, the throne room, all looking so magnificent in fact that it has been upgraded, from House to Palace; a proclamation has been made. The King, who has been pacing and coughing and rubbing his eyes on site intermittently for months now, has decided enough is enough: it's ready, he says. And the Count-Duke says, two weeks, Señor, and the mortar will be dry enough and the rooms will be habitable and healthy. It is *almost* ready. The Count-Duke pacifies the King with a small ceremony of presentation, a silver key to the new Royal Palace of Buen Retiro, on a silver plate. The King takes the plate from him, and then graciously, gives it back. The Count-Duke is the governor still; the keys are his, and his the locks, his the doors they open. The King is very good at this sort of gesture. (And when is the valido not on hand, anyway, to open any closed door the King would pass through? And to close and lock it behind him?)

So come December, the King is to make his official entrance, with the perennially underwhelmed Queen and the little Prince, too. The Count-Duke has been reviewing, rearranging, selecting menus, scheduling entertainments, hiring staff, firing staff, for days; swapping one picture at the last minute for another; moving this console to sit below that window instead; positioning the donations of more favoured, useful donors in more favourable, useful, visible positions; tasting the soup and adding salt to it, starching linen and flicking his duster, he may as well be. He bends stiffly to hold a stiff hand to a draught—he does feel a draught, these days. And it's December, and cold, and starting to rain. He rolls out rugs and hangs tapestries. He rustles and rolls through the tapestried rooms of his gift. Everywhere there is something to be done he is there already; on his pony out in the wet, trotting through the grounds, barking orders from under his flopping hat, the plumes sad and waterlogged hanging like a dog's ear, and it rains, and it rains.

It has rained for days. Even the turgid river has quickened its pace and gurgles brownly by. And out here beyond the city walls, where the soil is so stubbornly unabsorbently dry, the water runs and runs everywhere on the new stone, off the new stepped Dutch roofs, puddling the new planted gardens, splashing and steaming in the new lakes, soaking all the hunched and surly birds on their perches and all the bewildered animals brought from desert and jungle and plain to these dusty small and now soaking new dens; they sit and stomp and snarl in their own sodden dung, and flinch their whiskers and head-butt their horns and scratch and claw at the filth.

And it rains, and it rains. And still, come the grey appointed day, the King and Queen set out from the damp Alcázar and travel through the centre of the city in their grand damp procession under damp canopies through the dampened interest of their people, to make their grand entrance ... except there isn't one. The new palace is entered by a sort of side door, from which any old staircase gives access to the main floor. The Italians at court laugh when they see it. This austere block of a building, so Spanish, they report back—the King and his minister just sort of slip in ... no monumental portal, no glorious ascent for the Planet King! Where one might expect something magnificent, something carved, something marble—brick and tile for Felipe. Why not build some processional entrance from the forecourt? Oh, yes—because that's where they've put the menagerie!

So the court sidles in to the new palace and assembles in the great central courtyard, damply. Rank and privilege can be measured by degrees of dryness. The grandees, at least, can keep their hats on. Some of them merit a spot under an awning that their generous donations to the palace décor have paid for, a room in return for a view; thus the Secretary has filled the place with both furniture and enthusiasm. The grandees make themselves as visible as they can through the smir; make their place known, peering out at their peers to see where they have ranked, guessing what price has been paid for proximity. Who's bought their way to the front? The old families note how fitting it is that the new favourites should fill this new building that has no deep foundation, that they should raise their vulgar canopies at windows that give on to all the modern tat they've filled the rooms with to please the valido. Yes, they have to admit, as they mutter under their own awnings, we're close enough to see in, too, so who are we to talk; old money's just as worthless as new though, these days, or might be tomorrow, so we may as well spend it. Mutterings not voiced too loud because the Count-Duke's big-eared creatures are everywhere and when it rains like this you'll always find rodents running through the gutters.

And those of every rank and distinction, under their awnings, are straining to see through the rain, to see upon his balcony, below his canopy red and gold, behind the glass screen that the Count-Duke has had put up at some expense—brought and fitted in place uncracked in the last-minute near-dark dawn in the rain, directing the men who manoeuvred it himself— now behind this rain-lashed window can be seen, can just be seen, the King, watching the wet entertainments in the plaza below. In his golden-glassed philatory, perfectly still, bone-pale and chilly as a relic.

There are jousts and bullfights. The rain eases to drizzle in the afternoon and the King rides out and wins prizes. Then it starts again, sleety, and they go back in. The night comes on under cover of gloom, the purples greying and the grey purpling until it's dark out and the rain can be heard falling unseen beyond the plain square windows. They go to bed after plays, dancing, a banquet, and quiet comes down around midnight in the form of snow.

It snows, and snows. The King walks his rooms in the morning and approves the gifts so generously given to fill them. Outside, the snow; and inside, snow-grey light falling through the ordinary windows upon red, gleam, gold. If the new palace is, on the outside, perhaps a little stark, then that is because Spain has no taste for the grotesque. But within, within, if you have been invited indoors to come close to the King's presence ... All the King's esteemed and privileged guests are left with an impression so overwhelming that they can't seem to find a way later to describe it precisely, or else they begrudge the description—you had to be there. But whatever is here, they all agree there is a lot of it, and the King moves through it all in impassive approval. Each room opening off the next in perfect symmetry, tapestry upon tapestry and more paintings than walls they say. Frame upon frame upon frame through doorframe after doorframe, opening, opening, on, on. So who cares if it's brick and blocky and haphazard from the outside, if it's low and long and ordinary-windowed; because look, within, at the gifts this King has been given. Look at all this gold and silver and ivory and bronze, this walnut, pear wood, teak; look at all these objects, these exquisite inlaid carven cast and crafted solid objects. And if you're not allowed in you'll just have to imagine.

And the snow settles and fades. And then jousting in the sand-strewn slush, and prizes.

And the menagerie. The little Prince is thrilled. Snow, and presents, and now this! The world is arranged for his pleasure. One by one the gates are opened and out they charge or lope or stumble; a tiger, a lion, a bear. All Noah's ark and all Aesop's fables, says the poet; but the moral remains indistinct. The noise alone is terrible. Mewling and growling and braying and snarling, and the tearing of hide and flesh, and the snap and rip and gristle of bone and sinew and all the awful wetness of evisceration. The snow is muddied and bloodied and the creatures rear and slip and panic or roar and fall, one by one. And it stinks, if you have donated enough to be close enough to smell it: of caged fur, of fear, of blood, of animal breath, of torn gut, of bile and saliva, of caked and fresh dung. The bear beating her own head and turning circles, her fur a mass of mange and her snout rubbed raw on her own claws. The camel staggers and struggles to stand, spits and foams, and is easily felled. The lion rearing on his hind legs his haunches set for springing his jaw hugely opening shaking his foul mane, and the tiger rising to meet him and towering over and roaring horribly a sound that's louder than any of those nobles watching could imagine an animal making, the smell of that roar from her belly, and swatting the lion down. The stag lifts his head and bellows and falls butting and clattering in a mess of deep purple and red. The tiger, fatally distracted by her hunger, mad with choice; muffled in meaty nuzzling, the camel under her grunting and struggling to breathe, to rise, long neck lifting and arching, ribs expanding massively, once, twice, shuddering, still, slumping under the tiger's paws and jaw, but everyone is watching her last remaining enemy pacing, scraping, and then charge and gore and the tiger falling lets out a fearful caterwaul: the Castilian bull, by honest triumph or design, is the victor.

The King announces that he will do this bull the honour it would ask for if dumb animals could talk. He turns to his side and asks quietly for his gun, and lifts it to his shoulder and the bull falls and the brief report is so quickly absorbed in the last of the snow and the silence and the King's face so composed still and his body so unmoving looking down upon the last twitch of the beast, that all those watching can barely register that this has happened, until the little Prince applauds delighted, and then everyone else does— this noble kingly act of release, and God's pattern restored. The Count-Duke commends His Majesty and turns his head a fraction from the bloodshed. Hasn't the stomach for it.

X

Hazer, y hazer parecer/ Do, and appear to do

The Count-Duke, then—with the Secretary at his back, in his shadow—continues to oversee all: the new palace, the business of government, the life of the court, the needs of the King, his family, and his realms. In recognition of this service, unstinting, a portrait of the Count-Duke on horse-back is commissioned, complete with pink general's sash; a rare honour, to be placed in this pose, more usually reserved for royalty. An indulgence, which he has been permitted, and which the painter is permitted to indulge him in, and is hope-fully privately separately paid for. He sits hugely in the saddle looking back and down, the horse with its gleaming backside also turned to us, just about rearing despite the bulk of the rider; a glance before charging into a made-up battle that he didn't see because the Count-Duke has never seen battle. But he is nonetheless in command of armies; everything is under control, and the Count-Duke is the man to control it, with his baton, with his horsemanship, with his impressive moustache. He's sending them out to fight in all corners, and it's all going very well, very well, all his policies. And this is also the point of the scheme for the throne room that the painter is designing, on behalf of the Count-Duke—a Hall of Realms for the honour of the King.

A prince needs a place in which to learn princely virtue, and ideally—according to the fashion of the times (let it not be said that Spain is behind them)—a hall in which to illustrate the allegory of it: courage, temperance, piety, and strength, the virtues that are his inheritance; and of course, good taste. And every king needs a room to put his throne in. And there's no king greater, so there will be no hall that's grander than the throne room of the new Royal Palace. They say Spain's armies can't afford to fight, that the cost is too high; but, says the Count-Duke, look here at the King and his Queen and his father and son on their horses: look here and here, how the King defends and spreads the faith; how the disparate parts are to be united. Here, says the Count-Duke, here is the true history. How everything makes sense or will one day make sense if we wait and have patience and faith in God's plan. How, out of heresy and discord, there is harmony; and how treachery is dealt with. So— what was that? What's this little pamphlet of lies? It will make a touch paper for a fire to warm the feet of the King you kneel before.

The Chief Secretary, who carries always in his pocket Gracián's *Oracle*, advises: Do, and appear to do. Things don't pass for what they are, he says, but for what they seem. It's not enough to rule well, and widely, over this vast and prosperous empire—it must be seen. It must *seem*. There's to be more cloth, more draping, more lustre, more showmanship now. Curtains hung to veil and part and frame. The Count-Duke, heeding the advice of experts, gives instruction: enough with austerity. Within our own walls, within this palace, let's be splendid.

First: equestrian portraits, to hang at the head of a scheme that will celebrate, emphasise, insist upon, the King's dominion: his right to it and the rights of his ongoing lineage. He has an heir. The King on his horse, flanked by his parents on theirs, his wife the Queen—who bore his heir at last—by his side. The Queen poised, proud; impenetrable, and yet evidently not so, possibly even pregnant again under that curtain of skirts; a second son last year already lost and gone to join his four sisters; but the first, the heir, survives. So the boy too will be painted on his horse, to hang between his parents on his big-bellied pony; already he rides well, hunts well, already masterful, easy in the saddle as his father is.

As Master of the Horse, the Count-Duke has designed a programme to school the sons of the nobility, and he comes to the riding school at the new palace to oversee it as he oversees all as he is always everywhere, and the little Prince is his star pupil. He dotes upon him as a surrogate son and the only heir to his affection; always at the ready to hand him what he needs—a crop, a lance—to practise the arts of running things down, knocking things over, running them through; a boar, a man, a man of straw. How to march, how to joust, how to masquerade; how to halt and half halt, how to curvet and levade. In all seasons the boy is out running the course, tilting; even at Lent, the Count-Duke writes proudly to the Cardinal Infante, there's no stopping him, and so the Count-Duke is out there too, light-headed with fasting, jogging sorely alongside him in case he should fall. The painter makes an image of it: the Count-Duke in the riding school, receiving a lance to pass to the Prince; perhaps he's spreading himself too thin because although he's dressed for the occasion and the painter attends to the details of sash, hat, sleeve, these accessories, these objects, are more solid than the man himself, his limbs, his face, and even the bulk of him, the paint is thinned and you can almost see straight through him— he is fat but losing opacity and as the years pass he will grow ever more transparent, maybe one day in a thousand years' time he'll be nothing but a fat smear on the wall behind the boy he worked so hard for.

But the Prince takes on depth and solidity, filling out daily; he will be a king of substance, surely; there he is, the perfect little horseman, baton raised and face serious as a general's. In the background, the mountain they call La Maliciosa— but we heed no gloomy portents. There will be, must be, more in the line to follow. The King's sister has given birth to a daughter who will make a perfect match—the right faith, the right inheritance, the right blood. In this family tree so painfully, elaborately twined, these two new shoots are already in training. So for now there is a future as glorious as the glorious present and the glorious past, and the King's new throne room in the new palace will attest to this, and the painter is to do the attesting.

The painter rides out into the country and sits until the dust falls and he is alive in the clear high air, looks out over this vista, the hills, the different blending white and wisp of cloud and snow on the horizon, and thinks all of this, it is all the King's, until the eye can see no further. All the separate kingdoms of Spain he holds together; Castile spread around him and up to León; south to Andalusia, Seville, Granada, and beyond to Morocco; north to the Netherlands and the wars; west to Portugal where the painter's parents' people came from, until the land ends at the sea, and over it to the other side of the world, and the King owns that too, far seas and dark lands and from the earth, silver; east to Aragon, to the islands, and across the sea—to Italy, to Rome and the church we're knit into ... and draw a cross through it all and here at the centre, these mountains, this plain and the city they built here. And he brings this width and depth back to his canvas and works it onto the grey ground; the width and depth of air stretching out beyond the King, in command of this landscape and looking out beyond it to all his kingdoms and all that can't be seen from here and that the King and the painter have never and will never see. The horse curvets, the round of the flank and the forelegs rearing, sturdy, stable. Not easy to do. Firm and just, the rule, the line. Power and control; this is the meaning of the painting, of the whole scheme. The King in his place at the centre, looking out.

Perhaps there is a point upon the studio wall, or a window, that the painter directs the King's eyes to, and this single tile or square of sky is to stand for the world that the King in the painting looks out on.

One afternoon, while the painter's working at the background— grey-green shrubs, grey-blue rock, grey ground— he could ask his assistants to complete this part but there's a satisfying ease and facility to it and he wants to find that width, that depth, recalling it— the King arrives unannounced, with his little son swaggering behind him. The Prince's chamberlain gives a small shrug as he pulls the door closed. Both dressed for war with the pink general's sash, gold hair and thread and spurs. Leaning up against the studio walls the boy's grandfather and grandmother are already astride their half-formed horses, armour yet to shine, thread yet to gleam, eyes yet to see . . . There is much to be done, the painter's studio has been bustling these last months, his assistants industrious, he has deputised the detail of skirts and threads and folds, and clouds and hills, and they are very meticulous, and yet none of them, the painter has noted, quite a match for him— he thinks this as he works into the cloud, the mountain . . . For now the palace sleeps and he has skipped his siesta for a moment alone, and here they are, King and Prince, evidently also restless, come to see him. The King says, I have come to pretend to be king, Diego. I have come to sit upon my wooden horse so that we can show the world what a fine horseman I am, so my son can see what a great leader his father is. See how fine my son looks in his sash. Will they keep you from the battlefield too, my boy, I wonder? I meant to hunt today but the Count-Duke is otherwise engaged and the day is dull and the woods are dark and so I have come to ride my false horse here, to pretend to do the only thing I am really good at.

The Prince and the painter watch as he swings his leg across the upholstered block, always elegant, even in this mood. How, how is it your father is king? Do you know, Baltasar? I wake and I cannot remember how I came to be here, how I came to be in this dreary dark fortress beneath such fine sheets, although I've never slept on ... what do they sleep on? Straw? (The painter just stops himself scratching an involuntary, unseemly scratch; he's been sleeping in fine sheets too for a long while now.) I dream I am sleeping on a meadow beneath stars, Diego. Can one dream that one is sleeping, and dreaming? And how then can I know when I'm awake? I dream I am riding on a real horse, Diego, I feel it under me moving, and how then is this *block* more real than the real horse in my dream?

He jiggles up and down on the cushion obscenely, and the little Prince giggles and jiggles in a squat on the floor beside him; the King refrains from giggling. And then slumps, sighs, and takes the useless rein and pulls himself into a pose that is almost a mockery of the pose required of him; arms just a little too akimbo, back pulled up unnaturally straight, a child playing at being a knight, if it weren't for the sad countenance. The painter regards him. He says, if Your Majesty is disposed to sit for me today, I am honoured, as always. If Your Majesty would just— the arm a little more *so*——

And the King looks at him for a moment piteously and then nods and turns his head back and by the time his eyes are facing front to the realms framed in the window, the pose is perfect, and there he is: King again. Already thirty, in his prime. He sits just so for three hours more, without once letting his spirit slip, or without appearing to.

King, Queen, Prince on their horses, to hang above the throne; next, the long walls: narrative and allegory and battles, following the fashion. The painter calls on colleagues—he enlists even his ageing ailing rival, who manages this last task before departing, humbled, or humiliated and raging as death leads him from the court he's spent his life in. The painter calls in favours, offers incentives, has stipends provided, ensures payments. For the tasks of Hercules, he brings in gaunt Francisco, an old friend from Seville; the working of his endless fingers, stretched out thin—Francisco works fast and heads south again, back to his ever-expanding family and the next of his wives and the niche he's carved out of the dark for himself painting friars and monks. He can't quite play the part as his friend the painter can, not quite cut out for the cut and thrust of court—a kind, a mild man— what light this might cast on the painter's mildness, kindness?

Below Hercules' mythic triumphs, there are to be twelve recent victories depicted, and the painter can't get out of doing his part. He is to remake history, or to take a part in the shaping of it rather: Spinola taking Breda. He drafts and re-drafts it. He stands back from it, steps into it, watches himself doing it. What was it like—— what was it really like? The grey smoke of the siege rising in the distance; a rank of orderly lances against the blue-grey sky—— not all quite perpendicular because life's not like that, not so neatly composed. They were at siege for months, these soldiers. He sees their faces; he is interested in their ordinary faces, not just those of the leaders victorious and vanquished. But then again, for the sake of decorum, because they'll be out on public display after all and deserve their dignity, he fattens them up and cleans them down and it seems that conditions weren't as bad as all that; he decides they weren't starving and dirty and torn and worn out. He makes much of Spinola's well-groomed horse and its sleek and well-groomed arse—because the point is that the horse has turned to allow Spinola to graciously dismount as he acknowledges surrender, a new take on this theme, a somehow avuncular hand on the shoulder of his enemy— and also because he's got quite good at horses and their arses. It's the best of the twelve in the sequence by a long lance length; and when they come to see it, then, now, that's what they see; and——

Look— at the very edge of the canvas and the crowd, there is a well-kept, closely observed and observant courtier looking out—

So— there you are, Diego. Let's have a look at you. All these years unseen. Your hair's grown. Your beard filled out. You look older, of course; I like your posh hat. White feather and lace at the neck utterly unsoiled; you've bought this suit to be seen in, I think, and I think you've enjoyed painting it and painting yourself in it. Just a little flashy, maybe? But still understated in grey. I like your style. The eyes are still sharp and dark and more or less inscrutable . . . Half-shadowed and watching from under that elegant dove-grey hat. This is what you wanted, then? Yes, it's the best one, this clever arrangement of lances; and you, thirteen years a courtier, the best dressed man in the cohort. You don't need to sign it—who else could have done this?—but in place of a signature you leave in the corner, at the hooves of the horse and your boots, a folded scrap of blank paper that might have fallen from your pocket.

And at last everything's ready to be shown. The playwright writes a new play and the court comes to the new hall, which the play celebrates, to see it. The King, his Queen, his son, presiding. The Prince will one day be king and all this is for him. All around the Prince the noble feet are darkly finely shod, all stepping to their measure. Everyone is where they should be, where they have been put. And while the Prince wanders where he pleases, no one else does; maybe no one else can. His father, even— especially, in fact— never moves from his place once he's taken it. But Baltasar hasn't really tested the length of his leash. The dogs, when they are loosed, always come back. When they first let Canela go and she chased off into the woods he almost cried. But he didn't cry. And she came back. The Prince looks down. His own slippered feet are small and he walks and rides well. These are not outdoor shoes. He looks up, past the other shoes, past the stuffed and stockinged calves and the modest rosettes at the knees and the gloves and hats laid on the knees and past the hands and faces, past the whispers and the beards and the murmurs and the nods and mini-bows and glances aimed towards him. All of this is for him, this room, they are all here to see it and it is all for his instruction and all about him, and his destiny. His father on his horse and his mother on hers and a man who was king who was his grandfather who's dead, and his grandmother who's dead, also on their horses, and there he is too, up there in the dark, on his horse. He and his horse look very sleek and smart. Up there in the dark also he can see, just, in the lamplight, there are Hercules' massive feet, which are very different to his own feet, or Lezcano's or any of the other dwarves, and he hasn't seen anyone else's bare feet. They grip the earth. From that foundation Hercules rises, immovable as he wrestles and swings his club. He is the size of a whole man; there are ten of him. King Geryon: he gets him with his club. The Cretan Bull: beaten with his club. The Hydra's lizardy heads all smashed with a backhand club. The Erymanthian Boar: clubbed. One of Cerberus' heads chewing on a strap; Hercules strains to pull it free of the dog's jaws, ready with his club. Diverting the River Alpheus, one big muscly buttock shining, weight resting on his club. Wrestling. And then dying, afire in the darkness.

France has declared war. But he and his father are glorious victors—see?—and will win.

He was to have a little brother, not long ago, a while ago, but he's not, now. But he has a sister, little Anna instead, who is tiny. He has a new cousin in Vienna, he knows; he has been sent Mariana's miniature and carries her very tiny face as a charm. The scale of things is interesting.

The Count-Duke surveys the seating arrangements and sees that they are wanting. The back of the hall is crammed and jostling with people trying to get in, and jostle and cram breeds ill-feeling like crabs, jumping from one hot and wriggling body to another. But it won't take long to find a spot for everyone, if more cushions can be brought, if the men will stand, if we'll all just squeeze up. Room for everyone. The King and Queen can see the stage, yes? And the Prince is content to wander between them and play with the dwarves at their feet. And the Count-Duke's wife, she is quite comfortable there, just outside of the Queen's canopy, just behind her screen; and the Queen is being attended to, she is not long since her last laying-in (a tiny, very tiny daughter somewhere lies in the palace wailing; the Infanta Anna, watched over by the Queen's women and the other hooded one who always also watches). And the historian, the Bolognese, can stay by the wall here with the Count-Duke himself; the historian can take the Count-Duke's own seat, see, and he'll just use this little stool, and then they'll have the chance for a chat. The historian is to write the true history of the King, of his victories, an account of this splendid hall that celebrates them, now unveiled and thrown open.

So he folds himself onto the low velvet seat, all knees and angles like a mantis. He sits very straight, and the Count-Duke gingerly lowers his large backside down onto the footstool and reclines against the wall, leaning into the historian so that there is a voice just below and behind and very close to his ear all evening. The play unfolds upon an intricate stage; Cosimo Lotti, the famous engineer, has newly arrived from Florence, and the Count-Duke, keen to show him off, will indulge his every ingenuity. Actors, props, impromptu machineries in the waxy light of candles and silver lamps, lit most brilliantly; all brilliantly contrived it is. Around and above in the shadows the King's generals and their victories, Hercules labouring in the darkness, the King and Queen and their son on their horses, and below their own images the King and Queen in person watching, the Prince playing quietly, and on stage something is happening. Something about this Palace of Retreat and the magnificence of its buildings and things that have or will or might happen within its walls, its gardens; it is very hard to say exactly, the dialogue all forked with in-jokes and unknown allusions, the high hall echoey with whispers, and the Count-Duke just behind his ear, talking, talking; huge and sweaty and almost enveloping the insubstance of the Bolognese. He explains the scheme of decoration: the victories, Hercules, the horses— the lions— In the play there's a magician who has brought, for the pleasure and amusement of the King, all the wonders of the empire to his court; they say he made his entrance followed by twelve silver lions, who still sit in this hall and attend, obedient; this, the historian surmises, is meant as subtle praise— and, even more subtle, suspicion and insult? Isn't magic the work of the Devil?— but he can't see the Chief Secretary around just now and he'd ask the Count-Duke but he's speaking of the hermitage they visited today or will visit tomorrow or later when it's been built, he is extremely hard to tune out; the fountains, the lakes, and how the water was pumped through them or will be come summer time; how he'd heard of a similar scheme in Rome and borrowed it; how Cosmelotti, yes, the Florentine, you've heard of him?— he has all kinds of ideas for keeping their gardens green in all seasons, what a mind the man has, for all kinds of contraptions, just look at that stage, how he's lit it, how that bit moves there . . . a man is turned from the gate, the palace is a heavenly kingdom and will admit no Jews, and the Jew vows he will burn it to the ground; there's laughter and jeering and it seems a little weird, this, as jokes go, but the Count-Duke seems unfazed by this vision of his sacred palace burning, and undeterred . . . does his

guest know Rome? Such gardens ... and then the parrots ...
the parrots? Yes, that is what he's saying, the parrots in the
bird-house and the hens and something about a lady named
Doña Ana who has got in among the hutches somehow, so
white, so soft she is, so refined, how she likes to be tickled just
under her breast, her breasts he's talking about? This is not
the stiff propriety of the Spanish court that the historian has
come to be acquainted with ... tomorrow the Count-Duke will
personally bring him one of her eggs for breakfast, he gathers
them himself, ah, this makes more sense now.

Meanwhile something is happening with a lady onstage who
is very pleased with some flowers she's been given, it seems,
they are big and brilliant pink and just blooming and entirely
real and just today cut from the palace gardens— because of
the watering system, you see, there are flowers even in this cool
season, the Count-Duke notes— not paper flowers but just
plucked; artifice has come to the aid of nature and don't we all
need a helping hand, the historian thinks she's saying, and to
emphasise the point she gestures to her face which is made up
for the stage, features outlined and coloured and huge in the
wax light, although not much different to the other ladies or
most of the grandees and gallants either; red mouths and red
cheeks shine waxy where the light catches them in the shadows. Things seem to be resolving, they are surely resolving now,
it's been going on for hours or at least the Count-Duke has, he
is talking now about curtains or tapestries or rugs, he is talking
about paintings and perspective and possibly now poetry, and
yes, he is still talking about aviaries; and the historian, dark
hunched and gloomy like a cranky crow, feels his unbelonging
and would love to fly the coop now.

Yes, now there's music and a dance. So the play that seemed
to have probably celebrated the King's new palace appears to

be over, the hall is filled with voices, and a final bow, a last applause, and a new hush now settling; the poets are to read their verses. It's only right that the King should have a second palace near the city, says one; supposing the old fortress were to burn, supposing sickness were to sweep down upon it? Where would he go then? Where would we all go? The listeners feel the heat below their black cloaks, under their plain collars, the itch of flame or fever that might at any time be coming, feeling the rank draught of sickness, the beat of its contagious wings, ready to sweep down upon them; a fair argument, they must concede, uncomfortably. There is a bony clatter in the midst of their clapping, applause from a wizened hooded figure that the grandees leave a seat for, without quite seeing her. The poets are, what a surprise, universal in their approbation, an entirely spontaneous and doubtless genuine outpouring of approval for the palace and the Count-Duke and the King and the Prince, for this Hall of Princely Virtue, for the realms within it made by the brush. (How nice, that you should be acknowledged, murmurs the playwright to the painter; both are surely squashed in somewhere watching; and the painter nods at the newly knighted Don Pedro.)

The Bolognese, official historian, professional witness, makes his record: it was thus. He's already writing it, forming the lines as he's watching, from this corner, close to the door, in the shadows; hardly seen there, a shroud of a man as faceless as death who hangs near him always, grinning as she reads over his shoulder. It was, he writes, just as it is depicted here, just as the poets acclaim it: the splendour, the victory, the power, the control. Look how the King defends and spreads the faith; how the disparate parts are to be united. How the line is continuous from father to son. How, out of heresy and ugly discord, there is harmony; and how treachery is dealt with, trampled

underfoot. Here, here is the true history. At one shoulder the
valido's incessant murmur dictating; at the other, just beyond
hearing, a clatter, maybe a lungless laugh— yes, by all means,
set it all down, so it'll last.

The candles are extinguished, the hall empties out, Hercules
labours on in the darkness. Triangles of limbs like a yoga
sequence. Around the walls, iron balconies, lit up by a single
lamp, now; moving towards the end of the hall where the
King rides above his empty throne, his realms all about him.
His wife opposite, and between them his son, and his father
at his side. And his generals victorious all around the world,
in the Rhineland, in Genoa, in the Indies, in Brazil. Hercules
swinging over and over between them. And the lamp is borne
down the empty hall. There's Fernando Gíron, gouty and
ailing, giving orders from his chair: now dead. And Spinola,
twice, neatly bearded, gentlemanly, dead waiting for another
siege to end. The Duke of Feria, there and there and there,
thrice victorious and quite suddenly dead. And Fernández de
Córdoba, in the moment of triumph that preceded his failure;
retired to his estates, and just as the victory he hopes to be
remembered by is being hung, dead.

There's that fool Don Fadrique, who couldn't seem to pick
his battles wisely. Beyond this frame, beyond this hall, beyond
the palace— elsewhere in the city Don Fadrique languishes,
is old and dying in jail, imprisoned after a too-public set-to
with the Count-Duke, who would send him back to Brazil
half-cocked, he said. He said it too loudly behind too-thin
closed doors. He too loudly pointed out a wage discrepancy:
how much a general, an actual working general, makes, fighting in the field, and what it costs him, what risk to life and
limb he takes just to earn his living; and then how much the

Count-Duke earns sitting on his backside, however precariously he chooses to perch it.

Old and failing and shamed as he is, Don Fadrique is dead before he even knows the extent of his penalty: no offices, no estates, no legacy, everything stripped, even funerary honours. He goes unknowing into disgrace, led off into the fog befuddled, looking about him as if for something lost; the catafalque he thought he laid on has been dismantled under him.

In the painting he's holding a baton—the baton you used to see in his hand, the poet writes—to point to the King's triumph. Under the King's feet: Heresy, Discord, Treachery, writhing distorted and snarling. Disobedience and Impertinence presumably dispatched already. The poet's eulogy celebrates the victory and then can't quite make an end of him: This was Don Fadrique ... Don Fadrique de Toledo ... who—— and now ... and he ... and today he—— the poet crosses recrosses deliberates takes heart and baton in hand, redips his pen: And today undone in the cold shadows, he brings tears to our eyes, and fear to our lips. (In this court one shouldn't let fear past the lips. Better to flatter, if only from the teeth outward— so advises Gracián.)

And tonight in the cold shadows, all down this hall, silver lions stand guard. A gift from the lampholder. Muscle under silver skin twitching as the light moves, silver eyes watch his progress up and down the central aisle. He takes a seat casually on the dais and looks back down, the way he's come. The Hall of Realms: these realms made by the paintbrush, one of the more grovelling poets has written, in praise of the King's favourite painter. And money; also made by money, and influence, transmuted into gifts, into cloth of gold, into commissions, into loyalty, into silver creatures. The King's Secretary surveys it, from a throne he wouldn't wish for, not for all these painted realms before him. He and his lions watching. Assessing what's been done, what's still to do; what will be seen to be done; and what won't be. Yes, it's all coming along nicely. He rises noiselessly and pads out of the room silent, the eyes of his silver pride following.

XI

Sprezzatura/
Light work

The painter learns the new palace as he furnishes it— his latest
and seemingly endless task. The whole place scaled with paintings, glittering, all but overlapping and more or less fungible.
There are other palaces across the King's lands that stand empty
and stripped, their rooms denuded, so that every wall here can
be floor-to-ceiling gilt framing landscapes, still life, mountain
ranges and joints of meat and bunches of flowers, the glades of
Arcadia, anything innocuous and easy on the eye unless you
choose to look too long and see dead hares hanging, greening
oysters, fruit ever on the point of over-ripening, that first soft
sickly browning pucker on the orange skin, soft to touch, petals
droop and about to drop, everything is a memento mori if you
stop to look at it, but there is then always something else to
look at, some other small Jerome lost in picturesque wilderness,
some other Anthony tormented by entertaining devils and mad
distorted animals, some other pile of lemons, another hare's
corpse hanging. Such a rich superfluity of paintings this King
possesses, he can barely build enough walls to hang them—
such is the effect intended, the implication (all those other
naked walls, in other rooms, unseen, unused). And his nobles,

in emulation of the King's discerning eye, clamour to build
their own collections; and more wall space is made to fill with
the gifts that they select from these collections. The painter
sees the work of his old colleague, no more distinct than any
other, who died last year still fulminating. He walks among
them, so much production, so much expenditure of effort, for
what, for gaudy wallpaper, frame upon frame; he tries to see
them, to adjust his eye to the thing that is framed, each separate one. But then there can be little time for such reflection,
since the painter's duties are ever increasing, ever accumulating
as his stock rises and accesses granted, and he wanted that,
didn't he, what else is he here for. There's always more work to
be done as the palace expands and the King's wealth increases
impossibly, and needs to be spent on something, even on credit;
as if there wasn't enough stuff already, as if there wasn't enough
to be done already—

— the King would like to provide the Queen with something,
and would prevail upon the painter— as if he ever has even
a moment to take up his brush— something for her private
rooms in the new palace, something to amuse her. The Queen
seems to hate the place, because it's too hot or too chaotic or
because the Count-Duke built it. In keeping with the tenor of
the whole endeavour, she suggests, a suite of fools? Yes? Poor
Don John, for example, should be sent for— the fool, that is,
the fellow that's named for the bastard— for the King's great-
grandfather's bastard, yes; who else? And, oh, the buffoon
Barbarroja, that braggart—that might be amusing, something
in a military line, something a bit satirical—and perhaps they
might have the King's painter for the job, if he can spare the
time. As if he—— No hurry. Sometime before she expires
from breathing all this stuffy air and tedium. She says all this

very lightly, as if it's only badinage, and the King sends for the painter.

Since the Prince was born she has lost two more children. Fernando, a little brother for him who wasn't quite ready for the world and lasted only a day in it. The Prince's sister Anna lived almost a year. Margarita Catharina María Elisabeth Fernando Anna perhaps she counts them sometimes as a rosary; her husband prays for them, for their souls and his own, paying penance, fearing he's to blame, fearing the Queen might think so. His sins. The boy Juan José with the black hair, and all the rest of them. Wishing he could find a way to keep her safe and contented, away from rumour and gossip and the horrible growth of expectation weighing on her ever-emptying womb. Her husband comes to her and even as they go on, as they must, trying to make her heavier, he hopes he can find something to make her days lighter. And so he calls on the painter.

Don John of Austria shuffles into the studio under his plumed hat and the painter greets him. Timid, gentle, easy, the painter sees him, this man; so unlike the famous noble bastard of the last Spanish emperor, so unlike a commander that the joke of calling him that will never grow old. It works something like 'Slim' or 'Little', as in Little John. Where's your fleet, little Don John? And he'll smile and come up with some retort.

Gathered in to himself, head ducked, and always on the point of shivering—the outline of him shivered, shivering——the timid incline of the cocked hat; his staff, irresolute; the thinness of him and the slightness and his threadbare costume, that splendid worn anachronism. Tatty prop trophies at his feet. There's no fight in him, he bears the blows of others as if that is his role—and so it is.

A shy man; a shuffle of a man; his dusty hat awry. The painter watches; tremble running— through the fingers— through the staff— through the feather—— on through the painter's brush; the smile uncertain as it passes he catches at almost—— the narrow shuffle of the skinny legs, the feet. Behind him beyond him, beyond his understanding but seen dimly a sea battle a ship on fire masts and sails blazing cracking vanishing into paint swiped off into blue his insubstantial dream of victory—the Battle of Lepanto, the bastard of Austria's famous victory, seventy years past— glimpsed through an open door——

— Bursting through the open door in to the studio in turn— the braggart Barbarroja, Don John's old adversary, in history and in this court. These two buffoons once re-enacted their namesakes' great battle at Lepanto—for the pleasure of the grandees, with sticks for swords and sails on sticks and cymbals—and they have been stuck in these roles and these costumes ever since; although nothing now seems less likely, poor Don John deferential under that furious boggling glare. They are to offset one another: the bashful fool, the bellicose. In comes Barbarroja, sweating and burning in his own hot air, knocking away all trace of the shivering Don John, huffing away any fallen feather-frond.

The painter waits out all of Barbarroja's bluster, his ridiculous flattered vanity; if only the grandees were so combative, the King might hold onto his territories yet. The fool narrates his victories; he froths and champs, he would be out on the field again; why do we not strike here! and there!— he strikes with the side of his hand at invisible maps; he charges, he pivots, he can't help marching over every minute to inspect the canvas, where the painter has barely laid down a dim block of form; manoeuvring about the studio, knocking pots and whacking tables with his baton, bellowing orders, a caricature. And the painter waits until at last the ranting runs out of steam and the fool stands at attention, stock-still now, each breath flaring the hair out of his nostrils, cheeks and temples glowing, a spit of scarlet there, the high heroic shine of his red eyes staring out from his skull— staring out from the relentless battle within it. His red robe and Turkish cap, which he wears proudly, pirate warmonger, and doesn't know it's also the cap of a fool, unless that is the source of his fury—to be treated as a fool and not a warrior.

The Queen prefers the picture to the man himself and he's sent away soon after, too insufferable to have around. Or, but, also, because—— because yes, Barbarroja is a braggart; yes, he is obnoxious, and noisy, and perhaps actually mad; but, also, perhaps he has once too often taken too much liberty with the fools' limitless license, tested the bounds and found that there are limits after all to what the Count-Duke will tolerate; and it seems that the Count-Duke doesn't care for the freely offered advice of a great military strategist who was after all defeated and is after all mad and, or, only a fool.

The portrait could look like caricature after all, if you don't look too hard at it; lost in obscure exile, he becomes an old joke for the Queen's wall—

The Queen meanwhile grows round and pale and taut once more and, after yet more months of carefully cradling her belly, so fragile and egg-like, has given the King another daughter, strong, healthy, hopeful, and the new Infanta is to be baptised María Teresa, and as if—

— there wasn't enough to do already: d'Este, the Duke of Modena is coming to Madrid. He is to be godfather to little María Teresa; he is to be made a councillor, a viceroy, an admiral, and, please God, an ally, because in the world beyond la Corte the King needs all the help he can get. He is to be received as royalty; arrangements are to be made for his accommodation in the new palace— the painter will need to be involved in these arrangements, as if there wasn't—— He can have the Count-Duke's rooms, which are sumptuous and well appointed; the winter apartment is cosily brocaded; in summer he may be refreshed in rooms of cool white and gold. The rooms stand perpetually sumptuously empty, white and gold in summer, red and gold in winter; come looking and the Count-Duke is not to be found there, in any season. He is seen to leave the Alcázar early in the morning and he enters the palace grounds but he prefers, when he is here, the role of governor to valido; and so prefers to lodge in the governor's residence, the hermitage of San Juan, which is small and quiet and simple, where he can work, and also pray, when he has even a moment. So d'Este can use the Prime Minister's apart-ments—which are, after the King's, the most splendid—since he doesn't really use them anyway, really preferring the little hermitage apartment—and since by some oversight in the planning stages we have no guest quarters at the new palace ... The Chief Secretary, too, makes space, perhaps sleeping in his office, wherever that is, if he ever sleeps, and numerous others are as ever willing to offer up what's theirs, upon request, to accommodate the entourage.

So the palace is to be opened up to visitors, and the Count-Duke once again surveys his creation and just wonders ... They are indeed splendid, these rooms; and splendidly impressive; but he can't help but wonder if they couldn't be more ... just *more* so ... if perhaps there are embarrassing blank spaces, the backs of the doors for example, the windows that are closed up for winter ... and so the painter ensures through reshuffling and borrowing and commissioning and hiring that there is nowhere that the eye might end up resting, God forbid, on nothing.

And it also seems that their guest might be honoured by a portrait—a big one, why not, a big equestrian portrait with the new admiral's sash, that the King can keep at one of his residences to remind him that this true, this loyal ally and friend stands by him. That will be a regal gesture, won't it? And the Duke, upon arrival, admires the painter's efforts in the Hall of Realms, admires the King and his son and his father, and also elsewhere the Count-Duke, on their horses, admires the horse of Spinola at Breda and its shining powerful backside, and agrees that he would be honoured to sit for the King's personal painter, if the painter has the time to spare—— as if there—— which he does, of *course*, assures the Count-Duke. And perhaps a copy might be made for the Duke's own collection, if the thing turns out well? Oh it will, it will *certainly* turn out well, the Count-Duke assures him. No doubt it will, agrees the Duke's ambassador. If it turns out at all, it will turn out very well. The King's own painter, I have heard, is a talented and very expensive man. How effortlessly he executes his duties. He'll make you even more handsome than you are, than even *you* are, if he can find the time to finish it; he is a tardy exorbitant liar, but yes, no doubt, very talented.

The painter takes his deposit and makes a study, working quickly. The ambassador accuses him of flattery? So perhaps the Duke is not this handsome man; this youthful carefully barbered man, no trace of bearded shadow; with a fullness of mouth and health, with a gloss to his hair— his armour— a moustache not quite full upon the lip and a neat dark turn at the corner; light falls on the forehead and the smooth skin of the cheek, rarely has the painter rendered noble skin so flawless, almost royal skin. And smart, and shrewd, and maybe not quite at ease here, the painter observes; this truth sneaks through the dark pupil; and the handsome Duke approves, because he likes to be flattered or because he prizes truth, and admires a modern style, and he gives the painter a gold chain before he leaves, which the painter plans to wear on gala days, of which there will no doubt be many to come. The Duke leaves before the sash is even finished, which is done quickly, the work of minutes once he finds some minutes spare, a few strokes—not out of haste or laziness, actually, but because this is how he paints and that's what they've paid for, so that's what they're getting. But somehow then he doesn't ever quite get round to the larger work, let alone its copy, doesn't quite manage to seat the Duke up on the saddle, doesn't find time to make it down to the stables, things get piled up in the studio and the two large canvases already stretched become a bit buried, and they start to gather dust and when the Duke's ambassador leaves for Modena months later he takes the small portrait with him and suggests to the painter, smirking smoothly, that they call it quits at that. To which the painter agrees readily, relieved, distracted by other tasks already, and the King too by now otherwise preoccupied; this is how it goes these days, promises made and easily broken, and the King perhaps thinking better of it since the Duke's loyalty looks a little shaky anyway—so, no need to impress him, the ingrate; and also perhaps the King chooses not to press the matter because, surmises the painter, he'd rather avoid a conversation about overdue bills or any kind of payment. And then, instead, there are other works to be done—

— The Prince— the Prince— the Prince——— copies to be sent out to all corners, all his cousins and aunties and potential fiancées, just in case, keeping options open—

— The new lodge in the forest of El Pardo of course wants furnishing; with every new enclosure, a new blank wall. The King and his family come to hunt here, to practise the arts of war—a fitting activity for kings and princes, for generals in training—and so: hunting portraits. His brother (whom he misses, who is no longer at leisure to hunt); his son; the King himself, if he must; he supposes he must. So, no rest for the painter.

In the studio there is quiet, grey light, patient industry. The King, in his seat in the corner. He watches, approaches sometimes to watch the painter conjure, the loosely held long-handled brush— How do you do it, Diego. I wish you'd teach me, I wish there was time.

He watches; at the end of the long brush, coming into being—

— the Cardinal-Infante with his long fair face, smart, attentive, elongated ... the King's brother ready to hunt, back from the Netherlands. Brother, the King says, you return so quickly? Is the war over then? The painter at his side assessing the effect as they wait for the man on the canvas to stir and reply— Yes, the war is over! We won! ... They wait a while longer— The King strings out his charade— Tell me, what's the news, brother? Victory?— They say you want to steal our Netherlands from Spain, brother, steal it from under me, they say you're going to marry a French princess ... have you heard this, Diego?— the painter makes no reply, but offers an indulgent smile; Fernando remains mute. My brother it seems has nothing to say on the matter; quite right too, I wouldn't dignify it with an answer either ... The King puts two fingertips to his temple and rubs at the thin skin there, closes his eyes for a moment; an elegant, minimal gesture, but one of despair, nonetheless— These lies, these lies, honestly, Diego … and the painter feels embarrassed of his almost-smile, unsure of what his face should do or is doing, and moves forward again with long-handled brush and adds a line of light down the long nose; the King exclaims, Oh, it's only a painting, after all! I assure you, I thought the Cardinal was in the room with us; I assure you I was taken in.

This is not a new joke. It's hardly a joke at all, really, by the time of this iteration, but it restores the King's equilibrium, resets his expression—

—— a little tension about the mouth, as if he is holding his face that way, holding his lower lip stiff: the King: father, husband, brother, exemplary hunter, out in the country, in his— yes, better, wearing his hat—— pushed back on fair hair worn casually—— the one held in the King's hand dissolves into the full flat clouded grey sky. Just a man, wearing his hat, out on the hunt, luminous face against the dark green crown of leaves framing it and his hat—just a man and his melancholy dog—the paint goes on easy, thin and quick and fluid, brush racing halting ruffling lively and quick, light on soft leather metal wool just catching the long dog's brow, snout, the hangdog rim of his eyelid. They are fine, obedient, regal creatures, the royal dogs— he takes pleasure in attending to them, finding the best way to express their individual dogginess—

— placid, gentle, effortlessly noble, the little auburn Prince, light falling soft on chin and brow, on the fall of his newly full hair, and the hunting cap jauntily set—

— he finds his way to them, these different men and their different dogs, he finds time to work, the work that he loves, still, even if there's so little time, to finish anything— the King complains he doesn't finish anything—

Still, he'd like to be paid for this, at some point. There are of course proper procedures for these things. He sends an invoice, signed Painter to the King.

The painter is appointed Gentleman of the Wardrobe, for his continued good services, for the effortless grace with which he executes them. Another doorway he can pass through, another space to enter, cloth and lace and intimate items, the things of the King's private hours—such as they are, such as his privacy is; although no more money for it. And of course more duties to attend to, as if there weren't enough——

— Vessels to be brought, filled, emptied—

— Collars to be pressed—

— Mirrors to be shone—

— Doors, to be opened, to be closed and curtained, to be hung with paintings—

— So he's busy, very busy, the painter, at the moment. He is much called upon and he has his duties to perform and his commissions to fulfil and there are scraps and snatches recorded as he goes: receipts, invoices, payments made or promised, paintings sold or gifted, catalogues of works, inventories, bequeaths——

— And how much can be gleaned from this? In amongst it all I find that he finds time to paint a pelican; perhaps as a diversion; perhaps upon browsing Ripa (if he has a moment to browse his library, and if he owns it, which probably he does, or some other iconologia); some lost fable, or his own creation; perhaps observing in the aviary, there is sure to be a pelican in the Count-Duke's care. Perhaps, even, painted to please the Count-Duke, who loves birds, and also piety and self-sacrifice:

the pelican plucking the blood from her own breast to feed her brood, a sacrifice akin to Christ's, and a symbol therefore also of a new arising ... There are donkeys, with the pelican. But there are different orders of donkey: patient pious asses such as that which bore the Saviour and his mother, and witnessed his birth; or diabolical donkeys, full of ill-will and kicky; no way of knowing which these donkeys are, or were, now. There is also a bucket, significant enough to warrant inclusion in the title of the work as it's given later in an inventory, which is the painting's only trace, which is where I found it—Pelican with a Bucket and Donkeys ... How many donkeys? Perhaps the pelican with her beak buried in elegant fine-drawn feathers, soft and blood-stained breast; and the donkeys with their scruffy scumbled thick fur; looking on? Protective? Bothering her? Braying? Totally oblivious? The bucket— almost existing— I can almost see it, this solid object, how he'd do it, the handle, the dented rim and dull gleam, copper—— or then again tin—— or perhaps wooden even— the donkeys feeding from it or the pelican pouring her blood into it; no, no way of knowing, hopeless. This piece of frivolity or study from nature or high moral fable of the sort he's not normally given to making so maybe not that, this too hangs somewhere in the palace and is lost or burnt or stolen later, even the circumstances of its vanishing now obliterate and the donkeys wandered off into the wilderness of forgotten. I so much wish I could see it, and know why you made it, and what it meant; if it would offer some glimpse of you as I try to catch you in passing, find you in a catchlight or the placement of a mark—

— coming in the door of your home, late, to Juana; exhausted in the dim light, framed in dark; sitting down together and nodding off in your chair while she clears half-eaten morsels from around you; knowing you in rare moments; stay, rest, let me look at you; but he is ever self-effacing and immersed in his work and there is always—

— always work to be done, always more to be done—

XII

Zarzuela/
Song and dance

The Planet King in every season shines upon us— warms
and shines, as his emblem assures us; a comfort in the cold
months. And every year we are delivered, from the cold
and the darkness; the winds drop, the snow melts from the
mountains that surround us; each year spring will come, and
Easter, and the Lord will rise again; and then summer; and
every summer the King's retinue evacuates the Alcázar and
processes in a winding line of carriages carts and horses,
chamberlains and cooks, dogs and guns and hawks and hams
and swine strung up, musicians, dwarves and clowns and
men of pleasure, planking and lances and drapes and tables,
to take its leisure in the sap-scented airs of the Retiro. New
spaces, new buildings, still they proliferate, the Count-Duke's
follies—we make a joke of it, always a new place to celebrate,
and a new play and a party to celebrate it— What, another
hermitage, hidden away here in the undergrowth? Another
arbour? And here that Florentine magpie Cosmelot has made
a little plaza from some shiny bits and pieces. Another new
plaza? Why of course— A plaza for everybody, here at the
Retiro! Haven't you got one yet?

Every summer the King's in his splendid palace and so is his son, and all is right with the world. See?— In this time of abundance and God's glory—yes! Victory, and plenty, growth, success—all across the empire, that's what you'll find—every year the ships return with their splendid cargo—abundance in all things, flowing back to the centre. Cause enough for celebration. And every celebration must be prepared for— the Count-Duke, the Chief Secretary, the playwrights, the poets, the set dresser, the engineers, the cooks and grooms, moppers, shiners, scrubbers, sluicers, sharpeners, starchers, and of course the painter, all play their unseen parts. The tailors rush to complete their orders, botching costumes together with rapid stitches and threads rapidly snapped.

Here is the new arena: the painted loggia gleam and lustre just like jasper and bronze, by the light of six thousand lanterns. Rhinoceroses! Two oxen in ingenious disguise of hide and horns lead a triumphal march; the King will triumph! In peace, and war—be sure of it. Here is the King, saturnine, shining—

Here eighteen bulls of Castile dance to their bloody deaths, one after another on the dark wet ground—

Here are Venetian dances; below our masks of glitter and feathers and sequins, our exposed mouths are painted sticky red and our skulls bend close together; we are sophisticated, we are illicit and—

Here—come into the trees hooded—is a very private party; a host of courtesans have been employed to totter a gauntlet in nothing but their high heels and we each have a gun and a cache of sugarplums to shoot at them and revel on into the dew of a sticky dawn—

Here's the Coliseo, a new theatre, now, built by the Count-Duke within the palace grounds and almost like the theatres in the city. The layout the same, the balconies, the stew-pan for the ladies, the musketeers vying and primping, the same. All the thrills and catcalls and all the dirty jokes and dances, and less of the stabbing and punching and hunger. It will no longer be necessary for the King to make his way out incognito; he can be incognito here, within his own walls. We squeeze and jostle in and yes, we say, it's almost like the city. And the Knight of the Sad Countenance rides in on Rocinante— rides a real horse, say, why not, into the new Coliseo— and he is astounded—he takes ladies' maids for princesses and expresses his wonder, what beautiful ladies, what a palace this is, such a king it must belong to; and the nobles laugh because this great hall that the knight errant takes for a great hall is, in the play, only a humble stopping-place, these splendid silver-gilded balconies he sees are only a cow's byre; this King that he greets is the innkeeper really. The court are only puppets, and puppets are brought in dressed as the grandees with all their features and foibles and the knight tilts at them and tears them to pieces, and the grandees laugh to see themselves eviscerated and applaud him—

The whole court gets involved: taking each other's parts and the parts of their ladies and the ladies' maids. They all forget their lines, but the lines are terrible anyway. The painter— ah, there he is— takes the stage briefly, also, to please the King; he says 'married already!' or 'already dispossessed!' and is rewarded with a laugh, for the pun or for the sight of the stolid Sevillian in his wife's dress (an old one that she's had let out for him, on the promise of a replacement).

And Felipe in the audience, among this audience of only we privileged few, sits with hands on knees and claps them down from time to time to show his mirth. The King has an idea: Supposing for one afternoon there was a decree, that the ladies must come to the show without all their petticoats— because space is tight, and those petticoats in recent years are monthly growing in volume; because the King says so— and then, when they were all at their seats in the stew-pan, a barrel of mice was tipped in there right among them? The King's coterie, his closest confidantes, find the King's idea very, very funny, and act upon it at the first opportunity. Chaos ensues, and much merriment. For the grandees, anyway.

Here is a pathway into the dark gardens and though another evening's fallen, though so many evenings have passed—how many? we're not counting! we're not done yet— To the lake! they're crying, the chorus, and lead us with torches across a bridge to the island in the centre of the water to such sights, such wonders, as held Ulysses spellbound for years. Come, come into her lair, so cunningly lit; Circe is here, oh she is breathtaking, glamours and spells are woven around her, squibs and scents and apparitions— Cosmelot excels himself— so that when at last we go out into the starlit gardens it seems many nights have passed enchanted and we are stunned and bedazzled and a little light-headed with the smoky scented air and asking each other, how did he do that? And feeling how extraordinary, to share in this enchantment; and no one thinks to think what it might mean, that even Ulysses could be willingly spelled into staying on an island where everything is intoxicating and smells of ambergris and gunpowder—

Here is a hidden chamber in the back wall of the stage, opening to show the true King Segismundo— kept captive as a madman and brought forth from his tower to govern, as a ploy; and then he is told, it's only a dream, life is a dream, you've only dreamed you were king. But it's too late; the veil is rent; the dream is no less true than the waking nightmare and the rightful lunatic has already taken over the asylum. All somehow comes right in the end.

Of fools, we find in Ecclesiastes, the number is infinite; and Democritus tells us that the same is true of worlds; one can't help but wonder if the first of these infinities is concentrated here, in our own instance of the latter . . . And as Saint Paul says, we must become foolish in order to become wise. And so another summer advances and Pablillos leads the men of pleasure out, to dance into the streets for Corpus Christi. And we are all men of pleasure, for this festival. Here's the King riding out of the palace gates, upright and indulgent upon his horse, among his people; out from the Alcázar through the streets of the city dancing in motley behind friars in their hundreds bearing gold and silver effigies, dancing behind the effigies and before the King and his councillors bearing the Host, bearing the body of Christ through the streets of the city in grand celebration of the flesh, revelling. The bright lolling paste heads of dwarves and giants behind them, outsize, foreheads nodding as the necks within them roll and hold them just about upright dancing. The nodding foreheads shine with a sweat of egg-glaze as the heads within sweat into the damp smell of paper and plaster and glue, peering out through the teeth of a grin or a grimace; behind them the spine of the serpent winds through the streets, each articulation with its own set of legs poking out from the pasteboard body and trundled on wheels to bear its great weight, each part aglitter with its splendid scales; its eyes blaze with coloured foils and fire crackers, its teeth flash in the sun, its three tongues flick and lash at the ends of their levers, it flicks off hats with its tail in passing, the peasants who've come up from the country open-mouthed gasping, they yelp as it slithers through the dumb-show streets and the city kids mimic and gape and howl at these rustics and fall about laughing. The nobles applaud from their horses. Tricks and illusions feint and vanish and snap. The puff of sulphurous stink-bombs flung at and out of windows; the dandies toss gilded painted eggs in at the windows of carriages and the ladies cry out at the splash but it's rose-perfumed water that splashes their skirts and they're pleased to disdain it haughtily, a day's ordinary wages dissipating with each puff of perfume. A boy in a monkey-mask ties a wire across a narrow alley and hoots as his victims dance into his trap in a tangle of goats and ganders, of beaks and feathers and horns.

A monk spinning circles down the centre of the road,

bumping his way through, grabbing pastries from the tray of a bewildered seller and, with as many as he can hold in each sticky spittled hand, spins off down the street and onto his knees and with his habit flipped over his bare arse, on his knees and his elbows on the ground in the dust he's cramming his greasy sugared face at the fistfuls of pastries; he capers sticky-fingered after the ladies and pretends to mount them; he sings and prances. The King stares at his antics. He is a holy hermit, he has been many weeks out on the Sierra, they say, his bald pate flaming; he has earned the licence to frolic through the city as a holy fool.

And we process past the plays the abject madmen put on; their faces painted with ochre, cheeks daubed red and yellow, the yellow whites of their wide eyes, hair and habits shorn and washed where possible for the occasion; they pace out their motions, meticulous, spasmodic; jerkily, endlessly slowly, distractedly, wandering, in agitation; in their white clothes and their mouths hanging or muttering, their eyes wide or weeping or half-closed contented in the sunshine, their arms flailing or hugging or grasping or carefully remembering the motions; they stretch out in appeal to the King, or to Christ, to the body of Christ that has been in their mouths, the blood of Christ that has touched their tongues; or to no one, no king or god or world beyond the circle of their own arms, alone and gathered only into themselves and indifferent, weary, narcoleptic, eyelids swollen with slumber or peeled back raw and haunted with the effort of endless waking, the refusal night after night of nightmares; gathering alms which they receive graciously and hide away among their habits or toss aside forgetting for others to pick up and push between tight-closed lips ...

Their attendants gather and shepherd their flock and keep

them in line. They are God's children, they are not to be mocked or feared or chastised. They are unconstrained by prudence or propriety; they are free, to live each in their own world of irrational wonders which is also, maybe, the world of the miracle, maybe closer to God. It's a frightening liberty, this the King sees, although he might envy it. They are tabulated and categorised, there are so many ways to be mad— the simple, the deranged, the innocent delirious demented; the prophets and savants; the wolfmen that the dogs yelp back at; the speechless and the shrieking, the unutterably sad and insensate; the manic the frenzied the furious; the raving and deluded; the lunatic fits and outpourings and the peaceful ruminations of the calf-like idiot; nonsense and inaccessible inarticulate wisdom and cursing; all around voices, the voices of God and his angels who may or may not be fallen, may or may not be trusted, voices and visions out of brightness on the edge of blackness, blackness beneath bright; creatures with horns bleating, monkeys wearing man-suits and monkey masks pressing in pressing closer; windows speaking grating voices papery voices and eyes behind the grates and paper panes. And there is a number to the panes and to the paneless, to the closed and to the open, there is meaning there writ invisible on the yellow glass, the paper panes, and there is a number to the stones and the cracks, and there is an alleyway and there is a wall and there are doors in significant numbers but none of them none offers ingress or egress, there is no way out of this prison this madhouse this sepulchre this palace this labyrinth, no way but death and the promise of Heaven painless and the certainty of pain of Hell or of nothing of nothing of nothing— of what were we speaking—? The gratifying slide back into oblivion and everything blurring again in the tears in the colours in the brightanddarkness

in dreaming— back within better than outside looking on,
looking in, looking out as it expands inevitable inescapable
however you rend and tear at the veils there are always others
and no true light can shine through them they are endlessly
woven and rewoven by the ceaseless spiders hiding in the
corners that the light can't reach into, the spiders that hide
in the dark there and come out and creep into the corner of
the eye and crawl invisible no matter how hard how fast you
flick and you scratch, you scratch, with your bound mittened
hands rubbing light into the eyes and leaving filaments of
swaddle that scratch and scratch stuck between the eyelid
and the eyeball you can feel it a spider's leg even when the
lids are closed coming out of the red darkness behind them
do you know them the shapes of them almost but there aren't
there isn't a way to say it unspeakable all unsayable, and only
at carnival it makes a terrible sense, now, only here in the
streets in our paint and our dances can we be presented in
public outside exposed turned out from the inside and the
King is here or something there is some reason we're here the
flesh of the dead Christ that they have consumed dead flesh
in the mouth bite your tongue they must cover their mouths
if they won't close them or suck on their hands if they must
they must hush, or sing nicely. Mustn't shout or scratch.

So the city celebrates God's glory, even in these straitened
times—— but these, surely, are times of abundance— see,
there is bread and wine!— like a miracle flowing forth from the
bounty of the Lord and the King His anointed servant, wine
flows through the streets of la Corte! The city trips and reels
and capers after the Saviour's blood and body and the King and
his cousins cheered by the madmen in a wake of revelry, the
procession ascending all the way to the unassuming gates of the
new palace, which close upon the eggy chaos left behind it, and

the nobles leave the populace to their sticky stinking party just before they find that the wine's dried up and they can't afford more for the taxes and there isn't any left in the city anyway.

And ah— back— safe within the walls. How reassuring it is, to breathe again this carefully partitioned air, with each partitioned cube having its purpose; each with its doors to pass through, or not, as permitted. Back within the palace walls— and for this special festive occasion, the court will enjoy a merienda of fifty dishes! and the King and Queen will eat together! in public! with all of us! And wine is brought forth, no shortage here at the Retiro; and uneasy forced jollity—we are inwardly shaken by the madmen and what might have been revealed there out in the streets what they might have shown us if we thought too long about it or voiced that inward tremor or—— this brittle gaiety gives way to genuine goodwill as the wine flows. Or as genuine as we get here. And disquiet is returned to its safely labelled cell to start at ghosts cat-like.

If the soul is a labyrinth, then however gaily we might light it, we are all living in the formal, shadowed, melancholy complex that is Spain's; we are all prisoned within it. There are these bright and lamplit spaces wide within it, where everything is made visible—as if painted on a curtain that we draw over the invisible world which is death; which belongs to death; which is confusion and fear and unseen and what if it is, what if it is— meaningless— so we keep our eyes upon the stage and remain vigilant against the invisible. In desperate celebration in these frittered hours we stave off the inevitable; always grasping at some more brilliant prize that in the obtaining turns tawdry.

Go below the staterooms where the ceilings lower, the walls close in; there are corners and corridors and doors to cellars and

store-rooms, subterranean chambers; doors which might open
onto a closet fit only for a boy to sleep in, or a dark, sepulchral,
vaulted space without end, to find barrels of wine, or armour, or
game birds hanging, hams, whole sides of meat, tombs. Climb
up into the towers and turrets, into the roofs, winding up into
the pitched heights where the fools watch the sky, watch the
swallows circle. It is riddling—narrow, wide, high and deep—
this labyrinth of errors, of wrong corners, of cheats and liars at
every turn, traps at every turn. Where is the centre? Where is
the beast, where is the belly of the beast? Through every hall
and corridor, every hidden passage, leading round and back but
never out. There is only back in. Navigating in blind error in the
dark and never finding centre or exit. Another room brought
into existence and needing to be filled; an edifice built against
emptiness. Every throne room and every privy. The clang and
ferment of the kitchens and larders, the stores of grain and
fruit, the bread yeastily swelling and rising and poked into the
ovens, the massive pastries crenellating, the spit and hiss of car-
casses speared from bum to gullet, heads hanging and flopping
on slit necks as they turn, lips drawn tight over teeth from the
last of life passing, they are glazed and basted and garlanded,
dressed with apples in their mouths and feathers in their arses,
but none of these poor primped creatures is the beast. There are
bulls in the corrido, is it one of them, the beast? The icehouse
where they store the ice brought down from the mountains, is it
frozen in that pit, the beast? Ready to be chipped out when the
ladies call for refreshment—scraping with their little pointed
teeth, the ice melting pinkly down their fingers as a hairy brute
crashes in furious and covered in raspberry snow; think of this
and let out a laugh and the shriek of it echoes through the
palace, through all the dark places, and does it reach the beast?

There must be something monstrous. Something we all

step so carefully around, in prescribed circuits and measured counted steps. The grinning gallants, the buffoons too. Spot the difference. All of us laughing with our skulls showing. They think perhaps it's her, that old woman with her sickle and scythe waiting, pacing. But lift the skirts of death and see what she keeps there, her nothing. Not her. Something else then; something even she is guarding, circling. We all revolve around our Planet King, is it him? But there is nothing at the centre of a crown, even one you can't see. There is nothing at the centre of a skull that will outlast the flesh that covers it and the brain-meat within. Is that it then. Not death but nothing. Is that what's at the centre? If it is then yes, it is. It is monstrous.

This endless feast, this on-going zarzuela, this song and drama and feast and dance, this bottomless exuberance, kept within the palace walls could go on for years. That clatter in the background isn't bones or armour or lances, it is only cutlery being washed up in the kitchens. Supplies are seemingly limitless— enough— too much— of everything; of nothing——

Towards the end of this long and briefly passing sequinned decade the Count-Duke's patience is wearing very thin, and his head always aches, and his joints, and his heart; and he can't help but feel there might be other things to attend to; and yet, who built this palace in the first place? This pleasure-ground to keep the King ringed up in? And they've all bought into it, haven't they; they are all quite dazzled by the magnificent edifice that the Count-Duke has constructed around them, he has them all convinced, even the King. The Count-Duke says it so often he's almost convinced himself, even: everything will be fine; is fine. But he wakes in the dark having hardly slept and there's some dark awareness pressing on his chest and he worries; rising in the very early morning, distracted from his prayers, he worries; there's hysteria just the other side of hilarity—he wheezes and pulls air into his chest and self-medicates in secret—and what if when things turn back turvy-topsy nothing quite sits right? Things will be left upended or on a slight squint, the world won't be set right again . . .

And if the King is enlivened by these entertainments, he is brittle with it; as if keeping a mask on when the party has ended and the eyeholes are grubby round the sockets from fingering. He is never free of these obsequious creatures, pressing in on him; and every gesture he makes in their midst is a form of performance. They find all his jokes funny. They find all his pronouncements edifying. They find all his observations to be true. It sometimes exhausts him. His every thought celebrated and made flesh, made up into fine words and fine cloth and marvellous machineries; his every victory painted and performed; his every action transmuted the moment it transpires into staged allegory, into myth; over and again he sees this made-up version of himself intervening and solving all the ills that the world on the stage has suffered, a one-man deus ex machina; how neatly all order is restored; and then the curtain call and dancing—

— and he is worn out, worn out by all of it. The pageants and plays, all the fancy private parties, all the penances that attend them; the proximity. Worn out by the frenzy and sham of the Count-Duke's palace, which is so relentless, which is still so close to the city, which is still so crammed with grandees and the public wandering in the gardens, which is so hot and so stuffy in summer, as the Queen has observed so often to the Count-Duke's wife—

— and out in the streets, at carnival time, his people make use of their carnival licence to take pot-shots where they can, hoping to catch his upturned eye; he was offered a military cross made of tin, as cheap as a soldier's life; Saint Sebastian cleverly pin-cushioned, and one of his arrows pinned a sign to his heart to say he's a martyr to all these taxes fired from all sides; Saint Bartholomew carrying his long knife and a banner that said the King's levies have flayed him. The whole city stripped and emptied of substance by so many excises, out here, they tell him, we can bear no more of it—

— and the playwright, a knight now and off to war, fighting one of the King's many battles, comes back a little less willing to make work that is only an excuse for Cosmelotti's whizz-bang and dazzle. He would rather his words were heard than squibs and fireworks. He has lost a brother to those same wars. He urges the King to go to his troops. He should be out in the field; he should come out of his retreat and fight; he should be with his armies so that they can see his majesty and be led by him; Planet King, where is your warmth, your light shining? On waste ground; on empty woods; on sacrificial boars led onto the end of your lance; on the glorious field of victory that your bed is ... he doesn't write this but everyone knows it, however thoroughly the King repents he's still at it, and God punishes him for it, the King himself knows it: he is the soul of his country, and it's all his fault—

— and another note under the King's napkin, a whole satire in verse snuck under there; the King is Great, it says—like a Hole can be Great: the Emptier it is, the Greater it gets. The whole world sliding into that great big nothing. They say it was the short-sighted poet, that sharp and bitter man. No proof that he wrote it. But he hasn't been around much; he spends most of his time in his own place south of the city, and he sits among his books, reading, communing with the dead, listening with his glassed eyes to their advice and their advice is that they have none to give and they can't be of help. He writes hard satires of the courtly world he was briefly admitted to. He writes cruel words about the valido that favoured him for a while when it suited; has he anyone else to blame though, he likes to make himself difficult, he sees it as a vocation. He writes: fancy-dressed poverty; gold is poison; blond dirt. He circles the grave with his pen and the page grows blacker, he leaves his hourglass unturned, lets the hours pass uncounted, I do not wish them marked he writes and he sits reading and it sits unrunning and he is glass and dust.

The poet makes the mistake of coming into the city; they fetch him from a friend's house in the night, in his nightshirt, shivering, half-blind without his glasses and afraid of the dark now though he's spent his career writing out of, about, and into it. And after all those figurative prisons he's built, he can't write his way out of this one—

But still, the King admires a good line, and looks out from his fortress, from his grand house, from his palace, and thinks of it often, the poet's warning, more and more often: palaces are sepulchres. For an idle prince.

XIII

Las hilanderas/
Spinners

The Queen advises her husband that he should go to war, now. Everything's flying apart at the edges, chaos spreading, Catalonia, Portugal, Andalusia, the ongoing mess in the north, the Netherlands ... In the Netherlands, they hear, the Cardinal-Infante is exhausted. Is sick. Is vomiting bile. Is poisoned they say maybe. Is dead. His brother—— is dead. The Queen offers comfort—steady, wise, faithful Isabel, always standing by her King—— or just now supine, by her King, here in the Queen's chamber— and she says, go.

The Prime Minister would advise against his going to war, he thinks, he mumbles into the pillow, knowing they have said all this already; in the past that has been the Count-Duke's recommendation, that the King should keep safe in Madrid; the Count-Duke says ... The Queen raises herself on one elbow, motions out with one hand beyond the curtained bed for attendance— Husband, she says, the Prime Minister has, no doubt, your interests at heart. He has been a constant steward of your reputation and your honour all these years, and has ensured that you are seen as the just and faithful King I know you are. By all means, have another portrait painted. But also, it's no good, just being seen—you must act, now; you must *do*.

He has been spending more time in the Queen's chamber, of late; they have just one son, although he tries not to think about it this way; and often they talk late into the night and through the morning like this; and these days he doesn't so often seek out other diversions in the afternoons, he must conserve his energy, he is often tired, these days, although not all days, still, still he can't help himself some days, and at dawn with his wife he prays in their private chapel, they pray quietly together and he atones and she knows this, and the Count-Duke is not so much a feature of his early mornings— or his afternoons.

Her attendants, making quiet morning noises beyond this curtain, wake them from the barest sleep. They were talking into the early hours, murmuring of it, what must we do; it's time to go to war now, she said; no, now it's time to sleep; but in the morning . . . and dreams of war and battle dress, of borders, walking across borders, walking the canvas boundary of the hunt, dreams of his brother hunting, his brother some-where, lost in the woods somewhere, dreams of a shrouded woman who had found him, who would lead him to where she'd found him, dreams of a clearing, of her sickle cutting, of sickness, of her scythe . . . now it's morning and though he's barely slept on it, barely the briefest respite, troubled by these dreams of threatened borders— now waking the King wakes into this same preoccupation, worry, grief, with barely a second of suspended liberty between dream and waking; and waking, a woman beside him, again— has he—— the relief, it is his wife the Queen, no sin; and then the same conversation con-tinuing, the Queen saying, it's time now, and he remembers. Gather yourself. Go to Catalonia and quell that rebellion, too close to home for comfort. Rally your troops.

And where *are* all the King's creatures these days? And

where are his loyal cohorts? La Corte is so quiet, nowadays, since the war broke; where are they all hiding? Where are your valido's creatures? The grandees are all occupied, invisible, or unwell, come down with summer colds suddenly, retreated to the wainscot. They have grown too much accustomed to comforts, comfits, cushions. They are all expert huntsmen but the hunt is only a rehearsal for war and it seems they've all got stage fright, now; he's tried cajoling, appeals to honour; bribes, even, which sometimes work, to their dishonour, but also to his own ...

Felipe sighs, rolls onto his stomach. He should go, now, she says, and shame them with his example. Yes, he says, and feels her cool hand on his head, a cool weight on his crown. She says, On your way you should visit Ágreda and meet with the visionary abbess there and maybe pray with her, because you will be in need of God's grace, and maybe seek her counsel, because it seems you're in need of it, and if mine is not enough for you I think she'll back my corner. The Queen receives her chocolate from beyond the curtain and says go, go see Sor María; and then go to war. Lead your troops, as King Louis does (speaking, or not speaking, of shaming by example). I'll hold the fort.

⚜

In the north of the country a boy with black hair sees his future in the swallows and it is high and soaring and clever and quick and as he's always known, maybe, he is not just another clever schoolboy like his schoolfellows, those other bastards—he's the son of a king.

The King has his heir but needs a safeguard, in case of ... in case. The Queen remains unpregnant. The boy will be needed, the King foresees; he is going to need smart and loyal generals in the coming years— and the Netherlands without a governor, since his brother—— his brother ... since his brother.

The Queen graciously welcomes this new little knight, Don Juan José, to the court—he's made the new Grand Prior of the Order of St John at the age of just thirteen. Stitches him a sash perhaps and lays it over his shoulder and lays a hand on it and assures the boy that he'll be honoured as his namesake the Emperor's bastard was honoured before him, that he'll be her valued advisor, and a valued companion to her daughter, and a valued advisor to the heir, her son.

The Grand Prior's mother, his real mother, whom he doesn't remember, sits on her little stage, her little dais, her little throne at the window; mistress of half-lit shadows; her red hair growing dull in the dimness, though she is not so old; there is no sunlight to warm and shine her. Sits on her chair and watches from the window of her private palace for no one coming, and no one comes. She keeps within as he has asked her, keeps quiet as he has asked her, all these years, forsaking the stage and forsaking her son and friends fall away and these days, no one comes. Once her voice was heard by every cavalier and gallant in the city, her voice thrown out to the sky in the theatres slung between houses that she can't bring herself to visit now. Hardly going out and hurrying through the streets when she has to, unwilling to hear words written for her out of other women's mouths, wanting to cry them out over the heads of the audience from the back— over all their foolish over-dressed hairstyles— over the heckles and cat-calls over the thin simper of the girl who takes her part; wanting to yell out so that they all can hear the years of confine-ment in the tarnish of her once-golden voice; and fearing it, this urge, this noise rising unstoppable up to the top of her throat, clamping her teeth against it swallowing it back like bile or long-forgotten giddiness; keeping her eyes to the slops of the streets and not looking up. The terrible desire to be recognised, and the horror at the thought of it, laughed out of the hen-basket, cupped hands over stage whispers, La Calderona, there she goes, the King's whore, or once was.

So she mostly stays indoors. All that she needs is brought to her. They bring her food, she assumes, since she seems to still be living, presumably she puts it in her mouth and chews and swallows, but this must occur in the blank automatic hours of her existing and she feels herself to be stomachless, the once-stretched skin a little loose over nothing, fine silver trails still leave their trace where her belly was distended and would testify to what is gone, to what was taken, if she were to examine it, if anyone were to see it, were to see her skin, her hip bones beneath the skin, her red hair fading growing limp and thin. She avoids mirrors and prefers to undress in the dark.

She lives in untaxed luxury, in peace, in an elective hush; unheard, unvisited, unused, uncourted, unseen, unseen at her window, by the half-drawn curtain. Her heart's secret buried in a living tomb. That was her line once.

And now, she hears, unwilling to listen but the gossip of this city will insinuate through any opening left unguarded, the girl that brings clean linen, the girl that tends the brazier, the girl that brings the fucking soup the endless sludgy river of it, the man that always lingers, still, her mangy stinking cur, his smell that she's grown used to; they all can't help themselves, all in turn dying to tell her that the King has owned his thing of darkness, this unknown knight with the black hair, that he is brought back from the north to la Corte; and furthermore she learns, she receives word that the King, in his kindness, has found a home for La Calderona in the country.

They cross paths, maybe; her son on his way to be owned and promoted and knighted and draped with honours; the actress maybe even grateful, by now, for a habit and a veil, for a costume to make sense of the life she's wound up in, like bindings round her still full breasts, like a shroud. Or maybe absolutely furious at the waste of it.

So she enters the cloister and becomes one of them, uniform; enfolded into their quiet order, into the quiet ennui of their afternoons. And, having no option, La Calderona grows accustomed to her hen-coop. I'm not what I appear, nor do I look like what I really am; this was her line. This is another costume, and she grows accustomed. Her red hair covered and shorn. She adjusts to their rituals, their rhythms; newcomers shifting to the same cycle. For a few days in the month the convent is perhaps more than usually quiet as they bite their tongues. They confess: I have had unkind, unsisterly thoughts, Father. I have wanted to snap or strike, I have dropped a needle and wept in the impossible attempt to rethread it, I have given in to this woman's weakness, this devil in my unused womb. The old ones know it, see it coming from afar in the scratchy tempers and the blemished oily skin. They see the novices' scowls, the sympathetic frowns, as they go about their prayers and chores, pressing a hand to the midriff, finding below the folds of fabric the indent of the pelvic bone and pressing; no help. It must be borne, borne for years until the ache and the strain of resisting this devil is gone. The reminder of sin. The old ones give thanks for its passing. La Calderona, still young, still bleeding, is made prioress only a few months into her arrival, and the old ones accept that, also, as they accept all precepts from the Lord, and she isn't envied by the young ones, either—— I don't think; she is admired, there, and makes alliances; I would like her to have that— Say of me just this, she recites to herself sometimes: that I was and am a woman. This was her line.

(In the brothels of la Corte, too, there are slow weeks for business, women penned together falling to the same synchronous magic and the same curse. They don't bite their tongues in the brothels; they drop things and swear out loud; they snap and snipe at each other and the youngest novices—who are, some of them, very young, but won't be novice for long—cry for being snapped at. There are some of their visitors who don't mind or prefer it, and although this is prohibited there are some establishments, with discreet back doors, which are willing to bend the law; easily taken for readiness, in and out in a minute, the poultice re-applied when he's out of the room and she'll re-join the others and laugh about it. They lie around eating the sweets the nicer clients sometimes bring them, groan and shift and work their jaws, snap at each other and laugh at their own self-pity. The boss, past such things, eats and pats her tummy, which is bloaty only with dried fruit, envying their tender-breasted swelling. Or else, like the old nuns, glad to be rid of it.)

✝

So the King—on his way to the front—makes time for a small diversion, to seek the advice of another abbess, unblemished, untouched by his sin. Seek the advice of Sor María, the Queen advised: the abbess who is blessed with visions, who has heard the word of the Mother, who has been lifted by God to visit with the ignorant peoples of the King's distant lands.

Sor María filled with light, light lifting her, translocated over the wide ocean, to a place above or between—between old Spain and new, between innocence and wisdom, her soul hangs embodied; and both there and here she brings the message she is given, given by the Mother and the angels, speaking in ribbons scrolling and twisting around her. She is but a vessel; a mouthpiece; a receiver; a hollow thing, nothing; unworthy, she is nonetheless chosen to receive, to speak, to write the story of the Mother of the Lord; they have told her— the Lord has, the Mother, the angels speaking ribbons— they have told her that the people are ready to receive this message, the news of the mysteries that have been hidden and must remain mysterious; because such is the nature of the word of God, which is light, which revealed in its entirety would blind us with infinite guessless wisdom. And yet although the meaning as she can receive and convey it and as we can comprehend it will be partial and earthly and flawed by mortal understanding, still it is worth the endeavour; she will strive to hear, and the people in turn will be rewarded by the endeavour to receive it. The first intimations at the edge of things, she knows, recognises them when they have arrived already, does not know their beginning because they are always, the mysteries, present in the hidden light that surrounds us, glimpses she is given, the hum of the words of light that are already there beyond hearing; the light that is wisdom that is everywhere always even when hidden in shadow.

The King has come to see her. A day's ride away from the front, they walk in the convent garden; a small well-tended garden, sun-lit; and he feels that this is what her soul must be. And his is all tangled, all dried out; sordid scrub and weeds. He asks her for guidance, he says his wife the Queen has told him that he should come to seek her wisdom. She protests she is unworthy, an unworthy vessel. She sits down on a stone bench and looks up at him, straight into the sun it seems, without squinting her eyes, as if she can take more light than the rest of us, and he admires this, her narrow cheeks, her dark lidded eyes admitting so much light. He sits down beside her, and there they sit, their two straight backs. She begins to speak. She tells him: she has been abbess here since her mother passed, years ago now; for years she has borne this duty. She tells him: her mother established this convent in their home, her mother and her father and she all took orders; they were always very devout, her parents, and when she was a child she felt it hard on her, sometimes, but then she was called— the light touched her, God's light— and they followed suit, all three of them took orders and then her mother died and she was young when she came to be abbess; she felt herself unworthy, she tells him. Not ready. Better suited to obey than to command. Can the King understand that? She had since she was a girl been troubled, with visions, and with terror and doubt; she would find herself in a strange land and appearing to the King's new subjects there and she has heard since that they heard her, that they saw her, she was at once visible in both places, there and here at once; she saw the earth from above, the vast expanse of sea below, and knew that her Lord had lifted her and yet was terrified, and because of that terror, that lapse in trust, she doubted her fitness for this task. And she has often made penance for these doubts, because this is the task she has been appointed. Does the King understand her? She has been afraid, she is sometimes still afraid, and she must remind herself that the Devil feeds fear, he stokes the dirty ashes of it and blows upon the embers; but if she can only obey then the obedience acts as a balm, as a cooling draught and cleansing pure fire that leaves no ash or smut behind, and she will emerge stronger, with the strength she draws from obedience to her duty; which is the strength of knowing she is not alone, *because* she owes that duty; and she understands now that to command is to obey her calling. And so she has striven to obey, to command, however discouraged, however unfit she thought herself and ill-prepared. Does he understand? And she has often petitioned her elders: she has asked that they mistrust her and question her accounts because the Devil must always be guarded against and he is an excellent mimic and it is incumbent upon us, all of us, to test all things, to question what seems received wisdom. Because even a vessel of the divine can become broken or cracked. So we must always invite this, this questioning, and we must be open always to wisdom, as we must be ready always to receive the Lord.

The King understands her. But where is he to turn for wisdom? His brothers dead. His court of incompetent cowards. His Prime Minister ... Who can he trust? And she tells him: since your wife has sent you to me I'll offer what wisdom I can—for what it's worth, from one so unworthy; and my counsel is this: above all, trust yourself. You are King; you alone. That is your burden and duty. And perhaps the time has come, now, for the King to govern alone. To come out from the shadows of la Corte and warm and shine. The Lord made only one sun.

The King says, Sor María, my wife tells me the same thing; and the nun smiles and nods and says, She sent you here to pray, I think. So he prays with her in the convent's small chapel, thinks perhaps of making a gift to them, a painting ... thinks of the nuns of San Placido and their Christ ... He prays and yet he struggles still, to find comfort in the word of God, which the nun has told him will outlast all, all of creation, from the endless stars to the last insect, from the firmament to the fingers of—— he finds it hard, still, to release the hands of the world, to pull himself from its grip, he is still in the grip of his flesh ... He says none of this but suspects that she knows, which makes him feel worse, and he longs for that fiery balm that she spoke of to soothe the itch and prickle of shame, fear, desire, despair, all these human sins he hides within his radiant skin.

The King leaves Sor María to her garden, and her writings, her correspondence, and her prayers. She has promised to pray for him. And to write to him. And to the Queen.

⚜

Louis the King of France (Isabel's brother and also brother-in-law), belly swollen and doughy, skinny, bunged up, diarrheic, wastes away quite suddenly, and dies. His five-year-old son (the King's nephew) takes the throne, and within days defeats Spain in battle at Rocroi, clever boy——— well no, his mother, Anne (the King's sister, and sister-in-law), as regent takes the throne; and France is now in the ascendant. Perhaps after all there may be more than one sun.

⚜

Felipe, sinking, returns to the city with his brother's body. He returns to the Queen and she tells him how things are, how it's been at la Corte. Rancid with rumours and conspiracy and lies. Rebellions flaring, as they are across the empire, fraying and fractious at its edges ... The King and his government are not well looked upon. And— whose fault is that? Who is it that's advised the King, for all these years, who was it that said 'Flanders first'? And see where that's got us ... If a strategy is failing, only a fool would say— it will work if we keep it up but do it more so. We are losing. And we are almost bankrupt. And your valido, he won't listen. That man—you must have noticed—he grows louder and fatter and stranger. She fears for their son and the influences upon him. The Count-Duke's wife is his governess; does this not worry the King? Sor María has asked the same question? Well then, he should take note of this. He should take care who he speaks to. She can advise him on that; she has, in his absence, made sure of certain loyalties; she has prayed daily for him and heard the prayers of others. What has Sor María advised? Well, she is a wise woman. And pious. Pious, wise men should heed the wisdom of pious women. The Queen has prayed for him daily.

The King writes often to Sor María. He asks for strength, asks for wisdom, asks that the nuns of Ágreda do penance for him, for his sensuality, still insatiable; for which we are all punished. She writes that penance first requires effort from the sinner. She reminds him of King David and his harem. He thinks of her dark eyes looking up at him, into the sun, seeing through him. She sees him, he thinks, she sees the shadow under his radiant skin; she reminds him of his duty, of his sin. He needs her for this, he needs her as he needs his other women; differently, but increasingly. And he needs his Queen. He must trust someone. He goes to her chamber at night and he prays, in the mornings, with her; at her urging, he makes himself ready to govern alone.

The Count-Duke, meanwhile, washed out, fading, ever more transparent even as he grows fatter, is always back and forth, between Alcázar and Retiro; there is so much to maintain there— strewing bird-feed, making omelettes probably, building huts to pray in, for no one to pray in, a few desultory friars who keep there. It has been too hot over there, these last years; and there's no money; and the King is sick of it and the Queen always hated it but still the Count-Duke comes to pray here; he continues, in the midst of all his duties, all his cares and woes and those of the country and the King, to come to the Retiro almost daily, and prays and trots through the grounds and sees that the trees are correctly planted, sees that the gardens are laid and shaped and thriving, this land that requires such constant care, that if left to its own ends will only drain and dry and crumble and the leaves wilt and the fruit shrivel and drop unripened to be supped at by disheartened wasps, and it takes all his attention to see that all is kept alive and in order, that his birds are well and laying.

He is often alone there. He retains staff to maintain it but they tend to avert their paths, to busy themselves, or just hide, when they see him coming, when they hear him coming, shouting all the time at no one, blundering, wheezing, scratching his pate because his damned wig itches, and no lotion he concocts can soothe it. And the trees, despite all his efforts, are dying. And the grass is dying. And the fish look bloated and float wrong and wonky and the water is all silting up. His heart hurts. Everything dust and mud. Rugs and curtains clouted up with spent ash. He sneezes, he coughs. There's a fire in the royal apartments, even though there's no one in them, no hearth lit there, how has it happened, he sees the smoke rising, an augury, he remembers those poems that were read when the hall was crammed with courtiers, what if fire, what if sickness, on contagious wings ... he calls for water, they dredge up silty water from the many ponds and channels, he oversees everything, shouting, itching, overheated, and the fire is extinguished and then there's cold mucky wet ash to clean out and some choice pieces of the King's collection, he regrets to inform, are ruined. He has the furniture covered. His head hurts all the time and his joints hurt. He's dizzy, often. There's no one in the kitchens, the stoves and pots are cold, carbon-gritted, fat-rimed. He is massive and starving and has no appetite.

The menagerie empties slowly. The peacocks trail their trains in the dirt and turn grim and vicious, squalling. Doña Ana dies, as birds do, little brittle hearts they have; the Count-Duke finds her one morning; or he is met at the entrance to the complex, a keeper brings her body, limp and long as a rubber chicken, and she is buried or baked. The Count-Duke mourns. Soldiers are dying now in the north of the country and in Flanders and further afield and in all corners their armies make ready for defeat or retreat; and the Count-Duke still insisting, Flanders first! and the north is now a haemorrhage and the country bled as pale as the over-taxed undernourished meat they feed on; and here in his own retreat, in the birdhouse he comes to for warmth, succour, relief—the warm soft breast of a hen in the hand, the low contented trusting clucking—even here death has found him out and Doña Ana's black eyes are gone dark now. The Count-Duke finds he hasn't time, these days, to gather eggs in the morning—

— First thing the valido is there in the King's chamber. Up for hours, or hasn't slept; just come from prayers, all night at prayer. Seeking strength, seeking guidance, seeking solace. And knowing his strength is going, he has written to the King. The King—— his prince, the prince he's served since he was a petulant boy, the boy he's shaped into a man, a king, taught him everything, gave him everything he had— is standing at his console at the window, dressed already and expecting him, at this early hour; his draped bed as yet unmade, the curtained smell of sleep, a sweet foetid air of the night just passed still close in the room, but the King already risen, having had no need of his valido, to fetch his shirt, to call for a barber, to ready him for the day. This cloying close air, here; something anxious in it; something sick; it's him, maybe; something corrupt which must be purged. He has bathed, he has prayed, he sweats into his new shirt and defies the itch his scalp is screaming. He has come for his answer. He hesitates before the basilisk King— radiant, weary prince—and lowers himself to one swollen knee, unsteadily, steadying himself for a moment with one swollen hand to the floor, not quite falling, he lowers his head and coughs into his cheeks with jaw clamped closed and a little wet explosion spittles his lips, the blood in his temples beats and pounds. The King says get up, cousin. Stand up. No need for that, now. So the valido— the King's faithful servant— raises himself, painfully, can't raise his head, can't believe and knows what is coming now, blood swims dark behind his eyes and sounds a loud knell in his temples. The King holds out a paper and the Count-Duke recognises his own broken seal, his own broken signature scrawling the bottom of the page—— the King says, You have been our most faithful servant.

He knew and yet didn't expect this. His skull itches and pounds.

The King says, It is with regret that we accept your request.

Señor. (His broken name, a scrawl, is that his own signature, that mad imploring scrawl?)

Take it, the King says. I have no need to hold on to it. No need to share it with anyone. I'll make it known. Go home, cousin. Go back to your country. South, isn't it? You've told me often how peaceful it is there, how little time you have had for it. I hope you find it so. Peaceful.

The valido still can't raise his face to the King's cold pity, he is shaking, his hand as he takes the paper tremors, he stuffs and fumbles it into his doublet between two buttons so it smothers his hard-beating bilious heart. This foetid sweet air. His head still bowed he reaches for the King's hand to kiss it. The King, without moving, withdraws himself. He won't be touched. You may retire now, he says. And the Count-Duke retires from the room. Remember, Prince, how I kissed your pot, and carried it from the room for you? This man wearies me, you said.

The valido leaves the room and retires to the country, where he keeps dogs, and is mostly alone with his dogs, barking back at them. He tends his garden; he experiments with cuttings and imported seedlings, he devises schemes for irrigation. He makes study of the elements, he extracts ore, he melts and smelts and boils and cools. He invites the Chief Secretary to visit him in his exile and long into the night, they say, the pair of them are at their alembics. There have long been rumours about the Secretary— there in the shadows the whole time. For years there have been rumours— they say he's an alchemist, a magician, they say he has the King under his spell; and then there's those persistent rumours about the convent of San Placido and the nuns there ~~and the King~~—

They've been saying this stuff for years while the Secretary has been safe in the impenetrable shadow of his offices; but now that the Count-Duke is gone they are stripped from him. He is brought into the light of the Inquisition—God's light—and his sin is rightly punished and he vanishes into prison, absorbed at last into darkness.

The Count-Duke's librarian comes to visit the painter. Brings him a gift of a book, perhaps. They are old acquaintances, out of Seville; the librarian was witness at the painter's wedding. The painter offers refreshment and they sit by the brazier and wait for it to come, the painter turning pages; then drinks arrive and they sip a little; the painter clears his throat and asks, What will you do now?

The librarian shrugs. He can find some other place, some-where. Some private house maybe. There are always other libraries. Everyone has books these days. No cause for concern on his account. But what about the painter? The librarian asks in turn, What will *you* do now? Wasn't he your patron?

He was, the painter says. He once was. But I've been in the King's service for ... twenty years now. He has no cause to doubt my loyalty, whatever his doubts of the Count-Duke. (The painter is now Chamberlain to the King's Private Chambers; a role that brings him yet closer to the King and his various needs and dependencies, which brings him access to other doorways—rooms, closets, wardrobes; which brings more responsibilities; which brings no more salary. And then, pro-moted again, to Assistant Superintendent, which means a bit more of the same. Perhaps fancier hats.)

Of course, says the librarian. Look at de Haro, anyway— even the Count-Duke's nephew survives on his own merits; it seems he's next in line, the new valido—— Prime Minister, I should say. What do you think? He seems a safe pair of hands. Capable. Honourable. And, as you say, loyal.

The painter sips, nods, non-committal, thinking of his patron—— his former patron. The strange quiet of the court without the presence of him.

Not even loyalty, was it really, in the end, says the librar-ian. It was reputation, above all, wasn't it. It was a matter of perception. Competence. Sanity. Wasn't quite right, in the end.

The painter recalls him, the massive bulk of his back, his shoulders, his forehead; his tireless working. The sheer massive corporeal presence of him.

Still, they agree. For all his bombast and crazy and misguided scheming. Still, they agree. The poor man.

An idea for a painting: women spinning. The homes of women interest the painter, the solid objects and the movement in them. The spaces in which they cook, sit, serve, spin. Winding, weaving, cutting thread; pulling together tighter wheel to reel; they are working as ever fast and patient and steady, the spinners; circles in circles, reel to wheel; it's about women and what they do within walls and how their hands move, how the movement of their hands moves down and up through arms, neck, shoulders, back, hips, calves, and all the body, all the body spinning.

XIV

Truhanes/
Jesters and rogues

Here in Fraga with the King's entourage, the painter has set up a makeshift studio. Through a widened window frame they come to see the celebrity painter— yes, he is that now— they come to watch him at work, the painter to the King.

The King as general, come to Saragossa to appear before his troops. The King out of black, radiant in battle dress red white and gold. Here he is commemorated, against the dark grey ground, surveying the troops, luminous, shining on them, looking out upon them from—

— oh—

— but his eyes—

— Oh, heavy years upon him— His hooded shadowed eyes. Hollow temples, hollow sockets, heavy jaw— the painter sees and shows the years upon him, the weight of them. The painter believes in— what? In setting down the world as he sees it, as it passes; as everything passes. Including the smir and dazzle of silver-gold thread, the stitching, the broidered red coat; including sword at side, staff and hat in his hands, in command; all this on the periphery as you meet his eyes, these dark and hooded eyes. The King looking back at the artist, back at the troops, back at us the audience peering through the widened window as he comes into being, the usual quarter profile, the familiar stance, the usual sidelong eyes—oh, how they've fallen into shadow. The care that crosses the brow, pulling at the corner of the lids, deepening pale grey shadow etched out of his temple, under the thin fair skin; the skull under the skin—

This shade of care against the dazzle, this show of truth: he is staunch, your King, he is dedicated; it says majesty, sincerity, command. The King says— Good—we'll have it sent to the Queen. Isabel will rule with my image alongside her. Everyone she gives audience to will see: here I am out in the field, in my battle dress; her pride will inspire pride, her assurance will reassure them. To think of her gives me strength, he says. Now that we govern together, alone.

It says I am here; I was here. The King immobile stares back at himself.

I remember, he says, when you first came to me. When you painted me in an afternoon; when everyone was watching and you saw only me, it seemed; when you saw me as no one else was willing to. As a man; as a young man, as I must have been, though I don't know that I knew it.

The King stares back into his own immobile stare. Yes, you saw me; you still see me, he says. I thank you, Diego.

He stares. He says, Look at me. Look at my eyes. Is that how my eyes are?

He says . . . Well, good. Perhaps—I would like to go unseen for a while, I think. Perhaps you might find some other subject. Find some other knave, some other rogue, some other fool—

Such as—— El Primo, who is maybe a knave and rogue but no fool. He is an official of the court, the King's rubber-stamper, he stamps the King's signature upon the many papers that pass through his small precise official hands. He is here in Fraga to perform this duty, here in Fraga with his big book, bearing the stamp of the King with him. El Primo, which means the cousin—as the King calls anyone of rank—is part of the inner circle, and so feels entitled to look down upon the other dwarves, who serve as jesters, buffoons, entertainers. No, he's no fool. He took a bullet for the Count-Duke, once, a year or two ago. When the Count-Duke was still around and worth having a shot at.

The painter sees: El Primo's quick capacity; and pride in it; disdain in it. El Primo's grey gaze and a grey ground, the grey mountains laid in already, grey clouds. An illegible block of grey for the text on the page of the huge book he holds—his smallness makes it huger. Around him the stuff of his office: papers, glue-pot, loose-leaf ledger, pages bent back, each separate white page bright there against the grey, the black. He wields the King's mark.

Load the brush for the blackness of his hat. The painter rains excess paint onto the grey sky above him, black swipes like brimstone falling—— shoulders shaping lower, lower; excess off; an exercise in restraint, El Primo's dignified restraint. Encased in the black of the court from shoe to neat black sock to high hat-brim.

Swipes, swipes and loads and swipes—— shoulders narrower, lower—— higher, the hat—— the precise outline of the mass of his black hat— high brimmed— high crowned, and the forehead high below it. In the background the mountains. Pages I'd like to flip through. The smell of glue-pots. Of bindings, of book spines. White page ready for stamping. Ready for a mark. Prepare a grey ground. Clean off your brush.

☦

Back in Madrid, Isabel governs with her husband in his battle dress beside her. She wonders, perhaps, sometimes, what he's up to, how he's taking to life as a soldier, where he takes his soldier's pleasures; or not. Prays for him. Perhaps misses him, looks to his image and consults it and looks forward to his return, or is quite content to run things, quite capable, with her women about her. In the autumn she grows tired and one more—patient, cowled, cold—draws close, to attend her.

Back in Madrid it's winter, and quiet in la Corte; doors kept closed and curtains drawn against the draught; the grandees all slunk back to their estates to avoid being enlisted, or sitting around forming spiritless factions, writing forgotten verses; since there's no parties or tilting, there's not much to do anyway; a skeleton crew of grooms rides the remaining horses in circles to keep them in trim; and in summer war's the only theatre, and no feast but field rations, and each winter, the King returns from the front, a little older, another heavy year upon him, in his eyes.

Back in Madrid, the painter's studio is at work making copies of the Prince in the riding school, to be sent out as gifts for his father's allies—see how as a child he was already fitted, already in practice for war: there's the Prince, as he was then, a little more solid perhaps—— and where the Count-Duke stood on hand to serve the little Prince's every need there is only a blank wall. As if he was never there. The painter complicit in this reworked history, although having no direct hand in it. (The ghost of the Count-Duke in the first version continues to efface.)

And the painter, back at court, having no official commission and time on his hands in the King's absence, takes him at his word and seeks out the truhanes, the jesters, the fools. The men of pleasure, so they call them; the men of the court who are employed to entertain and distract and beguile; to tumble and riff and reveal a truth made palatable with a punchline. They are small, some of them, and some of them twisted or turned inward, and some of them are kept as companions to the children and some are perpetual children themselves; they are dressed up as soldiers; they are cleverly expert in rhetoric; they are funny at punning; they are clowns and acrobats; they are whatever the court finds novel, they are at the mercy and whim of a court with little outlet otherwise for caprice. They are someone to love, if you long to show affection; something to dote on, like a loved dog; something to poke fun at and play jokes on. They are confidantes and punchbags. They are always present, they have been here all along, in nursery and chamber and dining rooms, seated on a stool and ready to give pleasure. And they are still here, even in these times when there's little time to take it; waiting to be called upon, and not much acknowledged— except by the painter.

He observes—— he sees them. And the court as they see it; the world as they see it. This unquiet shadow-world of instabilities—the fools know that nothing's solid and consensus can't keep us forever from chaos—he inhabits it. He too can be anywhere, unobtrusive. Watching. Let the eyes soften, unfocus. Let the brush feel the softness of fabric folding, rumpling; let attention soften into the folds. Soft, soft. Soften the edges of this sheltered world, this lash-fringed world; open your mouth to it. Let your lips part. Let the muscles of your jaw soften, so long clamped shut. Let your tongue lie heavy. Silent. Let your limbs soften and fall; let your brush fall softly. Attend, but

gently. Light falls on the hands, brush falling lightly. Light on
the soft cheek and chin——

— Calabazas sits upon his bare stage, clasping his gourd and
smiling: there he is, sitting in a huddle in a crouch squatting,
one knee pulled up folded under holding his knee hugging it;
look how the gourd at his side set down has the shadow of a
flagon it's the same it's one or the other it's both it is not so
solid as you might expect of an object; smiling, grinning, half-
laughing. Looking somewhere past him somewhere elsewhere,
gaze diffuse, all clouded a mind clouded high and wide as sky.
He looks past the painter; his eyes wander to the window where
swallows fly and fall and he watches; swallows; oil of swallows
will clear the eyes, the apothecary says, and yet he cannot see,
cannot count them ... apothecary says the oil of swallows
taken before wine will act as prophylactic so you'll keep sober
no matter how much wine you swallow ... he gulps with gullet
open. Are you missing your gourd? It is here, Calabazas, and
he feels it set gently into his hands and hugs it but no, it isn't
thirst— it is a pun, you see, swallow swallow, the swallows,
I swallow, I will not bite and they will fly straight down
and circle in my stomach, open my mouth wide as a-a-aaah
casement and they'll fly straight in and I'll swallow, swallow,
swallow, you see haha a pun Don Diego— Only a dream, you
may say— but then what is only a play, only a poem, only a
painting, even? Calabazas smiles; and the painter loves him for
it; the charming blur of his smile—— and I love you for this,
Diego; for seeing it— and then——

— See Lezcano in the landscape his Prince hunts in;
Lezcano grown out of the nursery now, his rattle discarded,
his boy's dress put off, a grown man in a small country suit.

Out in the countryside, out in the mountains, out in the grey landscape, the grey ground. A blue lake in the distance. A thought in the distance. Out here in the mountains, a hermit in his shelter. The painter has a landscape he can call upon, a backdrop ready to go, and needn't leave the confines—— the comfort— of his studio to recall it. Same old grey mountains of the Guadarrama. La Maliciosa, over in the distance.

Contemplating something, Lezcano, lips parted and eyes unfocused, half-closed. Sock half-shuffled off like a mortal coil. Snakes in the mountains, maybe. His built-up shoe. His rumpled shirt. The blunt bulb-shine of his nose. The blank of his looking, half-seeing. Half-see him. Half-consciously holding his cards. Not a pose you'd hold long—not like El Primo, posing—a moment, half a moment, speaking or about to, head thrown back, half-open lips— half-closed lids— watching through half-closed eyes. The painter sees, this half-seeing. Sees the good clothes rumpled; Lezcano lets his sock fall. Imagine! To let a sock slip down, unashamedly. To go about unstarched, ankle bared to the world, and feel no dishonour in it; feel nothing of the indignity of a wrinkled sock. And be loved; and still be loved.

Here are no solid objects—— something in his fingers, loosely held— hard to see— hard to grasp. The feel of worn cards—— worn cards waxy under fingertips, oil of your fingers leaving traces and blending with the oil of others' skin, whoever has dealt this deck before you, who has played this deck, how will your hand fall out? Lezcano once played with the Prince; but the Prince will shortly put his games aside. If you could pick a card, any card, what might that mean then; is there a trick to it. King or knave or jester. A club to swing at boars and bulls, to beat the dogs of Hell with. A diamond to

adorn a sacred saint's heart. A heart that aches or loves or, just
an organ, pulses. A spade to dig a grave with—

See? Do you? Well then? Sitting for the painter, Sebastián
is asking, with his fists balled in his lap: What do you see,
painter? A jester? He is that, yes, he can be. Look at him, and
the Prince's dwarf looks right back. His eyes don't wander,
nor his thoughts. He's a prince's companion and he doesn't
joke around; unless the Prince is in the mood for jesting.
Dark, dark eyes and— the painter sees and catches— a canny
light in them. Full dark beard, thick dark hair and sharp dark
darts of moustache and looking out under thick dark brows,
the seriousness belied by the deep-grooved cheek, the trace
of his smile, of a wryness he sees there. Serious, sincere, but
not excessively earnest. A good companion for a boy—— but
barely a boy, now; a comrade, a clown, a wingman for a young
man. The Prince grown tall, furring on his mercifully good
chin; Sebastián wears the very fine cast-offs he's grown out
of. Red, for a change; a bright flame-red cape in the darkness,
against the dark grey ground. Cuffs, collar and cape—finer
than yours, painter. Scarlet and silk and lace? What of it? Ask
the Prince if a law's been broken.

The painter sees the long work that's gone into that fine
Flanders lace—— flecked onto the sleeve in seconds.

The Prince, idly wondering if the painter's nearly done. The
Prince idling about, straying from the corner where his father
likes to sit, watching Sebastián watching and being watched.
His gift of the cape is coming out nicely. You like it, Diego?
You must get bored of all this black. The Lord knows I do,
sighs the Prince. He comes to the painter's side, to scruti-
nise. Yes, you've caught him—Sebastián's very essence—how
quickly he's appearing! You've made him very handsome— but

he is, though, I know, you're not a flatterer. Who would care
if you failed to flatter a dwarf, though? I suppose you'd mind,
wouldn't you, Sebastián. Do you like to be handsome? You do,
actually, don't you; you're quite proud of it. Diego sees that, too.
Why do you hide your hands? I'm sure it makes life easier for
our painter. Hands are hard, aren't they? My drawing master
has been teaching me—your son-in-law, Diego, of course. I
like him very much.

The Prince peers closer while the painter steps away to load
his palette. This lace is just smears and daubs, isn't it. Diego,
aren't you clever.

How do you like his suit? Country green—like Sancho
Panza's. Oh, Sebastián, don't take umbrage. I know you're not a
fool. Only a truhán. Aren't you? A rogue? It follows, doesn't it,
that if you're Sancho, I'm his master. A mad knight. Deluded.
I'm to be a hero, don't you know. I'm to go with my father this
summer to war. In two weeks, we're leaving. And then when
we've won I'll come home and marry my cousin Mariana. She's
only ten. You painted her mother, my aunt, Diego. Was she
pretty? She's pretty in your portrait— and we know you don't
flatter. They say my cousin's like her. So I'm to marry my pretty
young cousin, once the war's won.

The Prince upends a copper basin, dons his helmet. And
later I'll be king. He pulls a long, mournful face and is suddenly his father, his father's sad countenance. Is it so funny,
Sebastián? So hard to believe?

He sets down the basin, pings the rim of it to hear it ring.
Come, let's go out to the yard and tilt, he says. Let's go tilt at
windmills. Let's go play soldiers. I'm going to war! (The Prince
is wired. Too much chocolate.) Let's put on our gear— you've
got your red cape on, I'll wear mine— and go out on the town,
like they say my father used to ... Let's find some women to

be chivalrous at. Let's stay out till we're quite, quite mad with love; oh let's stay up all night, let's push against the dark until it's light again— and then we'll go to bed at dawn and it will all have been a dream. I'm up for anything. Aren't you, Sebastián? Let's go see a play. Let's light torches. Let's write verses. Let's put masks on. Let's go dancing. Let's round up my troops, all the stupid boys and groomsmen who hang around this place, all the lads who aren't afraid of the dark, anyone who'd rather come carousing than stay in bed with blankey. Let's go into the woods. Let's swim in the fountains. Let's do all the things a hero should, and all the things a prince can—which is anything I like. Right? Ha, ha! I'm joking, yes, of course. Yes, I really am deluded.

He's back at the painter's side. Picks up a spare dry brush; wields it at his dwarf. En garde! Shall we have some swordplay, later? Have I told you? I made out my will today, and you're to have my sword, Sebastián. Two of them, actually; one to hunt with and one for dressing fancy.

He stands at the painter's side, mimics his stance.

Sebastián, a good model, doesn't take his eyes from the painter's. Thank you, Señorito. How do I look, then? he asks the Prince.

Superb, the Prince says. Diego really is clever. You look like yourself. Are you pleased? You'll have the two swords, and a dagger, and some other silver bits ... so you'll think of me, when you're out hunting and swaggering with your new friends, once I'm gone. So you'll remember me. He pulls the mournful face again.

Of course I'm joking. I'm not going to die.

The Prince doodles in the air, on his palm, with the brush. I did make my will today, though, he says quietly.

They leave again for Saragossa, tomorrow: the grandees who've been talked or bought into it; the King; the Prince. On their way, the Prince is to be sworn in as heir to Navarre; he is already heir to Castile, to Aragon, to Valencia, his father's kingdoms; he is sixteen—a soldier, a man, a husband soon; leaving behind a child's pleasures. A noble prince, with noble plans. Tonight, then, a celebration—a rare party, in these days—and at the Prince's request, the men of pleasure are invited to dine. A last release.

Lezcano, Calabazas, Don Antonio el Inglés, Sebastián, Don John—rumpled, wandering in smiles and lost, proudly plumed, smart, deferent—Pablillos even, in charge of the others; in the clear diction of an actor or a noble he acts as their host's proxy: drink up, drink it down, as your King has invited you; raise your glass to the Prince and to victory! They take their seats at a low table within sight of all the grandees and the King's household and the Queen's. This is an unheard-of treat—a kindness—a night off of sorts; no jibes or taunts or brickbats, so it seems; no need to perform; a relaxation of the endless exhausting calculation, the placement of each phrase upon an axis: amusing, apposite, appropriate, acceptable. No need to put on voices or put on airs, no need to make gestures or faces, no need for wise witticisms or asinine asides, no need, in short, to play the fool, and so despite their hats and caps, and despite their differences, they take their places and they drink together, and their glasses are bottomlessly filled from the dark-robed shadows, and Calabazas clutches onto his gourd, which is his and belongs to him, and drinks from one hand to the other from his cup and from his gourd alternately and his gourd too is magically refilling like a flagon from a fable. And the nobles all around them are indulgent, genial, inviting them to drink! drink up! A toast to the Prince! To victory!

And the men of pleasure are at leisure, laughing, lolling, besting each other and buffing shoulders and toasting, and the night is bottomless and bright with candles and cups and gold and silver thread, and the glitter of faceted glass, of glazed ceramic and suckling fat; platters and the dishes and the cruets and the salvers and the salt cellared in silver ships sailing in fleets down the centre of the tables and the carafes and the cups, the cups, the endless cups, and as if these last lean years of lack had been only a dream, the feast is endless—the ladling of garlic soup; the shoals and shoals of silver fish, butterflied and buttery; the flock of capons, ducks, pigeons, quails, their ghosts flown to an endless aviary in the afterlife leaving crisp and succulent corpses behind them; the larded lamb, the tongues of oxen mute and resting heavy on their silver palates; and the costly scents of spices, of saffron, of chocolate, shipped from the Americas, and the grapes and the oranges and plucking of seeds from pomegranates, the almond confections and sticky honeyed fruit and cakes, and with every course another cup. Every last scullery cupboard, every last store, every last river and nest and hide in every last corner of woodland has been scoured out.

And just as it ever was, every plate has its vetting and its ceremony; each course commencing with a bated wait to see, will
it pass muster. It becomes a sort of game to watch the spoon-
ful of soup, the morsel of meat pass the taster's lips (spoon,
fork, lips, never trembling), and the roll of the gullet and the
waiting, the watching—a temptation for a jester, a missed
opportunity, for gagging, spittle, foam, gkk ggkk clutching
with bugged eyes, but they have the night off and are busy
drinking—and the physician is sober and staid and isn't dead
yet, even by midnight when sweets are brought out and the
Prince is calling for a top-up of wine for himself and the fools.

And the men of pleasure are all lit up, laughing, buffeting,
bullying, and to better each other they start to squawk and
mimic, they are gaping fish, they are clucking capons, pigeons,
quails, baa! they are lambs and bruuuh they are bulls! And their
table in this close-set hall seems to have some space about it,
as if a little stage has been left for them; and Calabazas knows
there always is one; he thinks himself sometimes upon a stage
and looks about and sees beneath his feet the boards of it,
and he smiles; his vagrant thoughts evade him, wandering
askance with his astigmatic eyes; the world is dim and bright
and blurry, and sweetly swimming with wine— Calabazas
hugs his gourd and they pull at it and he pulls back and they
let go suddenly and he totters and tumbles from his stool and
some of the grandees laugh; so they all do it, all the fools on
an unspoken signal tumble back and roll and stand, some not
so steadily, some stumbling, and a dandy in a fancy suit bats
Antonio on the bottom and the stocky English dwarf flaps a
hand to mouth with widened eyes and turns his haughty head,
an expert coquette, and now they're all laughing. And someone
shouts, who can spin most prettily? And a few of them start
to pirouette and then a handkerchief is waving for a prize, or

as if for a bull, and they run and snort towards it and fall all over and how the nobles laugh. What else will they do? Top up their glasses! More wine! Calabazas, up from the floor lad, fill thy gourd! Calabazas smiles— Be merry, master, he says; be merry, my masters, while merry-make you may—day will follow this night, but night follows day . . .

XV

Desengaño/
Disillusion

Recall, if you will, gentlemen, the last decade's enchantments. Recall Circe in her chamber. Recall the revels and the pageants. Recall the boy and his bull; you recall that golden youth? Recall if you will, if you can bear it, how golden your own youth was, how enchanted. How thrilling, all those costumes, all those guises. A veil just barely parted, the wink and flitter of a lady's left eye. What's left of it all, now? Where are your costumes? Stuff for moths to crop, for mice to make homes of. Nothing but poor fabrics, rags. Recall that beggar dressed as a king. (Pablillos spreads his cloak to his sides and it is, indeed, looking worn and a little moth-eaten, and he's coming to resemble those philosophers he mimicked.) The veils will be lifted to show, underneath— what, do you think, gentlemen? The end of the world, they say, will be a great unveiling— *apocalipsis*, gentlemen. And ladies. Recall the nymph Calypso who kept Odysseus hidden. What's beneath the veil, then? Just skin, like anybody. Flesh, bones, like anybody. Let the light of truth fall upon us all, gentlemen, ladies (Pablillos reveals his ankles to curtsey, makes a weary attempt at a simper, his heart's not in it). Now is the time of unveiling. Now the veil of enchantment is lifted.

An enchantment is a lie, gentlemen; a deception. Let go of your enchantments. They are illusions. An illusion has no substance; it's a trick of the light. Choose, instead, the truth of disillusion. Desengaño. Life is a dream, if our playwright will permit me to remind you.

This stuff. These rags we're so glad of. These hangings hiding bare walls, covering these flimsy barriers of stone we build around us, against the vastness of it; but we've bricked it in with us, we've only closed walls around it, made chambers to contain it and then gilded them—that is, nothing, gentlemen. Empty air. Black atoms and shadows. No matter what matter we paper and gild these walls with, no matter what furnishings we drag and angle and shove through the doorways to sit on, to dine at, to fill up with knick-knacks, no matter how we shelve and carpet and furnish, we never fill aught but a fraction of that emptiness.

In short—do you understand?—it's all going to ground— to the grave— to shit— and always has been.

So face it bravely, gentlemen; be disenchanted. Behind and beneath everything: nothing.

Nothing but the grey ground.

Pablillos lays down his hand, reaches to the floor in a bow, and his enervated audience barely glance over. Pablillos, fevered, lays his cape aside. Exposed, unveiled. He has known she is coming; he has felt her coming closer, felt her relentless presence, in his own small chamber but everywhere else, also, in every procession and every performance; at table when he entertains; seated alongside the Queen, taking an empty throne—a dark unperceived double, reigning over them all. Pablillos knows her coming, sees her form beyond the dim veil covering his sight; pushes it aside, lets all fall, goes into the dark and the cold beyond it.

The King, returned from war, goes to his private chapel, alone, so that no one can hear the prayers he fails to offer; so that no one can hear the sin of his angry silence, his despair. He sits at his desk at his papers, rigid, numb. He writes to Sor María of his grief; of his almost unbearable grief. What is he to do with it? It is, he writes, the greatest defeat of his life, this grief—and he is at present much defeated, he returns from war a defeated man. What is he to do? Hourly—from one moment to the next—what is he to do with his heart, his face, his hands? His well-trained immobility is now a refuge—to move would be absurd. He has people as always to clothe and feed him and without them he might die, shiver or starve to death, because to do these things—dress, eat—is absurd. Everything is awkward and foolish on him; the wearing of gloves is a nonsense, the hat on his head feels ridiculous to him. Obscene, somehow, that he should wear a shirt and comb his hair and shave and eat soup when they are—— when his wife, his sister, his heir—— it can't be undone— he is going through the motions and can only give thanks that his motions are, as always, from one minute to the next, so clearly prescribed and defined. He moves dumbly and stiffly through his days but after all he always has; he is no one, hollow and wax as an effigy; not even that, even, because he has no livid painted visible wounds to show; there's no one to bear him through the streets to be pitied and no one to pity him. He is pale but he always is—luminous. He wears black but he always does. He prays. He orders ceremonies, masses, vigils. He mourns and Spain mourns with him. He finds no meaning in it. He seeks out God. Lipsius says God's ways are not to be comprehended. He says, Fuck Lipsius. Fuck G ... blasphemy, Felipe, to top it all? He is a sinner and all Spain suffers for his sins and everyone he loves will have his sins visited upon them while he goes on stuck in the fucking world, living. He writes to Sor María: My son is dead. My wife is dead. My younger sister, both my brothers. I know that despair is a sin. Very well; I live, as ever, in sin. I am defeated by this grief.

He prefers not to be painted, in this time. He still comes to the studio to watch the painter paint. The painter observes his dulling and saddening eyes, is relieved that he is not called upon to paint them.

The Prince died in Saragossa. Not in battle but of fever. And if he hadn't been brought into that unhealthy air ... but then again, it seems the air is unhealthy everywhere, since the Queen ... since the Queen died right here in la Corte of some other sickness, waiting for the King's return, and he was almost home, was on his way home ... His image that preceded him, a fool in battle dress, hanging by her empty throne ... How he loathes that general now, his usurper ... And now here he is, too late, back again from war to this empty, empty court and what little light there was is gone now. All enchantments ended. He sees the world for what it is, and it is— nothing; shams, shadows, bones. His sister dead in Vienna and he hadn't seen her since she left all those years ago, how could that have happened, how could those years have passed, they say she was poisoned, and can't prove it or name a culprit; anyway she died and they cut her open to free her poor child but what chance could such a child have, lifted into the world out of death and poison. Now he has only her painted ghost, all their painted ghosts, the curse of their perpetual silent ageless visibility; he moves through the rooms of his many buildings, castles, palaces, monasteries, houses, haunting their corners, a mourning ghost among ghosts.

He retreats to his hunting lodge, out in the forest, wanting close walls to confine him. High in the tower, images of wise men: doleful Aesop, merry Menippus. A difference of outlook only: despair of it or laugh but the world remains ridiculous and there's nothing you can do about it. These ancients, poor, humble, would scorn the vanity of this worldly court, and all its hunts and pageants and its wars; they'd moralise and mock. They look somewhat like fools, or else, the fools of this court are the only models that the painter can find for wise men. Solid objects: the bucket of a slave (they were slaves once), roll of paper, amphora not more solid than a wall painting on the painted wall. Their shadows behind them in their bare grey rooms. They are old, and tired of it.

Mars, too, in retirement in the high tower; a jester dressed as a god. A sluggard a slumped bum rakish-angled and drunk. His robes hanging off him and his muscles beginning to sag. This is what the god of war has come to. He is making the best of his reduced circumstances, it seems; smirking at the chaos

that he's left the world in, the whole world's a skirmish and
here he is slumped and ridiculous in only a helmet and a huge
moustache. Because these wars too will pass and the result will
be irreparable or seem so until the next war and the next and
the world will change again and live on in its damage until it
turns to change again, again, when all this lot are dead and
another army and another comes marching over the ground
won by another and over the bodies that have gone to mulch,
to dust, and over the hopeful daisies that they're pushing up,
always there are more to take up arms, we are born to it and so
we soldier on, and, or, get drunk.

The King comes often to this high room and he feels
their gazes on him, at the centre of all these silent watchers;
Menippus sardonic and mocking; Aesop, disappointed in him;
Mars, reduced to self-parody, inane and out of focus. And
there are ghosts, too, in the high tower; inescapable; ghosts
everywhere, their gazes on him. Well? Sebastián demands
(Sebastián mourns his Prince, too, but has no licence to say so;
he recalls the Prince and mourns the loss of all that boy's noble
plans, come to naught now). Lezcano would like to play cards.
Calabazas with his gourd and his skance eyes—Calabazas has
died, too, and didn't see her coming. The King's sister María
with her green hooded eyes—— skull under the skin— His
wife Isabel on her horse her clever mouth lips shrinking back
from it even now the skull under her skin— His son, his son
the Prince would go riding; is ready to ride out to war— his
sweet son with his sleepy dog— his son as a little general— the
fine hair like his own at the temples the livid pox on his skin
the skull under the—— his brother, both brothers, his almost
doubles, so like him, the same faces like a horrible mirror, they
hang around him so young and untouched and, he can say it
if no one else will—the painter's work attests to it— better

looking; untouched by sickness or war or age—he sees it in the true mirror, his age, his cheeks falling and hollowing, the hollow sockets, the—— under— oh— no one but ghosts and remote nuns to comfort him——

She's everywhere in these years, tireless, patient, always hungry, never satisfied, uncomplaining, knowing she need only wait, and she's always there, the King's most faithful attendant, at his shoulder, at his table, in his empty bed; he can't shake her—

His valido— the Count-Duke raving mad and dead in his exile and now governing Hell, writes the poet (freed in time to watch his old rival fall and taking what vengeance he can); and maybe he is, getting things organised down there, making things ready for his King— ever the faithful servant—

The poet, free but unable this time to make a comeback— the poet dies bitter, broken, his soul forever imprisoned—

The King's bastard's mother, she's dead also, he's been informed; years since he's seen La Calderona but he hears she's died quietly, abbess of her convent, such a waste, he has wasted so much in this world, women, prayers, time ... everything taken from him, everything ending the same way, everything passing—

— La Calderona's cur dies one day, probably, maybe drunk in some gutter untouched, no one wanting to move him and get his skin on them— but no one has thought of him in a long time, have they. Already forgotten.

✠

The King dines alone at the Alcázar, going through the motions, with only his physician, his closest attendants, his

Prime Minister (the worthy, dull de Haro, who doesn't stamp
or bellow or blood-let and barely warrants a mention). The
King dines on eggs since there's no meat to be had and in any
case he deserves no more than that. He writes to Sor María of
his penitence, his grief. His want for nothing. And there's not
much to go around; wages are owed; the cooks are on strike,
tired of making something out of nothing, for nothing.

All the wine is drunk and the bones gnawed clean and the
eggs are just for eating, not making bombs of, the stink dissipated, stink of sulphur or rose water, both. Rooms disused and
dust-sheeted, empty walls; apartments, annexes, whole houses
shut up, the cost of upkeep too much; the Queen's courtyard
closed up, the King will have no entry there; he has barricaded
this part of himself; he is done with that. He is as chill as a
chapel, as a mausoleum.

La Corte quiet now. La Corte keeps to itself. Barest whispers in the corridors, in the kitchens, in the mentideros. The
juntas all dismantled. There are conspiracies, and there are
inquisitions, and there are executions in the Plaza Mayor.
There aren't any parties or fireworks. The fools all sit quietly.
The theatres, in Isabel's honour, are closed; no stages thrown
up between houses; no plays for Holy Week; no comedies in
the Coliseo, which like the rest of the Retiro stands empty. The
rules are enforced. The courtiers go about scowling, suspicious,
hungry. Plain belts tightened around plain garments—not
much to put in the belly anyway. In the streets only beggars
and penitents; or, if there are gallants, their strut has lost its
swagger, the carriages are shabby, the ladies keep their blinds
closed and their veils on properly with no flirtatious winking
to be seen.

At the Retiro, the birds are all quiet now. The birds are all
dead in the aviary and now there's just the standard crabby

hens, for eggs and rubbery eating, and nothing left of all that fine plumage and no new down to feather a bed with. A hot wind blows through, like contagion, like failure. The interior left empty, the contents withdrawn, the gifts that furnished the rooms so richly removed to other residences, or covered over, or sold. Bare walls are exposed to the shuttered light, tapestries left to the moths. The emptiness of places where chairs were and people to sit in them; cold braziers; walls enclosing empty spaces and their small ordinary windows admitting little light. In the hall Hercules batters on in the dark, all the dead generals and their victories which now seem meaningless. The Secretary's lions have been melted down; the King's armies need all the metal they can get.

Everything's gone brown. No one walks the paths and they grow tangled with knots of weed. The water has soaked into the earth, dried up, and there are black unflowering limbs on the sick fruit trees dropping hard and bitter fruit—— this year the pear tree has died in my garden, and I'm helpless and can't reverse that, and I'm alarmed by the time that's passed, that I can't prevent passing, and I miss the blossom— And then there's a rose in my garden which, untended, grows fast and alarming in hideous profusion, strangling everything, stretching its thick thorny reaches into branches, pulling down trellises, grasping at the sky; one of those in a bower would throttle the memory or ghost of any lovers lingering—— No lovers here at the Retiro any longer, no leisure to be taken here, no love. Unloved it tangles, totters; the poor mortar that held it together starts to crumble; the buildings disassembled by fire, ruin, time— I am so sad today, looking out at the garden, and I am frightened—

✠

The painter looking on, living still, in the world; seeing it, seeing its surfaces, the things in it, the light on it, moving through it, and arranging it. This world of solid objects; but what he's in pursuit of now is— the texture of a moment, the layers, the trace of it— what the world looks like, passing through it, harder to grasp at than the brush held lightly in the hand.

The painter works now in the Prince's old chamber. A gift from the King. The Prince's eulogy made much of the boy's love of painting; of his good taste; elegant, unaffected, subtle, effortless: these words for the painter, and the work the Prince admired so. So far he's come, even at the death of a prince he gets a mention. It may be that the painter can offer the King some comfort, though he is the conjurer of all his ghosts; it may be that the King prefers to live among them; in any case he spends time, as ever, in the corner of the studio watching, and has arranged things so that the studio is also the room his son once lived in. It's a big room, Diego, he said. Going unused. Not likely to be used now. The painter did not say, There's no reason to think that, Señor—there is time, still. Because it's not his place to say it, maybe, but more because he sees that the King doesn't want that— doesn't want time, doesn't want anything, now. That he's done with all that. And also—what is worse—that he can't be allowed to be done with it, and will soon have to accept that. So the painter, tactful, says nothing and the King, after a silence, says as if to clarify— I don't wish to remarry, Diego; and the painter says nothing; and maybe that's a relief to the King, who isn't looking for hope or an answer. The painter doesn't ask, What can I do to help you, Señor. He just gets on with his work, quietly, and the King watches. It's a cool, grey room, high and dim in its corners, the painter's new studio. High recessed windows and a door with steps leading out to the back of it.

In his quiet corner of the painter's studio, the King contemplates: Do you recall that play of Don Pedro's? The poor savage kept in his prison far out in the woods and brought to court and told he is king; and then they tell him he was dreaming after all, that it was all a dream ... do you recall him? The painter says— Yes: Segismundo. But, Señor, he really was king; they locked him up because of a prophecy. And once they'd woken him to the truth they couldn't get rid of him.

That's right, says the King. I remember now. It was the poor savage they made of him that was the lie. Or ... kept locked up without books, without counsel, without ladies to amuse me, without my painter to make images of me, without my playwrights and my poets, what would I be but a savage also? Free of all of it.

The painter paints on—he is making a copy of the King—and forgets again the true King in his corner quietly watching and everything around him except the pale high quiet light falling on the canvas obliquely, the seeing-unseeing of the marks he's making, the knowing of the surface and the brush and the palette in his hand ...

Some hours or minutes later, the King says: I envy that savage, Diego.

The painter steps back from the depths of his painting, back from the surface. He says, Do you, Señor? And the King says, Oh, I don't know. Don't listen to me. I don't know what I mean. Where would I be after all, without my painter, without my portrait always hanging over me ... The King's face growing impossibly hangdog-longer with every pronouncement. Shadows pulling in around him in the corner, now. The painter doesn't say anything. Turns back to the same face on the canvas, lit from within by the undimmed light of royalty. God's light.

The King, exhausted, always exhausted, and now more than ever, exhausted by war and punished by it and fearing what will be left of him, perhaps, now his son is gone ... the King is thinking always on his legacy, thinking what he'd like to leave in the world, when at last he's out of it. And he watches the painter working, and hours pass in this way, and it occurs to him that this is perhaps the only pleasure left to him. That this is something his grandfather and his great-grandfather left him, something of worth, something he's proved worthy of even if he's failed in so much else, in his attempts to emulate and honour them, their legacy; the empire they left him, assaulted and frayed. But his good taste, his eye, he has that; that his son had, too, his son the little general there on his horse; if he'd only stayed here in la Corte ... Outlasting lands and empires, sashes and swords, all the mutable things of the world and its borders, outlasting his passage beyond that last boundary, something to remain behind him; this. This is what he might like to leave of himself. The painter will give him his legacy. Together they'll rehang the whole of the Alcázar; rehang the staterooms to reassure everyone that everything is fine. Flourishing.

He will found an academy of art. He will arrange his collection and offer it up, and new beauty will be brought into the world. How should it look? What might it contain? He asks the painter— How is it in Rome, how is it done there? There should be sculptures, casts; the ancient and the modern, alongside each other; continuity and newness, beauty made afresh; a casting back in time, oh unmessy heroic age; the perfection of marble flesh; God's work. This is how the painter can help him. Instead of portraits; he's done with portraits— Rome? Would that please you, Diego?

Twenty years since the painter sat in the gardens of the Villa Medici— in the hills above Rome among the grey-green trees, a statue, a shrine, a sheet hanging; an arch; passing strangers and the grey ground . . . and yet he still can breathe it now, for fragments of seconds, when in solitude, an unexpected catch of the grey-green air of the Roman hills; sculpted marble; ancient stone— how often he thinks of it. And he catches it now and is lifted, a hand on his breast to hide the tremble and the quiver and his head falls forward light and heavily in a bow to hide his face and pull himself back to the ground—

Rome? The painter gasps a laugh back, still bowed; straightens with his face straight and his head swims and he says— It would be my honour, I am as ever in your service, Señor.

Twenty years, though. When he was last in Rome . . . What has he done since? What has passed? Twenty-five years since he came to la Corte; twenty-five years lived within these walls, and new walls built around him for him to hang pictures on . . . His daughter is married. He is almost fifty. So is Juana. They have grandchildren, and his home is full of voices, and he is proud, no doubt, of his home and his family expanding and his gifted son-in-law; but how can it be, twenty-five years? Had he meant to do more, once? He's been so busy . . . Usher, Chamberlain, Superintendent . . . he is within the King's chambers. He has furnished their walls. He has made images of the King, of his dead brothers, his dead children—an act of resurrection, their perpetual images, the veins showing through fair skin, the wet on their lips, all the warmth and life his brush has touched into being, he has kept them in the world thus. They will outlive him, and the King, and all of us—— I've seen them, their living skin— how has this much life already passed, Diego? And every day, all your responsibilities, and you're always answerable and on call, and how then do you take yourself out of it, out of the daily necessary accounting, do your days pass by and another gone and still no painting and then a week's passed—and your hand heavy with guilt and obligation and the weariness of that. And your task is to make record of the world you're in and to add to that world, to make a new thing to hang in it, but this world is so full of things on walls that you wonder what the point is, if this new thing will endure—— but these are my anxieties, maybe not yours. Five years since I sat in that swing and felt that things were possible. Some new thing in the world ... How to make anything possible? How is it, so many years, how is *that* possible? Too fast in passing and nothing left behind ... but you, you'll leave something. Really something. If I could tell you. And you do; you do have time. You still have time. Go to Rome. Go to Rome. I've been waiting for this for you, knowing this is coming, looking forward to it, to getting you out of there and into the air to let you go— so go, Diego——

So go, Diego, the King says; you'll be missed, of course ... and the King looks around this room that his son slept in; and the painter, observing him, sees that the King can't ever get out of where and who he is and although he hasn't the right, the painter pities him.

The King sends him off with a magnanimous budget, to furnish the new academy, and is left alone in the empty court. Segismundo in reverse, retreating to his tower and taking refuge in a dream he isn't king.

XVI

Sfumato/
Smoke

And so the painter leaves the country for a second time, travelling with a company bound for Austria, to collect a new wife for the King—his private wish notwithstanding. The convoy travelling south, breathing through a handker-chief all through plaguey Andalusia; pale greying sweaty bodies by the roadside; exhausted by drought and sickness and heat. The painter and his companions press below their jaws, nervous, palping the glands to check for swelling; some of the party sicken and, wide-eyed and glassy, are left behind.

Through Andalusia and over the sea and landed on the other side, and on, alone with his own retinue, to Rome. We've been in the court so long. Is it possible now— to move outside of it, to see what's beyond it? The Medici gardens, the rest he took there, the grey-green evening— still here?— and maybe he's come back looking for it, maybe that's what he's back for—but there is so much to do, here; purchasing, acquiring, collecting, bartering, and then there's a Pope to paint, if he can find his way to an invitation … returning an older more important man, maybe he can't find his way back to the gardens—

— But anyway, he stays a while. He sees the way an artist might live here—feted, free to move; to show movement; people do move, here, unconstrained; flesh and skin; billows of colour blowing through the place. He enjoys his reception here, the ease of it, the civility, the release from the rigidity of his life in Madrid and the courtly machine he's caught in. Maybe seeing himself in another life and knowing he could never live it; maybe knowing all along that what he longs for here— he'd never be able to have it anyway, being so cautious by nature, so careful, so constrained by his own self. But maybe this is a rest from himself, too; made sweet with the melancholy of return, the knowing that this is only a suspension, not an escape. So knowing all this, when the King calls him home, he stays a little longer.

A moment's respite: a cup of coffee taken in the morning, rising early as his ingrained courtly habit is, standing on a balcony, leaning up against the balustrade, framed in these pillars and the sun appearing in the streets, pinkish light and stone. Thinking of how, back home, there would be duties to attend to, rooms to make ready, keys to turn, things things things to be placed in their places ready for the rituals and systems they precipitate; then the next thing then the next; the court is yet more anxiously shadowed and fraught and duty-bound than ever; observing its rituals in the face of disorder and chaos and closing its walls around itself against the plague and famine outside it; dark and sombre and lightless, hopeless, without and within those walls that close—

—— no; not thinking of that, no—— imagine a different kind of attention; imagine instead an opening out from this balcony's frame—

—— thinking of how, up this early in a foreign city, one feels oneself in possession of it; the feeling of near-possession you have, when you seem the only one awake, and that this is a day you're the first to partake of; the cool stone against his shoulder, the first fresh-scented warmth of the sun, the scent of cool stone warming; the touch of the cup on his lip; blowing on the dark surface, bitter steam rising from an oily whorl, warm moisture in his nostrils, his moustache; eyes closing briefly, as I have never seen them, since he must have them open to see and paint himself; but imagine the lids heavy and perhaps a shine on them, under the sun, and lilac-brown; behind him, through the open window, a curtained room, a bed just left, still warm; close; clothes discarded, clothes ready to be worn, the day almost ready to be worn, but not yet; for now, shirtsleeves, this morning stillness, sun, coffee, the empty street now just stirring, the first carts, shutters, clatter, cats; I wonder if you smoke, it's a moment for smoking, a moment centred, emptied; this unique sense of containment, the frail equilibrium of being only oneself, for a moment, in a foreign city; the sort of moment that seems just passing but that stays, indelible— sitting in late yellow sunshine a glass of cold salt sherry with three sips taken and the way the late light falls through the chill of the glass—— but that's mine, that was back in Madrid, Diego, and in the evening, when I was in your city long after you'd left it—— but something like that, for you, here, in Rome, with your coffee in the morning— I'd like to give you this, a moment, Diego, before you put your shoes and jacket and hat on, and head out to buy things and paint popes.

THREE

XVII

Darlo todo, y no dar nada/
Give everything, and give nothing

— Let's say early morning— the bright haze of an early summer morning— after a night at an inn; the last stop on a long journey, the dust of it washed off with the sweet water out of the plain, poured from a glazed ewer; out onto the last stretch of road; the rusted burnt earth, the pallid shadows of the hills in the haze in the early morning. Drawing close to the city, the way as ever is loud and busy; a festival mood; the theatres are re-opened; la Corte re-awakened—despite the war, the plague, the privation—because a new queen has come! and a new male heir surely coming.

The painter pays his tax at the gate, finds carriages waiting; takes one for himself, his retinue following. He breathes the different air, the higher, dryer air of the plain and the familiar and particular smell of the city, its struggling river, horse sweat, dust and slops; thinking of this journey taken—— this journey retaken, up through the country from the south to the city, here at the centre; that young hopeful man with the curl at the temple and the thin moustache, and his dark eyes and all that they've observed since in their near-thirty years of observing—and the past he's left behind him, all he's left

behind him— so, back again— this passage that's defined his
life; the path he's travelled; the past obscured in dust behind
him ... Traveller's thoughts, weary, rolling with the carriage
wheels, jolting over stone, half-formed ... Half-looking out
the window at the gallants, the veiled ladies, their tented
forms, their men stretching to take an elbow over ever-wider
skirts. Sad to have left Rome ... to have left Rome, again—
and all that he's left there, this time ... Down the Calle
Mayor, now, nearing the Alcázar, feeling the walls of the old
fortress closing, the court encroaching; things to attend to;
duties; to-do lists; everything, always there's everything, to
do; awaiting him, the young Queen to be painted, and the
King's daughter also—the Infanta María Teresa is thirteen
years old now and looking for a match; the academy, his
purchases, shipping, correspondence, all that; new acquisi-
tions; quality control, his studio making their copies: King,
Queen, Infanta ... Pope, from his own copy with him, from
the one he's left in Rome behind him; what he's brought back
with him: a sibyl, a goddess, her half-seen half-known half-
forgotten face already; what he's left behind him ... Rome ...
And then at home Francisca— when he last returned his
daughter had almost become a woman, in his absence; to
think of that girl with her blue ribbon now, now a matron and
the mother of his grandchildren ... his full and noisy home
and all the children and Juana, Juana, at home ... taking his
cloak. Juana admiring the chain he's been given, lifting it
from his neck to stow for safe-keeping; and her arms about
his neck and his life hung back around it. Resigning himself,
or ... Pale grey thoughts; just travel-weary and thinking grey
thoughts, thinking pale grey ground ... pale form ... purple
silk ... thinking not much——

In Rome he met a woman——

She said——

— He has brought back with him a sibyl; she holds a tablet, or a folio, half-vanishing into pale shadows, and if there's anything written on it—which she's pointing to, to draw our attention or to follow her own finger as she scans—then whatever she reads there is not for us; there's no text that's legible. I'd like to write onto it, the story of who the sibyl is. She's not like Juana, and not like Juana was in this role, all those years ago; she wears no costume, her hair isn't done up in pearls. She is in motion, she looks like she might have just risen from a bed or couch, in only a flimsy wrapping; her hair falling loose, woken by a vision that only she can see, only she can read its meaning; she is in the act of reading, or writing, or prophesying, parsing the invisible truth on the tabula rasa. She might be the excellent painter Flaminia—— his lover—— or just some other woman drafted in to model, or a figure from out of his mind— although he's not in the habit of inventing—— some other woman he's met on his travels, passing through, a foreign traveller—— oh I'd love to put myself there, to sit for you, Diego, but she's dark and beautiful, this sibyl, and looks nothing like me.

The shadow of her hand, her finger, on the pale page she points to, and that's all; there's nothing we can read here.

— She said— Perhaps stay just a little longer. And the painter said, yes. In Rome he met a woman—

— Outstretched, pale, her head propped on a hand to meet his eye in the mirror. He said, yes, I'm staying. In Italy he could arrange his model thus—at leisure, with her back turned, the long pale naked stretch of her, the mounds and dips of her. Her face a blur in the mirror.

She said, Will your King be very angry? (The King writing: now, come back. I mean it.) Another month passed. And another, and another. He said, No, not angry; he'll be sad. But he won't say so. Oh, you stoical Spaniards, she said.

Outstretched, on the purple silk, on the pale grey ground. She watches his reaction; she looks out at him, regarding him, flushed with her own exposure. She watches him looking and blushes and he paints the blush. From where the mirror sits, she sees him, not herself. He paints her as he might remember her, from a composite of her, as if she's already gone from him; or he from her, rather. Her face half-known, half-made in the mirror. He tells her, I'll remember—

— In Rome he met a painter named Flaminia Triunfi— and admired her—

— Flaminia, stretched out there watching in the mirror as he lays in the grey ground. You see, Diego, how it's done? With warmth, with light?— and he says, but there are always shadows—and she says yes, but they are warmer, they are softer than you see them; and things are not so separate, or needn't be. And she, with her greys, with her purples, with her pale flesh, soft, warm, also. Yes, like that, she says. You have seen me, she says; you do *see*, don't you. You are a true artist, Diego, she tells him. And what is true? he asks. And she then— what then?— she'd groan, Oh, I know, it's all shadow and sham … so sombre, so *sober*, my poor Spaniard. You, *Pictor Regis*— will you sign me? Now it's done, now you're done with me? No, not even your blank scrap … No need, I know. You know you'll be remembered, your work will, without your even putting your name to it. Yes, you'll be remembered. You're that good. That's true. I won't be. My brother, maybe. Maybe not. He's *not* that good.

But you are, he says. You are an excellent painter. She nods, only a little, keeping her head in position, meeting his eyes in the mirror; smiling a little, keeping her face still. Thank you. Yes, that's true too.

He told her, I'll remember. She watched him looking and blushed and on her half-made face he painted the blush——

—— But don't do that. I don't want to do that.

This is true: In Rome he met a woman named Flaminia Triunfi, a painter, and admired her. But Flaminia doesn't have to be his lover; she can be the nude if she wants to be; she can be the sibyl; but she is without question an excellent painter. So Flaminia, you were admired, in your time. I think you must have had fun, in the middle of things, in Rome; I imagine that people were a little scared of you and wanted to know you and wanted you to admire them; I don't care if you were beautiful; but I believe that you were brilliant since Diego said so and I'm sorry that there's no trace that your brush left on the world preserved, and you are remembered just because of that, because you met another painter who said that you were excellent.

This is also true: In Rome he met a woman——

— Another life, you could have had, Diego; a different path that I could write for you; the way not taken: No, you say, I am not coming back; I am an Academician. I am a virtuoso of the Pantheon. I will stay in Rome and my son-in-law can be your

painter. Juan Bautista will paint your Queen. Juan, take care
of my daughter; take care of all my grandchildren; come visit
some time. Francisca, look after your mother. Juana—— what,
Diego? What will you say to Juana?

But the King wrote: Come back. And again, and again. He
wrote: The King misses his painter—— The King is keen to
get our academy started—— He awaits the painter's report
on Rome and what he's seen and bought there—— The King
requires the painter to return and make a portrait of his new
wife. The King's niece has arrived from Austria, to be Queen.
And the King would have her portrait painted.

The painter wrote, Yes— soon; he would return soon.

He said— I'll have to go soon. She said, stay a little longer?
And she put a hand on her belly, the soft flesh just swelling.
There might be a little boy; a little boy in a blue sash over his
little boy's belly, in a pair of little putti's wings, all scrappy,
holding a mirror for her.

He said— A little longer. I do have to go, though.

Is that it, Diego?

In any case, he is back now; he is home; delayed and much later
than the King demanded, he passes in his carriage through la
Corte; back within the fortress, back within the walls; travel
weary, thinking not much.

✢

Frames and canvas ranged around the studio. Ready for
inspection, for finishing, for hanging, for storing, for sending on. In the warm long evening, the painter hears the key
turn and his door opens and closes; a figure detaches from

the gape of corridor shadow to step into the warm long
studio light—

He doesn't look like a newlywed. He looks more exhausted
than ever. A little tension about the mouth— as if he is holding
his face that way, holding his lower lip stiff. Ever more of an
effort. Still, as ever, perfectly turned out. He is a father, still, to
his daughter, and perhaps again imminently— perhaps a son.
He is a husband again. He is, again, a king complete.

He closes the door behind him, locks it; as ever courteous.
He seems a little uneasy, this incognito visitor, although this
of course unshown—but still the painter, knowing him, feels
it—perhaps a little awkward, taking up the old rituals of
acquaintance. For some reason, the King has had the painter
paid for all the works he's done over the years; all the commissions that have stacked up—in corridors, in other courts—all
the works hanging on walls—that huge deficit all at once
remunerated; perhaps he fears the painter will be discontented,
restless, in returning; has been away so long, so long in returning, despite the call; needs to be kept here, needs to feel needed,
so perhaps the King thinks.

Paintings leaned against the walls; paintings rolled for
transporting; the painter checking a catalogue. He has made
a purchase, on behalf of the King, just delivered: the collection
of King Charles of England, who has no further use for it, his
eyes having parted from his body along with the rest of his
head. The King inspects the haul. Once I envied that Prince, he
says; when he came to visit and was so cultured, so refined——
(when he snuck into the palace in disguise and they had to
entertain him for weeks and then get rid of him—the King
too delicate to recall that, now); and now I have these works,
that were chosen by that man whose good taste I envied, and
Charles . . . there but for the grace of God, of course. I was so

young, then. So unschooled. It was when we first met, was it not, that summer of his visit?

It was the reason I was kept waiting, the painter refrains from saying, making a mark against an entry on the page, all that long summer. You're right, it was, Señor, he says.

And how was Rome, Diego? Good to have you back. The King browsing, wandering the ramshackle gallery as the painter attempts to set things in order; acquainting himself with the years he's missed, with the new works, with the painter's progress. Perhaps he has come here, in those two missing years; or has felt unable to in the painter's absence, with only the studio at work making copies; no reason to drop by, with no taciturn painter for company, and the ghost of his son still lingering; and now there is a little awkwardness, in the old ritual of his visiting.

Frames leaned against the wall. Canvases stretched, primed, sketched, the tinta oscura already laid, the portrait copies, King King Infanta Queen Pope, their pale opaque forms in already wrought landscapes on block horses, in curtained interiors, awaiting finishing: animation, bloodflow, colour, catchlight— Juan Bautista's work, mostly, these days, and the studio under his direction. The painter examines and these unformed ghosts look on with their unshaped featureless faces, just-cast masks with their shadows for eyes, with their pallid hands unlined, semi-transparent and nailless and fingers undefined, like moles' paws. The King preferring not to examine his own ghost-selves, preparing to ride out to other courts on their horses, too closely. Stopping instead at the red irascible Pope in his world of red splendour— And how did you find our Papa, Diego? You were received well? I hear that this brutal thing pleased him . . .

— The painter undaunted by the dangerous glint of his eye; the Pope commended his honesty, rewarded him with a

chain, sent him home with a copy and a note to the King, a
recommendation, Señor, that this painter should be admitted
to the Order; the King knows all this, and hasn't mentioned
it, the note, the painter's petition, or the delay in his returning;
but he called and the painter came back, and brought this copy
with him; in Rome he was elected to the Pantheon, and to the
Accademia di San Luco— in Italy they value the work of their
artists ... he doesn't say this.

He was very generous, Señor, I was honoured ... he says, but
gives up, since the King has moved on already, having spotted
a canvas turned to the wall—a rag to a bull, this, guaranteed; a
warm keyboard to a cat—he can't resist it. But ... What's this,
Diego? May I? he asks with a gesture and—

— Oh, well now.

The King contrives to look without looking, an extraordinary trick with the eyes, and done without mirrors. This is
Venus, I think? The King knows a goddess when he half-sees
her—though she's not buxom, not rubicund. Outstretched long
and pale and unlike any statue in Rome that the painter might
have observed her from; more like a woman, a particular living
one. But nonetheless, she's also Love; she is Beauty. From the
corner of his eye he sees her, seeing him, in her mirror.

— And the painter remembers the blur of her blush, remembers her skin but not the feel of it, only the paint mixing on
the palette and how he had rarely had occasion to use so much
white and how she blushed when he said so, did she? He can't
remember her features in motion, if she yawned or laughed or
frowned, if she grew bored or tired of his looking at her. He
moved her arm—— there's a trace of where it once lay— but he
cannot remember physically lifting it from her side to reposi-
tion it; imagines the soft give of her skin and the warmth of it,
indoor summer warmth within so she's warm under her skin,

and the skin moist and cool from exposure. It is better, there, the arm, out of the way of the curve of her waist; perhaps he moved it later, when alone. Her little waist and the roundness of her and the rounding of her belly that he didn't stay to see . . . Her face in the mirror lovely and also ordinary, and indistinct; only the cheek, flushed, and the misplaced lights in her eyes; through a smear of memory, silver-grey . . .

The King continues his tour with all the appearance of insouciance, despite this apparition of a naked goddess, here in the chaste environs of the painter's studio, here within the walls of his fortress— I see you are even more the Apelles than we'd given you credit for . . .

In the playwright's new play, in honour of the painter's return, Apelles paints his master's concubine, and she falls in love with him, when she sees how he sees her; furious Alexander, after a good Stoical talking-to from Diogenes, concedes her. Give Everything, and Give Nothing—

— I'd no idea, says the King . . . but I suppose in Italy, such models are available . . . I suppose you'll exercise discretion, whoever she's meant for . . . I must say if I were Alexander and this were my concubine (he is still not looking directly at her) I'm not sure I'd part with her . . . But no, of course, I'm not asking to have her. What would my new wife say? And the King allows himself one of his quiet sighs, to show he makes a joke, although the laugh's largely gone out of them these days and it's mostly the sound of deflation.

(In the house of Martha and Maddalena: The child is swaddled in very fine clean linen of which Martha keeps a substantial supply, as she was instructed in the note he came with. Here in the soft yellow hush of the chamber that he sleeps in— sweetly sleeps in— wakes and bawls in— she sits down with him,

gurgling, wrapped in fine linen that she pushes gently from his tender face; she unpins her mourning dress, sets aside her simple veil, and sets him to her nipple. He feeds sometimes weakly, sometimes fiercely, and burps, as babies do—her black dresses all stained at the shoulder with milky sick. His little red face, his black hair, his helpless belching. His crying through the night, his little crumpled face among the softest lace and linens, like a pope's frock. Martha has heard talk of the famous portrait.

Light falling from the window on a world of solid objects. Soft sheen of eggshells. The shine on the jaw of a fish. In the widow Martha's house all is calm and industry— and wakeful bawling— she cleans, she cooks their simple meals, she and her widowed mother Maddalena at her shoulder, attending to their little grandee. She mashes chickpeas in the mortar, and feeds the child just a little at a time, offers the spoon and he eats gummily, is sick, grabs for her breast, hiccups and sucks. She speaks to him in her own language, his mother's language too, should she ever deign to drop around and have a conversation with him. If he were her own child, Martha's child—— but Martha's child is swaddled in a shroud, nowhere near so fine as this cloth, and Martha now sleeps in nice sheets that are far finer than the one they wound her husband in. Oh, death's a bitch. But Martha has Antonio to feed, for now at least. She rests here in her nursing chair, with one breast bared, with a nice linen napkin to mop up the spittle and sick, and Antonio today in his little lace cap is peaceful, and sweet.

He won't need her much longer, she knows this. She spoons mashed squash, semolina, squashed marrow, with a little bone spoon that won't hurt his sore gums. Teeth are coming. They'll come for him soon, and she'll be left alone, with a purse of coins and a load of unwashed linen. She can be seen at the window, neat in her cap, just the faintest stains on her mourning black; at the window she points and talks, talks and points. Un soldato. Un gatto. Un cane. Che vita da cani! Una carrozza, the horse goes clippety-clop. Un arrotino, the knives go shtrip-shtrap-shtrop. Un gatto ... e un gatto, un gatto, un gatto (this being Rome); e un cane. And Antonio says, ga. Ga gaga. Cacacaca! A dog; a cat, feeding on fish-scraps.)

XVIII

Querer por solo querer/
Love for love's sake

And so after these years of darkness— the King remarried
and there is light, there is hope!— there is colour— butterflies, ribbons, fans, rouge, the flush of youth, the brightness
of it, of the possible—the casements thrown open and light
let into the castle, into the labyrinth, we are lost no longer;
the windows open and looking out—out, from this darkness!
Theatres back up in the streets and the forecourt and out at the
Retiro; musicians and songs and dances; the dwarves tumble;
the fools quip. The girls run around the Alcázar, farthingales
notwithstanding—two cousins, the new Queen Mariana and
her stepdaughter, the Infanta María Teresa, just a couple of
years younger. They play bowls down the corridors. They race
turtles. They let birds fly in the halls. They antagonise their
lapdogs with ribbons and bows and combing, dangle baubles
above their primped brows and the little dogs leap and spring
and yap and the girls laugh and clap.

You know, the King writes to Sor María, I didn't want another
wife. You know I have married this— girl, she is but a girl—
for Spain only. This girl. She should have wed my son. And I

would have loved her, welcomed her, welcomed seeing her with him, a good match for him, two young people, they would have gone hawking, but I am tired, Sister, and youth and youth's vitality is a gift that's denied me, that's been taken from me, since ... You will say, God's ways are not for us to comprehend. You are right; I can't comprehend this. That I should find myself married to the wife meant for my son. That my losses should amount to this. And yet, if I turn my gaze upon myself and how I have lived, if I look upon myself without illusion, as we all must, then I know that this is my duty, my sacrifice, since for my sins we all are punished.

Please pray for me, for all of us, pray for an heir for Spain; and ask the sisters to pray for us, and for my daughter, and for my wife, he writes.

The King at work in the afternoon while María Teresa takes tea with her favourite truhán; quiet tidy Nicolasito, his neat teeth shining as he takes neat bites of what she proffers; they sit and sip sweet water and nibble at cakes; she pares a slice of pear for him; he refreshes her glass. It pleases the King to see his daughter happy. He writes to Sor María: She is smarter by the day, she is even of temper and sound in judgement, we seek a good match for her and I'm sure she will make one; if she can calm down just a little, she still makes such a hustle-bustle, ah, such a tumult; but then again, she is young still ...

What's to become of her, he wonders. He looks to her in these days when he is in need of some small measure of joy— the least portion of it is all he deserves, since he is a sinner—his happy, sanguine daughter, Isabel's daughter, the bright promise of her thriving despite all the black and yellow bile that keeps the court churning. She is so like his sister. And like Isabel. His only joy since Isabel—— If he could live out his days just watching his daughter at play with her dwarves; not ageing; not having to be sent off to marry some man she's not met; she would sit forever at this little table, eating cake with Nicolasito; and he could just watch her. This scene: Nico gracious, silent, smiling, this gentle happy daughter, the King's unsullied love, the pureness of it.

They are like a middle-aged country couple, taking their ease after a morning's labours, perhaps— changing sheets, sweeping the stables of their inn, perhaps— counting the barrels, balancing books, perhaps— and now at leisure, with the evening ahead of them. Simple refreshment. A rest, then a walk in the town, perhaps.

His daughter rises, out of this illusion; she goes through the process of rising: gingerly, she moves back from the table, taking care not to knock it with her skirt, which in the current style is made for very little movement, for very slow and stately movement—in spite of which his wife has been running about the corridors and taking his daughter with her; a silver bowl has already been dented, a porcelain vase smashed, the nose of Seneca has been re-attached but his bust will now be forever affronted. The skirting, the corners of the Alcázar have never been swept so thoroughly. And the King of course is glad of it, this new brightness; but also, he is tired. So he is glad of these moments, when his daughter is calm and quiet, when she is in command of her good judgement, and at ease with her neat companion.

And then the Queen, Mariana—come in from her walk and complaining that it's gloomy, why are they all so quiet.

And here it comes ... here is temper, stamp, hilarity, as the girls compete to win him ... They say, *Father* ... and *Husband*— wheedling together, needling at him—might we put on a play? Have our meninas act it? We could do *Love for Love's Sake.* There's a giant. Little Sarmiento on Velasco's shoulders ... Won't that be funny? Husband? Father? We're so *bored.* The Alcázar is *boring* (and his daughter, who had seemed so contented, is feigning yawns now ...) Can we go out to Aranjuez? And put on a play there? And have dancing? We've made this new dance up— And the girls twirl away and curt-sey and bow and with solemn faces with crimped lips twisting in the effort of solemnity they set up half a square and spurt into giggles as they make up the steps. And fools are enlisted to make up the foursome and the girls bustle each other and hustle nimble Nicolasito who taps and trips and spins and they all stamp and caper and tumble the steps and the room is filled with the Queen's loud laughter, all her teeth showing.

And the King says— My love, the Prime Minister and I, we are just in the middle of this ... ah ... if you would perhaps show your amusement in a more ... or, just, if you would show it *less* ... in a manner more becoming, to a lady, perhaps ...

The Queen pouts, flushes, sulks; If I'm not to laugh then send the fools out, she says. And bravely, against the embar-rassment of the reprimand, against the tearful sulk, brightly: Come on, my husband, why don't *you* dance with me? Come, cousin—that is, *daughter* (they giggle)— And we need a fourth—Don Luis, you'll dance?

And the King, concentrated on his papers, looks up with infinite unstressed patience, while de Haro stands patiently by; the King says— We are just a little busy, the Prime Minister and I; but perhaps later ... why don't you all have a walk in the gardens?

And the Queen says, I've *just had one.* Have you *tried* walk-ing those paths with a *massive skirt* on? Spanish fashion is so *weird.* Why can't we copy the French like everyone else does?

And the King says, Don Luis, make a note—we're to have

the paths widened. But please, my love, stay in the grounds.

— *Fine*, she says, if our public doesn't love me then I shan't go among them any more—

— And the gardeners, de Haro, while they're about it, might plant ... whichever flowers my wife favours.

And she says, You don't even *know*.

Well, which is it, then, my petal? We must learn each other; we have so much still to learn of each other, doesn't that please you? To embark upon this ... journey, together ... these first years of our marriage, which I am assured is to be ... long and ... fruitful?

And she says, I hate fruit. I hate flowers. I miss home.

De Haro, the King says— have spruce and fir trees planted. Make a new Black Forest for my Queen.

⚜

María Teresa, the painter sees, is flushed, harassed. She smiles to hide it. He can easily paint it out. But he might use just a little of this, transmuted; the colour, the shine of it. She should be young, happy or content if possible, healthy, fertile, willing, loved. She is some of these things. There is, on her cheek, a redness.

Butterflies in her hair. She is mutating, emerging, becoming a suitable bride—showing colours after her grub-like childhood in the dark, wrapped tight in the cocoon of the Alcázar and ready to wriggle free of it, to uncrumple and dry out into maturity—— but she is of course never crumpled, always pressed, steamed, crimped, curled, pristine, spread for display, a butterfly settled and arrested, unnatural, not stirring or closing or opening, not dipping or trembling, but lit there and stuck—might fly at any moment but won't, cannot— pinned by the painter's brush, pinned into place as his sitter.

Butterflies batting all around her head, she dreams them, their dust covering her, dirty glittering dust that she scrapes from the corners of her eyes on waking, hauling herself free of her sleep-cocoon, an imago. She is changing; she'll leave soon, when there's someone to take her, when one of her butterfly-selves finds an admirer and a place to settle; the painter and his studio are turning them out, the image of her, a whole flight of her spreading out across Europe.

She is thinking of Nico; thinking of his tongue. He has but half of one, having bit through it in a fall when they were children. She remembers it, his head smack on the floor, the spittle, the blood, as all hands turned to her, to shield her, while he lay bleeding and crying. But now she loves that blunted tongue. He is thought mute, but isn't. He just takes care over what he says, and to whom. She lets him call her Tess, or Techh, is how it sounds, his blunt tongue, his neat teeth. Every time he speaks she thinks of his tongue and the thick square blunt edge of it; touching it with the tip of hers; and all of her blushes. She looks at the painter but he is not watching her face or any of the small areas of her exposed skin; he is painting, she thinks, from the angle of his glances, her skirts. Sketching in the frame of them. Skirts so large that a man, a lithe and small man, might hide under them; and what unseemly mute unspoken never-to-*be*-spoken, barely thought of thing might there a tongue do? She feels a heat prickle and creep all the way from the damp sweat between her legs to her chest while the painter looks at her little foot in her little shoe.

When the painting is finished the blush is there for all to see, offset by the ribbons in her hair; it has become the flush of healthy femininity and high breeding, scentless, although sometimes she thinks he's put too much sinful shine in her eyes.

I think Juan José fancies me, whispers María Teresa.

Yuck. He's your *half-brother.*

I *know*, she says. But still— Or at least, he's pretending to. Very gracious and all gentlemanly. Half a prince. Maybe he's thinking, if he married me he'd get to be king. Since I'm the heir, for now, after all ... You'd better get on with it—making a boy for us. For all of us! For Spain! Otherwise it's on me ... and I'm not sure I'm ready to succeed my father. What would the grandees say. Last time a queen ruled they locked her up and called her mad. I mean, they actually called her 'the Mad'. I don't care for nicknames. Only you and your little womb can save us!

Don't worry, cousin, I'm sure we'll soon find you a husband, too, says the Queen sweetly, flapping her stepdaughter with a fan. All that time you've spent being painted, all those portraits, in which you do look *so* pretty. Unless ... *you* could have a baby with your *half-brother*, and maybe *he'd* get to be heir, then.

I don't want to talk about this any more, says the Infanta.

Me neither, the Queen says, sulkily.

Mariana likes to play with her cousin, her stepdaughter; likes to be silly and giggle with a girl who's her equal—— almost her equal, since she after all is Queen. But then again her cousin is the King's daughter, and heir presumptive, until the Queen can manage a son. She sees the way her husband dotes on his daughter, and sees how like her mother María Teresa is—how like the portraits of Isabel that still hang everywhere; and she sees how his face is different when he looks at his daughter even though it doesn't change in its arrangement. How the sadness becomes of a different order, more— at least I have you, daughter, than— this must be endured, as it is when he looks at her, his wife, even when—especially when—she's trying to please him, by being jolly, or being demure, or making a special effort to be a lady, with her face painted, or when they lie and—

— It's not *fair*, complains the Queen. If your brother hadn't died I could have had a young and sexy husband (Mariana likes to shock, to show that she has been in courts less boring and proper than this one). Now I have to go to bed with your dad and make babies *right now* and everyone's hanging around outside the curtains to check the job's done—can you imagine what that's like—oh, but no, of course you can't, my sweet virgin *daughter*— just *try* to imagine what it's like, all those people around rustling when you're, when you're trying to . . . (but here, her sophistication fails her). I only started bleeding last year, you know.

Me too, says María Teresa. I was quite early, I suppose. Everyone was delighted, as you can imagine.

Mariana smiles at her.

Maybe we'll fall in time with each other.

Like nuns do.

Or like in brothels. I bet that happens in brothels.

Yuck.

They make a few passes at the game they're playing; Mariana is better at the performance of it: the hand-gestures of thinking and the elegant placing of the pieces; but María Teresa is winning.

Do you think he still sleeps with courtesans?

He's my *dad*. Stop it.

Well, he's my husband. He does though, doesn't he? He does that. Your *boyfriend*'s living proof of it. Actually, he's not that bad-looking, your half-brother. That black hair; not quite one of us, is he; he looks a bit wild. You could do worse.

Stop it.

María Teresa throws a small chequer-piece, which narrowly misses her cousin/stepmother's cheek and rebounds off her hair, dislodging a bow. The Queen stands, furious, scoops a whole handful of pieces from the board, scuppering the layout of an imminent victory and ready for war . . .

— What's all this excitement, ladies? The King, on his way to siesta, straining for a light note out of exhaustion—longing for a rest, but that's not what he'll be getting . . .

Nothing, Husband, the Queen says, demurely; the high colour of temper in her cheeks, she thinks, might just be becoming, as if she blushes upon sight of her King— Is it time to rest?

On the way out she turns to see María Teresa making smoochy faces; she sticks her tongue out and takes her husband's arm, sweetly. Surprised, gratified, he pats her little hand.

Mariana, Queen of Spain, she must also stand and be painted; after all, they called the painter back for this; and there's hours of awkward silence in this massive skirt with all this *stuff* in her hair and they won't let her have anyone there to entertain her, since she's prone to laughter, and she tries, she tries, to look like a queen, but can only look sullen and grumpy and flushed, though she's done as she's told and stopped wearing rouge, but her skin flares and pulses with the sweat and the grease, it's hot all the time and the rooms are so stuffy and the skirts are so large, and she is vanishing to nothing in this cage, of skirt and court, all the laughter squeezed from her, and so there's that pout that they all have, she can't help it. And that's how the world's going to see her, because the painter won't lie or flatter, that's the image they'll repeat and repeat and repeat so that everyone can see the new Queen.

Mariana— poor Mariana—— should have a monkey; I think she deserves one. No record will be left of it, and the painter, preferring dogs, won't paint it; but it would so suit her, wouldn't it? So, a small gift: while her husband clasps his temples, Mariana runs through the halls with her monkey on her shoulder, on her back, laughing.

Mariana, fractious, in her marriage bed; Mariana lying with her husband— who's repented, and goes on repenting, of congress with so many women, surely some as young as she ... *Love for Love's Sake*, the play they're staging—that's a laugh—but she doesn't really feel like laughing ... her husband maybe thinking all the time of his son, who should be here, in his place, filling this place; he is filling the place of his son, where his son should be there is nothing, this nothing to be filled and made to make something— a son— Mariana crying maybe but she will do her duty, she will bear it, she was born to do her duty, to bear children, as she's always known. But it wasn't supposed to be like this; there should have been a few years' grace, a few years' getting-to-know-you, going hawking, at ease while they waited for the King to pop off and leave the throne to them—not dead yet though is he—it isn't fair—instead—— she should have been at ease here with her handsome young husband, the hunter, the horseman, whose ghost hangs everywhere ready to ride out; this family of twisted roots and branches. It was supposed to be: uncle/father-in-law; husband/cousin; and now that pattern's snapped, the tender brittle young branch snapped and she is made to twist herself upward to be regrafted, make a new shoot from this gnarled knot, this conjunction. And they bud and they blacken, bud and then fail to blossom or fruit; that is, Mariana time and again feels herself bleeding, wakes up in her blood, the bed wet; feels it starting under her skirts, the deep pain clamping in her, the sticky smelly mess of her failure, hot under her skirts and her skin feeling damp, clammy, feeling tingling with pale sweat at the temples and beneath her eyes like tears stinging a swelling sweat around her hairline all stuck with grease and powder and blood high in her cheeks under the rouge, colouring with panic and pain and shame and failure, rising up in her throat, sweat between her small breasts, down into her back soaking all her nice underthings, she dissolves where she stands and is only the costume she stands up in, and between her legs the wet itchy heat of blood when it shouldn't be, heavy and clot, her womb relinquishing again, again, the little monstrous homunculi that's tried to claw its home there, clawing its way out or simply falling, and she or someone, in the next hours, will have to tell him. Again. And he is always so sad, so kind, so Stoical.

And then she has a daughter. She lives. They name her Margarita.

XIX

La familia/
The family

A chamberlain at the painter's door—framed in the doorway in the yellow light—announces the arrival of the King. Today the King can't just let himself in, unannounced, and take his quiet seat in the corner; today he is here on official business. Today the King is the painter's subject, and must subject himself to observation. The King writes to Sor María: It's awful. All my old flesh and bones on show. And the painter is—phlegmatic, always. I can't bear it, sitting for him. His phlegmatic tact, his silent relentlessness. Who would have a painter for a mirror? You would say, turn your mind from worldly things, forego your vanity. But— I am getting old.

And the painter observes him, hesitating at the doorway— drawn, his pallor pasty and dull—and sees he will have to lend him radiance, today—and prepares to begin. The King, long accustomed to the ritual, comes forward and submits to the place prepared for him; Go away, he says to the creatures that wait on him; and his attendant closes, locks the door behind them.

The endless necessity of this: of preserving his image, of making a record of his years passing. No crowns for these

kings. And no sash, no sword, no papers even; just the King
against the dark grey ground; just the painter and the King—
just as it was on the day he first came to him; just as the
painter sees him. But now— these years— so long in passing,
so soon gone——— the fleshy chin grown heavier— the folds
of skin below; the pale skin that he brings a little colour to;
but the traces of tiredness and care ingrained, which he sees
and knows and won't obscure; it is his duty to make record
of the King's reign as it passes, and he won't, can't, compro-
mise—he is also, in this, an official of the court. His duty:
to show the world as he sees it; to show the dignity of the
King, to testify to his resilience. So he will brighten the skin,
but won't hide his tiredness. It's not unkindness. It's to say,
this man is majesty, he is prudent, temperate, just; but he is
also a man who has suffered, for you, for us all— and also for
himself and all that he's lost. The King is also just a man of
solid flesh. Look at his eyes.

The morning passes; the hours pass for the painter unheeded,
as he works— quickly, quietly; the King empties his mind and
blank, immobile, his heavy lids seem unblinking until—

— he lifts the back of a long hand to his mouth; the long
jaw pulls longer, hollowing the long cheeks, pulling the lips
down with it, which he does not allow to part, even behind
his hand.

Are you tired, Señor?

The King lowers his hand from his mouth— Not at all, not
at all. Why do you ask?

Forgive me, Señor; I thought I saw a yawn.

A king does not yawn. Does not expose his molars; does
not laugh or shout or indeed gape, like a madman, like a poor
fool. He breathes always through his nose (long deep profound
breaths, each one almost a sigh). His mouth opens only to eat,

and to speak, and does both of these things with restraint, with decorum.

But now when the King opens his mouth to speak he finds himself saying— A little, perhaps. I am a little tired, Diego. Excuse me.

Would you like to rest, Señor? We needn't go on with this.

Oh he would. He would like very much to rest; he would like to retreat to his corner and sit quietly here in the studio, watching the painter work, on— some other thing. Bring his daughter in. His … wife … oh, this yawning, this hollow in him …

He says: Not at all. If you'll tolerate my weary company, I shall endeavour not to yawn. I am sorry if my ragged visage taxes your brush, though, Diego; and he smiles his invisible smile to show this is a joke.

An hour or so more passes, silent. Observing. Heavy lids; heavy jaw; his brow, his brow bones— his eyes. His hooded shadowed hollowed eyes. Hollow temples, hollow sockets, depth of reddened dark he looks out from. The weight of care on the brow, the lids of the eyes pulled slack and low, deep grey shadow etched out of his temple, under the thin pale skin; the skull under the skin. It is a portrait of a man, just a man, a block of dark grey, the edges of him glistening. Glistening daubs for buttons. Seams and creases. Ragged, ragged, the edges of his pupils, his iris, ragged in his eyes …

As the painter stands back, wiping his brush, the King rises to examine the portrait. His … oh, his eyes … the painter stands by, phlegmatically.

He says, Perhaps, that's enough. It's finished enough. Let's not go on with it. I'm so tired of seeing myself in your mirrors, Diego— glancing to the door, and the mirror beside it, and meeting his own tired eyes in it. And the painter, alone, works on——

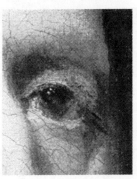

— He's in London now, this King. This old and tired and sad King— hanging alongside his younger grander self, that new father to a son in his new purple-brown and silver suit. And then look across to this portrait, so small and plain alongside it, and so much lost in the twenty years between them—the son, the wife, and hope, almost—just a man with no fancy threads or papers. Old father to a new daughter; just seams and creases and— his eyes. I can almost pretend he sees me, knows me, when I drop in: you again, he almost sighs. What's *your* petition? I come in and sit down and rest a minute; this cool gallery on a summer weekday afternoon, out of the busy city, come to sit alongside you and see your King, Diego, and how you saw him. How long has it been? I've been so flat, so tired; and then I don't understand where my time goes, so many small duties that make up the minutes of a year and then it's gone and it's gone and it's gone, you know how it is, I know you do; I think, at least, you would know what I mean. What am I doing; what will I do; what, in the end, will I have done? Thirty-five years you've been at court, now—as many as I've been alive for, this hot Tuesday afternoon. Not so old; but my skin bags and creases and I look tired all the time and I can't stop getting older. I'd hate to see what your honest brush would make of me. That's not true, of course. How I'd love you to see me. But then again, I can't bear all these mirrors. A glimpse of me; a lonely ghost on your periphery— But you're working now, don't mind me———

— He is always working. Another promotion, to High Chamberlain, overseeing all the court's quarters: reviewing the document, the King scrawls 'I wish it' across it. So that's that then. The King accustomed now to governing alone, and making his wishes known; and weary perhaps of the neat spaces left for his endless signatures. El Primo stamps it. The painter is installed in a new apartment, in the treasury, where the King keeps all his most valued possessions ... through a passageway full of unused images, waiting images, faces turned to the wall, half-extinct expinxit horses, works half-painted, unpainted—the painter can reach the Alcázar to perform his duties without having to go outside at all. But within the walls, now, he can open any door. He makes arrangements— he puts things in places— he ensures the smooth running of the world of the court and all its solid objects:

— He furnishes, he decorates; they are renovating. Always, they are renovating. He designs a grand new staircase. He designs an octagonal gallery. The stuff he bought in Rome at last arrives and he has it all hung on all eight sides and placed on pedestals and in niches—

— He arranges ceremonies. Festivals. Performances. Works with his old friend Don Pedro the playwright, and the Florentine Cosmelotti, to ensure all goes off with a suitable bang—

— He arranges accommodation. When guests come, he accommodates.

— He places chairs and tables. The lighting of braziers.

— He officiates at dinners, removing the cloths from the dishes.

— Deep in the cellars he walks with the cellar-keeper and inspects the wines—down where there's no finery, only plain tiling to save the walls from damp; no windows to fit with coloured glass, ceilings too distant from the light to warrant modelling; and no space for paintings, where they'd moulder unseen—

— He oversees the cleaning of the King's quarters, all their hidden cupboards and corners, the dust that gathers on sills and frames, on the doors, in every inset frame—

— He opens windows— he opens doors and—

— he closes doors and locks them.

He can go where he wishes, known but unobtrusive. He has a key that opens all the doors.

✢

The locks run smooth in the palace, because they are in constant use (and it is someone's duty to ensure they do so). The painter's cousin, his counterpart, the Queen's chamberlain José Nieto, can also open almost any door. José Nieto rises (early, as we all do) and opens the casements and lets the light in. He trims and points his beard. He unlocks the door of his chamber and locks it behind him, and puts this key away close to his breast, because, of all the keys, this one is his alone. He makes his way to Her Majesty's chambers and unlocks the first door (without knocking, with the privilege and right of passage) and greets the ladies who sit on cushions in this outer chamber and through a succession

of murmurs and curtseys and nods his presence is made
known to the Queen.

   She is a mother now; the little girl is five already. No more
monkey business. The Queen has made her life at la Corte,
as well as she can, arranging it around her, or allowing its
arrangement; submitting, worn down to something like calm-
ness by years and duty and confinement; putting up with it;
seeking some comfort in piety. And when the Queen wishes
to pray, or visit her daughter, or wherever she wishes to go that
day, José will go ahead of her and unlock any door that requires
unlocking (and he can find the key by touch, by instinct, he
never fits the wrong key to the wrong lock, all the bolts turn
smoothly), and opens any door she'd like to pass through, and
closes it behind her if she wants it closed, and waits on her,
attends her needs and awaits the completion of her business
there, from stateroom to chapel to water closet. The Queen
is often confined and when that is the case he can wait all
day for her summons, he can loiter in her outer chambers,
chatting to her ladies, who like his pointed eyes, his pointed
beard to pull at. José owns many pairs of gloves and every
day he sends the pair he's worn for cleaning and has trained
himself, he thinks, never to rub his nose or eyes or put a hand
to his mouth; always to remove the gloves before eating; but
still any tingle or sourness, something unexpectedly bitter or
sweet, any brief stinging or numbness, sets off a tiny panic in
him, and he thinks, poison. But he is hardly alone in that. He
is one of many who are tasked with preventing the King and
Queen from touching anything until someone else has done
so. Latches, keys, door handles.

José opens the door to the little Infanta's chambers. Margarita:
bright and sunny as a daisy, safe here, hope embodied in a

bright white dress. Privileged guests may come to the door-way—no further into her chamber—and watch her, thus framed; an exclusive audience to the private performance of her playing— of her life lived within this frame. The picture of a perfect gleaming princess, blonde white and gold; and everyone around her watching, to guard, to serve and preserve her—— And the picture too wants preserving, of course; the painter is called upon to preserve her image.

So she is escorted, close on all sides, to the studio, and he observes her: and she stands still, as she is told to, very per-fect, very like her dolls, the same clothes and china skin; she is good, obedient, trying to make her eyes glass, not to blink; the painter's eyes are kind and quiet and his studio is very silent; he has closed the door. The sun through the high win-dows and the outside she can't go into, preserving her safety and her white doll-princess skin; except sometimes she's allowed out with a parasol and a phalanx of servants. Her life within these windows and these guarded doors, framing her, this is all she's known, these frames, and she behaves well, she is good, she lives up to expectations . . . and for now, she is to stand still, and she stands still with her eyes open until they fill up, not spilling. She is to stand still; and that is tiring, though she's sure she can hide it; and she is very tired. Of all the people watching. The painter is very quiet. They love her when she's happy, and she is, mostly, and so she plays happily, plays her part, doll-princess, on whom they all depend for hope, for brightness. Her white skirts she mustn't dirty. Her white skin she mustn't smear, with rouge, with tears, with chocolate. Thirsty. Here in the studio in her white dress, in her blue, in her pink, on her own always with all the people watching. The painter, who says nothing, watching her, not unkindly, concentrating; she's not to put him off. She stands

still for him. She thinks of dancing. She thinks of her friends
and wonders if they're playing without her.

Do you like ices? she asks the painter. Because Mari-Barbola
loves ices! she tells him. She *loves* them. She's *always* to have
ices. Did you know, every day, she has a pound of ice brought
to her? (So the King has ensured, and without fail the Infanta's
dwarf has her ice, every summer day.) She likes them with
anise. I think those taste like medicine. I like peach. Which do
you like, Don Diego? (she is always polite, this little Princess,
and remembers that it's gracious to ask questions, show an
interest in her subjects). The painter doesn't answer. He is
concentrating.

She holds in a sigh, restrains a fidget; she is hot. She'd like
an ice, actually. She misses Mari-Barbola. Misses Nicolasito
who dances so prettily. Missing the life she doesn't know she's
missing, beyond the open door she can't step through, beyond
the windows to the gardens that from here she can't see. On
her own here with the nasty angry goddess and the man being
flayed, paintings she tries not to look at but can't keep her eyes
from rolling up to, her eyes filling, trying not to blink. She
hiccups, keeping her mouth closed. She says—— but doesn't.
Don't put him off. She is so thirsty. Isabel de Velasco is no
company at all, she is an utterly useless maid of honour, sitting
in the corner; Margarita tries to catch her eye and signal, she
is thirsty, bring a cup, but Isabel is miles away, lucky Isabel not
having to stand like this; she's a doll discarded on her chair
with her eyes half-closing, with her shiny black hair, not quite
so finely wrought and rare a doll as the Princess ... Margarita
sniffs. She sniffs again and there's unbecoming snot coming
and she has no hankie, Isabel has it. She shouldn't lift her hand.
She should keep her face still. But it isn't; she feels the corners
of her mouth twitch and tighten. Her throat strains sorely,

her neck, her jaw. Her eyes sting. And she sits down and she's sitting now and has let herself all crumble, her hands in her lap balled and she sniffs and hiccups hotly and she hits at her skirts rising in a cage around her with little lace-cuffed fists and she doesn't know what's happening or why she's sitting or what her hands are doing and when she opens her mouth she hiccups loudly and shouts I WANT—— I want— I'm LOOO-oonely. And now can't get her breath through all the snot and tears and the stuff of her skirts all their stupid hooped frames all round her and hot and frantic and embarrassed.

The painter has stopped painting. José, who has a key, has appeared at the door again. Isabel has woken up and come to her side with a belated hankie.

All going well? asks José. Poor kid. How long have you been going? Poor little rag-doll.

The painter hasn't had much to do with children; he leaves that to Juana (—— and also— in the house of Martha and Maddalena——)

Princess, he says. Shall we have a break now? Shall we call for Mari-Barbola and have ices? (There was something about ices, he heard her, but thinks he forgot to answer . . .) I shall have an orange one. If I may.

She is already quieter. Poor kid.

Which would you like?

Peach, she snuffles, from the depths of her skirts and her humiliation.

The painter sees: What can be seen through a door, a window, a picture frame. He can be anywhere; known, unobtrusive. He observes as he arranges—

— The dwarves and the jesters and the dogs of the court. Shifting and slumbers and dancing—

— the servants, attendants, the nuns, the nannies, the little ladies-in-waiting—

— the gods and mortals that hang on his studio walls; that he has hung there—

— the King— the Queen——

— his many mirrors—

— the light of his high windows. The shadows in the dim high corners.

— José Nieto in the doorway—the Queen's chamberlain, his cousin, his counterpart— framed in the light, pausing on the stairs to his door.

— the tiny Infanta: Margarita, the bright thing at the court's centre.

He observes, from the very midst of it; the elements of the court's composition. He is there at the centre; just off-centre.

☩

The King and Queen are sitting for their portrait, and the Queen is impatient and bored, and the King is sick of portraits. And the painter is doing what he can with this but, since he won't flatter, since he can't lie, it is not going to be fit for purpose: see how well-suited this couple are, how tranquilly they reign, together . . . see how mournful, how sullen—— no. This won't work.

So perhaps, we might bring some light in, some distraction? Perhaps we might send for a fool, a buffoon . . . or perhaps, even better—— José is in agreement. José now, pausing on the stair at the painter's doorway, letting a slant of light in— along with the Infanta, and her girls and dog and governess and dwarves. Here they all are. She comes into their midst and unites them; bright in the centre of the studio, of the court. The King and Queen, unfinished on the canvas, united now in their love for her— How is my favourite little jester? asks the King. How she's loved, this little Princess, by the girls, the dwarves, her parents; by the painter. You can see it by the light on her.

An idea for a painting, a frame for it: here they all are, just this moment stopped. The royal family assembled, here in this cool grey room—lofty, dim in its high and far corners—here in the painter's studio and the painter in their midst. The painter in plain black, reds on his palette ready for the details, cup and curtain and bows, blush. The circumstance of this moment, of a set of gestures— the gestures not arrested, but ongoing—— Stand back with your brush, Diego—observing— ready to make the first mark; so—

— Here they all are. Stand on the brink of the light and by this light regard them: maids-of-honour, dwarves, a sleeping dog. Daylight, flooding from the unseen window, falls knowingly upon them— lightly upon the lesser beings, touching only the borders of their contours, but falling fully on the face of the Infanta, her white-gold hair, her white skin, the white satin of her wide skirts. She is untouched by any shadow that might pass between her and the sun; untouched by the knowledge of the shadow that will claim her, and all of us, that has long since claimed her and all of them. Look though how they almost move, how they might easily at any moment join hands and dance a jig—that sinuous line of near-contact—Mariana Sarmiento dips beseeching with red beaker that the Princess is about to take—Isabel Velasco self-conscious, currying favour, looks where the Princess is looking, drops a careful curtsey—looking on from the shad-ows: a nun; a man not much more than collar and moustache and— the eye falls through the light on the line of Isabel's sleeve half-bright in the sunlight— Mari-Barbola who loves ices and on through gesture and bow to the poised balancing hands of Nicolasito——points a perfect slippered toe, a flick of a heel and a tip-tap-toe, kick of a heel and a tac, toe—— look, how Nicolasito seems already to be dancing—— a prod at the dog with a pointed toe— a line from toe to paw, corner to corner—elbow-crook to elbow-crook— angle of a hand and a hand and a hand that holds a brush, poised— ready to make a first mark. How the eye traces from frame to frame to frame: to begin from this dark corner, from these vanishing points: there's José Nieto, pausing at the threshold; and the mirror, just off-centre on the back wall by the doorway, full of borrowed light. Two dim ghosts of colour in it: the ageing King and his young, his very young, Queen. The painter has made many portraits of the man in the mirror, and this will be just about the last of them. A king of pale shadows, retreating at last into his own blurred image: indistinct, withdrawn, almost incidental, and yet there at the radiant off-centre of everything. And framed up high above them: Marsyas the musician, flayed; Arachne the spider; the mortal artist daring to show the world to itself so; to unpick the stitches and seams of God's creation, to show how it's done—then re-do it. In faultless imperfect reflection. Shattered world made whole out of shadow and points of light. Light falling and stopped at frame to frame to frame. Bright lines in the depths: the bevelled mirror; the grid of panels in the door, cast into relief by that strong external light which enters the room only as a crack of brightness, a brush-width of bright falling across the floor—— and the pale light is stopped by the bright edge of a canvas on its easel, outreaching all the heads of those below it, stretching up to the high dim ceiling. Just about the height of the painting itself, the painting that contains it, which is what it might be; the painting containing the moment of its own composition. José in the doorframe— King and Queen in mirror frame— back of the canvas frame; all enclosed in this frame: the perpetual present of this moment—the perpetual pastness of this moment; just stopped.

Look: here is the Infanta, here her meninas, her dwarves, whom she loves, and the dog. Her parents are here, watching—almost—only the dim mirrored trace of them; but he can see them. The painter. And here, says the painter, or says his painting, here in their midst, trusted, unremarked, in his dark discreet clothing, his dark direct discreet eye: here am I, with a canvas as tall as a room, to record it all. Look at the barest gesture of paint that his hand is; how the brush that made all this is just a brushstroke— So, Diego; there you are—

XX

Principe vero ea quae digna sunt cogitavit/
But he who is noble plans noble things

—— On this day in London I woke at dawn to thunder; storms
and flooding across the country have broken a sultry stretch,
a doldrum, the hottest September days in a century, and I feel
susceptible to portents; close; closing—

The Queen has another daughter, another little Princess, in
December. Soon carried off one cold night by infinitely patient,
cruel and gentle bony hands.

The King fasts and prays. His scientists read the stars;
read the signs that they are privy to; they promise him an
heir, before the new year is done. The King eats no meat,
only eggs on holy days. He trembles, in the chapel, unseen;
in the spring the Queen stops bleeding; in summer she
grows, she lies still in the heat, feels him stirring; autumn
ripening; they pray for fulfilment of this promise, this
prophecy. A healthy living son, of pure blood ... There
are storms through the autumn, and heat unbreaking, low
red moons distorted and bloating on the dry horizon; the
Queen grows big and red-cheeked, stretched and veined,
it must be a boy this time they tell him, because the shape

of the Queen's belly— because the swallows— because the stars; she is sick with the heat, she eats ices. The doors and windows are closed to vapours, to anything else that might get in, and in the dark corners she hears clattering; rattling; sighing. A sound like a blade stropping. She will have no crib prepared for him. She will receive no gifts. She will not speak of names for him. The King sits at her bedside praying until she sends him away, ashamed, and telling him he smells of eggs and it sickens her—the King prays and fasts—he is distracted, he seeks distraction for an hour or two and then a week of penance and fasting, pleading, that his wife, his family, his coming son and his country aren't punished for his sins ... A second full moon in a month, a fat red blue moon, they say it means nothing, nothing bad, no ill omen—

In November, he comes— the Queen has a son. Early in the morning, and earlier than they expected him; she throws the covers from her, eyes rolling, animal; frightened; waking from a bloody dream to find herself damp and cramping. She hears bells toll, she yells, make them silent! Fools crowd around her and pluck at strings and tinkle bells and rattle and chatter; go—AWAY— she screams, and the physicians and the midwives are patient and calming and hide their alarm and say— Almost, Your Majesty, he is nearly here; they dab and mop her scalding skin, they sop the blood from her; they haul at him and he is here; blue, skinny, glaucous; but— yes— breathing! He gulps a first breath and then bawls his arrival into the dawn. That is the sound of a man, the King says.

She, my wife, is my soulmate, the King writes to Sor María. The new Prince does well, he lives. My unsought solace. I think

of my boy who's departed, how bitter these years have been . . .
I thank God for this new chance. My wife brought him forth
in fever. She rests, I have faith, she will recover; I have faith
that perhaps I am forgiven . . . Pray for her. Pray for my son—

La Corte celebrates. They roast whole goats and, greasy, soot-
smeared, toast the future—in this strange season, this cold
clouded month with no stars to tell by—there is yet a future,
be sure of it! A boy, a prince, an heir! Spain's not finished
yet— No fear! Fill the cups— we're not done yet! Pass the
flagons—in the kitchens of the palace and the courtyards and
the forecourts, and in every inn, and tavern, and pastry shop,
and in the streets— bang the cups! Hammer it out! Cymbals
and drums! Bang the cups down on the benches and climb up
to dance! Pour wine, more wine! Let it all flow out! These years
of drear and quiet despair—banish them! Death—out with
you, we'll have none of you, you've no place in this dance! The
Devil is cast out of this court with a bang! Flares and torches!
The light's long gone but we make our own, light the long
night up and don't feel the chill— Take up your batons and
let's have dancing!

It goes off all the long noisy night— the new Prince bawling
and the Queen alone in her chamber, delirious, hearing it all,
the bawling and the brawling, beyond, beyond closed windows
doors and curtains, a great banging brawling party, and come
morning there's no cup left unturned, no bench left unbroken,
the whole place sacked, the whole of la Corte devastated by
this last fulfilled hope . . .

Weeks pass; her brow cools, she heals, she strengthens;
sorely, weakly, she rises, to see the masquerades, to see the bulls
fall, to see the tourneys, in his honour; and her son screams
and screams and they celebrate his healthy lungs; the King

receives congratulations, from every last gentleman, and each commends the new-born Prince's healthy lungs; they bear him through the streets bawling past masquerades, musicians, magicians making tricks, madmen dancing; they pour water on his forehead and name him—for his father, and for the future that's coming, now, that's promised now, to be prosperous—he is every last good prospect—we're redeemed, we aren't done yet, we live on to a new future, our new-born future!— the water on his skin makes him scream and the King, hearing, says Ah, my house smells of a man, now; now I've made a little man. Thank God.

A little man. He grows slowly. He bawls. He falls. He foams. His limbs fixed and rigid. His head bangs back, eyes rolled; the physicians gather round him, they fear what possesses him, and if it will release him; a pillow for his head and a bit for his teeth, and froth foams around it and he is silent, rigid, fighting his ghosts alone— whimpering— after long minutes he returns to them. And screams. He is the future. He won't fail them; the seers have promised. Why would they lie?

Felipe Prosper: his very tender skin. His noble radiant bloodless skin. How cloth chafes him. How heavy his clothes are. Don't dress him in metal collars, in armour, in damask, in starched lace. Hang him with baubles, hang him with charms. A tiny censer to ward off sickness, filled with spices to mask the smell of it; bells to warn off death; an amulet of jet to ward off darkness. A little horn to turn back evil eyes. He takes only bland pulp and sicks it back up again. Touch him only softly or he'll weep. Anyway he'll weep. Touch him and he quivers, yet craves to be held, for someone to hold him, but then can't bear it—unless you are very, very gentle. Quietly crying when the spoon's held to him, when it touches his tender lips. Quietly crying his hunger, all night crying, quietly, a crying that shouldn't be heard from a child, hopeless crying, terrible; a child shouldn't cry so quietly, resigned to it; a child that sees—— in the corner— where light won't reach—— She clacks and clucks at his crib, she busses his cheek with her cold knucklebones, as he chews weakly, toothless on his rattle. His very fair hair, his very fine hair, so thin on his thin scalp and sensitive to touch, his thin skin, the thin bones of his skull under his skin. He lives; he lives; another year and another; words come to him slowly; he doesn't name her but she's never far.

That darkness that is always behind all of us, the dark ground; the painter sees it in him, pities him, lets a little light in through a door cracked behind him. So he might leave, any second, it might mean— or as if someone has invisibly just come in, to wait on him. The darkness also in his haunted eyes. A little dog, the painter's favourite, who makes the Prince laugh and is soft enough to be petted. How he loves to rest his face against the dog's soft flank, feel his little bones, his little heart, his soft fine fur on the ridges of the skull under it; to be that little dog is his favourite game, or dream, for he can't go on all fours and get his knees bruised, he can't run about and risk falling . . . feels the falling, fears the black and brightening . . .

High whine of air around him; dust in his eyes; he can't go outside. He can't breathe the air—the common air too coarse for him, he can't— take it in— hiccoughs, cough, oh no, no, enough, enough— scrapes and rattles, half-set honey in his gullet, clay and crunch, scrabble for air, rasping, shudder, hiccoughcough— cough— and gulp and heave and spit up thick honey— the particulate air will harm him and he will scorch in the sun, his very tender skin; his scalp red-raw scorched in the sunshine. His skin shining, flaking, crystalline. His mitten-paws. In the night he bites them, in his dog-dreams, gnawing his hands, gnash and gnaw, they say try to ignore it, the itch between the fingers, under the skin. Wakes cold; shivering; convulsant; mid-conversion, any hour of night or day it might visit him; they say it's God's touch, not the other one. Dusk comes and he lies down exhausted and wakes in darkness, just a faint crack of light where she comes in; wakes cold and gnawing and weakly, What's wrong with me? he whimpers. But though they let and purge, salve and poultice, wind his hands in mittens, wrap him in soft fur and linen, no one can cure him. He burns and itches, wrenches and foams and retches. Everything's wrong with him.

The King has another son. He names him for his brother the Cardinal. The Infante Fernando. He prays: let him be a hunter, a gamesman, a rider; let him be smart and— pious— let him be healthy— let him— let him live, let him be, please let him be …

Don Juan José, the King's bastard, now governor of the Netherlands, is losing his grip on things. Losing his lands. Inch by mile. But clinging to this favour that he still enjoys, his father's distant favour; bides his time. They've found a match for his sister María Teresa, so he's heard. He's heard his little brother's sick. He hears things, sees things. He dreams of a king; he sees the King's unborn son made king—a son that's still to come— a helpless drooling child dragging himself onto the throne unable to walk and growing to a helpless drooling adult, hexed, a half-wit, the image of his father in a dark flawed glass, jaw jutting and drooling, indolent, filthy with his hair in knots unwashed, his mama sitting on his throne and pulling him onto her knee drooling while she chews his food for him. He sees him weak, bald, shrivelled, he sees the lovely young queen pulling at him, at nothing, a shrivelled flaccid thing with one blackened ball; he sees impotence and weakness and all Spain dying, all its gold tarnished; with a fool's foresight, in this nightmare he sees all this, the sands of the golden age almost run and, having flared bright, now pile up as ashes; and when they're done, Juan José will be ready to step forward through the ruins.

In October, the little Prince Fernando dies. Made it to a year, almost. But there's still little Felipe— Felipe Prosper still clutching his amulets, hung with his charms. The King is not hopeful; he is Stoical, as he must be. He schools himself: without hope or fear. He prays to be spared, to be spared all passion. He can't help it. Hoping; fear. He sits at his son's bedside when he sickens, and submits to God's will; he sees that this is God's will, his retribution, and offers up his sorrow; he writes to Sor

María: I know this now; that this is my burden, and I offer to God all that I have—I offer up my sorrow. He prays; does penance. He will never be done with this punishment. What can he do? What has he done?

He sits by his son's bedside, praying, unsleeping, fasting— he lives on the sips of soup he takes to test it's cool enough before he spoons it for his son. He sits thinking— these mordant thoughts— these daunted thoughts— what can he, what should, will he—— God's will, be done— a will to be re-written ... he dozes and half-dreams of sepulchres, of laby-rinths, he wanders them, seeking a centre, seeking a dark place to lie down in; he drowses, wakes to the stertorous gurgle of his son's laboured dreaming; he watches over his laboured sleep, breathing, still; twitching ...

What will he leave behind? What sort of kingdom, and what sort of heir? What monument is he to have, if he is not to be remembered like his father? His father went to his rest magnificently; if we were to be cruel we might say it was the most magnificent thing he'd ever done. Laid out upon a bier so magnificently massive it broke the floor of the chapel. Glorious, famous, faithful; prudent, continent and meek; liberal, religious, pious, clement; just, victorious; peaceful and benign; honourable; truthful. These are the marble virtues that watched over his catafalque, vast and unassailable; the King recalls those marble statues now, their gestures, the arch dignity of their faces, their emblems, lit from below by hun-dreds of candles, kept lit at great expense by the monks of San Jerónimo. Black velvet lining the walls, absorbing all of this expensive light; a black, velvet quiet, as peat-soft as the grave; we should all hope to pass so softly, in such opulence. And now his body waits upon his soul's return. As all the King's ances-tors await judgement, and the King, too, in time. He recites,

he paces round them in his mind, now; these words, these
monuments—piety, clemency—victory! Truly, continence—
honour . . . he will honour them; he will make peace with them;
his fathers and his sons to come; make a place of rest for them.
Glory! Fame . . . what's to be said of him . . . Peace . . .

He will have a place made ready for them. Here's what he'll
leave: a richly furnished hole in the ground for them to rest
in, below the basilica of the Escorial, below the monastery his
grandfather built. If the soul is a labyrinth, then here, the King
has found his way to the centre of it; has hollowed it out here,
a chamber, buried below the holy heart of his grandfather's
house, carved out of the slagheap soil. He has the tomb finished in marble, purple-black and red, dark and rich, and there
are niches for his father, his grandfather, the emperor before
them, their wives (those that made heirs, at least; and a place
for Isabel, she will rest here, even though their son—— their
son); and their bodies are carried down to their niches and Oh,
ye dry bones, hear the word of the Lord, says Ezekiel, while the
weight of them is borne downward—not much weight to them,
to their dry bones, but the boxes that house them are marble
and must be carefully borne—to await that final irrefutable
word; and here below this monastery is a place for all his dead,
all his children new-born and surviving a few minutes months
or years, and increasingly now when not at his son's bedside the
King buries himself in this place of retreat that his grandfather
built; here beneath it; and here too is a niche for his own bones.

He comes alone and no one will seek him out there, he
goes to the place that is waiting for him and lies down where
his coffin will be. There is always this death, and the knowledge of death, here at the centre. He descends, down into the
dark marble, black, green, red, bronze. Dark here. Cool here.
Although he bears a candle with him the chamber has the

smell of lightless places, of underground places; marble and darkness, cool, unbreathed air, bodies here unbreathing. But: one breathes. Lies down upon his marble bier of cool smooth blood-red stone, and listens to his breath, that breathes on behalf of all of them; lies here long enough that everything slows to silence and only, if he listens, his breath, his slowing heartbeat, his harnessed heart. Trussed and caged in the prison of his body, his ribs, his bones, his blood against his skull under his skin. His eyes soften. Skull large and heavy against the stone. Dark red in the darkness. Dark green veins. Cold marble skin. His wife lying above him, heart stopped. He prays, his lips move, his hands fold on his chest over his heart. A long way from heaven, down here; the whole holy weight of the basilica above him. They are all ascended; must have ascended; the specific particulate arrangement of their souls, the particular temporal moment of their souls on earth, passed now, gone into the unknown, and his soul here alone. This is where he's headed, in the end——

They'll make a pantheon for the princes, later; for all his children, Margarita Catharina María Elisabeth Fernando Anna María Fernando ... Felipe ... for Baltasar Carlos a special tomb upon which is engraved: But he who is noble plans noble things—

XXI

Isla de los Faisanes/
Île des Faisans/
Isle of Pheasants

The painter is tireless. Arranging, placing, accommodating. He is to make all the arrangements for the Infanta's wedding. He is indispensable. Right in their midst, right at the just off-centre of everything. So, now, you have what you wanted? If Juana asks then perhaps he says yes, more or less, I have what I wanted.

But Juana—and the painter—they are grieving. Francisca has died, giving birth to their seventh grandchild. Perhaps they are a comfort to each other, growing older; and they have at least their grandchildren around them; and their son-in-law, Juan Bautista, who has lived in his house all these years and learned from him, who has been his student and as near as he's had to a son— but—— Perhaps he doesn't say to Juana, out loud— Always something's missing. Always a door unopened— or closed forever now. Places he could have been; things left behind him. What's past, what he's parted with; the things he's given, the things he's sold. Pale half-forgotten form, outstretched on purple silk, a grey ground. In Rome ... He can't quite remember her face, now.

He had a son, in Rome. His name was Antonio. That's all I know of him.

The painter petitions the King. He writes: I would like to return to Rome, Señor. He receives no reply.

The King in his place in the painter's studio; the painter works up to it, having waited—having had no response— he says, Perhaps you will understand, Señor, there is a woman there; she's mother to my son. Or no—— He says——

— I would like to see her again—

— I would like to see my—

— meet my son——

— I have been so bound to my duties to you that I have neglected my duty as a man.

No—— he says, I will find gifts for your daughter, wedding gifts; gifts to send to France; he says nothing of his son who—

— he's never met——

— had no chance to meet——

— is buried in Rome . . .

— He doesn't say— I'm a painter. Anyone could plump your cushions. Let me go to Rome. He makes a request, properly and politely.

The King says: No. I need you here. You can't go. There's work to be done.

Very well, Señor, he says; phlegmatic. Goes about his business, knowing, clever, discreet, courtly. Dutiful. Noble— surely.

He opens doors, closes them. Has the mirrors cleaned. His own eye in the mirror; his own dark doublet, unadorned. His noble eye. His noble name.

He petitions the King——

— You would be a knight, then, Diego? Why? Does it mean so much, to be called noble, to have a red cross to stamp it? Another gold chain around you? Do you care so much, what they think of you?

But of course you do. I do.

You want them to acknowledge that your work is as worthy as a poet's, as a playwright's—your friend the playwright with the red cross praises painting, above all other arts; he envies you, he says, he elevates your art——

You want them to acknowledge you. Is that it?

You want, after all these years, the King to acknowledge you, to exercise his power in your favour, to demonstrate, by making an exception for you, that you are exceptional.

And so after much petitioning, much lobbying, much gathering of signatures and testimony and supporters—the Pope, even, for God's sake—much creative genealogy, sending back to Seville for deeds and proofs, that noble old surname and no, no conversos, Christian all the way back—much argument to say he's never, *as such*, taken payment for the work of his hands—— that is, painting is a noble art, a work of eye and mind; he is akin to a poet, not an artisan (and whether he believes this or not, he scrubs his cuticles and makes the case)— the King makes his decree: *I wish it*— and he gets his red cross, painted (so they say) by the King's own hand where he stands in the midst of the family— there's the last mark——

You have what you wanted?

In October the French ride into la Corte and right into the court, into the fortress in their frills and ruffs and colours, as if they hadn't even time to put on riding gear and came straight from the ongoing Parisian soiree to convey Louis' impatience, his eagerness, to marry the King's daughter. And they are received in the same spirit, Spain not to be outdone. A last burst of majesty; a last best hope, of legacy, of something lasting. The King, in private, disgusted. But, he explains to his daughter— We can't keep fighting. It must be done. So we'll do it with style, with splendour. We'll show those flashy ars ... aristos. Oh, your fiancé excepted, I'm sure, my dear. María Teresa brave among her butterflies. The King in marble agony. Selling his daughter to this vulgar Bourbon— arsehole—— he says it to himself, silently. For the sake of Spain, for the world, for peace. Honour. Prudence. Clemency. Planet King.

The painter oversees the motion of this orrery; puts wheels in motion; assembles, overhead, the constellations—in the galleries of the Alcázar, in the new Hall of Mirrors, a new scheme to be hung, in honour of the forthcoming nuptial. He guides the visitors through the halls of his arrangement. Here are Arachne's women, spinning, winding, weaving, cutting thread— stand away and you'll see it, the threads

pulling and the whole thing pulling together tighter wheel
to reel; fast and patient and steady— stand here and you see
it, the whole scene wheeling left to right, turning, pulling
out and around like the thread as it spins, circles in circles, reel to wheel; they see that strength is beauty in the
movement of hands and down and up through arms, neck,
shoulders, back, hips, calves, and all the body, all the body
spinning—— They see that love is strength is beauty they
see Venus triumph; they see Adonis, all but overwhelmed
here. Reds and flesh and gold. They see themselves reflected,
multiplied, surrounded by infinities of love, the limbs of
women, and love reflected back upon them, enfolding in
endless red recursion.

The playwright takes up the cue, and writes a play for an
epithalamium—in which Love triumphs, and Peace triumphs,
and Mars ends impotent, a sluggard, a bum. In a darkened
grotto dwell Fear, Suspicion, Anger; Jealousy dwells there;
Desengaño is chained in a gruesome green darkness; Love
triumphs over these, her enemies. Not hope, exactly, but an end
to disillusion. They see the goddess Venus married to Adonis,
her pretty mortal husband. The bride ascends, draped gauzily,
triumphant; her groom looks on adoring. The French, with
raised painted eyebrows, applaud the machinery, applaud the
goddess rising.

María Teresa will be married on the border, on the Isle of
Pheasants. The painter is to make a realm between their
two realms, for them to meet in. He sets off with a carefully
chosen crew making fast for the North, for Bidassoa. On the
way, he makes short stops to prepare for the King's stopping;
he ensures accommodation, he ensures regular, comfortable,
secure rest; he has all the doors on all the inns checked and

fixed by his own carpenter; thief-proof, assassin-proof; he is the man for doorways. And who can pass through them.

Behind him the King, his daughter, and all the family. And the court—the courtiers—the administrators, and the attendants—and more than a hundred wagons, and a hundred horses, and more than a thousand mules; and doctors and barbers and cooks and waiters; and almost everything the King owns. Miles and miles and miles of it. And all along the length of it, relics are brought forth; peasants dance with swords and hidalgos scrape up gifts for them, open their estates to them; through the mountains, bonfires mark their passage. This spectacle, the King passing, the country out to see him pass. Streamers and dancing and wine. Feasts of what little they have; animals slaughtered and roasted on spits at the roadside; pheasants in dozens thrown into the pot as a tribute; they cross themselves as they pass through the country, the knights with their red crosses, and make prayers and donations at every chapel, every shrine; and the peasants and the farmers and the struggling hidalgos offer prayers in turn as they pass— for peace, for plenty, for a long and fruitful marriage. And everyone, every one of the grandees and courtiers and guests of the court has a bed and a safe door to guard it, and the horses have stables and the grooms and the servants have straw to sleep on and something to drink. Twenty miles of stuff and baggage. And stopping every ten. The arithmetic alone! Clever painter. Who has arrived on the island and is at work on the pavilions. He is tireless. He seems tireless.

Going deep into this low, foetid border country, brown, yellow, marshy; seeking solid footing upon which to raise pavilions; cicadas loud in the evenings and clouds of mosquitoes gathering, spreading and flattening, rising and spiralling, whining, on their nasty thirsty whim; in the night not sleeping in the low air listening to the whine of them; versions and reversions, recursions; the night terrible; hot and droning; all the distance he's come, all there is to do here, he must be up early and on form in the morning and he must sleep so he looks presentable so he can think and see and point straight with clean and steady hands to instruct them and he goes over what needs doing which he has already set out and made a list of but might have forgotten something and maybe needs—— he's actually forgotten all the gifts, all the gifts in his keeping, the diamond-studded fleece, the gold watch with diamonds, the jewels, the thieves are out there and the door's not safe he's left them in a tent or can't think where to find them and no, he's awake—— but everything is fine; he'll go to sleep. It was good, wasn't it? What he's done. A palace full of paintings. Close, eyes closed now; Argus with all eyes closed now; all eyes closed now; Mercury creeping. Oh, he needs to sleep.

Everyone waking bitten, itching, miserable, ready to put on a show. Reputation is all. No scratching. They won't be outshone. The King has arrived with his daughter.

Two kings meet in a pavilion made by the painter for the purpose. Every toe pointed; gold, ruffled, trimmed and bowed French feet; where there is an ankle, a knee, a wrist, a shoulder, there is a puff or a pompom or a ruffle trimtrim; cascades of hair in curls. And plain black-slippered Spanish feet, unadorned. The Spanish sober, dun-coloured, with their red crosses and their plain white collars. The French King a succession of fringed dandelion pelmets of red and orange and gold, a beruffed Chinese puppet. Planet King radiant with black bow at his wrist, dark cloak, gold. The bride a width of white. The painter has made this scene and now from within, regards it. Closed in by painted views of the countryside framed on either side. The kings reflected in a window pane, in tentative accord with heads inclined. Beyond the window, a small atrium, and a cut-out in the canvas, and a square of the real sky.

In a pavilion made by the painter for the purpose, the King meets with his sister Anne; here on the Isle of Pheasants where they were both married and last parted. They are older, irretrievably older. The King comes to her, without reaching, without touching. Asks, Am I grown so old and terrible, can you not bear to look at me? You've seen this man's portrait of me (the painter is here, quietly, with his red cross)—that's bad enough. Is the truth so much the worse, that you should weep? Oh, Anne. These forty years. These wars. The Devil. The Devil hates us. We should have followed the example of our parents, and just been quiet, and prayed . . . but the times, the Devil, wouldn't allow it. Little mother, he says, not reaching for her— Little mother, as he once called her, after theirs died. It's been so long since you cared for us all. And all the younger ones you cared for . . . our brothers and our sister . . . and there's just us left, now. No, no. Please . . . I can't receive your kiss. Please don't touch me. I will not weep. Oh, sister, it is hard, to see you weep. It's been cruel. These forty years. But your son, and my daughter—we'll set it right, now.

María Teresa is here, to be presented to her mother-in-law—impressed by her pearls and diamonds and her pretty pointed lace ruff, and by her composure, and by her tears. But María Teresa is also half-drawn to a threshold, here; they are playing a game with her attention. Because here is a door left ajar, and beyond it, her husband, watching. So through this contrivance of a happenstance they are permitted to peek at each other for this first time. The Infanta pale and puffy, anxious and itching; with every effort of her will standing still, on show, for the Prince—to whom she's married already, a cousin having served as his proxy, so that she can step across— this border that the painter's made the mark of—

Here is the threshold still to cross. Here is the boundary drawn. Louis regards her. And passing across to him, here is her life, enframed; what can be seen through a door, a picture frame: a retreat into closed rooms, with her dwarves. She comes to him virginity intact, which pleases him at first; and her tactful gracious aunt ensures privacy for the taking of it; but in the years that follow she is not much touched. And if she weren't to step across it? But she has no choice, what side of the border she stands on, and the barrier must be broached, and she must step across it— And so she'll step out of the painter's sight, out of the King's, for always.

Thank you, for this, for all your work, Diego, the King says. It went well, I think. Don't you think? So—we've both lost a daughter now. I know, it's not the same. She is still living. I thank God for it. But I wonder if there's time; if I will see her again. It's not the same, I know; I know how much . . . The King turns his eyes, his eyes full of years, on the painter— I see what you mean, Señor, says the painter to the King.

They pack up; they dismantle the pavilion, make a bonfire of the wood, roll up the canvas, package up the gifts, the jewels, put on their travelling clothes and turn back, back to la Corte, leaving behind the new Queen of France; leaving behind, to the north, the new peace that they've forged there, and yet, in their passing, something defeated-seeming, this retreat. Say an old hidalgo watches them pass, out on his old skinny horse with his friend, roped in as squire, beside him. Watching the procession; in reverse a little shabby now, a little shambling and slow, the best is spent, things discarded in their path; holding together the show. The squire asks, Shall we follow? Shall we seek favour?

Seek fortune with that king who's passing? And the ladies? And those gallants, and the fools? Seek adventure with them?

— Sure, the squire says. Adventure; advancement ... whichever ...

But no, the knight says; look closer, my friend; that court you see, they are only players. Only players dressed up as courtiers and their leading man as king. Look how the fools are hot and tired, walking with their caps off, keeping something in reserve for the next show. Look there, that figure with them, in her dark robe, playing Death. And he turns his old horse homeward.

The painter on the way home, all the way home, ensuring their accommodation; checking the doors are secure; almost home now; ready for a rest; very tired. Sleeps readily, every night, on straw-stuffed mattresses, palettes, rock-hard, grey ground ... at the edge of consciousness, Mercury creeping through Argus' dreams to steal them; the moment before he ends it. Rest and forget for a moment, before it comes, before it's ended. Swipe of light a glimmer in his dreaming sight at top right. Displaced dream-light; rest, rest now; it's

coming, see the glimmer of it. This hung too in the Hall of
Mirrors. All eyes all closed now. Your last work— close to
rest, now—

— on his way home; at every inn they stop at, all the beds
arranged and thinking only of his own, of his home—— in
Madrid, Juana receives a message: her husband's dead.

Expinxit

Say early morning; the high plain, high summer. Long days of travel. Dry air. La Corte half-shadowed in the haze of dawn. Swallows circle the golden tower of the Alcázar. The road of kicked-up dust, fraught already, the beasts, the bounty of the country, the court returning back to itself, ready for a rest, drowsy in the soporific dawn-warmth and wheel-turn clop and whinny, travel-weary ... now all the revels are done, all the arranging and placing, and there's peace, and a living heir, Felipe still living, and a young Queen who'll surely bear another son, and the promise of continuity and this afternoon a sound sleep. The dust of the road washed clean with cool water. The painter exhausted, ready for his bed; thinking of his waiting wife, maybe— thinking of the next thing, a chance to paint, maybe, after all this arranging, accounting ... thinking of a place, of places, of placing, returning to his place here resigned to it ... Arrange himself into a portrait maybe, an account of himself with his red cross. Long after noon and the city already slumbering by the time they've passed the gate ...

He comes into the house and breathes the cooler air, the dim indoor light of siesta; darkness; the windows are covered— for mourning? In exhausted panic he calls out for Juana— Juana's here hearing stirring waking dreaming of him in a deep grieving sleep, or fitful dreaming grief; thinks she is dreaming— he is here, home ... She comes to and sees he is there, in the doorway, in the flesh, in the dimness of the afternoon shrouded, coming towards her, saying her name. Is it you? Are you well? she asks; Who else? he says— what's going on? Is everyone ... Who ... Why are you laughing? *You*, she says— we thought it was you. Everyone's fine, here. Everyone's here. And now you, too— back from the—— north. We heard ... You ... but, well it seems they were mistaken ... you're well? The painter tired, bewildered— I'm ... yes, quite well— only I'm a little ... I'm very tired. Let me lie down and sleep, if no one's died.

—— Not yet— not quite yet. I'd like to leave you here, sleeping— ready to start again, to make your next mark— and they were only mistaken. To leave you lying in peace and not in fever. Not to let you lie down weakly only a week later with heat in your heart and your gut, in vapour and sweat, in thirst and weakness and small breathing; to keep you from the week of fever after. Not to have the poor King shattered and send his physician for you and not to allow that man in to see you and say there's nothing to be done— I would withhold that diagnosis. Stay your hand before the will is signed, reject your resignation. But to leave you sleeping ... Mercury creeping, into half-dreaming, to steal you— you saw him coming; swallows falling; eyes closed and hot in their sockets rolling under the lids the skin the skull under the skin; she's there, in her dark corner, always waiting—— Not to let her lead you off, and not to see Juana follow you, only days after. Not to see you buried, even if it's as a nobleman (what you wanted?)— not to be left asking what it was like, what's it like where you are, not to let your bones be lost so that I can't even visit them; not to let you vanish yet, not quite yet—

—— but yet some last ceremony— I'll retrace—— Say mid-April (another year gone); approaching the rain-fresh

city— looking for a last mark— for a way to make it; for something remaining. Back to Madrid, to find a way to leave you,
or to leave a space for you, or—— I walk through the Retiro
sneezing, the horse chestnuts are flowering; I see your name
there on the plaque on the house where there used to be the
house you lived in and as I stand there again looking up at it
and hoping for something a boy on a skateboard clatters past
close enough to make me yelp and that will be caught on his
friend's camera footage and none of this would make sense to
you. I circle. A glass of fino in the dimness of a bar while the
rain falls; tapping my bent-clipped pen. I walk out into the
rainfall and wonder why I'm delaying, why I put it off, the
reason to be here, to see what I came for— so I make my way
in the rain and there you are immobile on your plinth, outside
the gallery, and the sun's coming out and I go in. To see what
you saw— once more. Calabazas' sweet smile and the scribble
of ships at Lepanto and the shuffled hooves of the horses and
Jesus' head dipped and the bleeding from the nails one for each
of his feet; the grey empty spaces they stand in, the nobles, the
fools, the barest line where floor meets wall and the shadows,
and a glove hanging from a hand; the scraps of blank paper
you litter in corners; the slug-trail shine of the King's outline
and the poor drooped King unwilting still as you see him, just
a man, as you observe him, phlegmatic (I am still shattered,
he wrote of your loss, in a margin); Argus asleep and Mercury
creeping and these women spinning a thread between them
and the cats curled at the feet of the spinners, and the warmth
and light around them; and sleepy dog and hangdog hound;
the shine in the eye of Barbarroja, the shine of Vulcan's eye;
Apollo's very blue sandal . . . Still this scintilla this scintillation
and these shifts and this stillness, this catchlight this eyetooth,
this holding this hollow, this solid object and this not so solid,

this bauble this bow this butterfly, this fringe of lace this lash this moustache, feathers, plumes, horsetail flicking from a proud shining backside; this upright lance and this one angled, this tangent, this man at Breda in glowing white inspecting his nails or hiding his tears and this hand on his shoulder a comrade or in comfort and the very sharp catchlight in the eye of the man looking out at us and the barest suggestion of a watching eye behind him; and you, sidelong, in your grey hat; and all these things and still and looking . . . I see the air above the Medici garden. And I find kept in a glass case a letter you've signed and the pace and flow of the ink of it your actual hand and the place where you weight the upstroke of the V and the ink has thickened and the twirl and flourish of the last Z crossed up and through. And then you, with your red cross, that they say the King painted on for you—why not if you'd like that—see you seeing yourself, almost smiling, and sort of sardonic, and I grin back at you as if we shared a joke. You, still in the world. The raw edge of the canvas stretched on the frame and the light on it and the edge of this frame, and this frame, this mirror, this frame—— And the man at the threshold, and the bright behind him. I keep glancing, moving off, stopping. Don't want the last time I look to be the last time. How can I, how can I—— And then here the marks of your brush where you swiped the paint off, the true mark of your hand— so that I am close to tears, when I thought I meant to laugh— and I'm here, this morning in April, still a bit sneezing, and I'll have to leave eventually but you— about to make your mark, the first, the last—— here you almost are.

- Get notebook out

- Tele training

-

Image credits

Acknowledgements

My thanks to—

— Granta Books, and particularly Laura Barber, for her smart, sharp, tactful and sympathetic editing, for which I am endlessly grateful. Also for keeping the eggs in and rescuing the dog.

— Jenny Hewson for her unstinting support, intelligence, humour, encouragement and friendship; I'm glad you're in my corner. And all at RCW, and particularly David Miller—I'm sorry it comes too late.

— Scarlett Thomas, David Flusfeder, Will Norman, Vybarr Cregan-Reid, Ariane Mildenberg, David Marston, Catherine Gandhi, Jonathan Holt, Ruby Radburn, Patrick Hudson, Adam Biles—thanks for hearing and/or listening to parts of this, for your thoughts, and for the various and sometimes multiple occasions when you have listened to me moaning on about it, and for the invaluable advice and support that helped me keep going.

— Koenraad Claes for guidance on the speech and manners of a Brabanter—I hope I have done some justice to research kindly conducted beyond the call of duty.

— Rachel Horsley, Steve Noyes, Chris Scott and Jane Shankar, my excellent PhD students.

— The University of Kent, for allowing me to go to Madrid.

— Alistair, for space, and time, and company on many a pilgrimage, and love and patience.

— My lovely family, who have always backed me; especially my parents Mike and Margaret, grandmother Nancy, and sister Lucy, who is a proper historian, and always asks the right questions. Thank you.